Secrets in Death

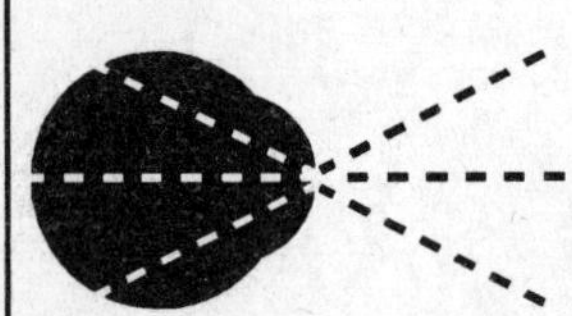

This Large Print Book carries the Seal of Approval of N.A.V.H.

Secrets in Death

J. D. Robb

WHEELER PUBLISHING
A part of Gale, a Cengage Company

Farmington Hills, Mich • San Francisco • New York • Waterville, Maine
Meriden, Conn • Mason, Ohio • Chicago

Wheeler Publishing, a part of Gale, a Cengage Company.

Wheeler Publishing Large Print Hardcover.
The text of this Large Print edition is unabridged.
Other aspects of the book may vary from the original edition.
Set in 16 pt. Plantin.

LIBRARY OF CONGRESS CIP DATA ON FILE.
CATALOGUING IN PUBLICATION FOR THIS BOOK
IS AVAILABLE FROM THE LIBRARY OF CONGRESS

ISBN-13: 978-1-4328-4158-4 (hardcover)
ISBN-10: 1-4328-4158-0 (hardcover)

Published in 2017 by arrangement with Macmillan Publishing Group, LLC/St. Martin's Press

Printed in the United States of America
1 2 3 4 5 6 7 21 20 19 18 17

Three may keep a secret,
if two of them are dead.

— Benjamin Franklin

Gossip needn't be false to be evil — there's a lot of truth that shouldn't be passed around.

— Frank A. Clark

1

It wouldn't kill her.

Probably wouldn't kill her.

Eyebrows knit together beneath a snowflake cap, Lieutenant Eve Dallas strode through the flood of people on the crowded sidewalk with thoughts nearly as bitter as the February wind.

She'd rather be back in her vehicle and driving home through the jam of other vehicles. Down to it, she'd rather engage in mortal combat in some downtown alleyway with a Zeused-up chemi-head than head for some fussy fern bar.

But a deal was a deal, and she'd run out of excuses — reasons, she self-corrected. She'd had solid reasons to put this deal off.

Like murder.

A murder cop dealt with murder and all it entailed. Not fancy drinks and small talk.

Resigned, she stuffed her hands — she'd forgotten her damn gloves again — in the pockets of her long leather coat that snapped and billowed around her long legs. Her gaze scanned as she hiked the two blocks, brown and canny cop's eyes on alert. Maybe she'd spot a street thief; Christ knew plenty of tourists clipped by with their wallets all but hanging out saying: Take me.

Not her fault if she had to make an arrest and put this little meet off, again.

But apparently the snatchers and pickers had taken the evening off.

She reminded herself drinks with Dr. Garnet DeWinter, fashion plate, forensic anthropologist, and mild irritant, couldn't annoy or bore her to actual death.

And if death by boredom equaled a potential risk, surely they had come up with a cure by 2061.

Thirty minutes, she vowed. Forty max, and she'd be done. Deal complete.

She stopped in front of the bar, a tall, rangy woman in flat, sturdy ankle boots, a long black coat, and the incongruous ski cap with a snowflake shimmering over her choppy brown hair and knitted eyebrows.

DU VIN.

Stupid name for a bar, she thought, her wide mouth twisting in derision. Snooty French name for a bar.

She wondered if Roarke owned it, because

her husband owned damn near everything else. She'd rather be having a drink with him. At home.

But she wasn't.

She reached for the door, remembered the snowflake cap. She yanked it off, stuffed it in her pocket to maintain a little dignity.

She stepped out of the noise and rush of downtown New York, into the fern- and flower-decked noise of the trendy, overpriced drinking hole.

The bar itself, a dull and elegant silver, swept itself into an S curve along the facing wall. Mirrored shelves filled with shiny bottles backed it. On the top shelf exotic red flowers spilled out of black-and-white checked pots.

Stools with black-and-white checked seats lined the front. An ass filled every seat while other patrons crowded in, keeping the trio of bartenders busy.

The generous space, artistically lit by silver pendants twisted into floral shapes, provided room for high tops, low tops, booths, and the waitstaff, dressed in sharply severe black, moving among them.

Just under the drone of sound generated by voices, clinking glassware, and the *click* of shoes on the polished floor, the music system lilted with some throaty-voiced woman singing in French.

It all struck Eve as entirely too . . . everything.

Her instinctive scan of the room paused on a blonde — striking features, a lush tumble of hair, a curvy body packed into a bright pink skin suit with high-heeled boots as green as her eyes.

It only took a beat for her to recognize the gossip reporter — or, as Larinda Mars termed herself — the social information reporter. The last thing Eve wanted, other than some weird French drink, was to find herself an on-air item on Channel Seventy-Five.

At the moment, Mars appeared much too focused on her table companion to notice Eve's entrance. Mid-thirties, mixed race, slickly polished looks, wavy brown hair, and blue eyes that looked as annoyed as she herself felt.

Business suit — not off-the-rack — high-end wrist unit.

His face didn't ring for her, but as long as he kept Larinda Mars's attention on him, Eve figured she owed him one.

The hostess, bold red hair swept up into a sleek, headache-inducing twist, approached with a practiced smile.

"Good evening, do you have a reservation?"

"I don't know. I'm here to meet somebody. Maybe she got hung up." Please God.

"Might she have made a reservation?"

"I don't know. DeWinter."

"Oh, yes, Dr. DeWinter. She's here. I think she went down to freshen up. Let me show you to your table."

"Fine."

At least they headed to the opposite end of the bar from Mars.

"Would you like to check your coat?"

"No, I've got it." Eve slid into the booth, onto the checked seat. A wall — head-high when she sat, and topped with more flowerpots — separated the booth from another section of tables.

The cop in her would have preferred a seat giving her a full visual radius of everything, everybody.

But she only had to handle it for thirty minutes.

A single glass of something pink and frothy stood on the other side of the table.

"Cesca will be taking care of you this evening," the hostess announced. "She'll be right with you."

"Yeah, thanks."

Thirty minutes, Eve promised herself as

she unwound her scarf — knitted by her partner's artistic hands — stuffed it in her coat pocket. Accepting her fate, she shrugged out of her coat as the waitress, her hair a short, blunt swing of purple, stepped to the booth.

"Good evening, I'm Cesca, and I'll be your server. What can I get for you?"

Eve considered ordering a cheap American beer, just to be contrary. "Wine, red's fine."

"A glass, a half bottle, or a bottle?"

"Just a glass."

Cesca tapped a remote on her belt. The screen on the separating wall of the booth came on, and displayed a list — a long list — of red wines by the glass.

"Would you like some time to decide?"

"No . . ." Eve knew a little about wines. A woman couldn't live with Roarke and not absorb some basic knowledge. She tapped a cabernet she knew she'd had at home, and knew came from one of Roarke's vineyards.

"Oh, that's a lovely wine. I'll have it brought right out to you. Would you care for any appetizers, hors d'oeuvres, accompaniments?"

"No. No, thanks."

The young waitress never lost her smile. "If you change your mind, we have a lovely selection — you can order from the screen.

I'll get your wine."

Even as she stepped away, Eve saw DeWinter walk through a doorway at the far end of the bar.

DeWinter wore a body-skimming dress, nearly the same tone as the waitress's hair, and matched the outfit with tall, supple boots in a silver gray — with killer, wire-thin heels.

Her lips, dyed a red that edged toward purple, curved when she spotted Eve, and humor lit her eyes — a cool, crystal blue against the smooth caramel tone of her skin.

With her dark hair sleek, her stride confident, she crossed the polished floor, slid gracefully into the booth.

She said, "Alone at last."

"Funny."

"I expected a text telling me you had to cancel."

"No DBs to deal with tonight."

"That's cheery."

"Won't last."

"No, but then what would you and I do if it did? You need a drink."

"One's coming."

DeWinter picked up her own, leaned back as she sipped. "I love the drinks here. This one, the Nuage Rose, is a favorite. What's yours?"

"First time here. I'm sticking with red wine."

"I assumed you'd been here before since Roarke owns it."

Figured, Eve thought. "If I hit every place Roarke owns, just in the city, I wouldn't have time to do anything else."

"You've got a point. It's a favorite of mine." Obviously relaxed, DeWinter glanced around as she drank. "Close to work, beautiful decor, great people watching, and excellent service."

As if to prove the last, Cesca set Eve's wine on the table.

"You didn't order any, but . . ." Cesca held out a black plate filled with thin, golden sticks.

"Olive straws. Cesca, you know my weakness. Thanks," DeWinter said.

"No problem." The waitress set down the straws, two little plates, some fancy napkins. "Just let me know if you need anything."

"They're terrific," DeWinter told Eve, placing a few on her plate.

No point in being rude, Eve decided — plus they looked pretty damn good. And were, she thought when she sampled one.

"Why don't we just get to it." DeWinter nibbled on an olive straw. "I don't need everyone to like me. I don't even need to know why the people who don't, don't. You know as well as I: When you're in a position of authority, some don't. And when you're a woman in that position, even though we're in the second half of the twenty-first century, that just adds to it."

She paused to drink again.

"But, even though you and I don't and likely won't work together routinely, there has been and will be times we do."

With a shrug DeWinter gestured with her drink. "I can get around that, as can you. We're both professionals, and good at what we do. But we also have personal connections."

Eve gave the wine a try — really good — while she studied DeWinter's striking face. "Did you practice all that?"

Though one perfect eyebrow shot up, DeWinter maintained the same even tone. "No, but I've had plenty of time to think about it. So . . . I'm friendly with some of your friends. Nadine, Mavis, for instance. Friendly enough that Mavis and Leonardo had my daughter and me to Bella's birthday party. And wasn't that an event?"

"For Mavis, Tuesday mornings are events."

"That's part of her charm and appeal. I like her quite a bit. I understand she's one of your people —"

"She doesn't belong to me," Eve interrupted.

"She's part — a key part — of your circle. A very tight circle. You're careful who comes into that circle, and I respect that. I don't expect you and I will be the B of Bs, but —"

"The what?"

"Sorry, my daughter's influence." Humor, the genuine sort, brightened her face. "Best of besties. We can maintain a professional relationship, but I'm curious what it is about me that irritates you."

"I don't think about it."

Lips curved, DeWinter took another sip of her frothy drink. "Maybe, for the purpose of this exercise, you could."

For the life of her, Eve couldn't see why it mattered. She shrugged. "I don't know you. You're good at your work. Really good. That's all I need."

"I'm pushy, and so are you."

"Okay."

"We don't necessarily approach a case the same way, but we have the same goals."

"No argument."

"You're not the type of person I'd look for, for a friend, being you're rude more often than not, single-minded, and manage to be a hard-ass and a tight-ass at the same time."

Though the tight-ass comment annoyed, Eve let it go. "Then what are we doing here?"

Shifting, DeWinter leaned forward just a little. "You also inspire amazing and unquestionable loyalty, not only in those who work under you, but in your personal life. You have a man I respect and admire quite a bit madly in love with you."

Eve crunched into another olive straw. "Maybe he likes rude hard-asses."

"He must. But I also know him to be a superior judge of character, a man who studies and sees the big picture. And I see that close circle of friends, the diversity of them. I'm a small-details-open-the-big-picture sort of person, so I'm curious."

Casually, DeWinter picked up another olive straw. "Is it Morris?" DeWinter waited a beat, nodded. "A big part of it is Li then. He's also one of yours."

A quick frisson of annoyance ran straight up her spine. "Morris is his own man."

"He is, but he's part of that circle, and the loyalty there is a solid two-way street. We're friends, Li and I. We're companions. We're not bedmates."

"It's none of my —"

"Business? That's bullshit, tight-ass." She laughed then at the flash in Eve's eyes. "I don't expect you're called that to your face often."

"Not unless the other party wants their face bloodied."

"I appreciate your restraint. I care about Li, as a friend. And though he's about as perfect a specimen, inside and out, as it gets — and I'm pretty damn good myself — we're not drawn to each other that way."

She glanced away for a moment, gave a small sigh. "I'll admit, I've half wished we were a few times, but we're simply not. On either side. I didn't know Amaryllis, but I do know Li loved her, loved her deeply. You know about loving deeply, and you know how the loss of her leveled him. You were there for him when it did. You're still there for him."

Eve knew the sound of bullshit, and she knew the sound of truth. What she heard was truth. It loosened her stiffened spine.

"He's still grieving," Eve said. "Not as much, not the way he was, but he's still grieving."

"Yes, he is. And part of him may always. We met each other at a time we both needed and wanted a friend and companion, without the complications of sex. We have a lot in common, and he's become a very good friend to my daughter, who's the love of my life. I'm not looking for Li to fill some void in me. I'm not, in fact, looking for anyone to do that, as I don't have a void, and have no intention of complicating my baby's life by inserting someone into it, on that level."

She paused a moment, sighed again. "Though I do miss sex. Regardless, Miranda is my first, my last, and my all. Li's delightful with her, and I think she also helps him find more light, more comfort.

"She wanted to meet you."

"Me? Why?"

"She's heard your name, and she's seen you on screen — it's hard to block the crime channels, the Internet, when she's a clever girl and very interested. Plus, you and Roarke gave Bella the dollhouse at the party. Major hit. But you left before I could bring her over to you."

"We had an incident."

"I'm aware. I heard. And the officer who was injured?"

"On medical leave. He'll be all right."

"I'm glad to hear it."

"We came back," Eve added. "To the party."

"Yes, Li mentioned that, but we'd already left. She had a school project that still needed — according to her — some fine-tuning. I don't have designs on Li, and he doesn't have feelings for me that go beyond friendship. So whatever problem you have with me, I hope you can take that out of the mix."

"Okay." Eve drank a little wine, considered. "I don't know you, and what I do know I don't really get. You strike me as a snob, and one with her own tight ass who's plenty puffed up about all the letters after her name."

DeWinter's back went up like a bright red flag. "I'm not a snob!"

"What's that thing you're drinking, the thing you named with a snooty French accent?"

"I like this drink, and I speak French. That doesn't make me a snob."

Amused now — who knew that was all it took to get under DeWinter's skin? — Eve plowed on. "And you — what's the word — swirl around in your coordinated outfits."

"You're wearing six-thousand-dollar boots."

"I am not." Appalled, Eve stuck one foot out, stared. "God." She probably was. "The difference is, I wouldn't have a clue how much your boots cost, only that nobody with any sense would wear them when they're going to stand on them for hours at a time."

DeWinter's face, her voice, registered absolute astonishment. "Your problem with me is how I dress?"

"It's systemic," Eve decided on the spot.

"Systemic, my ass." DeWinter wagged a straw at Eve before crunching it. "You've formed an opinion of me on surface appearance, and you're a better cop than that."

"You're too quick to preen in front of the cameras."

"I don't preen. And that's rich coming from you when one of your closest friends is a reporter — and you get plenty of screen time."

"When it's advantageous to an investigation."

"She wrote a damn book about you. And the vid adapted from it is up for Oscars."

"No, she wrote a damn book about the Icoves." Eve held up a hand. "You stole a dog."

"Oh, for Christ's sake."

"You stole a dog," Eve continued, "because it was being neglected and abused, and nobody else would do anything about it. You kept the dog. I believe in serve and protect, and when somebody — even a dog — is being abused, somebody needs to stop it. You did. That's a point for you."

"My dog's a point for me?"

"Yeah, and maybe Morris has shifted to the other side because I know when somebody's bullshitting me, and you're not. And you've been good for him. When I look at it, at him, I'm not going to say otherwise. He's steadier, and maybe part of that's having you to hang with."

"I care about him."

"I got that. Doesn't make you less of a snob or a media hound, but I got that."

On a huff, DeWinter sat back again. "I swear to God, here and now, I don't know why I half like you."

"Back at you. Since I figure half is good enough, that should do it. I need to get home."

"You haven't finished your wine —" DeWinter began.

They both looked over at the sound of glass striking the floor. DeWinter looked away again, picked up her drink.

"No point in wasting —"

It's as far as she got before Eve surged up.

Larinda Mars no longer sat in a booth, nor did her companion. Instead she walked like a drunk over the polished floor, her shoes crunching on broken glass from a tray she'd knocked over when she'd run straight into a waiter.

Her eyes, both dazed and dull, stared straight ahead as she weaved and shuffled. And blood soaked the right sleeve of her pink skin suit, dripping a thin river onto the floor.

Eve rushed for her, shoving people aside. Someone started to scream.

Mars's eyes rolled back as she pitched forward. Eve caught her before she hit the floor, so they went down together.

"DeWinter!" Eve snapped as she fought to pull the tight sleeve away and find the source of the blood.

"I'm here, I'm here. Put pressure on it."

"Where?"

DeWinter dropped down, pressed both hands on Mars's right biceps. "We need to cut the sleeve away. I need something to make a tourniquet. She's lost a lot of blood."

Jumping up, Eve dug in her pocket for a penknife. "Use this. You!" She grabbed one of the waitstaff. "Nobody leaves."

"I can't —"

"Lock the damn door." As she spoke, she dragged off her belt. "You!" She pointed at one of the bartenders as people panicked, scrambled. "Call nine-one-one. Now. We need medicals."

"I'm a doctor, I'm a doctor." A man

fought his way through the crowd.

"So am I," DeWinter said as she cut away the sleeve. "I don't have a pulse."

"Brachial artery." The man straddled Mars, began to pump her chest. "Get that tourniquet on. If we can keep her going . . . Tell the MTs we need blood. O-neg. She needs a transfusion."

Eve left the victim to the medicals, dealt with the crowd.

"Everybody stay where you are!" She whipped out her badge, held it up. "I'm a cop. Take a seat, give the doctors room." She stepped over as a man in a cashmere topcoat tried to shove the waitress away from the door. "I said take a seat."

"You have no authority to —"

She shoved her jacket back to reveal her weapon. "Wanna bet?"

He gave her a look of intense dislike, but stalked over to the bar, stood.

"Nobody out," Eve repeated. "Nobody in but cops and medicals."

"We won't need the medicals." DeWinter, her hands wet with blood, sat back on her heels. "She's gone."

No DBs? Eve thought as she took out her 'link to call it in.

No, it didn't last.

■ ■ ■ ■

She had a bar full of people; one might be a murderer. Though she suspected whoever'd sliced Mars was long gone. Still, she needed to deal with what she had.

"Quiet down!" Her order cut down on most of the noise. "I need everybody to remain in their seats, or remain where they are."

"I want to go home." At the sobbing shout Eve simply nodded.

"I understand, and will try to get everyone out of here as soon as possible. For now, I need this table and this table to move in an orderly fashion to that area of the room."

"There's so much blood," someone murmured.

"Yeah, and that's why I need you to move. Take your things, and move to the north side of the room. Please."

"Why are you in charge?" someone shouted. "You can't keep us here."

Eve simply held up her badge. "This is a police badge. I'm Lieutenant Dallas, NYPSD, and this is now a police investigation."

"Um, ma'am?" The waitress at the door

raised her hand.

"Lieutenant."

"Well, the MTs are here — I can see them pulling up."

"Let them in. Please move to the north side."

A woman stood up, picked up her purse with a shaky hand. And passed out cold. Since that started a fresh wave of panic and shouting, Eve ignored it, turned to the MTs who rushed in.

"Deal with the fainter," she said, gesturing. "It's too late for the bleeder. Listen up! I can take names and statements here, then send you on your way, or I can call for a wagon, have every single one of you transported to Central, and deal with it there. Your choice. If you want to get out of here, quiet down. And you people at these tables, move it."

"I'm not leaving my girlfriend."

Eve studied the man who'd caught the fainter on her way down. "No problem. Give the MTs room to bring her around. I'd suggest you shield her eyes from the blood, help her move to the north side. And somebody with a chair on that side, give it up for — What's her name?"

"Marlee."

"Give Marlee a chair." She turned to one

of the bartenders. "How about some water for her?"

"Um. The police are here."

Thank Christ, Eve thought. "Let them in, and go ahead and move over to the north. Thanks."

A couple of beat droids, Eve identified as they stepped in. A whole lot better than nothing. "I need to secure this scene. These people at these tables need to move to the north side. Get them some chairs."

"Yes, sir."

"Can't we find something to cover her?"

At the doctor's question, both Eve and DeWinter said, "No," in unison. Eve lifted her eyebrows at DeWinter.

"I'm sorry," DeWinter continued, "I didn't get your name."

"Sterling, Bryce Sterling."

"Dr. Sterling, I want to thank you for what you did here. We can't cover her, as it may compromise forensic evidence."

"I've got shields coming," Eve added. And a field kit, as hers was two blocks down in the trunk of her car. "Who's in charge of the bar?"

"I am." One of the bartenders raised her hand. "I'm the manager on duty."

"Name?"

"Emily. Emily Francis."

"Ms. Francis, I don't see any security cams in this area."

"No, we don't have interior cams. Just on the exterior."

"Is there another exit?"

"There's an exit to the alley. It's . . ." She pointed behind her. "From the kitchen."

"Is anyone in the back?"

"I — I was." A man — really hardly more than a boy — lifted a hand. "I was in the storeroom, and I heard screaming, so I ran in."

"We were in the kitchen."

A group of three, all wearing white bib aprons, stood together near the swinging doors behind the bar.

"Anybody back there now?"

"No. But I need to make sure everything's turned off. Can I?"

"Name?"

"I'm Curt — ah, Curtis Liebowitz."

"First, did anyone come through the kitchen in the last hour, and go out the alley door?"

"Uh-uh. I mean no. We would've seen them."

"Go ahead, Curt, and come right back. Okay." She turned back. "Here's what's going to happen. These officers are going to start taking names, contact information, and statements. When they, or the officers now on their way to this location, are satisfied with that information, you'll be free to go."

She gestured one of the droids over.

"I want to know who was seated at the booths in front and behind the vic, at the tables nearest her booth — if they're still on scene. I want those individuals held."

"Yes, sir."

"Get started. Emily, right?"

"Yes."

Eve leaned in a bit, lowered her voice. "Do you know who owns this bar?"

"Yes. Yes, I do."

"Do you know who I am?"

"Yes. I didn't until you said your name, but —"

"Good. I need you to help me keep the staff calm and ordered. I'd like you to have your most reliable waitperson help you distribute water or soft drinks to the customers still in the bar. Can you do that?"

"Yeah. Lieutenant? I know the . . . her. Ms. Mars. Larinda Mars."

"Personally?"

"No, I mean, not really. I mean she's a regular. And she's on screen. The gossip channel."

A steady one, Eve thought. She'd expect no less from one of Roarke's business managers. "I don't see the man she was with here in the bar."

"I think he left before . . . before she came up from the bathroom. I mean she went through there, and that leads down to the restrooms, so I assume she went there."

"Do you know who she was with?"

"No, but I can find out. He paid for the drinks. He charged them. I think he used his 'link app. I can check."

"I'd appreciate if you'd do that, and have a couple of reliables pass out drinks. No alcohol, okay?"

"Got it."

"Who served them?"

"That's Kyle's booth." Emily looked around, gesturing with her chin. "He's over there with Cesca and Malory."

"Okay, go ahead and check that charge for me."

Eve stepped back to the body, crouched down. "I've got a field kit coming, but in the meanwhile we've ID'd her — from the primary, and from the manager of the bar — as Larinda Mars."

"I knew she looked familiar," DeWinter added. "I've seen her reports."

"We have TOD as verified on my recorder by both you and Dr. Sterling."

"You had your recorder on?" DeWinter

demanded.

"Relax. Jesus. I engaged it when she came staggering out with blood dripping everywhere. Dr. Sterling, in your medical opinion, how long does it take someone, given her height, weight, to bleed out from a cut to — you said brachial artery?"

"It depends. It might only take a couple minutes. It might take longer, between eight and twelve. Realistically, she was dead before we saw her. We simply couldn't have saved her, as she'd already lost too much blood."

"Okay. Say somebody slices this artery. What's the immediate response?"

"Depending, again, it would gush with every heartbeat. If it was only nicked or partially cut, it would leak more slowly. Without treatment, there would be confusion, disorientation, shock, increasing with blood loss until unconsciousness and death."

"All right. I'm going to get your contact information, your statement. Then you can go back to the kitchen, clean up if you want. I'll clear that. After, you're free to go, with thanks."

"My wife is here. She's . . ."

"I'll see that she's interviewed right away, so you can leave together."

As she straightened, one of the droids opened the door for her partner and her partner's main man.

Detective Peabody wore a pom-pom hat over her currently flippy dark hair. EDD ace Detective McNab's red coat and plaid airboots lit up the bar like fireworks.

Eve moved to them quickly, held up a finger to hold off questions. "Peabody, I need you to get the statement and contact information of the guy next to the DB. He's a doctor. His wife's in the crowd, and I need her interviewed next so they can be released. After, take the waitstaff. They're likely to have seen more. McNab, the manager is Emily Francis — the brunette behind the bar. She'll tell you where to find the security feed. Exterior only on this place."

She took the field kit from him. "I've got shields coming, so let them in, curtain off the body asap. I'm heading downstairs, the most likely site of the attack."

"Just one question?" Peabody held up a single finger. "What the hell happened?"

"Looks like somebody decided to cut off the social information network. Keep this crowd in line," she added, then strode off, moving around the blood trail so as not to compromise it more than it already was.

2

Eve followed the blood trail across a short hall, down a steep flight of steps to another longer sort of vestibule with restrooms — painted doors with *Femmes* on one above a stylized female silhouette, and *Hommes* on the other, with a male silhouette.

The blood led to the female. She paused, pulled a can of Seal-It from her kit, coated her hands, her boots. Eased open the door.

Blood, an arterial spray, she assumed, slashed across a wall painted in pale gold, over a section of the wide, framed mirror above a long silver trough with curvy silver faucets.

It pooled on the floor, where it had already begun to congeal.

Stepping over, Eve opened the large pink handbag hung on a hook by the trough. Rifled through.

"Victim left her purse, ID inside verifies. Also holding pepper spray, panic button, and lookie here, an illegal stunner. Indications the vic was either paranoid or had reason to carry defensive tools.

"And that's likely her lip dye on the shelf under the mirror."

She verified same, setting up a marker, testing the dye tube for prints, running them. Then bagged the tube, sealing and marking it.

"She came in to use the facilities. Stood here, putting on lip dye, fluffing up. Most likely the attacker followed her in. Lying in wait seems a stretch. Had to have the weapon, though the attack itself may have been spur-of-the-moment. Pull the weapon, cut the arm. One wound from my brief on-site exam, so the attacker either knew where to cut or got seriously lucky. I lean heavy toward knew where.

"Did she scream?"

Eve imagined it, brought the picture into her mind of Mars standing in front of the mirror.

The door opens, she thought, and Mars sees the killer in the mirror.

Turns, certainly turns, according to the pattern of the spatter.

"If she screamed, she didn't scream loud enough for us to hear her upstairs. The attacker . . . if he or she avoided getting any blood on his or her person, that's not luck, either. Knew where to stand to avoid the spray. Or covered any spray with a coat. Might have washed any blood on the hands in the damn sink right here. Might have worn gloves, then taken them off."

She closed her eyes a moment, tried to bring back the goings, the comings upstairs while she sat having a damn drink.

Shaking her head, she studied the room again.

"Four stalls. All swank. No signs of struggle, no signs of an altercation. Everything neat and clean and ordered — except for the blood."

An argument, maybe, she thought. Her drinks companion, someone else. Someone else having drinks. Someone who trailed her into the bar.

A lot of possibilities.

She took a sample of the blood for her own kit. The sweepers, she thought, would deal with the rest.

And now she dealt with something she'd put off. She tagged Roarke.

His face came on her 'link screen. Those impossibly blue eyes. That slow smile just for her, curving that beautifully sculpted mouth.

"Lieutenant. And how's Garnet?"

"DeWinter's upstairs in your place. Du Vin."

"Ah, so you went for a touch of France." His voice held that lyrical touch of Ireland. "How do you like it?"

"I liked it okay, until I caught a case."

"Ah, well. I'm sorry for the dead, and for myself, as I expect you won't be starting for home for a while yet."

"Yeah, not for a while. I mean I literally caught a case. As in: I caught her as she went down, and before she died on the really nice floor of your French bar."

The smile vanished; those bold blue eyes turned cool. "There's been a murder in my place?"

"I'm down in the women's bathroom. You're going to have to repaint the walls."

"I'm on my way."

"I'm going to say, for form, there's no need for you to come here. But you don't need to say, for form, why there is. I'll see you when you get here. Sorry."

"So am I."

He clicked off.

As she dropped her 'link back into her pocket, Peabody opened the door.

Brown eyes scanned the room. "Well, we know where it went down."

"We do."

"Shields are here and in place. It's helped calm people down, but we've got a lot of nerves up there. Do you want me to take the body or statements?"

"Statements, for now. I told the droids to cull out people who sat nearest her booth. Take those. She was having a drink with someone. Male, mixed race, late thirties, wavy brown hair, blue eyes. Rich — expensive dark gray suit, ah . . . blue shirt, blue-and-gray patterned tie with some red in it. Pricey-looking wrist unit. Silver or white gold."

"How close were you?"

"Not close enough, apparently, but I got a decent enough look at him. They didn't seem to be having a happy talk from his expression."

"You know who the DB is, right?"

"Yeah. Larinda Mars, scandal queen. I'll verify that officially. The manager should have the companion's name by now. Take the statements. I'll get that and run it."

"Sweepers?"

"Yeah, call them in, and the morgue team."

Eve took a last look around, walked over to bag the purse. "Too damn big for an evidence bag, even the jumbo." To solve it, she dumped the contents in a bag, marked and sealed, stuffed the purse in another.

She carted it all up, went directly to Emily. "Have you got any sort of a box, with a lid?"

"In my office. I'll get you one. Lieutenant, the man who had drinks with Ms. Mars is Fabio Bellami. I have his contact information. I made a copy of the readout."

Eve took it. "Thanks, that's very helpful."

"I'll get the box."

Eve slipped the paper into her pocket. It was past time to give the victim some attention.

DeWinter slipped off the stool where she'd waited.

"Is there something I can do?"

Eve glanced at the white curtain. "I don't think this is a job for a forensic anthropologist."

"I was here. I had her blood on my hands. Can I help?"

Eve glanced at the people still bunched together on the north side. "Sterling's still here."

"He's been cleared to go, along with his wife, but he stayed to help someone through a full-blown panic attack — and another fainting spell. I think he must be a very good doctor. And I think if we'd gotten to the victim even five minutes sooner, we might have saved her. That's pure conjecture, of course."

"Conjecture can be useful." She held out a can of Seal-It. "Seal up."

"Sorry, what?"

"If you want to help, seal up. You've already got some blood on your boots."

DeWinter glanced down. "Damn it." But she sealed up.

And then moved behind the shielding with Eve.

Eve crouched, took her Identi-pad from her kit, pressed it to the victim's thumb. "Victim is identified as Mars, Larinda, age thirty-seven —"

"I don't think so," DeWinter interjected, earning a cool stare from Eve. "I can certainly verify that, but it's my opinion the victim is between forty and forty-five."

"So noted. The victim's official identification information lists her age at thirty-seven. She resides at 265 Park Avenue, Penthouse 3. Single — no marriage or cohabs on record, no offspring. Hand me the gauge. I need to verify TOD."

As DeWinter looked for it in the kit, Eve checked the victim for other injuries. "The arm appears to be the only injury. ME to verify." She took the gauge DeWinter held out. "TOD eighteen-forty-three, which jibes with my live record. Victim suffered an injury to the brachial artery in her right arm. The appearance of the wound indicates a sharp instrument slicing through the material of the sleeve and into the flesh."

Eve hunkered back. "She made it up here from the bathroom. Whoever cut her hit her in the bathroom. She got out, down to the steps, came up, down another hall, got several steps into the bar before she went down."

"Do you want my opinion?"

"That's why I let you in here."

"She wouldn't have felt disoriented at first — not the first few seconds, even up to half a minute, depending on what Li — Dr. Morris — finds regarding the damage to the artery. It's possible she made it out of the restroom, even to the steps before she began to feel seriously confused, woozy."

"Blood trail's heavier on the lower part of the steps, and there are some smears — likely from her hand — on the walls."

"Bracing herself. Maybe gathering herself or just standing on the steps unsure — confused. Then continuing up, a kind of instinctive process. Her brain was deprived of blood, like her heart."

"Besides you, and medicals, maybe soldiers, maybe cops, how many people are going to think — even plan — to go for that spot? That artery? You've got a sharp, you go for the throat, the heart, and drop them where they stand. More time to get gone that way, too."

"Are you asking or just thinking out loud?"

"Both."

"The throat's effective," De Winter confirmed, "but very messy, especially in a public place. The heart takes more precision. The brachial is a long artery, so increases the target. An inch lower, or higher? You'd get the same result. Not so with the heart."

"Got that. Good, and I agree."

"As for who might know, there's this interesting tool. They call it the Internet."

"Yeah, yeah, anybody can find out anything. But you have to be looking."

"But you do think the killer was looking." DeWinter looked down at Mars again. "For her."

"Most likely. She left her purse — and her wallet in it with cash and credit, her 'link. She's wearing jewelry that looks like it's worth the steal. They didn't bother. So that eliminates that motive."

Eve pushed up. "We'll see what she has to say to Morris. Have Peabody take your statement."

"Mine?"

"You're a wit, DeWinter, so yeah. Let's be thorough. Then you should go home. Your kid's probably wondering where you are."

"I texted her I'd be late. And no, I didn't tell her why."

"Good. Go spell it out for Peabody, and go home. You did what you could, for her, and afterward. I followed her blood trail, and I'm with Sterling. She was dead before she dropped. Her brain just hadn't gotten the memo yet."

"I've never actually seen someone die," DeWinter admitted. "It's different, going into the field, examining remains, or having bones on my table at the lab. Yes, I'll go home. I want to hug my daughter. Can you keep me updated on the investigation?"

"I can do that."

After DeWinter stepped outside the curtain, Eve took another moment to study the dead.

She hadn't thought of Larinda Mars in years, and when she had thought of her at that time, had felt little more than a mild distaste and contempt.

Obviously someone had felt a great deal more.

"Who'd you piss off, Mars?"

Still shielded, she took out her PPC and

began a run on Fabio Bellami.

She stepped out and nearly into Roarke as he reached forward to part the shield.

"You made good time. I need you to hold a minute."

She carried the evidence bags she'd taken inside the curtain to the box Emily set on the bar. After setting the bags in, she pulled securing tape out of her kit, sealed the box, marked it.

"Larinda Mars," Roarke said.

"Yeah." She looked over, noting that the number of witnesses had diminished by more than half. Peabody sat with DeWinter. "I'll run it through for you, but I want to clear these people out. We're going to have to shut your place down for a while."

"Understood."

"McNab should have the exterior feed, and I'm going to need to go over that. Interior feed would've helped a lot."

"Patrons don't like being on camera in a high-end pub. And we find murder a very rare activity here."

His voice was clipped, cool. She couldn't blame him for it.

"Also understood. I need to finish getting statements. The morgue team's on its way, and so are the sweepers. You're going to need to hold on awhile longer."

She let in the morgue team herself, and the sweepers. Directed both groups. By the time they were at their work only a handful of people remained in the chairs and booths, all staff.

She sat down with Cesca.

"I'm sorry I didn't recognize you before," Cesca began.

"Why should you? You didn't have Ms. Mars's table, but did you know her?"

"She comes in a couple times a week. Sometimes more. She likes that booth — she likes Kyle. He's usually her server."

"Did you see her go downstairs?"

"No. I did notice Kyle turning the booth — clearing the glasses. We were pretty busy. We usually are between five-thirty and seven-thirty — the after-work crowd. You and Dr. DeWinter didn't want much, but a lot of my tables did, so I was, you know, hopping."

"I noticed. Did you see Ms. Mars come in, from downstairs? Before she collapsed?"

"I heard the crash — you know the glass breaking when she . . . and I looked over, like you do, and I saw her, and somebody screamed, and you were running over. I didn't really see . . . It didn't register, I guess. The blood, until she fell and you grabbed her. I felt a little bit sick for a minute. I've never seen blood like that. Then lots of people were screaming or yelling, and my head was all . . ." She circled her fingers in the air around her wedge of purple hair. "So I put my head between my knees until I didn't feel so dizzy. You said to stand by the door and all that. It helped. Having something to do."

"You did fine. Have you seen Ms. Mars in here with the man she was with tonight?"

"I don't think so. He didn't look familiar. And he was really frosty, so it feels like I'd remember. But you get busy, and when it's not your table . . ."

"Okay. Your contact info's on record here, isn't it?"

"Sure. They have to have all that for payroll, and in case they need you to come in off schedule."

"Then you can go on home. Somebody'll be in touch about when you can come back to work."

"Can I stay until Sherry can go? She's one of the cooks. We're roommates. I don't want to go home alone. I just really feel, you know, a little whacked."

"Sure. Do you want transportation home?"

"We only live four blocks away. But I'll just wait for her."

"No problem. Do you want some water? A soda?"

Cesca's eyes filled. "I'm supposed to wait on you."

"You held up, Cesca. You did fine."

"I wouldn't mind a Coke." She wiped at her eyes.

"Okay."

Eve moved off, signaled to Roarke. "See the girl with purple hair? She's Cesca, one of your waitstaff. She's solid. And she could use a Coke."

"I'll take care of it."

Eve moved on to Kyle. She recognized him, had watched him stop by Mars's booth. Now she sat next to him as he gnawed on a thumbnail.

"I'm Lieutenant Dallas."

"Yeah, you said. I know. I'm Kyle. I'm Kyle Spinder."

His eyes, full of nerves, angled away, closed, when the morgue team rolled out the gurney with its black body bag.

"Oh man, oh God, oh man."

"Breathe slow, in and out."

"I never saw anybody dead before. I never did. Except on screen, in vids and games and shit. Stuff, sorry."

"Okay. You waited on Ms. Mars and Mr. Bellami tonight."

"Kir Royale — that's her drink. He stuck with mineral water, twist of lime. She ordered the caviar — toast points. He didn't have any."

"Have they been in together before tonight?"

"I never waited on him. Never saw him. She comes in a lot, meets people. She's always nice to me, sometimes slips me some cash. She never pays — the tab, I mean. She meets people who pay the tab, but she'd slip me some cash sometimes."

"What were they talking about?"

Now he looked pained. "I'm not supposed to talk about what customers talk about."

"This time it's different. This time it's a murder investigation."

Those nervous eyes popped wide. "Are you sure? Maybe she had an accident. Maybe."

"It's my job to be sure. Now, what were they talking about?"

"His play, I think. I sort of tune it out because, honest, you're not supposed to talk about what you hear. But they were talking some about this play he's producing — I think. And some girls, maybe something about illegals. His wife? Maybe? They would stop talking about it when I went up to them, so I didn't hear all that much. They kept it down — she usually keeps it down. So did he — sometimes the other person doesn't keep it down as much, but he did."

"How would you describe them together? Friendly?"

Now he shook his head. "I guess not so friendly. She smiles a lot, but . . . He wasn't real happy, if I had to say. He looked pissed — sorry, annoyed, a little mad. I guess maybe they argued some, but they kept it down."

"Who left the booth first?"

"She did — I kept my eye on the booth in case they wanted another round. We were busy, but I kept an eye, and I saw her get up, head downstairs. Mostly she goes before she leaves — down to the bathroom, I mean. Then I was busy, and when I noticed again, he was gone. I checked my meter, and he'd paid the bill, so I bused the table."

"About how long was that? When you noticed he was gone and bused the table?"

"I'm not real sure. Not that long. Five or ten minutes, I guess. Probably like five minutes, maybe. Another of my tables paid out, so I bused that one, and when I carried the tray over to the station, I sort of turned to say something to Bent — ah, Bentley behind the bar — and she . . . she bumped into me, threw me off, and I got my balance, but then I saw her, and the blood, and I dropped the tray. I dropped it, and then everything was whack."

"Before that, did you notice anybody else go downstairs or come upstairs?"

"I don't think I did. I try to keep an eye on my stations and none of my customers did, except Ms. Mars. I got — I got — I got her blood on me. See? When she bumped into me, I got blood on me."

"Yeah, I see. What we're going to do is get you a clean shirt, and we're going to take that one in with us."

"I didn't kill her." His face went sheet white, with high red flags on his cheeks. "I swear!"

"I don't think that. I think you were doing your job. I'm going to get you a shirt, then you can go."

"I liked her. She was always nice to me."

"Just wait here."

Once again, she went to Roarke. "That kid needs a clean shirt and somewhere to change. I need to take the one he's wearing into evidence. The vic walked into him, got blood on him. He's a little shaky."

"I'll see to it."

"And one more? Would you get your manager to pull out anyone who paid their bill between eighteen-thirty and eighteen-forty-one?"

"All right."

They cleared the bar until only cops and sweepers remained.

Gratefully, Eve took the coffee Roarke brought her in an oversized white cup and saucer. "Thanks."

With it, she sat to organize her thoughts.

Roarke sat across from her, waited.

"You brought a ride?"

"I did."

"Would you trust Peabody and McNab with it?"

"I would."

"Peabody!"

"Sir!" Peabody gulped down the last of a fancy latte as she worked on her notes.

"I need you and McNab to take that box to Central, log it in. I want McNab to go over her 'link and any other electronics in there. I want a full report on same, asap. I want you to start running the names in her address book, or whatever she has. Send me a copy. You can take Roarke's ride. Where is it?" she asked him.

"It's in the alley, in the rear of the building." He rattled off its codes.

"Park it in my slot. Roarke can have somebody pick it up. McNab, anything pertinent on the cams?"

"Nobody went in or out of the rear door." He rubbed idly at his earlobe and its forest of hoops. "Numerous in and out the front during the pertinent time frame. I'm pretty sure I've got the guy — from the description given — she was sitting with. Only from the back, but it looks like he walked out at eighteen-forty. Five others, also only viewed from the back, left at eighteen-thirty-eight. Three males, two females, who appeared to be in a group. And two females left at eighteen-forty-one."

"Shoot me a copy of that, and all the wit statements."

"Are you coming into Central?" Peabody asked her.

"No, I'm going to go visit her drinking buddy, then I'll work from home unless we break this. Morgue first stop in the morning, Peabody. Meet me there unless you hear otherwise."

"There goes breakfast. 'All the dish, served with a silver spoon.' "

"What?"

"Oh, her slogan — the vic's. Larinda Mars's *Who's Doing What* show: 'All the dish, served with a silver spoon.' Not that I watch that sort of thing," she added, a little too piously. "You just hear stuff."

"Right. Get gone. Wait, how did you and

McNab get here so fast? You were off nearly an hour before I called you in."

"I stayed at Central doing some paperwork until McNab cleared. He had one hanging. We were just walking out when you tagged me."

"Handy. Appreciate the assist, McNab."

"Where the She-Body goes, I go. I'm driving."

"Nuh-uh." Peabody leaped up, chased him out the back.

"I need to secure and lock the doors," Eve told Roarke. "You've got a nice place here — on the fancy edge for me, but nice, and quality staff. It'll be nice again."

He glanced down at the pool of blood, the river of it running from pool to stairway.

"I thought very, very little of Larinda Mars, and what I did think was with sneering derision at best. But someone spilled her blood on my floor. I trust you to find justice for her. And I'll find it for my place, and the people who make their livings working in it."

He looked around again, then picked up Eve's coat. "Let's lock up, then you can begin to fill me in on the blanks I haven't filled in myself."

She put a hand on his arm, then, since they were alone, moved it to his cheek. "I know you're pissed."

"Bloody well right I am."

"It happened in your place," Eve said, framing his face firmly. "And it happened under my goddamn nose. Believe me when I say I'm as pissed as you are. Justice, yeah, it comes first and last for the victim. But it's fucking personal for me, too. Under my nose, goddamn it."

He framed her face in turn, smiled just a little. "So here we are, all pissed off, and likely to give this particular dead woman more of our sweat than she deserved in life."

"Murder levels that."

"It does." He kissed her lightly, then rested his brow on hers. "Aye, it does. So we'll both do what needs doing until it's done."

3

The wind had snarled from bitter to outright mean. On its bitch slap wafted the scents of boiled soy dogs, roasted chestnuts, and frigid humanity.

Eve filled Roarke in, bare bones for now, as they traveled the two blocks to her car.

"I'm amazed she got out of the loo. She must have lost a half liter or more in there," Roarke said.

Still pissed, Eve thought, and who could blame him? "The doctor who assisted, and DeWinter agreed: Mars was mostly dead when she stumbled into the bar. She bled a damn river on the stairs. They gave her twelve minutes, tops, from the point of attack, but they didn't see that blood trail. I'm betting half that, or less. And the wound . . ."

When they reached the car, she rattled off the address, let him take the wheel.

"It wasn't that severe. Not visibly. A slice."

She demonstrated, swiping a finger over her biceps. "Not especially deep. It's a damn efficient way to kill. Economic. One quick slice, walk away, and — what I gather — her heart does the rest, just pumps out the blood with every beat."

Taking out her PPC, she glanced at Roarke. "What do you know, if anything, about Fabio Bellami?"

"A bit. I've met him a handful of times. Third — or it may be fourth — generation money. International banking with some tentacles in broadcasting and entertainment. Bellami's into the entertainment end of things, I believe. Theater primarily. And though he had a reputation as a wastrel in his youth, appears to have steadied up since his marriage."

" 'Wastrel'?"

Roarke lifted a shoulder. "It fits. Squandering his trust fund, buzzing about the globe and off-planet to clubs and other rich-boy hangouts, and causing enough trouble to require payoffs and restitution. He had a taste for women — often a few at the same time, so the stories go — along with drink and illegals."

"Sounds like Mars's type of story line."

"Would have been but, as I said, he's left that lifestyle behind. He's produced a couple of well-received plays, become involved in charitable causes, and appears well married if what I've heard is accurate."

"So, reformed?"

Roarke sent her a genuine smile. "It happens to the worst of us."

She couldn't argue with reformation, since she'd married a Dublin street rat and wildly successful thief — former. But she also knew habits were hard to break.

"Maybe he slipped, and she caught wind. Or maybe she was just pressuring him for juice. Either way he didn't like it. Their waiter was clear on that — and the couple of times I paid attention to them, Bellami didn't look happy to be there."

She sat back. "But he was there. Why does a rich, successful, reformed wild child meet with a gossip reporter at a fancy French bar? And why does said gossip reporter frequent said bar — downtown bar, when she lives on Park Avenue, uptown?"

"We have a superior wine list."

"She went for the Kir Royale. And I bet there are fancy, upscale bars a lot closer to her place, or to Channel Seventy-Five. You probably own them."

"Maybe one or two. She may have frequented those as well. Mixing it up."

"Maybe." She chewed it over while Roarke

hunted for parking. Once he'd bagged a space, she got out, studied the area until he joined her on the sidewalk. "Nice neighborhood."

"Not far from our own." He took her hand. "You know, there are spare gloves for you in the dash box."

"I forgot. Why am I wearing six-thousand-dollar boots?"

Brows lifted, Roarke looked down, studied them. "To protect your feet in both a practical and fashionable manner."

"I could do that for a couple hundred bucks."

"Debatable. How do you know they're six-thousand-dollar boots?"

"Because DeWinter said they were." As they walked, she poked a finger into his arm. "She dinged me on it, and I didn't have a decent comeback. That's three large a boot, for God's sake."

"I believe your math is correct. I expect they're comfortable."

"Yeah, they're comfortable, but —"

"And sturdy, as you prefer," he continued smoothly. "I imagine if necessary — as it often is — you could chase a suspect several blocks in those." He brought the hand he held to his lips. "My cop spends a good portion of her day on her feet, walking these streets and chasing bad guys. I have a fondness for those feet, and consider good boots as essential in your daily pursuits as your weapon."

"For six grand they ought to be gold-plated," she muttered.

"Far too heavy," he said easily. "And you'd surely end up with blisters. Here we are."

She dropped the argument she wouldn't win — for now anyway — and studied the stone building with its curvy concrete trim. Three stories, long, narrow windows, ornately studded double doors of dark, aged wood.

"How old do you figure?"

"Late nineteeth century. It was a residence, then a bank. It survived the Urban Wars intact, and morphed into a high-fashion boutique for a time, but the owners failed to maintain it."

"It's yours?'

"It was. I sold it a few years ago."

"You sold it to Bellami?"

"More accurately my representatives sold it to his representatives, and now it's a residence again. One that appears well tended. I find that satisfying."

"I bet you made a tidy profit, too."

The smile he pulled out for her equaled pure sin. "Darling, how else could I afford to keep my wife in six-thousand-dollar boots?"

"You're a real funny guy."

"I live for your laughter." With her hand still in his, he tugged her up the trio of stairs to the double doors.

Top-of-the-line security, she noted, including full-sweep cams.

At the press of a buzzer, the computer-generated voice answered.

Good evening. How may I assist you?

"Lieutenant Dallas, NYPSD." Eve held up her badge. "And Roarke, expert consultant, civilian. I need to speak with Fabio Bellami."

One moment, please, while I verify your identification . . .

Your identification has been verified. Please produce identification for Roarke, expert consultant, civilian.

"Thorough," Eve commented, smirking a little when Roarke took out his ID.

Thank you. Please wait while Mr. Bellami is notified.

"When's the last time you spoke with Bellami?" Eve asked.

"A year, or more. I know more *of* him than know him."

The right side of the doors opened. The woman wore slim black pants and a sweater.

Her pale blond hair, drawn back in a smooth tail, left her quietly pretty face unframed.

"Please come in." Her voice carried the faintest accent. Maybe Scandinavian, Eve thought. "Mr. and Mrs. Bellami are in the living room. May I take your coats?"

"No, thanks." Eve scanned the entrance. Lofty ceilings with fancy exposed beams and a tiered chandelier that mated rust-colored iron with sparkling crystal. Some art — dreamy landscapes — a couple of chairs that looked old and were painted a bold red, a cream-colored table holding a trio of vases, in varying heights where rainbows of flowers spilled.

It said rich, classy, and secure.

They walked over a floor of gold-toned wood through a wide brick archway.

Bellami rose from his seat on a high-backed love seat of shimmery blue. He wore, Eve noted, the same suit and tie as he had in Du Vin.

"Roarke. A pleasure, and a surprise."

A surprise, Eve judged as he crossed over to shake Roarke's hand. But the anxiety in his eyes didn't denote pleasure. "And Lieutenant. It's lovely to meet you. DeAnna, Eve Dallas and Roarke. My wife, DeAnna."

When she started to level herself off the love seat — and to Eve's eye she'd need a pulley and tackle, as she was hugely, amazingly pregnant — Bellami jabbed a finger at her.

"You sit."

DeAnna laughed, deep brown eyes sparkling with humor in a face, Eve decided, that owed some of its current roundness to the same reason her belly humped out in a considerable mountain.

"I will, as it would probably take me ten minutes to get up on my own. Please sit down. Fabio, get our guests a drink."

"That's all right," Eve began, but she caught something in Bellami's eyes. What might have been a plea. "Actually, coffee would be great."

"I'll take care of that."

DeAnna beamed at the blonde. "Thanks, Lanie. I can sit here with my weak tea and be jealous."

"When are you due?" Roarke said conversationally as he nudged Eve into a chair.

"March twenty-first."

At Eve's expression — it had to be shocked — DeAnna laughed again. The sound managed to be full-throated and musical at the same time. "But we're told to be ready in a couple of weeks. We've having triplets, and they come early. Thank God."

"There are *three* in there?" Eve heard herself say, then immediately apologized. "Sorry."

"Don't be. Fabio and I had the same reaction when we found out. And all girls. Poor Fabio. He'll be surrounded."

"I can't wait."

He looked as if he meant it, Eve mused.

"We have a mutual acquaintance," DeAnna said to Eve. "Well, more than an acquaintance for you, as I understand you're very good friends. Mavis Freestone."

"You know Mavis?"

"I do. Before this . . ." She circled her hands on her stupendous belly. "She and I performed together at a fund-raiser. She's marvelous. Unique and marvelous."

"She's all that."

Something — some*things* — moved inside DeAnna's belly — visibly. Uneasy with that, Eve concentrated on her face. Shadows of fatigue under those dark eyes, and a pallor under the olive skin.

The blonde came in with a coffee service. Bellami rose to take it from her, murmured to her. She nodded.

"Doctor's orders," Bellami said, setting down the tray.

"Oh, but I'm just sitting here."

"Come on now, Mama." Lanie crossed to

her, got an arm around DeAnna, and helped launch her to standing. "Bed rest means bed. Your babies are tired."

"They don't feel tired." She rested her hand on them again. "I'm sorry," she said to Roarke and Eve. "I'm at the stage where I eat, sleep, and waddle. And not a lot of waddling right now. I hope you'll come back when I'm not being sent off to bed."

"It was lovely to meet you." Rising, Roarke took her hand. "Stay well."

"I'm doing all I can. Good night."

She did waddle, Eve noted. Who wouldn't with that front-end load?

"I'm sorry if that seemed abrupt. She's had some complications, and she's on modified bed rest for the duration now. And the doctor made it clear she's not to be upset or stressed."

He looked after his wife another moment, then poured out the coffee. "I'm assuming since you're here — I'm aware of what you do, Lieutenant — something's very wrong. Did something happen to one of my family, or DeAnna's?"

"No. Just black's fine." She took the cup, waited for him to serve Roarke and sit again. "You had drinks with Larinda Mars this evening."

"I . . . Yes."

"Can you tell me what time you left Du Vin?"

"About six-thirty, quarter to seven, somewhere around there. I think was home by about seven. Why?"

"What's your relationship with Ms. Mars?"

Everything in his face tightened. "We have no relationship."

"Yet you spent nearly an hour together over drinks."

He picked up the brandy he'd set aside when they'd come in. "You could call it a business meeting."

"What sort of business?"

"Mine. If Mars is determined to cause trouble, I'll have my lawyers deal with her. I won't have my wife upset. If she's filed some sort of complaint or made some accusation, I —"

"She's dead."

Eve said it flatly, watched for reaction.

"I don't care what she . . . What?" Now his face went slack, as if from a gut punch. "What did you say?"

"I said Larinda Mars is dead."

He simply stared, showing confusion. "But we were just . . ." Confusion flashed into shock. "Oh God. My God. I left the bar. She was still there. Someone had to see me leave — there must be security. I was home around seven, by seven-fifteen. House security will show that. Lanie will verify that. Please, don't question DeAnna. Please, don't upset her."

He shoved off the love seat, rubbing his fingers on his temples as he paced. "She left the table — we were done and she left — not the bar. She went downstairs. The restroom, I assume. I sat there for another minute or two, then I paid the bill and left. I paid the bill, got my coat, and left. She hadn't come back. I came straight home. I took a cab. I'm sure you can check that.

"When was she killed?"

"You assume she was killed?"

"You said she's dead. You're Homicide. Yes, I assume." He snapped it out, then quickly looked toward the archway. Took a long breath. "She was alive when I left the bar."

"She was attacked in the bar. Downstairs."

"Attacked?" He sat again. "I'm not surprised. She was a vulture, a vampire. I couldn't be the only one."

"The only one?"

"Who detested her. I barely knew her, and detested her. If she was attacked, someone must have heard, or seen. I couldn't have sat there more than two or three minutes after she got up. I couldn't have been in the bar a full five minutes after she got up. How could I follow her down and beat her to death — or wring her neck — and get back out in five minutes?"

Eve eyed him coolly. "Is that what you wanted to do? Beat her to death or wring her neck?"

"The thought occurred," he muttered, then shut his eyes. "I should get my lawyers. I know better, but —" Opening his eyes again, he looked toward the archway. "I'll tell you everything — freely. I only ask that you don't involve my wife. A couple of weeks, they say. Longer is better, but in a couple of weeks, we'll be in the clear if she goes into labor. Please, we need that time."

"I've no reason to speak to your wife about this. Unless you killed Larinda Mars."

"I haven't killed anyone. I've done some stupid things, careless, reckless things in my life, but I've never killed anyone. She was blackmailing me."

"For?"

"Before I met DeAnna, I did those stupid, careless, reckless things routinely. I reveled in doing them, in shocking people — particularly my family. Spoiled, entitled." He shook his head. "If I drank, it was with the purpose of getting drunk. If I used, it was to get as high as possible. Every time. I wasn't an alcoholic or an addict. I used substances, and people, because I could. I was going nowhere, and that's just where I wanted to be.

"Then I met DeAnna. There are moments, there are people, who change your life, who save it. DeAnna changed mine. Saved mine."

"She would have been a bright light on Broadway when you met her," Roarke calculated. "A star, full of talent and promise."

"Yes. Gorgeous, talented, a shining prize in the box. And I thought, I'll have one of those."

He pressed his lips together in a show of self-disgust.

"That's just how I thought of it. She wouldn't be had, not DeAnna. She saw me for what I was — careless, callous — and blew me off. That posed a challenge, so I pursued. I got nowhere with her," he said with a small smile. "I began to see her not as a shiny prize in the box but a puzzle. Then as a person. I wanted to prove something to her, and to myself. I found a play.

"An old friend of mine had a play, and couldn't get anyone to look at it," Bellami explained. "I looked. And I asked DeAnna to look. She did, and she talked to my friend, met with him, with me. We worked. I worked, for the first time in my life, really. And that was a revelation. I was good at it, actually good at it, and I liked being good at it. I began to mend some fences. I began to live a life. I produced that play, and it did all right. It didn't shake the theater world, but it did all right. I produced another, and it did all right. My friend wrote another play, a really good one, and working on it, asking for DeAnna's input, we, well, found each other. She fell in love with me. I was already in love with her. We built a life, we're building a family. She helped me earn the trust and respect of my parents again, of my grandparents, my sister. She helped me earn respect for myself."

"All that's in the past," Eve said. "How could Mars blackmail you about things your wife, your family, really anyone who cared to look, already knew?"

"A couple months ago — early December — DeAnna took a weekend with a couple of her college friends. She was so tired, so worn-out, and this trip — a retreat, a health spa just a short drive out of the city — came highly recommended. Her doctor approved, in fact, he told us it would do her a lot of good. The night she left I went downtown to see a singer we were considering for the new play. We — my friend and I — wanted to see how she performed in front of an audience. We met at the club, and halfway through the first set, he got tagged. The person identified herself as a nurse at Clinton Memorial, and said his mother had taken ill. Not an emergency, but she'd been given some medication and had asked them to contact him, to ask him to come and take her home. She gets terrible migraines, and if one triggers she can get very ill. He had to go, and I decided to stay, see the rest of the show, told him to tag me if it turned out to be more serious.

"I remember listening to her sing, watching her — imagining her in the part. I remember I started to feel . . . off. Mildly dizzy even sitting down, a bit queasy. I remember leaving cash on the table because I wanted to get out, out in the air.

"The next I remember, I woke upstairs, in my own bed. A raging headache, the smell of booze-sweat, the taste in my mouth. I remember those mornings very well."

Pausing, he stared down at his hands. "I'd had one brandy — one. I wanted a clear head to rate the performance. And I rarely have more than two drinks, ever. I don't remember leaving the club or getting home or going to bed. I had never had a blackout, not even when I abused everything that could be abused. I told myself either the brandy or the quick meal I'd had before had made me ill. But . . . I could smell perfume on me — stale perfume, and not my wife's. I ignored it, I pushed it away and showered it away, and . . ."

"You think you were drugged."

"I know it." Eyes fierce now, he jerked his head up. "I know it now absolutely. But even back then? I spoke with my friend later that day and he was furious. He'd gone to the hospital. His mother had never been there. No nurse had contacted him. He went to his mother's apartment, and she was fine. They — someone had wanted me alone. At that time we both thought it was just some sick joke. I even thought it might have been pulled off by one of the crowd I used to run with. It would be something we'd do for a laugh."

"And now?" Eve prompted.

"I agreed to meet Mars, as she'd hounded me. She'd started to insinuate I'd want to know what she knew — before everyone else knew. It's a reality of my industry, that playing ball with her sort has to be done — to an extent. So I met her at the bar. She warned me to be careful how I reacted, what

I said. 'It's crowded, isn't it,' she said. A lot of people here. A lot of people to gossip. She showed me a vid. She had a video of me, and two women in the bed I share with my wife. We were . . . in my wife's bed."

He'd gone pale and closed his eyes, struggling for composure.

"I would never — I love my wife. I would never do that to her. I'm not that person anymore. I told her — Mars — that it never happened. It was faked. She said it could and would be verified, and to add to that, she had witnesses who saw me leave the club — she had the name, the date, the time — with those two women. Drunk and fondling them. Getting in a cab together."

"What about your house security?"

"I checked that the morning I woke up, after the club. I wanted to see when I got home, in what sort of condition. It had been turned off, by remote. By my code. Barely an hour after J.C., my friend, got that tag. Tonight, Mars said she knew DeAnna was very delicate, very fragile, how upsetting it would be for her to have to face this terrible gossip, this awful proof of my infidelity. How it would ruin my reputation, too, one I'd patched together. It would show everyone, including my wife, I was still a user, still a fraud.

"Then she turned and smiled at the waiter. I couldn't even hear what they said to each other. My head was full of noise. I wanted to reach across the table and snap her neck. Just break it like a twig. She leaned toward me, still smiling, and said nobody had to know. She was good at keeping secrets — for friends."

He pressed his fingers to his eyes. "Sorry, I need some water."

"Why don't I get that for you?" Roarke rose. "The kitchen?" He gestured toward the back of the house, got a nod.

"How much did she want?"

He sat back, eyes closed. "She said friends do favors for each other. She'd do this one for me, and I'd pay her back. I didn't raise my voice. I was screaming inside, but I didn't raise my voice. I said I hadn't done this. She'd set me up. She sat there, smiling, sipping her drink. Said the video would prove I did, and who'd believe she'd set me up, someone with my history? It would be eight thousand this month. I was stunned at how little, then she explained. Next month six thousand, the following seven, and we'd vary the payments. Didn't I want to write this down? I just sat there. She . . ."

He trailed off when Roarke came back with a tall glass of water, iced. "Thanks.

Thanks. God." He drank, breathed, drank. "She said if I fed her other secrets, good information, that would lower the payment for that particular month. It would be my choice: cash or information. And no one would ever see the vid, no one would ever know. My wife would be blissfully ignorant of my deception, we'd have our sweet little babies and go on as we were. As long as I paid.

"I know there was more. Arguing, carefully arguing. I can't remember it all. It's like being in a play, and forgetting your lines. I said she'd have her blood money, but I'd never give her information, never put anyone else through what she was putting me through. She said I'd be surprised how that attitude evolves over time. For now I could meet her in two days, same time, same place, with cash. That's when she got up, said she was going to freshen up before she left, and I could pay the check. She walked away.

"I didn't kill her. I wanted to hurt her, but . . . what would it do to DeAnna? It would all come out, and I'd throw us both into a scandal. She needs to be happy, to be calm. The babies. We're having triplets. My girls are inside my wife. I wouldn't risk them, even for the satisfaction of hurting that bitch."

"Where's your brachial artery?" Eve tossed out.

His eyebrows drew together. "I don't know what that is."

"Do you know much about anatomy?"

"I know where everything is, more or less. I know a hell of a lot more about the female reproductive system than I'd like to, frankly. Artery? Like the heart?"

"Not exactly. I won't speak to your wife, and I'll do whatever I can do to keep this out of the media."

Tears swam into his eyes. "Thank you. I'll do whatever you need me to do."

"I need the name and contact number of your friend — the one who went to the club with you. I need any and all communications you've had with Mars. It's likely I'll need to speak to you again, and I'll expect your cooperation."

"You'll have it."

"If you've lied to me, I'll find out."

"I haven't. I wouldn't risk my wife, our daughters."

"It happens I believe you on that."

When they walked back outside, Roarke slipped an arm around Eve. "You felt for him, and so did I."

"I believe he loves his wife, and I think Mars targeted him — rich, former womanizer with a lot to lose — managed to have someone slip something into his drink. Which means she'd stalked him, watched him, picked her time. Wife's gone for a couple of days — the threesome looks even worse in the marriage bed."

"You don't believe he killed her."

"My hard lean is he was blindsided. He still has some doubts about his worth, especially after waking up from a blackout, and she counted on all that. He didn't walk into that bar with a plan to kill, and I lean — fairly heavily — that her killer did. I also believe if she'd continued to bleed Bellami — threaten his wife, his family, his life — he would have eventually done her harm.

"But he didn't do her harm tonight."

"But someone else she's bled — as, obviously, this is her business plan — did harm her tonight."

Eve nodded. "Think about it. You bleed me, I bleed you, bitch. It's downright poetic. Why the hell don't people come to the cops?"

"Oh, let me count the ways." He tugged her back when she pulled away. "I see your side of it, Lieutenant, but it's a difficult leap for someone to come to a cop and confess they've embezzled, cheated, covered up some crime or misadventure. Blackmailers, as you very well know, depend on just that behavior. You just pay me, and I keep your secret."

"And they never stop. You never stop the bleeding."

"You're absolutely right, but those in the middle of it have the hope it will, somehow. Those who can afford to pay? It's just money compared to what else they might lose."

"Or information," she added. "I'm betting she bled plenty of that. Lowers the cash flow for the weasel, makes it easier to keep weaseling. It's just gossip."

She dropped into the car, put her head back. "Or favors," she considered. "Like slipping something into some guy's drink at a club. No way she'd have risked doing that herself. Maybe she hired the LCs, but that's easy. Unlikely Bellami's friend," she considered. "We'll check the story, check him, but it's tough seeing a friend ruin the lives of two people who helped him launch his career."

"She might have had something on the friend as well."

"Yeah, winding that around, but unless I find he's a scumbag, I don't see it. Triplets, for God's sake."

She shuddered once.

"I need to see her place. It's on Park."

"You need food. So do I."

"Oh. Yeah. Probably."

"We'll stop for — God help me — a pizza, then on to Park."

"That'll work."

4

As Eve considered a couple of slices and a tube of Pepsi — no wine on duty — the perfect meal, she figured she owed Roarke points for reminding her to have a meal in the first place.

And the forty minutes or so spent on eating it gave her time to reorganize the current data in her mind.

"You're in the women's room," she began as she took the passenger seat once again.

"Then I hope all the women therein are nubile and scantily clad."

"Perv." She waved a finger in the air. "Reboot. I'm in the women's room. Another female walks in, I don't react, barely notice, keep doing what I'm doing."

"Men imagine that to be grooming yourself and the other nubiles while scantily clad. The loo version of the classic pillow fight."

"I repeat the perv comment."

"I'm forced to say you're wrong — not necessarily re the perv, but in your setup. If you're in there, Lieutenant, and another female walks in, you'd not only notice but be fully capable of describing her in minute detail with a single glance out of those cop's eyes of yours."

"Okay, a civilian female is in the women's room, another female walks in. She doesn't think twice about it. A man walks in, she reacts. Possibly amusement if she's not alone in there or if said man looks embarrassed and backs out again. Possibly outrage if she's inclined in that direction, anxiety or fear if he appears threatening. But she reacts, notices, and is on guard."

"So you lean toward a female killer?"

"Not necessarily. Those are generalities. Specifically, Mars is in the women's room, someone walks in. A female, she doesn't necessarily react — unless she knows said female. A male, she reacts, one way or the other. If she knows him, she probably leans toward amused or interested. If it's one of her marks, which is a hell of a lot more logical than some random killer strolling in and slicing some random woman — plus, according to statements, she used the bar regularly — she has another sort of reaction. Maybe amusement, maybe annoyance, maybe curiosity, depending on her attitude toward said mark. But she's not afraid."

"Why do you conclude that?"

"Her lip dye's on the shelf in front of the mirror. She hung her purse on the handy hook, took out her lip dye — and she had fresh on when she collapsed, so she used it. So he walks in. She either keeps putting it on, or closes it, sets it on the shelf. She's got pepper spray, a panic button, *and* an illegal stunner in her purse, open and within easy reach, but she doesn't go for any of them — her purse was organized, no jumble like you might get if you're grabbing out a weapon or a defense. And she puts the lip stuff down."

Eve could see it clearly enough in her head. The sweep of blond hair, the pink skin suit, the pink lips to match.

"I need Morris to verify, but both logic and my on-scene assessment say she faced her killer when he cut her. So she set down the lip gunk, turned. She's like: Well, mark of mine, did you make a wrong turn? If he's smart, he just steps up to her, slices, steps back out of the initial spray. Maybe he holds there for a few seconds, maybe he files a sweet, sweet memory of the shock on her face, of her slapping a hand over the wound, of the blood pumping out. Then he books it. It has to be fast. The place is crowded, and somebody else might come in."

She frowned as Roarke drove uptown on Park. "He — or she — isn't real smart. Real smart would have been to bring something along to block the door, let her bleed out in there, give himself more time, possibly more time. But in any case, the killer bolts — keeps it easy and casual when he gets back upstairs, strolls right out. Button up the coat if you got any blood on you — a few drops is almost inevitable, and Bellami didn't have even a drop. Same suit and shirt and tie he wore in the bar."

"You don't suspect him in any case."

"No, but that's one more reason why. Minutes, it all takes just a couple minutes. Slice, step back, walk out, up, out. It's likely she staggered out shortly behind, a little panic at first, then confusion, weakness. A couple more minutes and she staggers into the bar. Another minute, she's dead.

"If the killer's female, she may not have recognized her. If the killer's male, she did. I'll run probability, but that's how I see it."

He pulled up in front of a tall spear of a building that read gold in the streetlights. At the entrance, within a deep inward curve of glass, a doorman stood in hunter green livery with gold trim.

The doorman — woman, Eve corrected — strode to the car even as they got out. Her DLE didn't look like much, deliberately and deceptively, and earned a single glance of quiet derision.

"Good evening. Are you visiting one of our residents?"

Eve held up her badge. The doorwoman gave it a long blink out of blossom blue eyes. "Can I help you with something, Lieutenant?"

"I need to get into Larinda Mars's unit."

"I don't believe Ms. Mars is currently in residence."

"No, and she won't be, as she's currently in residence at the morgue."

Now the mouth, dyed a soft, conservative neutral, dropped open. "I'm sorry, are you saying Ms. Mars is dead?"

"Since she's residing and not working at or visiting the morgue, yeah, I'm saying she's dead. I need to get into her unit."

"I . . ." She streamed out a breath the wind whisked away, sucked another in. "I can help you with that." Though she gave the DLE another pained glance, she said nothing, led the way to the curved glass doors.

Inside was warm air and a blinding plethora of gold. Gold urns full of spiky, lethal-looking vegetation and flowers red and glossy enough to have been painted with blood, gold tables, a central chandelier formed of snaking twists of metallic gold. More bloodred, topped with gold marble, for the security counter.

The woman behind it offered a polite, professional smile that turned into a rounded O when she spotted Roarke.

"Give me a second," the doorman said, going to consult with the lobby clerk.

The lobby clerk let out a gasp that edged close to a squeal, hissed out a bunch of questions. The doorman merely shook her head, then signaled Eve over.

"We're going to need to scan and verify your identification, Lieutenant."

Eve took out her badge, held it out for the mini-scanner.

"Okay. Um." The clerk gave Eve a wide-eyed stare.

"How about you clear us up?" Eve suggested.

"Oh, yeah, sure. But . . . is Ms. Mars really dead and all?"

"She's really dead and all."

"Golly."

"Did she get many visitors?"

"Well, we're not really supposed to discuss our residents or their guests."

"Police investigation." Eve waved the badge in front of the clerk's wide eyes.

"I guess she did. I mean, she had some, and she had parties and stuff. Deliveries. A lot of deliveries, right, Becca?"

"Plenty," the doorwoman confirmed.

"How about regulars?"

"Well . . . I think she was dating Mitch L. Day. He's the host of *Second Cup* on Seventy-Five. He's kind of dreamy. But I guess, mostly, she gave parties and got deliveries."

"Did she ever have any trouble here? Altercations, arguments?"

Now the clerk bit her bottom lip. "Well . . . I guess I don't think she and the Wilburs got along very well. They have the penthouse opposite hers. She and Mrs. Wilbur wouldn't speak or even ride up in the same elevator if they came into the lobby at the same time. And she — ah, Ms. Mars — lodged two complaints with the management that the Wilbur kids were disruptive. They're really not, and the units are fully soundproofed."

"They're good kids," the doorwoman put in. "She's half a bitch."

"Becca!"

In response, Becca shrugged. "You know she is — was — Roxie."

Eve turned to Becca. "Only half?"

"I know it's not chill to say bad things about the dead, but police investigation, right?"

"That's right."

Becca adjusted her cap. "She flashed that barracuda smile plenty, and butter wouldn't melt. But she tried pumping me for gossip on other residents, and guests, too. Tried to bribe me for it."

"How much?"

Becca's mouth twisted in a sneer. "A hundred a pop for anything she could use on air. Double that if she could make a special out of it. She didn't like when I turned her down — I'm not going to compromise the privacy of the people in my building. And I wouldn't with hers, either, except . . ."

"Police investigation."

"Yeah, that. After I turned her down — and I know Luke and Gio did, too — they're on the door, day shifts — she stiffed me. Us. Not another tip out of her. You turned her down, Rox."

"I had to." The lobby clerk bit her lip again. "You're supposed to accommodate the residents, but golly, that's against the rules. I could lose my job. Plus, you know, it's just not nice."

"Did she ever threaten either of you?"

"She filed a complaint against me." Becca's jaw tightened. "She didn't get anywhere with it. I had to talk to the manager about it, but I had a couple dozen resident commendations against her one complaint. And I told the manager about the bribe. Luke and Gio backed me up there. Roxie, too."

Now Becca smiled — showing a little barracuda herself. "I think the manager had a talk with Ms. Mars after because she never gave me any more trouble. I'm sorry she's dead — a person doesn't deserve to die for being half a bitch. But I'm not sorry she's not going to be in residence."

"Okay. I appreciate the cooperation. If you'd clear us up."

"Sure, right away. I have to log in to make a copy of her swipes. It'll only take a minute."

"I've got a master," Eve said. And a master B and E man if I need one.

"Oh, okay. Elevator three will take you up to her main entrance. Fifty-second floor. Penthouse."

"Got it."

With Roarke she walked to and into a gold — natch — elevator.

"Interesting," Roarke said.

"Not a bit surprising. You don't own this place."

"Why do you assume that?"

"The doorwoman didn't recognize you. Lobby clerk did, but just because you're rich and frosty. Plus, that lobby is really ugly. You wouldn't have a really ugly lobby."

"I appreciate your confidence. I wouldn't term it ugly as much as obsessively tacky."

"Whichever. I'll have to run this Mitchell Day, have a chat with him."

"That's Mitch L., initial *L.,* Day."

"Seriously?"

Roarke nodded as the elevator doors opened. "He hosts a late-morning talk show."

Mystified, Eve shook her head. "Why do people watch shows where other people sit around and talk?"

"There are some who actually enjoy conversations. I know that's a shock to you."

"If you're watching on screen, you're not even having a conversation. You're more eavesdropping." She pulled out her master, frowned in consideration. "Huh. Okay, I get that."

"Of course you do."

"Aren't eaves the things on the sides of buildings? How do you drop them, and what does that have to do with listening in on other people's conversations?"

He drew a blank, found himself intrigued. "I'll be sure to look it up."

"Language — which conversations are made of — doesn't make any sense half the time."

She keyed in with her master, opened the door.

To pitch-dark.

"Lights on, full," she ordered.

They blasted on to reveal a spacious living area, carpeted in pale rose. Furnishings hit the sharp and edgy of I'm-trendy-*now* with a lot of chrome and glass, splashy modern art, a pair of long, low gel benches in lieu of sofas.

An entertainment screen dominated one wall, floor-to-ceiling floating shelves another. On the shelves dozens of photos of Mars looked out. In most, she posed with someone — the fact that Eve actually recognized some of the faces told her all if not most were celebrities or luminaries of some sort.

The windows that would look out on Park Avenue bore heavy drapes in the same tone as the carpet with the addition of fussy, feathery trim in a deeper hue.

"A building like this is going to have privacy screens on the windows. She not only adds those curtain things, but keeps them closed. For somebody who made a living poking holes in others' privacy, she guarded her own."

"She'd know just how easily the boundaries of privacy could be breached," Roarke commented. "It's a space for entertaining," he continued as he wandered. "But certainly not for relaxing. It's tasteful, in the way a high-end ultra-contemporary furniture showroom would be, but without warmth or personality. Still, she certainly knew how to invest her gain, ill-gotten or not."

Eve scanned the room. "Where?"

"Well, take that painting there. That would be a Scarboro — an original. It would go for about two hundred."

"Dollars?"

"Thousands thereof."

"That?" Stunned, Eve walked closer, studied the splotches of crimson and orange over and around jagged lines of purple and blue. "Are you kidding me? Bella could do better."

"Art's what you make of it," he said lightly. "Certainly not my particular taste," he added as he moved to stand with her. "Though in my time I certainly . . ." He trailed off, amused at himself for momentarily forgetting her lapel recorder — currently engaged. "Ah, well, days gone by."

She shot him a look, understanding perfectly that he'd stolen more than his share of paintings — splotchy and otherwise — in days gone by.

"Take any electronics you come across. I'll take the bedroom."

There were two, though one now served as an office with a large white workstation, a generous desk chair in leather nearly as pink as the skin suit in which its owner had died. Lots more photos, she noted, some shiny awards, and all manner of dust catchers.

Bowls, bottles, a collection of shiny glass eggs on little stands, fancy little boxes.

She'd leave the office to Roarke for now. Bedrooms, she thought, tended to serve as spaces people considered safe, private, off-limits. And often held the secrets.

She hadn't skimped on the bed, Eve mused. The headboard, white, padded, rose nearly to the ceiling, curved in at the sides. Candy pink covered the bed, along with a mountain range of fancy, fussy pillows.

More jarring art — how did she sleep? — a gel bench at the foot of the bed, a mirrored chest with more colorful bottles arranged on it. A glance in the en suite showed her a long trough of a tub big enough for three good friends, a large glass shower with multi-jets, a long counter with double sinks shaped like full-blown roses and fed with waterfall faucets, a drying tube. A toilet and bidet stood discreetly behind white sliding doors.

The wall-spanning mirror over the counter turned into a view screen by remote or voice command.

The ledge surrounding three sides of the tub held candles in clear glass bowls and a trio of slim, ornate pitchers.

Cabinets under the counter opened to drawers filled with beauty products and tools.

She'd come back to it.

For now she went back to the bed, opened the drawer on the bedside table. She took out two tablets, one full size, one mini. Swiped, found them both passcoded.

Deciding she'd let Roarke take a pass at them, she set them on the bed rather than bagging them, moved around to the far side of the bed.

"Party time," she announced after opening the drawer.

Sex toys, enhancers, lotions, and lubes filled the drawer.

She lifted out a two-ended vibrator, noted it offered both warm and cool. It had a self-lube feature, and a control marked *Ecstacy.*

Curious, she flipped it on, brows rising when nubs popped out as it whirled in various directions and speeds.

Roarke started in, then just leaned on the doorjamb and grinned. "Now, there's a picture."

Vibrator still humming and whirling, she looked over. "There's this port on it. I think it's for VR, so you can hook into the program while you do yourself. Packs a lot into a small, compact package."

She turned it off, set it aside.

"In addition we have a variety pack of condoms — stay safe — nipple clamps, cock rings, a couple gel vibrators, lubes, cuffs, your classic ball gag, cord restraints, blah-blah, hard-on pills, strap-ons, and a few illegals, including Rabbit."

"An active sex life."

"Solo and with friends by the look of it. Tablets over there, passcoded."

"I'll look at them. She has droids — the human replica variety and a couple of small robotics. The replica has been in sleep mode since noon — that's its standard programming. It's also programmed for sex, which is not at all surprising. Its name is Henri, and though it has other wardrobe, at the moment it's garbed in a loincloth."

"What? Like the jungle guy?"

"Yes, like the jungle guy."

"Takes all kinds." She angled her head, giving Roarke a long study.

"You're picturing me in a loincloth. I feel so cheap."

"Nothing cheap about you, pal. She's got an office across the hall. Data and comm center."

"I saw it, yes, and I'll get to it. She has a tablet in the kitchen. It reads as a social calendar. Parties, openings, premieres, lunch and dinner dates. Henri says it's part of his programming to keep it updated. The 'link in the kitchen is also his tool. A scroll through indicates its communication with caterers, reservations, ordering supplies, that sort of thing."

"Okay. I'll bag them anyway, and EDD can go through them."

"Then I'll take a look at the office."

Eve rose to take the closet. Enormous, packed, with a vanity alcove and separate shoe closet, it boasted such perfect organization Eve decided Henri took care of this, too.

Plenty of lingerie and sexy underwear in the built-in drawers — and an entire section just for belts.

Just belts — she marveled. Another for

scarves. Yet another for the winter season's hats and gloves.

Evening wear, on-camera wear, cocktail wear, snazzy day wear, all carefully cataloged on the closet comp, with clear notations on what had been worn where.

She worked her way through it, painstakingly, and found the safe.

"Now maybe we've got something."

Crouching down, she studied it, wondered if she could crack it. She'd developed and honed some skills since Roarke had started teaching her. No question he could open it in a fraction of the time, but —

She continued to study the safe as she pulled out her signaling 'link.

"Dallas."

"Peabody. McNab finally got through her purse electronics. We stopped for some food, but the real time suck? Seriously shielded. Even fail-safed."

"What did you find?"

"She had a jammer on the 'link, to block logging any tags, so he's got to work on that one. The PPC's encrypted, but we've been working there. We think we might have the key. Dallas, we think she was blackmailing people."

"Do tell."

"Yeah, it's . . ." On screen, Peabody's

expression dropped into a pout. "You knew that already?"

"Yeah — Bellami confirmed, and he's low to off the list. But clearly he wasn't her first or only mark, so let's get more."

"Working on it, but even what we've broken down so far? It's like code names, or pet names. Not actual names. We've got some dates, some amounts. She doesn't list them as either, but that's what rings."

"Get what you can, send me whatever it is. Knock off and go home when you think you've done all that makes sense for tonight."

"We've got some juice left."

"We're at her place now. I've got a safe here. Let's see what she locked away."

"Is Roarke cracking it?"

Annoyance shimmered. "He's busy. I'm on this."

"But . . . okay."

Only more annoyed, Eve clicked off, scowled at the safe.

"You'll need tools for that one," Roarke commented.

She sent him a steely stare. "If you keep sneaking up on people, you could get stunned."

He crouched down with her, kissed her cheek. "You know how it excites me when you threaten to use your weapon."

She ignored that and focused on the safe. "Why do I need tools? I've got that app you put on my 'link."

"This model — its mechanism is a bit more sophisticated than that."

"Because it wants her thumbprint?"

"That's one. I can work it so it won't get what it wants and still opens. It's a three-stage system. First a code, which can be numeric or a word, a phrase. Or a combination, which would be recommended. Then the thumbprint, then another code. It's professional grade, in that it's rarely for home use."

She stared at the safe again. "Yours?"

"It is, yes, which is why I'll be able to get around it. Still, if I'd known, I'd have the proper device. I'll have to improvise, so it'll take a bit of time."

He gave her a nudge. "Shove up now, and give me some room."

No point in letting pride get in the way of progress, she decided, and got up to continue her search of the closet.

"She has ten zillion clothes and, according to the comp, hardly wears anything more than once. Maybe two or three times on the regular stuff. Evening stuff, one time, all of it. She's had some of these fancy dresses for three years, only worn once. Why does she keep them?"

He didn't answer; she didn't expect he would, not while he was muttering, not while whatever device he was using hummed.

"A lot of the shoes, not worn period. Some worn once. She's got a couple months' worth of underwear. Who owns sixty pairs of underwear? Even you don't have sixty."

"Ah, there you are, my lovely."

"What?"

"Not you, though you are lovely." He inched back, stayed cross-legged on the closet floor. "You can open it now."

"You said it would take time."

"A bit, and it did."

She sat beside him, opened the door.

"Whoa."

Stacks of bills filled an entire section. Eve pulled one out. "Hundreds of thousand-dollar wraps. There has to be . . ."

As she tried to calculate, Roarke measured the stash using his hands. "If they're all the same wrap, you'd have about a million."

"She's got a freaking million dollars in her closet safe?"

"It's an excellent safe."

"Says the man who cracked it in under

ten." She drew out a leather jewelry case from another stack, another section, opened it to the flash and fire of diamonds. "Real?" she asked Roarke.

He took it, examined it under the light. "I don't happen to have a loupe on me, but yes, quite real. Excellent cut and color. Somewhere around . . . fifteen carats. Fifty thousand, I'd say, depending on where she got it."

She pulled out a leather box, found diamond drop earrings.

"Quite nice," Roarke said. "They'd look well on you. I can estimate, Eve, but from the amount here, you're better off with a reputable jeweler."

Still, curious, he slipped a larger box out of yet another section, admired the emerald-and-diamond cuff. "Lovely craftsmanship on this. If all the pieces in here come to the quality we've seen so far, she has well over in jewelry what she has in cash. I repeat, the woman knew how to invest."

She held out her hand. He closed the box, kissed her cheek again, and handed the box to her.

And grinned when she opened it again, just to check.

"Everything back in. I'm not going to transport all this in my damn car. Lock it back up."

She put the necklace case in, the earring case.

Roarke tapped her shoulder, opened his hand. The earrings sparkled in his palm.

She wanted to laugh, but only rolled her eyes.

Grinning, he dropped them into her outstretched hand. "Haven't lost my touch."

"I'll give you some touch," she parried as she stowed the earrings.

"I'm counting on it. Give me a moment and I'll reboot the safe."

"Reboot it?"

"I'll reprogram it so it takes your codes, your print. Another bit of time, and then when you have it transported, you'll be able to open it without any fuss."

She finished up the closet while he worked.

"First code?"

She used her badge number, then followed instructions and pressed her right thumb to the pad.

"Second code?"

"Sticky fingers."

He laughed, programmed it in. Shut the safe.

"And done."

"Office?"

"It appears to be all business — her legitimate business. Work and work-related communications, work and work-related data — stories done or in progress, research — which could lead you somewhere, I suppose. Personal finances," he continued, "which do not include a million in cash or purchases of this sort of jewelry. While she does well enough in her field, she couldn't afford any of this, the art, the jewelry, the furnishings. Even the rent here's a bit of a stretch."

As she'd concluded the same, Eve nodded slowly. "Which says her side business pays a lot better."

"I'd certainly say so."

"Okay, let's go through the rest to see if there are any hidey-holes or anything of interest. Then that's it here until I have the safe and electronics picked up."

They rose together.

"And I don't have two months' worth of underwear."

"I'm glad to hear it."

"I think the wardrobe is a matter of being seen or photographed, doing an event in a certain outfit and not wanting to be photographed in it again."

"You were listening."

"Always. As for why she keeps things she

hasn't worn in two or three years, I think we could speculate that, in some areas, she was a bit of a hoarder."

"With clothes, jewelry, money, but not with, you know, stuff. Hoarders usually go for stuff."

"A selective hoarder?"

Eve shrugged. "Yeah, maybe."

But she couldn't say if it bothered her strictly because of her own sensibilities, or because of her cop instincts.

5

On the drive home, Eve juggled work on her PPC with communications to and from Peabody. She glanced up briefly when Roarke drove through the gates, struck by how the winterscape of trees and grounds and the blank, dark sky set off the fanciful rise of stone, the spears of turrets, and the spread of terraces in the house that had become her home.

Like a black-and-white photograph, she thought, of some otherworldly castle.

"Is it Irish?" she wondered.

"Is what?"

"The house. You know, the design. Like one of those preserved places tourists go to so they can see how people lived, or the ruins of what used to be that you see all over the place."

He studied the house himself as he wound down the drive. "During my education — and that would be through Summerset — I learned considerable history, whether I wanted to or not. He's one who believes your origins, who and what you come from, matter. Even if it's a contrast to what you choose to make of yourself."

He parked, sat a moment. "I already had a love of books by the time he took me in. That copy of Yeats I found in an alley in Dublin, and squirreled away so the old man wouldn't take it, sell it. Or burn it just to spite me. The words — the sound of them once you'd figured them out, on the tongue or in the head — were just a marvel to me. So, being a canny sort, Summerset used books on me."

"How?" she asked as they got out of opposite sides of the car.

"He had a collection of his own, and I was given access to them — on the provision I could discuss them after. Lessons, always, but I didn't see them as such, but only conversations."

The winter wind danced through his hair as he walked to her. "And novelties," he added, "as conversations with adults hadn't been part of my usual. He introduced me to the concept of libraries, and how I could borrow books. Now and again, he'd buy a book for me, a kind of reward, as I wasn't allowed to steal them."

They walked in on that, finding Summerset himself standing in the large foyer, a stick man in black, with the pudge of a cat at his feet.

"So it was fine with him if you stole cars, money, picked pockets, but books were on the forbidden list of loot?"

"One must have one's standards," Summerset said. "I trust you've had a meal of some sort."

"We have, thanks." Roarke removed his coat, which Summerset took from him even as Eve tossed hers over the newel post. Galahad trotted forward to wind himself through three pair of legs.

"Standards? I'm betting most people would rather have the contents of their wallets than a book that ended up on the shelf."

In that way he had, Summerset looked down his blade of a nose. "Books feed the mind and the spirit. We —"

" 'Don't take bread from the hand of a hungry man,' " Roarke finished.

Summerset gave Roarke a nod of approval. "You learned well. But then, your mind and spirit both had a voracious appetite. If your body has an appetite, there's pie. I had some time on my hands today and a nice basket of apples from New Zealand."

She had a weakness for pie, enough of one to overshadow any sarcasm she might have leveled.

Besides, they were only a couple days away from Summerset's winter vacation.

"There's always an appetite for pie," Roarke said as they started up the stairs. "Good night."

"Why New Zealand?" Eve demanded as the cat jogged up beside them. "We have apples from here. We're the Big Apple."

"Because it's February, and he'd prefer organic, naturally grown over agridomes or sims."

"It's February in New Zealand, right?"

"It is, but it's in the Southern Hemisphere, which means it's summer."

"How can it be summer?" Frustration shimmered all around her. "It's freaking February."

Simply delighted with her, Roarke draped an arm over her shoulders and, knowing her, headed to her office. "As with the time zones that baffle and annoy you, it's all about the planet, darling, its rotation and orbit. In the Northern Hemisphere freaking February equals winter. In the Southern Hemisphere, summer. You can't change the basic laws of science to your own rather adorable logic."

"Well, it's stupid, and it's no wonder people are perpetually fucked up, as nobody can depend on something as basic as February. Which is already screwed up because it insists on having less days, then adding one like a little prize every four years even though everybody wants February to get the hell over so we can move on."

Adorable, he thought again, and really unassailable logic. "Who would argue with that?"

"And anyway —" She broke off.

It still gave her a little jolt to walk into her office, to see everything changed. For the better, she thought, for a whole hell of a lot better. But still, a jolt.

"Never mind," she decided. "It all got me off track. I don't get what books have to do with the house, the design."

"Ah, yes, and I'll explain. First, I know you want to set up your board, but I think we've earned some wine."

He walked over, selected a bottle from the storage behind the wall while Eve drew out her board.

"Books, history, and Summerset saw to it that Irish history was included. So illustrations, descriptions, photographs of great houses, forts, castles, ruins, and so on. I'd think, I'll have that one day, and build it just as I like. A great house in a great city with towers and treasure rooms, and every comfort I could devise."

With a smile, he poured the wine. "Sometimes, in more fanciful moods, it might have run to moats and drawbridges as well."

He brought her the wine, tapped his glass to hers. "But you asked is it Irish, this house. When I began to build it, I had — or thought I had — left Ireland behind me. So much of my life there had been brutal, even bloody. I felt no ties there — so I believed. And yet, this house I built springs from those books, those dreams, those needs and ambitions. It comes from Ireland, and so do I.

"Summerset was right. It matters who and what we come from."

He felt her stiffen, saw her eyes go flat.

"It matters, Eve, that you came from monsters. Matters," he continued, gripping her chin in his hand, "because, coming from them, you chose to make yourself into a woman who hunts the monsters. Not for vengeance, as would surely have been my choice, but for justice. I built a house. You built a hero."

"I built a cop," she corrected, relaxing again. "Had some help there, same as you. And you don't give me hours of your time on an investigation for vengeance. If we don't always toe the same line on justice, we do on truth. And you work with me for truth."

His eyes stayed warm on hers as he skimmed his thumb over the shallow dent in her chin. "It wouldn't have been my choice once, but then I met you, and loved you, and things changed. Like summer in February."

Another truth, she knew, and it touched her, but she poked a finger in his belly. "Making it sound poetic doesn't change how it's screwed up."

"And yet." He kissed her. "We have pie."

"That's a bonus. But I need to get things set up before any pie."

"And I need to check on some matters, as I left the work abruptly. Once I do, and you do as well, it's my fondest wish — next to apple pie — to dip my fingers into the victim's financials."

"Always happy to grant those wishes."

"I'll come work on the auxiliary when I'm done with my own."

On his way to his adjoining office, he ordered the fireplace on medium flame.

Another jolt. She had a fireplace in her office.

Mentally rubbing her hands together, she

headed for the kickingest of kick-ass command centers.

Though she still had some trouble with the more advanced tech, she managed, generating what she needed from notes, her recording, official data, and carefully built her murder board, her murder book.

And completed the report she'd begun in the car.

She sent copies to her partner, her commander, and, after a moment's thought, to Mira. As straightforward as this case seemed, it never hurt to have the department's shrink and top profiler cued in.

When Roarke came back, she sat, boots up on her desk, still nursing the same glass of wine, watching the last moments of Mars's life on the wall screen while the cat stretched out, full-length, on a curve of the command counter.

Roarke stood, slipped his hands in his pockets, studied as she did.

"Take another look," she said to Roarke. "I'm looking for any sign the killer hung around. A lot of satisfaction to be gained by watching your target go down. I looked, and didn't find a discarded weapon, but the sweepers' report isn't in yet. So I might have missed it."

"Unlikely."

"Unlikely's not impossible. Computer, replay, half speed."

Roarke saw several glasses shatter on the floor, the waiter Eve had interviewed wobbling as he tried to balance the tray and more glasses fell.

The image jerked — Eve leaping up, he thought.

He heard a laugh cut off in midstream, and the first screams. A man at a table shoved up, knocking his chair over. A woman standing at the bar glanced over, dropped her own glass, and lurched backward.

Larinda Mars, her right arm a sleeve of blood, continued her sleepwalker's shuffle into the bar, her pupils so dilated her eyes read black. The image bobbled as Eve rushed toward the dying woman.

In the periphery, people froze. Some dropped to the ground, some started forward as if to try to assist, others moved away.

The screen began to fill with Mars as Eve rushed closer: the red blood flowing out against the bold pink, the mouth — yes, freshly dyed — slack, the eyes already sightless.

The sounds continued — panic, fear, confusion — as Eve's hands and arms showed on screen, grabbing on as Mars collapsed.

"Nobody sticks out," she said.

"You do. The glasses hadn't finished hitting the floor when you hit record," he pointed out. "You reached her in under five seconds. That's excellent reaction time, even for a cop, and I'd venture to say whoever killed her didn't expect to have a cop in the bar, one who'd react so quickly, who'd engage her recorder."

He ordered the recording to run again, studied the bystanders as he knew she had.

"No, nobody else stands out within recorder view. Still, it's possible the killer might have strolled back up to the bar, ordered another drink to enjoy while someone discovered her body, or she managed to do what she did and come upstairs again. But if so, he or she didn't show any reaction but the expected. Or weren't visible on the recording."

"Agreed. Computer, display exterior security feed, Du Vin, as previously cued."

Acknowledged.

"This is where I lean," Eve told him as they watched a group of five depart. "This is just two minutes and change before Mars bumped the waiter on her way back into the bar. Under three before TOD. I'll get better numbers from Morris tomorrow, but the doctor who assisted, and DeWinter, say with a wound like that she could have lived for maybe four to twelve minutes without treatment. I'm thinking closer to the four from the amount of blood she lost on the way up. So, less than three minutes before TOD he walks out. Give the killer three minutes to slice, to react, to exit the bathroom, get upstairs, walk out."

"I expect you timed that yourself."

"At a couple speeds," she confirmed. "Plenty of time. More than enough time. This group strikes me more than the others we have because it's off-balance: three males, two females. The best way to get out without raising much notice on a search like this? A group."

Roarke studied the recording again. "That may be, but people do socialize in uneven numbers, and it would count as a lucky break for a group to leave just as he — as I assume you're thinking the third male — wanted that cover."

"We'll find out. I'm looking at this one, too. He'd have cut it closer. Eighteen seconds before I hit record. Left alone. Then there are two females who left seventy-three seconds before record. I want to talk to Morris, and we'll definitely talk to all of these once we ID them through bar tabs, but look at the group again. The five."

Roarke leaned a hip on her command center, watched again.

"Female far right," Eve said. "Her head's turned just a little toward male second right, and his toward hers. Female center, male far left, inside shoulders close. They're holding hands. Center female's leaning forward a bit, her body's turned, again a bit, toward her right, like she's engaged with what the two on her right are doing or saying, while the male on her left . . . there! His head goes back, his shoulders shake a little. Like he's laughing at something."

"All right, yes, I see that now. And also see the third man is just a step behind them and, from this rear view at least, doesn't appear engaged with what the other four are saying."

"Could be he's just the odd man out, ready to call it a night, thinking of something else. Could be a lot of things, but he's the only one of the males wearing a hat — ski cap pulled over his hair. His shoulders are hunched, he's wearing gloves. Yeah, yeah, it's cold, but you can't get hair color, you can't get skin color. And he tacks left with them, still a couple steps behind, until they're out of cam range. They don't glance back at him."

She ordered a replay, froze it. "Still . . . could be a female," she mused. "This reads male from the camera angle, from the build, the type of coat, but it could be a female."

"Dark topcoat, dark ski cap, what looks like suit pants — dark again, and good dress shoes or half boots — more masculine in style."

"Could be female," Eve repeated. "Reads male, but that could be deliberate. I'm going to dig into the bar tabs. You can play with the vic's financials."

"Wishes come true. Let's top that off with pie. You're in my way," Roarke said to the cat, who turned his head, blinked his bicolored eyes, and seemed disinclined to move.

To solve the issue, Roarke hefted him, carted him to the sleep chair. Galahad rolled over, stretched, then curled up to take a nap.

By the time Roarke had stripped off his tie and suit jacket, Eve had two slices of warm apple pie, topped with vanilla ice cream, on the counter.

"I love this thing." She took mugs of black coffee out of her command center's mini AutoChef. "Frigging love this thing. Computer, list receipts provided by Du Vin from eighteen hundred to eighteen-forty-three.

Not going to pay the tab too long before the attack, can't have paid it after she came in bleeding, but we'll keep the window a bit wider.

"Oh God!"

Roarke glanced over quickly, saw her eyes closed in bliss even as she forked up more pie. "This is *pie.* Seriously, you need to get him to make another one before he goes on vacation. We absolutely need a backup on this. He's got three days — well, no, two, because today's over, essentially."

She ate another bite, slowly now, reminding herself to savor it. "Two days, right?"

"Yes, they leave in three days, which leaves them two."

"They? Who are they?"

"Summerset and Ivanna."

"What? What? She's going? They're going on vacation *together*?"

"At least the Australian portion." He sampled the pie and had to agree. There should be more.

"But . . . they'll have sex." She could actually feel the blood drain out of her head. "You know they'll have sex. With each other. Why did you have to tell me? Why did you have to put that in my head when I'm having pie?"

"You asked about the timing, I confirmed.

I didn't say anything about sex."

"You knew he was taking a woman he has a *history* with, and you didn't think they'd have sex?"

She slapped fingers to her eye as it began to twitch.

For a moment, Roarke said nothing, then sighed. "I acknowledged the probability in some vague and distant corner of my intellect, but I didn't actively visualize it until bloody well now, so thanks for that."

He scowled down at his plate. "This is putting me off my pie."

"Nothing could put me off this pie, not even Summerset sex. But, God."

"Say no more about it. I'm deadly serious." He pulled a leather strip out of his pocket, tied his hair back into a stub of a tail.

Letting pie and coffee soothe away the weird thoughts and images, Eve began to pick through the bar receipts.

In her designated time frame she found only one cash payment, and the itemized receipt management provided listed.

Two mineral waters, the first according to the time stamp ordered four minutes after Mars placed her drink order.

Just water, she thought. No caffeine to make you jumpy, no alcohol to slow your reaction times. Two waters, and a serving of spiced almonds. Just enough to hold a table for one without causing any interest.

She culled through, found what had to be the group of four. Eight drinks, two fancy appetizers — group size. She ran the name on the credit card.

Jonah R. Ongar

She ran him, sat back, drumming her fingers on the counter. After printing out ID shots, she rose, walked to her board to add them.

"You have something?" Roarke asked her.

"Two of the four — and it was a group of four. Four types of drinks times two orders of same. This one paid for the table, so we'll have a talk. Ongar is thirty-two, single, no marriages on record, currently cohabbed with Cheyenne Case, thirty-one, mixed race — who I'm betting was one of the four at the table. She's city government, works in procurement. He's one of the legal team for the *New York Times.* No major criminal bumps on either. She's been arrested a few times in protests, and he's got a D and D that's a decade old — and just happened to come down on his twenty-first birthday. They live downtown, about six blocks from the bar."

Eve sat, studied the new faces on her

board. "I'll talk to them tomorrow. And I've got this guy." She ordered another printout. "The single walk out, according to the credit receipt. I also have a wit statement from the guy he was drinking with. Business associates, discussing a mutual project over drinks. The wit stayed back to take a 'link tag that came through just as they were about to leave. Associate had another meet — wit states this — so went on his way. Wit took the tag, a personal one from his sister, which we'll confirm easily enough. They look clear to me, but we'll check them."

Still, she added them to the board.

"The two women who left together?"

"Mallie Baxter paid — they each had one drink and the straw things DeWinter likes. Mixed-race female, age twenty-six, one former cohab, no marriages. Assistant manager at some downtown boutique. No criminal. Again, looks clear, but we could have a partnership. One covers the bar area, one follows her down, does the job."

"The third man in the group of five?"

"Paid cash — the only one who paid cash in the time period I set up. Two mineral waters and some fancy nuts. First water order minutes after Mars ordered her drink. I get a time stamp on his cash payment, six minutes, twelve seconds before I engaged my recorder. I need to know who served him the drinks, get a description."

"Put up the receipt."

Eve called it up on screen.

"He ordered and paid through the menu app — that's the clever way to do this," Roarke told her. "Minimal contact with waitstaff."

"How can you tell?"

"There's a code for it on the receipt. And for the section as well. Give me a minute."

He did something on the computer, waited a beat. "I've got the section here and, according to the schedule, Cesca Garlini had it tonight."

"She waited on us. He was in the same section."

"On screen," Roarke ordered, and the table layout for the bar flashed on. "Where were you?"

She snagged a laser pointer. "This booth. DeWinter already had her drink on the table, so I sat with my back to the door. I thought about switching — it just bothers me — but figured she'd just make a thing. Ah, Mars was here, her back to me. Or more her side. Where was the third man?"

"Here. A two top — high top. That's behind you."

She closed her eyes, tried to bring it back.

Walking in, doing that automatic, instinctive scan of the area. "You've got a lot of flowers and ferny things. And fancy bottles. A wall along the side of the booths with flowerpots on it. I couldn't get a view of the room over it. Somebody . . . impression only. I can't see him because he's behind the damn flowers."

Frustrated, she dragged a hand through her hair.

She'd been right *there.*

"He's been in there before," she continued. "He had to have been in there before to pick the perfect spot to watch her without drawing any attention, having the cover. That's her favorite table. She sits there in that booth when she comes in. He had to know that. He copped one of the less desired tables, wouldn't you say?"

"Quieter," Roarke pointed out. "More private."

"Most people want the action in a bar, the noise — unless they want privacy. So if it's for privacy, it's usually a table for two. But a solo . . . I don't know. I'd say it would be an easier table to snag at that time of day. Right after work, people are blowing off steam. It's a big crowd, it's a happy vibe. But he wants the quieter spot, more secluded — and a high top. Better vantage point."

She shoved up, paced. "But this is good. Narrowing it down. Maybe I didn't see the son of a bitch even when he had to walk a few feet in back of me to get to the stairs, but it's going to be this guy. And we know who waited on him."

When she grabbed for her 'link, Roarke sighed.

"Eve, it's past midnight. You can't tag that poor girl now."

"She's young. She's probably still awake." But his quiet stare had her muttering a curse, stuffing her 'link back into her pocket. "In the morning."

"As a reward for your consideration, I'll fill you in on what I have — so far — on the financials."

"It better be good."

"I think you'll like it. Under her own name, she has a healthy portfolio. Some conservative stocks, bonds, and annuities meticulously managed by a very solid firm. No surprises. She keeps enough fluid to cover expenses very much in line with her income. A bit indulgent, as one might expect, in certain areas. Salons, fashion, entertainment. Though she's also careful to debit Channel Seventy-Five for travel, considerable wardrobe, and salon treatments, entertainment, and so on. All this is, again, meticulously listed for tax purposes."

"Now give me the juice."

"So far, and I haven't been at it long, I've found two other accounts. She did a reasonably decent job covering them, and they'd likely slip by — obviously have done — any standard check. The first is under the name Lorilie Saturn."

"That's too damn silly to be clever."

"That may be, but it worked for her. It's out of Argentina — which is a fine haven for accounts people don't want reported to the U.S. tax hounds. It holds just over three million at the moment. She uses its debit feature for purchases — which, from the listings, are exclusive to art and jewelry. During the past three years, more than ten million has come in and gone out."

"That's not chump change."

"Well now, it's all relative, isn't it? The second is under Linda Venus, so it's a theme we have going."

"A damn solar system," Eve muttered.

"This one is off-planet, another haven, and she uses it strictly for cash. In and out. She can go to any number of financial outlets in New York, or anywhere else for that matter, and as long as the in and the out is under ten thousand, it goes unreported."

"Yeah, yeah, like the amounts she laid out to Bellami. Always under ten large."

"Exactly. She would deposit, say, eight thousand, then have that funneled to her other hidden account, or leave it. She might withdraw five or six thousand in cash and skip away whistling a tune. There's considerable more action in this account. Often daily deposits and withdrawals or transfers. At the moment, this account holds six million and change.

"From her legitimate account," he went on, "she pays her rent and fees, her taxes, and the usual expenses one has, to live the sort of life her genuine income allows. However, there's another monthly amount drawn out of the Venus account — the same amount at the end of each month. Fifty-two hundred dollars."

"She's got another place. That's rent or mortgage on another place."

"I'd lean there. But as it's taken out in cash, and so far I haven't found where — or indeed if — it's funneled elsewhere, we can't be sure. And we can't trace it."

"Why would she want another place? Why another place?" Eve mumbled as she paced. "Hoarder. That's what you said. She's a bit of a hoarder. Maybe the other place is for the stuff. The stuff she doesn't keep in her apartment where she entertains."

She stopped pacing, fisted her hands on her hips as she studied Mars's ID shot.

"Yeah, that could play. It's one thing to have your closet packed with clothes, and a safe packed with cash and jewelry. Nobody sees that — or if somebody sees the clothes they just think: Wow, she's got a lot of clothes. But if you've got the place jammed with furniture and art and other crap, they notice.

"They talk, wonder."

She circled again. "She wouldn't meet marks there. That's stupid. You don't want to meet them anywhere that's tied to you. She's got the swank digs, so she doesn't need more swank digs. She needs someplace to keep secrets. Secrets, that's her thing. She needs a place to keep her own, away from where she lets people in.

"We'll find it." Eve turned back to the board, staring at Larinda's glossy, perfect ID shot again. "We'll find it."

"It's unlikely her killer knew of it." Roarke opted for a brandy. "Or why not find a way to kill her while she was there, where her body wouldn't be discovered for days or longer?"

"If he knew about it, had any brains, he'd have found a way to get into it and find something there to leverage against her. But we find it, we might find something that leads to whoever killed her." She rubbed her eyes. "And it's too soon, even with the lean heavy, to absolutely conclude it's rent or mortgage."

"We can lean while I put all this on auto. We'll likely have more data by morning. You need to set it down, get some sleep."

Not set it down so much as let it cook, she thought.

6

It started to cook, at least simmer, as they started to the bedroom.

"Gossip wasn't only the way she made her living, right? It was also what propelled her into celebrity circles. Arguably that's what made her a kind of celebrity. But, from my really brief interaction with her, it seems to me digging it up — not just covering the shine, the glossy stuff — uncovering the dirt was her main deal. And not just professionally. She enjoyed mining for secrets."

"And it paid her," Roarke pointed out, "under and over the table."

"Right."

Eve got another little jolt walking into the bedroom — the reconfigured, remodeled, redecorated bedroom. With that big, elaborate bed.

She didn't generally go for the elaborate, and couldn't figure out why that bed, those massive turned posts, the fancy head- and footboards carved with Celtic symbols, so appealed to her.

But it did.

She took off her jacket, tossed it over a chair while her mind flipped back to Mars.

"She was good at it, personally and professionally, over and under the table. That takes contacts, ways in and under and through. A kind of network."

"I'd agree with that." Roarke sat to remove his shoes while she unhooked her weapon harness. "The sort you pay in cash or in favors — likely both. A good reason to have a nice stack of cash available — but not a cool million."

"And contacts who were also marks. Find me some dirt, and I'll keep yours under the bed."

"Rug. Under the *rug,*" Roarke corrected with a smile, "but the same concept."

"Lots of enemies, so was she stupid enough not to take standard precautions?" Eve unstrapped her clutch piece, stowed it with her primary weapon. "The old: If anything happens to me, the file I have on you — in a secure location — will be made public. But that line only holds until somebody cracks, can't take the pressure anymore, can't bear the expense, handle the guilt. A mark who cracked, high probability, but not the only probability," she said as Roarke switched on the fire.

A low simmer of flames, a golden wave of warmth.

"Someone whose secret she exposed. A career, a reputation, a relationship damaged."

"Yeah. I'm thinking of tapping Nadine there. She'd have a handle on that angle, or could get one. And I doubt they much liked each other."

"Our Nadine," Roarke said as he stripped off his shirt, "is a reporter with standards and ethics. Ambition and pursuit of a story are key elements, but so are those standards and ethics. Mars, I would say even without what we've learned, was the polar opposite."

"It also helps they work at the same station. Nadine will know who to talk to, and who I need to talk to. That's on my list for tomorrow. But there are other probabilities for the pool of potential killers."

"Which is already deep."

Eve let out a sound of cynical amusement. "It ain't no wading pool, pal. Marks that refused to be marks. She couldn't have hit the target every time. Nobody's that good, nobody's that lucky. She had to miss a certain percentage of the time — and even a miss makes an enemy. She misses, keeps digging, and the mark says enough of that shit, sister."

"Well then." He watched her grab a sleep shirt, thought it a shame to cover that long, lean body. "If that's a line of thinking, I should tell you she shot and missed with me."

He continued to watch as the material floated down. Then abruptly, she yanked and her head popped out.

"What? What? She tried to shake you down? When? Christ."

"About three years ago, shortly before our wedding."

She just gaped at him. "And you're just telling me?"

"Darling Eve, if I told you about everyone who tried, in various ways, to shake me down, milk me, exploit some dubious connection, or issue threats — veiled or overt — we'd talk of little else."

He sent her an easy smile. "Do you tell me about everyone who threatens to make you pay, in one way or the other, for doing your job?"

She started to claim that was different, but realized it really wasn't.

Still.

"She's dead, murdered. I'm primary. And you've been consulting on this almost from the jump. Now you tell me she targeted you?"

"Well, her aim was poor so she missed entirely, and it was years ago. I honestly didn't think anything of it until you widened that pool."

"I need the details." She dropped down to sit on the side of the bed. "I need to see if this compromises anything."

"I don't see how it would, but . . ." He sat next to her. "She'd been wrangling for an interview, had pushed for one a few times before, but ran into Caro. I can tell you I wasn't even aware of the wrangling or pushing, as Caro wouldn't bother me with that sort of thing."

Eve thought of his sharp and efficient admin. "No, she wouldn't. I may have to verify that, just to cover the bases."

"I expect Caro has a file on it, somewhere. In any case, Mars finally got around Caro and approached me directly when we both attended . . . Christ if I remember, some event or other. You weren't with me, but I needed to put in an appearance. Ah, the library," he remembered. "The New York City Library, a fund-raiser."

"Okay, that's the when and the where. I need the what."

"I'm pulling it back — I haven't thought

of it since, after all. As I recall, she came up to me, very charming, asked if she could have a word. She said she needed an exclusive on our wedding, pitched it as the event of the year or some such thing, how her viewers counted on her to give them a window into glamour. She nattered on quite a bit as I recall about her various plans, a couples interview, individual ones, a tease of your dress, and so on — Honestly, Eve, I don't remember all of it, as I had no intention of giving her what she wanted, and said just that."

"Okay, I get that. But give me what you can."

"Well, she dropped the charm when I said no, changed tactics, and that I remember clearly enough. She said she could make it the event of the year, all glamour and swoon — or she could make things uncomfortable."

He picked up Eve's hand, ran a thumb around her wedding ring. "She didn't worry me, but I heard her out, on her certainty that a man in my position would have a lot he'd rather those viewers of hers weren't privy to, and that my bride-to-be's reputation and standing with the NYPSD could be damaged with the wrong word in the right ear. I should understand her power to sway public opinion."

"Nothing specific?" Eve prodded.

"Not at all. She had nothing, and I know a bluff when I hear one. And that's well beside the fact that I don't leave traces or footprints for some gossipmonger to follow. She didn't worry me. She did annoy the bloody hell out of me. And while I didn't care for her intimating she'd try to muck things up for you, I had no concerns there, either. You know how to handle a git."

Eve relaxed. "You went Scary Roarke on her."

He tapped Eve lightly between the eyes. "I was remarkably pleasant."

"Scary Roarke," Eve repeated.

"I asked if she enjoyed her work, to which she — rather smugly — assured me she did, adding that she was very good at it. So I simply outlined a hypothetical. What did she think might happen to her own career if I were to have a whim and buy Channel Seventy-Five?"

Eve let out a half laugh. "Perfect."

"It'd be an interesting acquisition. How easy it would be, should I be interested enough to do so, to break her current contract and plant seeds that would root in such a way that she'd be fortunate to find a job as a gofer in broadcasting at some third-rate station in Bumfuck?"

"You said 'Bumfuck'?"

"To the best of my recollection. I explained my interest would definitely pique if the right person — and I knew so many people — whispered in my ear that she was scratching about in my business or my bride-to-be's."

She could hear him say it all, in the brutally cold and pleasant tone he could whip out like a deadly weapon.

"Did she piss herself?"

"I couldn't say, but she did leave rather abruptly. I kept a few ears out for a space of time, and she opted not to scratch about. So that was the end of it. A single and brief conversation nearly three years ago."

"Okay, good. I'll need to give Whitney a condensed version of that, but I don't see any compromise or conflict of interest. She didn't make a specific threat or ask for payment?"

"No."

"Then it would be hard to stretch that pool wide and deep enough for you to even dip a toe in." Still, she punched him lightly in the chest. "You should've told me — if not back then, now."

"I just did," he pointed out. "And I didn't think of it even when the blackmail became a motive, as I never thought of it as blackmail. More as rudeness, and a pathetic attempt to intimidate."

"Nobody intimidates Scary Roarke." She swung a leg over, straddling him.

Pleased with the light in her eyes, he slid his hands up her legs, under the thin shirt. "Would you like to try?"

"You can be Scary Roarke. I'll be Bitch Cop."

"We are what we are," he said and, gripping the back of her head, pulled her in for a long, possessive kiss.

"You don't scare me," she murmured. And added teeth.

"You haven't read me my rights."

Since he'd stripped down to his boxers already, it was easy to find him, to free him, to lift her hips and, lowering them again, take him in.

All the way in.

"No rights for you, ace." His fingers dug into her shoulders as her hips moved, slow, a teasing rock. "Just hard labor."

"And when I make you tremble?"

Still moving, still rocking, she dared him. "Try it."

Eyes on hers, he slid a hand down to where they joined, pressing and playing his fingers, and shooting her system to a gasping peak.

She bowed back, helpless, not trembling but quaking until she tumbled down again, her head dropping to his shoulder.

"Tricky," she managed.

"I know how to handle my cop."

Her lips curved against his throat. "I know how to handle my criminal."

"Never convicted."

Laughing, she trailed her lips up his throat, over his jaw, to tease his lips, those wonderfully, perfectly shaped lips. All the while her hips moved, slow to languorous, arousing to torturous.

His hands glided up her sides — slim and strong — and over her breasts — soft and firm. Her heart beating under his palms; her nipples peaking under the brush of his thumbs.

When she bowed back again, he captured the soft and firm in his mouth, felt that heart pulse inside him. All but tasted it. And still she moved, moved, moved until the blood pounded under his skin.

Until his world whittled down to the taste of her, the feel, the heat, the all of her.

She flowed up to him again, smooth as water, cupped his face, near to destroyed him with a kiss before she eased back, stared into his eyes.

"Come with me."

Quickening now, quickening.

"I'm with you, *a ghrá.*"

Her eyes, the deep gold pools of them. Her hips in tireless, glorious motion.

"Let go first." Her breath tore; her eyes never wavered. "Let go first."

Control, already tenuous, slipped away from him, a frayed rope that gave way to fling him off a cliff.

He heard her, a low, broken cry of release as he fell. He caught her against him as she fell after him.

She went limp, soft melted wax, and the sound she made was a long, purring sigh.

"I won." She sighed again when he lay back with her pressed to his heart. "Bitch Cop wins."

"I'll concede the round. But demand a rematch."

"I'll take you on again."

Eyes closed, a hand stroking her back, he smiled. Her words tended to slur when she was all but asleep.

He managed to maneuver them lengthwise on the bed, shifting her until she curled up against him. She muttered something incomprehensible, so he stroked her back again.

"Not to worry now," he whispered. "Lights off."

In the dark he felt the cat land on the bed, pad over, circle twice, then curl his considerable bulk in the small of Eve's back.

Not to worry now, he thought again. This was as good as any man could wish for.

He gave the cat a stroke, then draped an arm over his wife and slept.

When Eve woke, the cat had switched allegiances and lay sprawled over Roarke's lap. Roarke, dressed for another conquer-the-world day, sat on the new sofa in the sitting area, drinking coffee — mmm, coffee — working on his PPC. On the wall screen the day's stocks and other mysterious financial information moved in a silent scroll.

She sat up, brain still fuzzed, spotted her discarded sleep shirt at the foot of the bed. She crawled over to retrieve it.

"Well now, that's a fine sight to greet a man first thing in the morning."

She grunted, dragged the shirt over her head.

"Even that."

She stumbled her way to the bar he'd left open for her, programmed coffee. Decided after the first gulp she'd be able to function.

"How many 'link conferences already in the bag this morning?"

"Only two." Eyebrows arched, he glanced over. "Back-to-back they were, so essentially one."

She grunted again and went to shower. While the hot jetted water pumped more life into her, Eve outlined the start of her day.

Check on any search results here. In the field, morgue, and Morris first, then the waitress — potential for consult with police artist on description. Briefing, Peabody and McNab. Briefing, Commander Whitney. Contact Nadine.

And she had to be prepared to deal with the media. One of their own was dead — they'd push hard.

She came out, grateful for the chocolate-brown cashmere robe, and eyed the two dome-covered plates on the table.

She thought, Oatmeal. Damn it.

Still, he'd set a pot of coffee on the table, and she was ready for a second.

She poured, sat. "I want to check on the search results before I head out."

"I already have. No other accounts. No real property, so far, tied to any we have. I've gone down another level."

"Okay."

When he lifted the domes, rather than the expected oatmeal —

"Waffles! How come?"

"You won."

"Score!" She immediately drowned hers in syrup.

Galahad, banished from the sofa, began what Eve thought of as a commando crawl toward the waffles.

"Forget it," she told him even before Roarke could give him the eye. "You didn't win anything."

He rolled onto his back, lazily switching his tail, as if contemplating the ceiling.

"We got lucky." She ate waffles and felt lucky all around.

"How so?"

"Not only did Mars manage to get upstairs — though some bladder in the bar would have required emptying before too much longer anyway. But she managed to get upstairs. And there's a cop right there. That's a couple of lucky breaks for the investigation, and bad ones for the killer. Just have to make them work for us."

She ate more waffles. "Plus, you own the place, and that's another break because the manager's smart and competent — and co-operative. And the staff's smooth. I'm hoping to have the next round of luck with the waitress. If we can get a sketch of the killer, that'll tie it up pretty nice."

She studied her next bite of waffles. "Why do they call it a waffle iron?"

He cut another bite. "Because it presses the batter?"

"But does it? Does it really? They're not flat, and isn't that the goal with pressing and ironing? They're sort of puffy with dents in them. Pancakes, I get the name. It's batter, you pour it on a pan, and you've got yourself a pancake. What sort of name is *waffle* — were they just not sure what it was, so they, you know, waffled? Or does it mean something?"

"The question will haunt me now."

"Ha." She ate the bite, deciding that whatever the name, it went down just fine. "I need to hook up with Nadine, go by Seventy-Five to talk to people. Sometimes Trina's there. Lurking around with all her gunk and goo and paint."

Roarke gave her knee a bolstering pat. "Don't be a coward, Lieutenant."

Scowling, Eve polished off her breakfast. "Lurking," she repeated. "And I'll lay down fifty right now, if she's lurking, she's going to want to do stuff to my hair, and that leads to doing other stuff. She gave me the hard eye when we went to Bella's birthday deal

— I know when she's giving me that look. I've got to slap some of that cream gunk on my face before I go. She'll know if I don't. She just knows. It's creepy."

Rising, she headed to the closet.

This, she feared, would always give her a jolt. The remodel had swollen the space, expanded it, added stuff — like a computer.

She gave the closet comp the hard eye.

Damned if she'd use a stupid computer to put clothes on her ass.

Brown, she decided. The brown robe was good, so brown was good.

She grabbed a jacket, turned to the pants and trouser area, reached for brown, stopped, reached a couple of choices over. Not only brown — maybe a darker brown like the robe, but it had a line of still-darker leather down the outside of the legs, along the pockets.

She had a weakness for leather.

She didn't want to try to think about what went with the browns, so she searched through the built-ins until she found a white sweater. Not snow-white, she thought as she began to dress, but sort of like the color of the oatmeal she hadn't had to eat that morning.

That sort of made it brown, too. Nice, easy brown.

Belt, boots, done.

She walked out to retrieve her weapon harness, clutch piece, restraints, and everything she carried on her person, her belt, in pockets.

She caught Roarke's eye as she strapped on her clutch piece.

"What?" Part of her wanted to whine. "Forget it. I'm not changing."

"On the contrary. I was just thinking you look very professional, with an edge."

She glanced toward the mirror, thought she looked normal. "And that's good?"

"That's you, Lieutenant."

"Then it works. I'm heading out, so —"

He gestured with his coffee. "You forgot to slap your face."

"Slap my . . . Oh, crap."

She dashed into the bathroom, dug out the face cream. Slapped it on.

Took a second or two to stare at herself. She, a trained observer, and one who damn well knew her own face, couldn't see a damn bit of difference.

But Trina would know. Yeah, it was creepy.

She dashed out again.

"I'm going to be like ten in my office, finishing up there, then I'm in the field."

"I've one or two things yet to see to here myself. I'd appreciate if you'd keep me updated on this case, and any progress you make. My place, after all."

"I'll do that."

She walked over, kissed him. "I'll text you if I learn anything you'd want to know."

He pulled her back for another. "Take care of my cop."

"That's Bitch Cop."

"Not to me — unless it's to my advantage."

"It's always to mine."

7

Ad blimps chugged through washed-out winter skies blasting hype for midwinter sales. As if, Eve thought as she pushed through traffic, nobody had anything better to do than shop.

And if the cost of winter coats could be *Slashed! Sixty Percent Off!* in February, why didn't stores charge less for them in, say, October, and move the damn inventory?

Just because certain people could toss around four figures for a pair of boots? To borrow from ancient slang, that was whack.

She glanced down at the boots currently on her feet, told herself not to think about it. Reminded herself those boots would likely see considerable mileage before the closet fairies disappeared them.

And she had a killer to catch.

As she bulled her way downtown, she decided to multitask and tagged Nadine.

It didn't surprise her to see Nadine Furst,

dogged crime-beat reporter, bestselling crime writer, and all-around smart girl, come on screen within seconds.

Not camera ready for a change, Eve mused, and with her streaky blond hair sleek and wet.

"Get you out of the shower?"

"Nearly. If you're heading into Central, I'll be there in thirty."

"I'm not. I'm in the field."

"The morgue then." Face naked, eyes hard, Nadine nodded. "A visit to Larinda."

"Figured you heard."

"Of course I heard." As she spoke, she moved. Eve saw a blur of Nadine's swanky new bedroom in her swanky new apartment. "Just like I heard you were on scene when it happened — Roarke's bar. I need a one-on-one, and I need it this morning."

"I need an interview — official," Eve countered, "and I need it this morning."

Movement stopped. "With me? Why?"

Eve noted Nadine now stood in her closet — nearly as big as her own, and even more ruthlessly organized.

"I'll get to that during the interview. I have to come to the station anyway. I'll talk to you there. About two hours, so be there."

"I want that one-on-one, Dallas. Larinda was — loosely — an associate, a coworker.

The station's already all over this, and I'm the top crime reporter — on screen and in the field."

"We'll talk," Eve repeated. "Two hours."

And clicked off.

She'd be annoyed, Eve thought. And she'd push for the one-on-one. Which Eve already intended to give her — and which Nadine already knew she'd get.

But the steps of investigation came first.

She continued multitasking as she strode down the white, echoing tunnel of the morgue.

Cesca the waitress came on screen, heavy-eyed, purple hair tousled. "Um," she said.

"I'm sorry to tag you so early," Eve began. "I need a follow-up with you. I'd like you to come into Central."

"Into . . ." The heavy eyes popped wide. "Am I in trouble? Am I a, what, like a *suspect*?"

"Neither. You may be able to help in our investigation. I can arrange for transportation if you need it."

"No. No, I can . . . Now?"

"How about in an hour? If you come through the main entrance, go to the first security desk. I'm going to have you cleared up to me."

"Okay. Okay. But . . . Can I bring a friend?

I don't want to come by myself. Is that okay? Wow." She shoved and pushed at her wedge of hair. "I'm so nervous."

"You can bring whoever you want, and there's no reason to be nervous. I can come to your place, but this saves me some time. I'd appreciate it."

"Okay. Okay." Cesca pushed at her purple hair again, and didn't look convinced. "You didn't catch the killer yet?"

"I'm working on it. An hour," Eve said, clicking off as she reached the doors to Morris's theater.

Today's music, hard-edged rock — beat low. Morris, a clear cape over a navy suit with thin, metallic red stripes, stood over Larinda Mars.

His hair slicked back from his interesting face to form a looped braid twined in that same metallic red. The red — mirrored in his tie — told Eve grief hadn't dogged him when he'd chosen today's wardrobe.

DeWinter, just being DeWinter, she supposed, earned some points for that.

Larinda, her chest spread open, lay naked on the stainless-steel slab.

If the dead had concerns about modesty, those who stood for them couldn't accommodate it.

"I wasn't able to finish with her last

night." Morris studied a readout on his lab comp. "I had a suicide pact — neither of them old enough for a legal brew. Baxter and Trueheart caught it," he said, glancing back toward his wall of drawers. "All evidence supports they considered themselves — with the influence of illegals — a Romeo and Juliet who would only find happiness in death. It's sad they failed to understand what they based their decision on wasn't a romance, but a tragedy."

"I never got it. A couple of kids take a look at each other and decide they're crazy in love while their families are like the Coys and McHats."

"Hatfields and McCoys," Morris corrected, the sorrow in his dark, exotic eyes fading to amusement. "Or in this case the Montagues and Capulets."

"Whatever. Stupid. So they both end up dead — self-terminations in the old 'can't be with you, I'll die instead.' "

She stuck her hands in her pockets, scanned the drawers. "I figure people who haven't dealt with death up close don't get it ends life and any and all potential therein. And even when life sucks wide, it can get better. Anyway, this one didn't self-terminate."

"No, indeed. A single cut to the brachial

artery with a sharp, smooth blade. A scalpel. There are no other wounds, offensive or defensive."

"The angle. Face-to-face?"

"That's my conclusion. It would take only a second." He lifted a scalpel off his tray, flicked his wrist. "And done."

"The medicals on scene speculated about the time frame for her to bleed out without intervention. What's your take?"

"I discussed that with Garnet last night."

"You . . . okay."

He set the scalpel down. "She contacted me. As you surely understand, she felt both frustration and guilt that she'd been right there, and could do nothing to save the victim, even with the assistance of another doctor, and you."

"Mars didn't last ten seconds after she went down." But Eve did get it, absolutely.

"And you wouldn't have changed that, as I explained to Garnet, if you'd reached her sooner. Both Garnet and the doctor who tried to help assumed, certainly hoped for, a slower leak."

"They didn't see the bathroom, the spatter. She lost a pint — more — before she got out the door."

"The initial gush and spray." Morris nodded. "She might have died then and there, within a minute or two, but — Conversely, we'll say, you sever your arm, through an attack or due to an accident."

"I'd rather not."

"Who could blame you," Morris said easily. "However, with this amputation, your brachial artery gushes with your heartbeat. Pulse and gush. Why don't you die? Many who sever limbs are saved — most, in fact — and the severed limb can be reattached with excellent results."

"Still rather keep all mine where they are."

"That's the hope. With the insult of a severed limb, the blood vessels compress, slowing the blood loss long enough for treatment — if treatment comes. In this case, there was some compression. Enough it allowed her to walk as far as she did, to try to get help."

"How much time?"

"I'd estimate she lived for about four minutes, perhaps five. But she passed the point of saving within about ninety seconds. The blood loss was too severe, confirmed by your on-scene record. Without immediate intervention from that point, she was the walking dead."

And Morris smiled. "A marvelous, classic screen series."

"What?"

"*The Walking Dead.* Have you seen it?"

"No."

"Zombie apocalypse, fascinating. You'd like it. But to Larinda here, a severed hand would have given her a better chance to survive than what would appear to be a smaller injury."

"He — fairly sure on he — could have stepped out, held the door shut for thirty seconds. Really wouldn't have to bother," she thought out loud as she circled the slab. "Even if she managed to get out and up the stairs in, say, a minute, nobody's going to wade through the panic and — what? Do what?"

"Tourniquet off the blood flow — the flow that's pumping out with every heartbeat. Just as you and the medicals attempted. Or cauterize the wound. Administer a transfusion."

"Not going to happen in thirty seconds. Or ninety."

She glanced at her wrist unit, then mimed slicing her arm.

"What do I do? That initial gush. I'm stunned, pissed. Look at my skin suit. What the fuck! I probably stumble back, grab at the wound. You son of a bitch. But he steps out, closes the door."

"You're already woozy," Morris told her.

"Your reactions are slowed within only seconds."

"Right, so I stagger for the door, lightheaded, maybe still too pissed to really be scared. I stumble toward the steps — it's a good five feet. Already past the sixty-seconds mark by then. Maybe I try to call out. It's noisy up there, and I'm weak. I pull myself up by the rail, brace a hand on the wall because I'm so dizzy. Maybe I grip the wound again, trying to stop the bleeding, but I can't stop it. By the time I get up eighteen stairs, I'm past that two-minute mark. I still have to get to the doorway."

"The blood's no longer feeding your brain."

"Not thinking now," Eve murmured. "It's just blind, animal instinct that keeps me moving forward. Really, I died back on the stairs. Zombie time," she said and made him smile again.

"Basically."

"Three minutes minimum before she made it into the bar." She nodded at her wrist unit. "The suspect I'm leaning toward left the bar under two minutes before TOD, so likely no more than five minutes after the attack, likely nearer to four. He just had to walk up the stairs, across the bar, and out the door. I'd say he planned it out, timed it.

He got lucky, as two couples were leaving as he did, but that was just a bonus."

She intended to go back to the bar, do another round of timing the walk, at a brisk New York pace, from the restroom to the door. Just to nail it down.

But now she looked down at Mars. "Did she tell you anything else I can use?"

"As far as useful, you'll be the judge, but she has a lot to say. I can tell you that though her official data lists her age as thirty-seven, I'd say she's solidly a decade older."

Eve frowned, slid her hands in her pockets. "DeWinter said the same. Still, a lot of people find a way to fudge their age. And she's in entertainment."

"Yes, however . . ." He let that go a moment as Peabody hustled in.

"It's just now eight!"

"We started early," Eve told her, noting her partner kept her line of sight several inches above the open chest on the slab. "Morris concludes she died roughly four minutes after the attack."

"That's fast."

"And he tells me she's about ten years older than her ID claims."

Peabody lowered her gaze to Mars's face. "Mid-forties then. She looks more like mid-thirties."

"And so she should," Morris confirmed. "She's had considerable work done. Face and body. And yes, many people do," he added before Eve could comment. "But not all that many have complete facial reconstruction."

"Reconstruction." Now he had Eve's full attention. "How can you tell?"

"There are always little signs, even with exceptional work. And some I can feel by manipulating. The computer screening verifies. Her chin, her nose, her brow, even her eye sockets, her cheekbones — all underwent reconstruction."

"Peabody, check and see if she was in any sort of major accident."

"Her body," Morris continued. "Breast enhancement, body sculpting that includes a butt lift, belly tuck — regular on both, as those treatments require tune-ups. Arm sculpting as well as calf implants."

"Implants. On her calves?"

"To give the appearance of good muscle tone. She's opted for a permanent bikini cut on the pubis."

"That has to hurt," Peabody muttered as she searched on her PPC.

"Also had the hair permanently removed from her legs, armpits. Plumping treatment

— very recently — on the lips. Skin resurfacing. Again, I'd say with some regularity, and that's full body, not only her face. She's undergone sterilization, and has not given birth. Ah, and her hair? Root system coloring. She's not a natural blonde, and undergoes what would be twice-yearly treatments to maintain this color."

"I've heard about that." Peabody lowered her PPC. "It's not only a major ouch unless you pay to go under, but costs about ten grand and requires a two-day stay. No major accidents, Dallas. No major injuries, right back to childhood."

"So she opted for a new face." Intrigued, Eve once again circled the body. "Can you tell how long ago, for the reconstruction?"

"I'll need to run more tests."

"And would they include giving me a picture of what she looked like before?"

Now Morris frowned. "I might be able to simulate, to an extent. Calculating margins and most probables. It's not —"

"Wait. Better idea." She yanked out her PPC. "Did you tell DeWinter about the reconstruction, the age difference?"

"No, of course I didn't." He looked mildly insulted. "You're the primary. You get my conclusions and observations."

"I didn't mean it like a poke. I just —

Forensic anthro. You can work with her on it, right?"

"I . . . Of course." Glancing down at Mars, that faint irritation changed to interest. He nodded. "Yes, we can work on this. I should have thought of it myself."

"How about you tag her, tell her what we're after and why?"

"I will, though I'm curious as to the why. Why it matters what she once looked like."

"Because if she changed her whole damn face, it might be she changed her name, her data, and everything on there's bogus. People don't become somebody else unless there's a reason. The reason may have a bearing on who killed her."

"This is why you're the murder cop and I'm the dead doctor. I'll ask Garnet to join the investigative team." Once again, he looked down at Mars. "I suspect she'll need to take our subject down to the bone."

Peabody said, quietly, "Eew."

"I'll clear it. She's got no living next of kin listed. Nobody to ask for permission. Let's find out who the hell she really was. Thanks, Morris. I like your tie," she said as she headed out.

More stunned than surprised she'd comment on any sort of fashion, he laughed. "Thank you."

"I'm heading into Central, which means I'm about to get my eyes burned by whatever Jenkinson's tied around his neck. So I thought I should tell you I liked yours."

Peabody jogged to catch up. "McNab made headway on the electronics, and he's back at it this morning. His brain needed a rest — I had to bring the hammer down on him. He'd been working an e-case for the last four days, almost twenty-four/seven until it broke yesterday. I can tell when he's hitting the line, and he was sliding over it. He needed some sack time, some solid down."

"No problem."

"He did say she paid a lot of scratch for security on her e-toys. Serious scratch. He likes that sort of challenge, and he peeled away some layers. He'll have the rest pulled today."

Peabody dropped into the passenger seat. "Can I have coffee?"

Eve held up two fingers. Using the in-dash, Peabody programmed one black, one coffee regular. Handed the black to Dallas.

"I think he's a little burnt."

Eve glanced over. "What?"

"I think McNab's a little burnt. He's been on the roll one way or the other for close to a month. Jumped in to help Callendar on a case, and he's assisted on ours. Santiago asked him to take some e-stuff. He doesn't say no — he loves the e-stuff, and the work. But, honest, his skinny ass is dragging some. Hell, more than some."

Peabody's brows knitted, digging a worry line between them. "I want to get him to take a couple-three days. Maybe surprise him with a mini-cation. When we close this down, is there any problem with me taking some leave? Three days?"

"No. No problem."

"Solid." Nodding decisively, she drank her coffee. "I'm going to put in for it, and talk to Feeney. We've got enough saved up to afford one of those three-day packages somewhere warm."

It occurred to Eve that Peabody had never before said anything about McNab being burnt or tired, had never before expressed a single concern in that direction. So she obviously had real worry.

"Take five days. You're not on the roll on Sundays unless we're working something hot. And Saturdays are rotated. Rotate out, leave after shift on a Friday. If he's dragging, five days gives him time to bounce back, and vacate. And neither of you use up more than three days' leave."

"We could do that. We could just stay

home for the weekend, sleep, then do the package. A five-day package really ups the ante, but if we —"

"It's warm in Mexico."

Peabody laughed. "Yeah, it is — and sunny, with beaches. But a cross-continent package adds to it. You can get some pretty sweet bargains in the Bahamas if you know where to look. I've been checking."

Eve drummed her fingers on the wheel. "You can use the villa on the west coast of Mexico. Roarke will get you a shuttle to and from."

"What?" The unexpected gesture had Peabody nearly spilling her coffee. "Seriously? But no, I'm not —"

"It's no big deal."

"Are you kidding? It's a mega deal." Peabody's stunned breath whooshed out, then in again. "A mongo mega deal. Big, giant gratitude, but I wasn't fishing for a freebie. We've got some saved."

"I know you weren't fishing. You didn't have your fishing face on."

"I don't have a fishing face."

"You have a fishing face." Eve did her best to mimic it with big, innocent puppy eyes, a shy, winsome smile.

"I absolutely don't make that face."

"You do when you're fishing. And you

weren't wearing that face, so you weren't. You were wearing your worried face. If McNab's burnt, some of the burn is from working my investigations. Take the villa, the shuttle, and the five days."

When Eve pulled into Central's garage, into her slot, Peabody just sat.

"Hugging would annoy you."

"Keep your hands off me," Eve warned.

"I'm too grateful to annoy you, even though in my head I'm giving you a big, sloppy hug. He needs a break, Dallas. He'd never admit it, but he needs a break. Thanks to the ultra of thanks."

"It's Roarke's villa," Eve said, but as she started to get out, Peabody put a hand on her arm.

"Thanks."

"You're welcome."

They got out, headed for the elevator. "When I get over being humbled and grateful, I'm going to start dancing. Five days at a swank villa in Mexico."

"Dance internally."

"I have to because doing it for real would also annoy you, and too much gratitude." As they stepped into the elevator, Peabody's face lit with a grin. "Okay, there it goes. My internal boogie. I'm mentally hugging you again."

"Did you cop a feel this time?"

"Just a little one. Affectionately."

"I'm mentally kicking my boot up your ass."

"Right now? Even that feels good." Unable to hold it in, Peabody boogied her hips. "O-fucking-lé!"

As the elevator stopped, filled with cops, stopped, filled with more, Eve muscled her way off, shifting to the glides.

"If we've finished internal dancing and ass kicking, we might take a moment to discuss a murder investigation."

"You're the boss," Peabody said with mad cheer. "The maggiest of mag bosses."

"Right. Well, this mag boss has a waitress — Cesca — coming in. Tag Yancy for a consult with her. The timing's too slick for the third male in that group leaving not to be our killer. Sitting right behind me," she muttered. "Son of a bitch, I want him for that insult alone. When we're done with the waitress, we're heading to Seventy-Five. We talk to people, have her work electronics taken in. And I want a sit-down with Nadine. If she doesn't know some of Mars's bullshit, she'll find out. I expect the media to hammer this one, and I'll need to report to Whitney, probably juggle something with Kyung."

Kyung, the media liaison — and not an asshole — would juggle back.

"At some point, we need to go by the lab, give DeWinter a push on the facial reconstruction."

She swung into Homicide.

Finding herself right about Jenkinson's tie didn't dull the glare of what looked like urine-colored sperm squiggling over virulent purple.

As he worked both his 'link and his comp, she held back any comment. Instead she crossed to Baxter's desk.

No sperm tie for Baxter; his had purple stripes against gray and set off his snappy gray suit.

"I heard you caught and closed a double."

"Yeah. Babies, boss, a couple of babies who'll never grow up."

"You're solid on the double suicide?"

"Yeah." He heaved out a breath. "She snuck him into the house, into her room. They took enough tranqs to put them down if not out, and before they went down they zip-tied plastic bags over each other's heads. Laid down and took the long sleep."

"They left notes." Newly minted detective Trueheart spoke up from his desk. "Full intent spelled out, LT. Nobody wanted them to be together in life, so they'd be together eternally in death."

"Her mother found them," Baxter continued. "She generally checked on the kid at least once a night, as said kid had started sneaking out, or sneaking the boy in. Good families. A couple of kids taking a wrong turn and bringing out the worst in each other."

"File it, move on."

"Working on it."

It's all you could do, Eve thought, and walked to her office.

She'd barely begun to set up her board when Peabody came in.

"The waitress is here. She brought a friend."

"Yeah, I told her she could."

"He's the one who had the vic's table."

"Spinder, right? Kyle. Better yet. Let's set them up in Interview. Find what's open."

She went back to her board, put up both waiters' photos. Wished for coffee but, following Peabody's confirmation text, walked out and down to Interview C.

She found Cesca and Kyle huddled at the table, clutching hands.

"This is where you interrogate people." Cesca's voice shook like a leaf clinging to a branch in a windstorm. "You said I wasn't in trouble."

"You're not," Eve assured her. "We're in this room because it's quiet and private, that's all."

"Maybe we should get a lawyer."

Eve glanced at Kyle when he spoke up. "You can. And we can talk somewhere else if the room bothers you. I have no reason to suspect either of you — and I wouldn't be talking to you together if I did. We believe Cesca waited on someone we do suspect."

Now Cesca let out a squeak and clutched at her throat. "I served the killer?"

"It's a line of investigation we're following, and we'd like your help."

"Why don't I get you something to drink?" Peabody proposed in what Eve recognized as her calm-the-waters voice.

"Can I have a fizzy? The flavor doesn't matter. I like all of them." Cesca looked all around. "You've had killers in here?"

"Yeah, but not right now. Kyle, drink?"

"Fizzy's good. Cherry's best."

"I'll go get that."

Eve sat when Peabody went out. She set down her tablet, brought up the floor plan for Du Vin. "This station. Station fifteen."

"Fifteen. Gosh, we were so busy. Can I think a minute?"

"Take your time."

Cesca closed her eyes, tapped her finger

in the air. "That's you and Dr. DeWinter. That's the three ladies from East Washington on a girl trip — they were really nice, having a lot of fun together. Chatty. That's Mr. Hardy and Mr. Franks — they're regulars and work just down the block. And that's . . . Okay."

She opened her eyes. "A single, a guy, but I didn't really see him."

"Your station," Eve reminded her.

"Yeah, but he ordered digital, paid cash. He had on . . . a hat. A watch cap kind of thing, and he worked on his PPC the whole time. Mineral water — a couple of them, and some nuts. He didn't eat them."

"How old was he?"

Cesca shook her head. "I guess I'm not really sure. We were busy, and he didn't want service, even waved me away when I asked if I could get him something else."

"Skin color?"

"I . . ." Now she squeezed her eyes shut. "He could've been white or mixed race. Maybe. I'm sorry. He sat like this."

She shifted, hunched over, lowered her head. "I think he kept his coat on. I think. And see, we're trained to leave customers alone if they want to be left alone. We get some who come in to work a little while they have a drink. I thought he was like that."

Peabody brought in a drink caddy, set down two fizzies, offered Eve a tube of Pepsi.

"How about his voice?"

"Oh, I don't think he said anything. Yeah, I'm pretty sure he didn't say anything. I didn't interact with him because he didn't want to be bothered, right? I mean with someone like Dr. DeWinter or Mr. Hardy or Mr. Franks, you make a little conversation, and you can joke around some. Be personable. Someone like him, you leave him alone unless he calls you over. He never called me over."

Eve glanced at Peabody as she cracked her tube of Pepsi.

"Did you see him get up from the table?" Peabody asked.

"No. I guess he was there for a half hour — forty minutes, maybe. I saw he'd left, so I went back, found the cash. He hadn't called for his bill, and really should have, but he left cash that covered it and a decent enough tip, considering. So I generated a bill and cashed him out."

She twisted her fingers together, gave another wide-eyed look at Eve. "I'm not helping. I'm sorry, but . . . Oh! He had a scarf — I remember that. I remember he had a gray scarf, because I wondered why he didn't take it off, wasn't he getting hot."

"I wish I'd seen him," Kyle put in. "I mean I might've seen him, but I wouldn't know because I don't know what he looked like. There were other customers in there with hats and coats and scarves. It's been really cold."

He brooded into his fizzy. "She was nice to me. Ms. Mars."

Eve tried different angles, different questions, but ran into a blank wall. So blank she saw no point in pulling Yancy into it.

She let them go, checked the time. "I'm going to update the commander, then I want to talk to Nadine. We'll wind around to the guy who paid the check in the group of four our suspect merged with."

"They could have gotten a better look."

Eve reran the security feed in her mind, the way he'd stayed a couple of steps back, the way the other four engaged with each other.

"We won't count on it."

8

After getting the come-ahead from her commander, Eve went straight up to Whitney's office. He sat, a big man behind a big desk, with the city he served rising through the window at his back.

He served it well, she thought. As solid as they came.

"Sir."

"Lieutenant. Do you have anything to add to your initial report?"

"We've just interviewed a witness, a waitress who was assigned to the table we believe the suspect occupied. It looks like a dead end, Commander. She's willing and cooperative, but she just didn't get a good look at him. He used the auto-menu, avoided contact, wore concealing clothing, and paid cash — which he left on the table without calling for his bill. I have a few more lines to tug there, and will do so today. This unsub fits the timing, the timing confirmed by the ME."

She could, and would, put all of this in an official report, but she wanted to do a verbal, privately, with full disclosure.

"Sir, three years ago during the investigation of the murders committed by C. J. Morse, I met and spoke with Larinda Mars. She offered some insight and information on Morse, and in the quid pro quo she demanded for same, I allowed her to attend a party Roarke held during that period — on the provision she brought in no cameras or mics."

Whitney steepled his fingers, tapping them together. "Was there anything in that conversation that applies or impinges upon your current investigation?"

"No, sir. She didn't like Morse, clearly, and was more than happy to give me personally damaging information on him. She wanted an interview with me — and with Roarke. I had ignored her requests up to that point, and continued to do so afterward. Roarke did the same, though he advised me she once tried to corner him at a fund-raiser in the spring following my conversation with her."

Whitney lowered his hands, kept his eyes level with hers. "And does this apply?"

"Only in that Roarke reports she insinuated a sort of media-style blackmail. That she would be forced to dig up information that might damage his and my reputations if he didn't cooperate. And this applies, as evidence supports she used various forms of blackmail, and this stands as a strong motive for her murder."

Whitney sat back, hands steepled again, fingertips lightly tapping the chin of his wide, dark face. "How did Roarke respond to her insinuations?"

"He suggested he might find buying Channel Seventy-Five an interesting investment, thereby terminating her employment. And suggested how difficult it might be for her to find other employment as a gofer for a broadcaster. In Bumfuck."

Whitney's lips twitched slightly, but his eyes stayed sober and steady. "Am I to assume there was no further contact or communication between Mars and Roarke, or you and Mars?"

"You can be assured there was not, sir. However, if we assume, and I do, she kept files on her marks, and on potential marks, Roarke's name and my own might be in them."

"As may mine, or our chief of police, our mayor."

At his response, the tension in her shoulders eased. "I've contacted Nadine Furst, and will speak with her — as well as others at Channel Seventy-Five. Someone Mars worked with or around may have some information on where she might have kept her data. Detective McNab is working with the electronics taken from her handbag on scene, and I've arranged for those at her apartment to be brought in. I'll do the same with those at Seventy-Five, though I suspect they'll cite freedom of the press and demand a warrant."

He only nodded. "I'll arrange for the warrant. As I'm sure you expect, the media is pushing hard for information. This is not only one of their own, and a kind of minor celebrity, but you were on scene when she was attacked, when she died. It's a setup made for clicks and bytes and ratings, and you'll need to address it. Kyung should be here any moment now."

"I understand it requires addressing, Commander, though so far I haven't received demands or requests for interviews or information, except from Nadine when I contacted her."

"Because Kyung immediately had any such demands or requests relayed to his office."

Not only not an asshole, Eve thought, but

an advantage.

"I'd like to pursue the leads and direction I have, as quickly as possible, and avoid, until I have more data, speaking to the media. If —"

She stopped when Kyung walked in.

"Lieutenant. Commander."

"Kyung. The lieutenant prefers to stand, but you're welcome to have a seat."

"Hopefully, this won't take much of the lieutenant's time, or yours."

He looked like a media liaison, Eve mused, polished and attractive, tall and just distinguished enough in his slate-gray suit. But — at least so far — he'd proven he understood actual cop work had priority over feeding the ever-hungry media.

"Larinda Mars," he continued, smooth as always, "was a recognizable name and face in her field of social information." He paused, noting Eve's curled lip. "You can call it gossip, her peers and associates can do so, even her viewership, but it falls to me to be more politic there. As she generated excellent ratings, her employer will devote considerable on-air and blog time to her life, her death, this investigation. Other media outlets will do the same. As you're also a recognizable name and face in your field, this adds not only to the initial frenzy, but will give that frenzy legs. We'll need your name and your face, your presence to funnel the data we want funneled, and in the way we want it funneled."

It just annoyed the crap out of her. Knowing he spoke the truth didn't cut through the annoyance or the crap. "The more time I spend funneling, the less time I spend actually finding who killed her and stopping the frenzy."

"Trust me, when you find who killed her, the frenzy will simply take another avenue." Always reasonable, Kyung spread his hands. "This will play for a while. I can and will write a statement — for your approval — and distribute that. But you'll need to hold a media conference, and as soon as possible. This afternoon, latest."

"I need to get to Seventy-Five, asap. I need to talk to her associates, her bosses, her staff. She'll have her blackmail files somewhere, and they may be at the station."

"It would be best, for now, if her alleged blackmail wasn't made public." Kyung glanced at Whitney, got a nod of agreement.

"I'm not going to discuss pertinent investigation details, for crap's sake."

Kyung merely inclined his head. "Precisely."

"I contacted Nadine Furst, and I'm meeting her there. She's crime beat and good at it — and she'll hold whatever I tell her to hold."

Kyung winged up an eyebrow. "You agreed to an interview?"

"I get her to dig into Mars from her angles, and I give her a one-on-one."

"This morning?" He held up a finger before she could answer. "This could work very well, all around. You give Nadine — as she represents Seventy-Five — a first exclusive. Seventy-Five, after all, represents Larinda Mars's family. Nadine also acts as the pool reporter, and agrees to that, agrees to share content of the interview with the other media."

"I don't know if she'll go with that."

"You'll convince her," Kyung said equably. "She knows how it works. She gets first exclusive, and she'll have control — with my input — of what's shared. You will have fed the beast for this morning. And the afternoon media conference will keep it fed for the time being."

He smiled. "Win-win."

It was sort of devious, Eve thought. She had to admire it.

Plus, it bought her a little more field time.

"I'll make it happen."

"I'm sure you will. Lieutenant, when it

does come out — as it will — that she used blackmail to gather information, the information that generated her ratings and her own celebrity? Her peers and associates will turn on her. And that will generate yet another kind of frenzy."

"Why she got dead doesn't make her any less murdered. It doesn't make the person who killed her any less deserving of a cage. I don't care what her peers think of her. Hell, I don't care what *I* think of her. Nobody had the right to kill her."

Obviously satisfied, Kyung smiled at her. "Knowing you'd say exactly that, in exactly that tone, to a room full of cameras and mics, is why you make my job so interesting."

"Glad to help."

He laughed. "I'll write the statement, text you the draft. Please ask Nadine to contact me once you've agreed to terms."

"Okay." She turned back to Whitney. "Sir?"

"You're dismissed, Lieutenant. I'll get your warrant, and Kyung and I will coordinate on the media. Keep me updated."

All in all, Eve thought on her way out, it could've been a lot worse. She started to pull out her comm, to tell Peabody to meet her in the garage, then decided to make one more stop first.

The Electronic Detectives Division spewed out color and movement like a Broadway musical produced by caffeine-hyped teenagers.

Everybody bounced, jiggled, hip bumped, and swiveled — often at the same time — and they all wore outfits that made Jenkinson's tie fetish come off as a conservative choice.

She saw neon stripes, glowing polka dots, animated shirts, and a plethora of wildly patterned airboots.

To escape the assault on the senses, she moved fast toward Feeney's office.

The captain of this madhouse, and her former partner, sat on the edge of his desk, frowning at his wall screen.

Maybe his toe tapped, but it tapped inside an old brown shoe.

Which lined up well with his rumpled brown suit, his plain, and reassuringly ugly, brown tie. Maybe his explosion of wiry, silver-dashed ginger hair added color, but it topped a lived-in face.

A cop's face.

His saggy basset hound eyes shifted toward her. "Heard one landed right at your feet, kid."

"She did."

"The wife'll be sad about it. She loves the gossip shows. Can't blame her," he said with a shrug. "Investigations run on evidence, evidence comes from leads, and a lot of leads come straight from gossip."

She hadn't thought of it quite like that, but couldn't argue. And that, she mused, was why a bounce off Feeney never failed to be worthwhile.

"She used gossip to hammer people to give her more gossip and cash or have their secrets exposed."

"Yeah, McNab's working on digging some of that out of her electronics."

"Actually, that's what I wanted to talk to you about."

"I'll give the kid a hand when I finish up in here. I've got her apartment electronics coming in. You going out for her studio shit?"

"Yeah, from here. But I wanted to talk to you about McNab."

Feeney reached into a wobbly bowl — one of Mrs. Feeney's creations — took a handful of candied almonds. Gestured to the bowl in an invitation to share, but Eve shook her head.

"You can have him on the team," Feeney said. "He's clear."

"Peabody —" Thinking of how cops loved

gossip, just like Feeney's wife, she shut the door. "Peabody says he's burnt — and I could see she was genuinely worried."

Frowning, Feeney rubbed his jaw. "She ain't wrong. He's been working a big one, complicated, and just closed it. Gave some time to a couple of the other boys." They were all *boys* to Feeney, no matter the chromosomes. "I'm putting him in for a commendation for the one he closed."

Fully aware Feeney didn't hand out commendations like candied almonds, she smiled a little. "Good for him."

Feeney jabbed a finger at her. "I told him after he nailed it down yesterday to go home and sleep, and take the next forty-eight off."

"It's on me he didn't. I pulled Peabody in when they were leaving."

"He came in with her instead of getting the shut-eye. Lovebirds," he said with a sorry shake of his head. "I can put the boot down, take him off, order him to take the forty-eight."

"Would he go home and sleep?"

"He'd argue and he'd bitch until I put the boot down harder. Then he'd sulk."

Because she saw it the same way, she nodded. "I offered Peabody a thing after she laid this out, and I should've cleared it with you first."

He popped another almond. "What thing?"

"I said after we close this one — because she wouldn't budge until this is cleared, even with the boot, any more than McNab — to take five days by rotating a Saturday, taking the regular off Sunday, and the next three as vacation days. They could take one of Roarke's shuttles to the villa in Mexico. He's yours, not mine, and he may not be up for a five-day leave."

Feeney scratched just above his collarbone. "I'd rather give him the five than see him really burnt and end up pushing him out for twice that. Or having him screw up because his head's not right. It's a good thing. I've got no problem clearing him for it."

"Good, that's good. Peabody's juiced. She got shiny-eyed at the idea of getting him away for a while."

"Lovebirds," he said again, eating more nuts. "Keep me up with the progress on what you've got, and I'll fix his schedule. He's a good kid. Lovebird shit aside, I've gotta say he's a better cop, got more solid footing, since he's been cooing with Peabody."

"Really?"

"Settled him down. Gave him a center."

She thought of McNab's wardrobe, his earlobe full of rings, the way he bounced. *Settled down* wouldn't have been the term she'd have applied.

But she did agree that, under it all, he was a solid cop.

"Okay. I've got to get going."

"I'll give him a hand anyway." Feeney's gaze shifted morosely back to his screen. "When I finish this bitch."

As she drove to Seventy-Five, Eve ticked off what needed to be done. "Peabody, run this Mitch L. Day character. I didn't get to that."

"On it."

As Peabody all but sang the two words, Eve gave her a wary glance. "What's up with you?"

"Just feeling pretty mag. Due to loose pants — not really any looser, but still loose — and your absofab offer of Mexico, I'm hitting this shop on my way home tonight, and buying this outfit I've had my eye on. It's all flowy and swirly. It's Mexico perfecto."

"Wow. That's just the best news ever!"

Even Eve's exaggerated sarcasm didn't dent Peabody's mood. "It has these adorbs little ribbons for straps, so when McNab tugs them, *whoosh,* I'm naked."

Eve's eyes went to slits. "And this, this is how you repay me?"

"I didn't hug you. Mitch L. Day — officially Mitchell Edwin Dayton — age thirty-eight, Murray Hill address. One divorce — no offspring. Currently married to Sashay DuPris, age thirty-two."

"So he's married and was bouncing on Mars."

"Updated data says DuPris, a model — oh, I've seen her — resides at an Upper East Side address. It doesn't list them as officially separated. She's major high fashion, Dallas, big-time. Back to him, no offspring in current marriage. Employed at Seventy-Five, on-air personality, since 2055. No criminal. A lot of traffic violations. He's originally from Minnesota. Huh, farm boy. His parents — forty-five years married — own and operate a farm. Two siblings.

"Do you want more? I can always find dish on on-air personalities."

"That's enough for now," Eve said as she wound her way through the parking complex for Seventy-Five.

She dealt with security — in the lot, at the door — noted all the humans wore black armbands. And the screens in the visitor's lobby all showed Mars at various splashy events wearing various splashy gowns and outfits.

Eve stopped at the next security station, badged the operator.

"Nadine Furst. She's expecting us."

"Yes, Lieutenant, you're already cleared. Do you need an escort or do you remember the way?"

"I remember."

She also remembered her way to the newsroom, and where she'd first met Mars.

She aimed there first. There the screens showed various world events, reporters doing remotes, and one screen dedicated to Mars.

But if she remembered the desk correctly — and she was damn sure she did — someone else occupied it.

The man sat in shirtsleeves, his suit jacket draped over the back of his chair. Sharp cheekbones all but sliced through his taut, dark skin, while his hair formed a perfect skullcap of ebony.

"NYPSD." Eve held up her badge. "I'm looking for Larinda Mars's desk."

"It'd be in her office." He rose, offered a hand. "Barry Hewitt, political beat. It's nice to meet you, even under the circumstances, Lieutenant. Ms. Mars has her own office. I'd be happy to show you, but I know Bebe's going to want to speak to you."

"Who's Bebe?"

His reaction, a slow blink, showed a bit of stupefied surprise she wouldn't just know. "Bebe Hewitt? Majority owner and head of broadcasting? And my aunt," he added with a half smile. "I know she's juggling a lot of fires right now, but she'd want to talk to you. I can take you to her offices."

"Lead the way." Eve ignored the hot glances, the murmurs as she and Peabody went with Hewitt.

"Every reporter in here would kill for an exclusive with you."

"If they did that, I'd arrest them."

"Ha!"

"When did Mars get her own office?"

"A couple years ago. I'd just moved up from the pool — utility player. My aunt wanted me seasoned before I got a shot at political. I'm still mostly covering city council and minor protests, but I'm getting there."

"Did you know Mars?"

"Not really. I mean not to socialize or jaw with, right? Low rung here, and a different beat. Same channel, get me, but those are different rungs on different ladders in different worlds."

He escorted them into an elevator, took

out a swipe card. "I do get this perk. I can go direct to Bebe's floor. I don't suppose you could get me a meet with Chief Tibble."

"Not my function, sorry."

"You gotta try." He stepped out into a glossy, plush reception area with low gel sofas, privacy chairs, more screens, and a curved counter manned by three perfectly beautiful people.

"Hey, Vi, can you let Ms. Hewitt know Lieutenant Dallas and Detective Peabody are here? Loved the vid," he told Peabody.

"Me, too."

"I hope you catch whoever killed Larinda. She was a real fixture around here."

The perfectly beautiful Vi stood up. "I'll take you to Ms. Hewitt."

"Good luck," Hewitt said, strolling back to the elevator.

Instead of a big, important office beyond several small, important offices, Vi led them to a very big, very important-looking conference room.

A woman — those scalpel-sharp cheekbones ran in the family — sat at the head of a long, highly polished red table. She wore black, and her hair, also black, was styled in a smooth coil at the nape of her long, slender neck.

On the table sat a basket of muffins, a

platter of fruit, a couple of pots that smelled like pretty decent coffee. Five people sat around the table, working industriously with their tablets as she snapped out orders.

"Get started. Talk to Kit if you have any questions. Michael, I want to see that retrospective before noon. Now, I need the room."

All five got to their feet, some still tapping and swiping, and hurried out.

"Bebe Hewitt." She rose, a commanding six feet in her heels, willow slim with sharp, assessing eyes of icy blue. "I would have come to you if you hadn't come to me. Please, sit, there's coffee."

"Before we get started, my partner needs access to Ms. Mars's office. We'll need to have her electronics taken in to Central."

"I can't accommodate that, without a warrant."

"A warrant's being issued."

"Good. When it is, and legal verifies it, you'll have what you need. Believe me, I don't want to impede your investigation in any way, but I can't violate Larinda's rights, or the rights of the free media. I need more coffee."

She pulled over a pot, poured. "Our responsibilities aren't that different."

"Aren't they?"

Bebe studied Eve with those cool blue eyes. "We both serve the public. I believe in what we do here. I respect what you do. And I'm not stupid enough not to appreciate that you — and you as well, Detective — are damn good screen."

She closed her eyes a moment, drank. "Larinda's assistant is Ross Burkoff. He should be helpful to you. I'm reasonably sure he handled a great deal of her personal business as well as professional."

"We'll speak with him. I also need to speak with Mitch L. Day."

Bebe let out a small sound that ended in a quick smirk. "That didn't take long. His office is directly across from Larinda's."

Eve recognized the meaning behind the smirk. "You're aware they're involved."

Now Bebe's smirk deepened, but there was a touch of annoyance in it. "The place is crawling with reporters — and I was one myself for a lot of years. Their involvement was a poorly kept secret until a few weeks ago, when Mitch's wife kicked him out."

"How pissed off was the wife?"

"Sashay? She doesn't get pissed — that might put lines in her face. She discards and moves on. She didn't care about Larinda any more than you'd care about a cloud rolling over the sun for a minute. You wait until it's gone. And Mitch? He was like a chipped wineglass." Bebe lifted her shoulders. "You wouldn't keep the glass once it's chipped, right? You just toss it out, get another."

"Who else was Mars close to?"

"I don't know that she was 'close' to anyone particularly."

"You didn't like her."

Bebe took some time with her coffee, not hedging to Eve's mind, but aligning her thoughts into words first. "She was superior at her work, had an amazing network of contacts, an enthusiastic fan base — and she knew how to keep them happy and tuning in. She had a strong and appealing onscreen presence, and her ratings were stellar — and growing. She will be missed, and she'll be very hard to replace. And no, I didn't like her."

Bebe added a shrug. "I didn't have to like her. I imagine you work with and respect the work of any number of people you don't like on a personal level."

"Why didn't you like her?"

"Offscreen, off camera, away from the public, she was a piranha. Careless with people, with feelings. Full of herself, full of demands — most of which I'd meet because she brought in revenue. She earned her own show, her specials, her fussy accommodations and travel demands. She lured in the talent and gave the viewers what they wanted.

"She was a soaring diva and often a pain in my ass, but she leaves a hole in my house that's going to take time to fill."

"Why don't you tell me where you were last night at eighteen-forty?"

"Really?" After a quick blink of surprise — much like her nephew's — Bebe let out a genuine laugh. "I'm much too smart to kill one of my golden geese, but let me think . . . What time is that in English? I can never make the translation in my head."

"Sorry. Six-forty."

"That's easy. I was having dinner — pre-theater — with my husband, my brother and his wife, and my parents, who're visiting from St. Thomas. We had six o'clock reservations at Andre's. Curtain was at eight. I got the text about Larinda right before curtain. Do you need the names and contacts of my alibis?"

"No, just wondering. Who sent you the text?"

She opened her mouth, shut it, seemed to consider. "One of our reporters — the metro beat. He'd gotten a tip from someone who'd been in the bar when it happened.

He's not going to give you that name, Lieutenant, and he wasn't the only one who got tagged from the bar. I hadn't reached the lobby, turned my 'link back from vibrate when other tags from other reporters started coming in, as I know they started coming in to my competitors."

"Okay." Eve glanced down at her own signaling 'link. "That's the warrant. Peabody, get a printout — two copies — for Ms. Hewitt and her legal department."

"I'll have them look it over right away."

"Good. Then my partner will expect access to the office and anything else that pertains to this investigation."

"I locked down her office personally — I did so last night — to ensure no one went in, disturbed anything. Reporters," Bebe said again. "If I'd been young and eager, I might have snuck in to see what I could find. No one's been in. She always locked her office, and the security scan showed no one had gone in since she did so at five-ten yesterday evening."

"Thank you for your time. We may need more of it." Eve rose. "Peabody, you have this. I'll be speaking with Nadine Furst."

Now Bebe's lips curved. "I hoped you would be. I respect your relationship with Nadine, as I respect her. I'll be very disappointed in her if she doesn't talk you into an exclusive."

With a shrug, Eve started for the door, stopped.

"I get the impression you're just not all that surprised someone killed Mars."

"She made her living on glitz and glamour with one hand, and on dirty little secrets with the other."

" 'Dirty little secrets'?" Eve repeated, turning back.

"Exposing the affair of some wholesome screen star, or the illegals use, the taste for underage bedmates. She could damage the glossy image — and did when she dug up the dirt. It's why the viewers clung to the screen — for the gloss and the dirt. She could be fearless in exposing icons. It's not surprising someone violently objected. Icons have fans, after all, and the word *fan* is short for *fanatic.*"

Interesting, Eve thought as she left. And an angle. Blackmail hit stronger for her, but a fanatic wasn't a bad alternate.

9

"Take the reporter — the metro beat reporter — and hang tight for her legal to clear the warrant," Eve told Peabody. "Make sure Mars's office is locked down — add a seal to it."

"On that."

They split off with Eve heading toward Nadine's territory.

Nadine didn't just rate an office. As a top-flight screen reporter, one with her own top-rated weekly show, a bestseller, and an Oscar-nominated vid under her belt, she claimed an office, another for her admin, and an array of cubes for her research and production teams.

Eve wouldn't deny that having a friend — and one she trusted — with that sort of media clout didn't hurt.

She got as far as the admin, a sharp-looking, pint-sized redhead wearing an ear 'link, carrying a handheld, and working with fast fingers on a mini tablet.

"Hey. Hold." She tapped her ear 'link, shot up a finger to signal Eve. "Nadine had to get to makeup. She's got about twenty before she needs to be on set. I can get somebody to show you the way."

"I remember it."

Eve veered off, past more offices, an open area filled with desks, alive with screens, another huddle of cubes. People rushed in a dozen directions, urgency in every step, talking incessantly, to each other, on 'links, into recorders.

A media version (less weirdly dressed) of EDD.

Corridors narrowed, snaked into an area packed with racks jammed with clothes, shelves stacked with shoes where someone plied a puffing steamer over a black suit jacket.

She wound her way to makeup.

Reflected in the mirrored wall behind the long counter, Nadine sat in a high-backed swivel chair, fully draped in a blue cape, eyes closed as she mumbled to herself.

To Eve's annoyance — she *knew* it — and considerable unease, Trina stood in front of Nadine, swiping a brush over Nadine's cheek.

Trina said, "Yo," and gave Eve a slit-eyed

stare in the glass that increased the unease.

Nadine's eyes popped open. "You're late," she snapped.

"Gee, I must've lost track of time while I was strolling along Fifth Avenue window-shopping."

Obviously not amused, Nadine, snarled, "You're not the only one with an agenda or a timetable."

"I'm the only one with a DB in the morgue."

"I've got to be on screen talking about it in under twenty. I need that one-on-one."

"And I need information. Do you want to waste time bitching or get down to it?"

"Save the bitching and the rest," Trina ordered. "I've got to do your lips."

Nadine stared hard at Eve in the mirror, but kept quiet as Trina used some sort of pencil thing to outline Nadine's lips.

Why did she have to draw what was already there? Eve wondered. Who came up with that rule?

"Decent coffee in the AC," Trina said as she worked. "Going with a dark rose," she continued to Nadine. "Matte. You don't want a big punch or fussy for this, right? Serious lips, not glam."

Eve got coffee while Trina mixed color from three different tubes on a white square.

She applied the blended color with a brush. Stepped back, tilted her head in a way that had Eve wondering why the piled-up tower of red-swirled black hair didn't tumble off her head.

She squeezed something clear onto another square, used yet another brush, and painted it over the lip color.

Eve couldn't see any difference.

Working briskly, Trina smooshed yet another brush into almost invisible powder, swirled it over Nadine's entire face, snatched up a bottle of something, and spritzed what looked like a vapor over that.

She said, "Check it," and whipped the cape away.

In her somber yet stylish black suit, Nadine studied herself in the glass. "Trina, you're a genius."

"Fucking A."

"We can do the setup in my office," Nadine began, but Eve simply shook her head.

"Badge first. What was your relationship with Mars?"

"Oh, for Christ's crying sake."

"I need to clear some decks, Nadine. I'm going to give you what you want, but I need what I need." She flicked a glance at Trina. "You don't have to be here."

"Yeah, I do." She held up another cape. "Sit, and I'll deal with your hair while you get what you get."

"No."

Trina tipped that hair-heavy head again. The tower stayed firm. "I do it here and now or I come to your place and give you a full treatment, which anybody with eyes can see you could use."

Just as Eve feared. "I'm working."

"You're working and that's talking and you can talk sitting on your ass."

"Oh, sit down, for God's sake." Nadine threw up her hands. "A trim and shape isn't torture. And neither of us has time to waste."

"So you say," Eve muttered. "I'm going to ask questions. You might not want the person who paints up your face to hear your answers."

"About Larinda Mars?" Nadine's snort didn't fit her serious-reporter image. "Please. I've got absolutely nothing to hide, from you, from Trina, or anyone." To prove it, Nadine took another seat. "You need what you need, I need what I need. Sit down and give Trina what she needs, and we're good."

Eve didn't like it, but she sat, as the idea of Trina wheedling into her house — and she damn well would — equaled a lot worse.

She immediately felt ridiculous when Trina whipped the cape over her. "Your relationship with Mars," Eve repeated, balking when Trina picked up a bottle and started spraying the contents on her hair. "What's that? Why? Stop it!"

"Do you want to ask me questions or ask Nadine questions? It's just water." Trina rolled her eyes, currently royal purple framed in thick black lashes tipped with red.

"I didn't have a relationship with Mars," Nadine began. "We worked in entirely different areas. I never worked with her, and we didn't drink from the same pool."

"Not entirely true," Eve corrected, trying to ignore whatever was happening to her hair. "She was gossip — a lot of that drank from the celebrity and entertainment pools. You joined that pool with the book and the vid. And you're up for a whatsit."

"Oscar."

"Why Oscar? Why not Harold? Or Tod?"

"There's an actual answer for that, but I'll skip it because you have a point on the other." Nadine swiveled her chair Eve's way. "I gave her a couple of interviews attached to the book, and the vid, along the way, as it was to my advantage, and because I'm a good soldier. The station wanted it. But that's not a relationship."

"You'd have been at some of the same events, parties."

"Yes. We didn't really socialize. I didn't like her, if that's what you're after. She's dead, and I'm sorry, but I don't like her any more now than I did when she was breathing."

"Why?" She asked for form, for procedure. Eve knew Nadine well enough to understand just why.

"Because she was sneaky, underhanded — which aren't actual flaws in a reporter — but add disloyal, toss in shaky ethics, and top it off with downright mean. She booted two interns just this past year, sent them both off in tears. Fired her last assistant and went out of her way to bad-mouth her to screw with her chances of getting another job."

"I need those names."

"You don't seriously believe —"

"I need them. What else, who else?"

Taking a minute to settle, Nadine breathed out slow. "She went after my people — my admin, my researchers. Subtly and not-so, because they wouldn't give her information on me. And she tried strong-arming me to get to you."

Forgetting Trina, Eve swiveled in the chair

to face Nadine directly. "When? How?"

As they sat face-to-face in front of the mirror, Nadine's foxy green eyes met Eve's.

"The first time? After you saved my life — the first time there, too. After you kept Morse, that prick, from killing me. She brought me a damn fruit basket, tried to play the concerned colleague, which was bullshit so thick she could have smothered in it."

"You know your bullshit," Trina said as she worked, earning a quick smile from Nadine.

"I definitely do. What she wanted was dish, and I could respect that to a point. I was, for her purpose, a story. But she wanted details about you and Roarke, wanted more access to you, into your home, into your personal lives, and I said no — not through me. She . . ."

Nadine rolled her fingers in the air. "We'll say intimated she could spin the story of my experience, and what happened that night, to twist us all up. Maybe we all set Morse up, maybe you had a reason to want him taken down. I told her to fuck off and spin away. She didn't like it."

"Never occurred to you to mention it to me?"

Nadine sent Eve a straight, heated stare.

"I handle my own."

"Okay. Did she come back on you?"

"No, and I shrugged it off. Until the book hit, and the vid deal. She pushed again, hard. Pointed out to me a handful of stories in the tabloids about my personal life, the speculation you and I banged each other or —"

"What?" Eve jerked sharply enough to have Trina mutter a curse. "You and me?"

"That rippled along for a few weeks." The annoyance on Nadine's face shifted to sheer humor. "Don't you pay *any* attention?"

"Not to crap like that." Eve wasn't quite sure if she should be amused or embarrassed.

"Sometimes you made a Roarke sandwich," Trina put in. "Yummy mmm-mmm."

Throwing back her perfectly groomed head, Nadine laughed. "Hard to argue with the delicious potential of that one. It's the bottom-feeder gossip that baits clicks, then dies, Dallas. It's tabloid bait. Her point to me? She'd fed that bottom, and could keep doing so unless I cooperated."

Maybe she didn't pay any attention, but Eve got the system. "You told her to fuck off."

"I did better. I let her listen to the recording I'd made of our conversation where she'd told me she'd violated Seventy-Five's rules of conduct, where she'd threatened me, attempted to extort me, which opened her to both criminal and civil action."

Abruptly, Nadine shoved up from the chair. "Who the hell did she think she was dealing with?" The heated question came with a wide-arm gesture for emphasis. "I told her — and kept the recording going — that if she continued, if I so much as heard a whisper of her continuing to smear my reputation, yours, Roarke's, to abuse or pressure any of my staff — or anyone else I learned of — I'd take the recording straight to the top. And if she wasn't terminated immediately, I'd give the station a choice — her or me. And just who did she think they'd stick with?"

"Why didn't you go to the top then and there?"

"Maybe I should have," Nadine admitted. "I didn't like her. I sure as hell didn't respect her. But . . . she had a place here, Dallas. She was part of Seventy-Five. Unless she gave me no choice, I didn't want to make the station choose, or set her off on some vindictive spree. She backed off, so I didn't have to."

"You've still got the recording."

"Of course I do."

"I'm going to need that. Who else did she push or threaten or try to exploit?"

Nadine dropped into a chair again, lifted a hand, nearly raked it through her hair until she remembered her on-screen appearance.

"Am I getting the one-on-one — here, this morning?"

"I said I'd give you what you needed."

"Fine. Hold on." Nadine stood again, pulled out her 'link, and walked out of the room.

"She's gotta go on screen and say nice things about an asshole," Trina commented, still snipping. "A lot of assholes in the world though, and most of them probably have some nice parts in there. She had good skin, took care of it. That's something nice to say."

Eve tried to swivel again so she could see Trina in the mirror, but Trina locked the chair in place. "Hold still, I'm fine-tuning."

"How do you know about her skin? Mars?"

"I did her face and hair a few times. She tried buying me away from Nadine. As if." Trina snorted off the idea of it and kept snipping. "I got my own place, and I do this gig because I like it. Mostly I just do Nadine up for *Now,* unless we got something big like this. And I don't work for that sort. She comes into the salon, that's one thing."

Eve read worlds in the tone. "What do you know, Trina?"

Trina released the chair, turned Eve to face the mirror. "I know you've got good hair, and you can thank me for looking after it."

Eve honestly couldn't see much difference, which actually counted in Trina's favor. "What and who did she talk about when she sat in here?"

Trina's ruby-red lips — with three tiny stars at the left corner — pokered up. She lifted her hands into a point over the chair, brought them down like a pyramid.

"What's that?"

"That's the Cone of Silence. Somebody sits in my chair, that's what they're sitting in." Trina's chin jutted up, held firm as stone. "That's the integrity of the chair."

"Murder evaporates the Cone of Silence."

"Maybe." Those same lips pursed in thought as Trina picked up one of the brushes.

"Keep that stuff away from me."

"You're going on screen. Nadine's got the serious reporter look. You need some kick-ass."

"I am a kick-ass."

"I know that, you know that." Using the brush for emphasis, Trina pointed the end at Eve. "Which is how I know how to make sure everybody else does. You don't like it after, it comes off. But if you want me to break the C of S, I need the incentive. C of S is sacred shit."

She set down the brush, opened a drawer, took out a small tool. "Your eyebrows need shaping. She tried to wheedle info out of me — just like you are now, right? Sugar-time though, not hard-ass like you. All smiles and just-us-girls shit. I said how I couldn't tell her anything about anybody, just like I couldn't tell anybody anything about her."

Trina paused, met Eve's eyes in the mirror with her purple ones. Whatever their color, those eyes transmitted sincere emotion. "She poked at me about Mavis, Dallas — like I'd *ever* give anybody anything about Mavis. No matter what or who. Ever."

Now those eyes fired hot. Another point in Trina's favor, Eve conceded. Her absolute loyalty to a friend.

"I know that," Eve said, to smooth her out a little. "I know that without a single shake."

"Right. Okay." Trina breathed out. "So. She said how she'd pay me for a vid of

Mavis and Leonardo and Bella at home. When she saw that pissed me off, she tried saying she meant with their permission. But she didn't."

Listening, considering, Eve tolerated the buzzing at her eyebrows.

"Did she ever threaten you, Trina? I need it straight."

"No." Stopping her work for an instant, Trina swiped a hand over her heart. "Arrow straight there, solid. More she tried to be the girlfriend, you know what I'm saying? Dropped little digs about Nadine not appreciating me enough. How she'd pay me more on the side than I got here, working with Nadine. She worked you in to the conversation once or twice, just how she'd heard I did your hair for something, and wondered what it was like."

She set the tool down, looked at Eve. "Cone of Silence. Absolute."

No question, Eve thought. No question whatsoever, whatever the pain in the ass. "Appreciated."

"Appreciated or not, that's my line, get it? I don't cross it. She finally got that. Maybe because I didn't tell anybody any of the shit she tried to bribe out of me."

"She stopped pushing you on it," Eve prompted.

"Yeah. So she'd still come in when I was here, not every time, but enough, ask me to buff her up. She'd work her 'link instead of talking to me because she'd figured out I had nothing to say. You get that, too, people who think of you more like a droid.

"Close your eyes. It's the eyes that say kick-ass on screen. I'd hear her talking to somebody, making an appointment," Trina continued. "But sometimes it was the way, like 'you'd better be there when I say, have what I want, or you'll pay for it' — that kind of bitch tone."

"Names."

Trina hesitated, sighed hard. "I think one was Annie Knight."

"She works here?"

"Hell no. Don't you know anything that's now? Jeezus-pleezus — sneezus! She's queen of talk screen. Practically built *Talk TV* with her own self. Top-rated late-night talk show twelve years running. Maybe more than, who knows? Anyway, I think one of them might've been her. I tuned Larinda out until I heard her say the name, 'cause I really like *Knight at Night.* Okay, open your eyes and hold still."

She came at Eve's eyes with a wand. "None of that weird stuff. Like the red you've got on."

"If I used color on your lashes, I'd go with a hint of green — pop top-shelf whiskey eyes, but this is for kick-ass, not for sexy. I know another she said was Wylee Stamford."

Eve's gaze shifted, had Trina pulling back the wand and cursing.

"Mets. Third baseman. Hit three-seven-five last season. That Wylee Stamford?"

Trina pressed her painted lips together in a satisfied smirk. "I guess you know something about something. He's got one fine ass on him, that Wylee. Yeah, that's who I'm saying she said. And she had that snake-hiss tone on her. Mostly otherwise she didn't use names. It was honey, sweetcheeks, dickwad — depending on the mood. Hey, Peabody."

"You're getting makeup!" Two steps into the room, Peabody gawked.

"Not by choice."

"You got your hair done!"

"I did not. She just —" Eve mimed snapping scissors.

"I want makeup!"

This exclamation slid straight into a whine.

"I got time. Nearly done with her." Trina waved a finger toward a chair. "Take a seat."

"This isn't a day at the damn spa. Status," Eve demanded.

"Mars's office is fully secured. Warrant is with legal, and I'm told it should clear through within the next fifteen. I tracked down the reporter — a Mickey Bullion. He confirmed the tag came from someone in the bar, but is reluctant to name the source."

As she spoke, Peabody moved in a little closer, to examine Trina's work on Eve. Eve shoved her back again.

"It wasn't hard to do a run," Peabody added, unabashed, "and find out his brother was on our list of wits. I spoke with him — Randy Bullion — and he confirmed he'd contacted his brother after we released him. Mostly Bullion the reporter's steamed he didn't get the tag soon enough to break the story, and Seventy-Five got scooped. I don't think there's anything there, Dallas."

Trina caught Eve's chin in the vise of one hand.

"I don't want the lip gunk."

"It'll balance the eyes," Trina insisted. "Did I say it comes off if you don't like it? Shut it a minute."

Peabody's shoulders raised up in a kind of self hug. "Oooh, I love this rosy lip on your palette!"

"Just mixed that for Nadine. It'd work on you. I think we go for a natural palette for you today — serious yet approachable cop."

Though she kept Eve's chin wedged, she switched brushes, swiped something over the cheeks, swiped something else. And something else until Eve visualized punching Trina in one of her black-and-red-lashed eyes.

"There." She turned Eve to the mirror. "Kick-ass, I-don't-have-time-to-fuck-around cop."

Prepared for the worst, Eve scowled. But . . . maybe her lips were a couple shades deeper — but it still looked like her mouth. Maybe her eyes read more intense, but basically, as with the hair, she couldn't see a lot of difference.

"Okay. Get this thing off me, and tell me who and what else."

"I didn't do her that much. Look, mostly everybody knew she was banging Mitch L. He's got his own stylist, and I'm not here that time of day, so I don't know the guy. Mitch L., I mean. But I do know Mitch L. was previously banging one of his interns — Monicka Poole. That was on the serious down low, but then he started banging Larinda, and the intern got the axe, and she cried on her friend's shoulder who happens to use my salon and she told me about it. Which means I told you and violated another C of S."

"Not really," Peabody said, rubbing Trina's arm in sympathy. "You're not violating a Cone of Silence when you have to tell the police."

"It doesn't feel right."

"She bled out, Trina."

Eve quashed her instinct to object to Peabody giving Trina too many details.

"Whoever she was, whatever she did, somebody killed her in a way that meant she bled to death trying to get help. Maybe it was only a few minutes, but it probably felt like hours to her."

"She was a bitch," Trina mumbled. "But . . . Crap, this is hard to say — it's like Mega C of S. She'd had some real serious work done."

"How do you know?" Eve demanded.

Trina rolled those purple, black-and-red-framed eyes. "Well, Jesus! I did her face, maybe a dozen times. You think I don't know when I've got my hands on somebody's face who's had serious work? Just like I know you haven't slapped that serum or moisturizer on yours more than maybe a dozen times in the last couple months."

She gave Eve a dark look. "Keep that up, you're going to need some serious work yourself. You got Mr. Frosty Extreme banging you, and you can't be bothered with basic self-care? What's your main damage?"

"Don't start on me, and don't worry about the Mega C of S. We already knew about the serious work."

Relief all but breathed over Trina's face. "Solid?"

"You think I don't know my job?" Eve countered. Trina smirked.

"Kick ass. I gotta say something, get it off my chest. Once I started to screw up her look — easy to do, you just use the wrong foundation or colors. It was because she tried to hit me up about Mavis and the baby, and it pissed me off so hard. But I couldn't do it, even then. Too much professional pride to fuck it up, even though I really wanted to. I could've made her look like a vampire under the lights. And now she's dead."

Eve saw Peabody about to speak, but shook her head. "You can't have too much professional pride. If you could, I might walk away from this investigation now that I know she tried to get to Mavis and the baby, because it pisses me off hard. But I won't. We do our jobs."

Nadine rushed back in. "All right, they're using filler to cover my scheduled spot, and hyping the upcoming one-on-one. A live one-on-one."

"I didn't agree to —"

"Live, my office. You look good," she added. "Hey, Peabody. Let's go. I've got a camera setting things up."

"It's going to be quick," Eve warned. "I've got on my I-don't-have-time-to-fuck-around face."

At Trina's cackle of laughter, Eve started out. "Peabody, ten minutes, Mars's office. They damn well better be finished screwing around with the warrant."

"You can do me in ten, right?" Eve heard Peabody say.

"Babycakes, I can make you a star in ten."

"I need a jump on the media conference." Nadine hustled past offices, down halls, through open areas, on her staggering black heels.

"I'm going to give you what I can give you. Exclusive and ahead of the rest, but you have to pool some of the info."

The staggering black heels skidded to a stop. "Wait just a damn —"

"Kyung set the terms here," Eve interrupted. "And it works. You control how much you share, and you get that edge. Which takes the time and edge off me for the media conference later today. You get the jump, Nadine, decide what you throw in the pool, and you can work out the fine lines with Kyung."

"There are going to be some very fine lines."

"Work it out," Eve said dismissively, then added the bonus round. "And I'm going to give you more, off the record, that you don't have to share. You're going to want to start digging, Nadine, and you're going to want to give a couple people you trust some shovels."

"All right." Nadine held up a finger, walked in a tight circle as she considered the pros and cons. "I'll toss some into the pool after I talk to Kyung. We'll work that out. You're going to tell me, I can already feel it, Larinda pushed somebody too far — poked the wrong bear trying to get to the honey."

"More like a herd of bears."

"I don't think bears have herds. What do they have? Why do I care?"

Nadine swung into her office, where her cameraman fiddled with some sort of light on a pole, adjusted a kind of umbrella. Nadine closed the door. "You there." She pointed to a chair, then put in an earbud while the cameraman set up a second camera on a tripod.

"They wanted this in-studio," Nadine said as she sat, angled toward the second camera.

"But I didn't want to argue with you about that. The producer will toggle between cameras as we talk, as it works in the booth, and on screen. You just talk to me, as usual.

"I want sharp focus, no softening filters," she told the cameraman, all business. "This isn't a memorial, it's straight news. I'm going to ask you about what happened in the bar — what you saw, did. You were a witness as well as being the primary. I'll ask the usual. Leads, suspects, progress, but I'm going to lead off with the eyewitness."

"I'm not going to give you every detail, anything that applies to the ongoing that could compromise it."

"Understood." Nadine laid a finger on her earpiece. "They're about to throw it to me . . . We're on in five, four . . ." She held a hand below camera level to show Eve three, two, one.

"This is Nadine Furst. With me is Lieutenant Eve Dallas, who has agreed to give Channel Seventy-Five an exclusive interview on the shocking and tragic death of our own Larinda Mars. Lieutenant Dallas, will you confirm you were actually in Du Vin, a popular downtown bar, when Larinda was attacked?"

"I can. I was off duty, meeting a colleague."

"Will you tell us, as an experienced investigator, as a witness, what transpired?"

Eve laid out what she'd decided to tell the media, answered Nadine's questions. Yes, they'd interviewed the individual the victim had drinks with before the attack. No, that individual wasn't a suspect at this time. They played the usual game of pitch and bat away on investigative details. And planted the seed — as she wanted the killer to know — they believed the victim had been target specific, and might have been followed into the bar.

"The fact that an NYPSD officer was on scene has given us an advantage. The investigation began immediately, and will continue with all possible resources. I can't tell you any more at this time."

Recognizing the signal, Nadine nodded. "Thank you, Lieutenant, and let me express particular gratitude from everyone here at Channel Seventy-Five for your dedication in the pursuit of the person responsible for the violent act that has taken the life of one of our family.

"And we're clear."

Nadine sat back. "You danced around a lot of that."

"Open and active. Ditch the camera."

"Sam, would you take them out?"

Eve tapped her ear. Smiling, Nadine removed her earbud. "And this."

Eve sat, silent, until they were alone.

"You can share we interviewed all the staff at the bar, and reinterviewed two this morning. Mars was a regular, and we've spoken to her usual waiter twice. We don't, at this time, suspect anyone on the staff."

"Okay, good."

"Now. Off the record until I give you the green."

"Understood."

"She may not have been who she said she was."

"That's not understood."

"She had substantial face and body work."

Almost amused, Nadine sat back. "Dallas, a lot of people, especially on-screen talent, have face and body work."

"Substantial. Altering."

Nadine's sharp green eyes narrowed. "As in she changed her face?"

"DeWinter is working on a possible reconstruction. If she can pull it off, we'll know, and may be able to identify, who she was before she was Larinda Mars."

"That's interesting. Still, she wouldn't be the first to want to change faces. And yet . . ."

"And yet. She's got a cache of about a

million in cash in her home safe."

"A million?" Nadine's shoulders shot straight. "Cash?"

"And jewelry worth easily as much. Art Roarke says is up there, too. Two underground accounts — so far. Several million each."

"How the hell did she —" Breaking off, Nadine held up a hand. "She didn't just try to extort for information, for contacts, for career enhancement. Straight blackmail?"

Handy, Eve thought, when you didn't have to spell it all out. "She's going to have tallied up a long enemies list, and some on that list are going to be right here, at Seventy-Five. So, when I say give shovels to people you trust, I mean trust implicitly. We believe her killer to be a male, but that doesn't mean he's not connected to a female she blackmailed. And I trust you, Nadine, to tell me if you dig up something on somebody here at Seventy-Five."

"Squeezing me," she replied.

"Killing, killing like this particularly — planned, cool enough to kill in a public place — takes a certain mind-set. Once you have that mind-set, it's easier to have it again. If you dig up anything, you tell me, or you risk putting not just yourself but whoever has the shovel in danger."

"Damn it." Nadine pushed to her feet, walked over to a friggie, yanked out a water bottle. "Damn it. I know you're right, but it's not a snap, Dallas. I didn't give two hot fucks about Larinda, but when I said 'our family'? That's absolute truth. A lot of people here are family to me."

"And if one of them's a killer, he needs to pay for it. He made a choice." Eve rose. "If you feel you can't do the digging or ask anyone here to do it with you, that's your choice. I won't hold it against you."

"You went after cops — and that's your family — when they crossed the line."

"That was my choice."

Nodding, Nadine took a long, slow sip of water. She paced a moment, sipping again, weighing it all.

"I'm in," she said firmly. "I'm in because I can't not be. It may give me some bad moments, but I'm all in. And yes, if I find something that points to someone here, as much as it grates, I'll tell you."

Lowering the bottle, she heaved out a breath. "I can't say I hated her guts. I didn't care enough to hate her guts, and maybe that's harsher in a way. But I care plenty about doing my job, and what's right about my job, to do this."

"Figured. Watch your six."

Now Nadine smiled. "I wonder what happened to the delicious young Bruno. Anyway, I'll watch my six."

"Good. I've got work."

"That makes two of us."

10

Eve intended to deal with Mars's office first. As she rounded the corner, she saw Peabody standing in the corridor admiring her newly painted face in a little hand mirror.

"Put that damn thing away."

Peabody batted newly lushed and darkened lashes. "But I look so pretty."

"We'll see how pretty you look after I pop you in one of your Trina'd eyes."

Unabashed, Peabody batted them again. "We went subtle with Baby Fawn on the lids, and a touch of Mocha in the crease. But I really love the Forest Shadows liner." Peabody risked one more peek before the mirror disappeared into a pocket. "Besides, I used my time wisely, and after Trina told me about Annie Knight, I had her tap her associate who's in makeup at *Knight at Night* for Knight's schedule. She's slated to be in her studio and offices all day."

"Add her to our list." Eve turned to the

sealed door. "And let's track down Wylee Stamford."

"Is he one of Mars's marks? Entertainment again?"

Truly stunned, Eve turned back around. "Jesus, Peabody, sports. Mets. Third baseman. King of the double play."

"Oh, yeah, yeah. He's the one with the really cute butt. Well, a lot of them have cute butts. It's the uniforms, maybe."

"I die a little," Eve grumbled, starting to unseal the door again.

"Hold on. Mitch L. Day's heading this way."

Eve glanced over. He rang a bell now — she'd seen that classic golden-boy face with its dazzling smile splashed across maxibuses.

He shot her one now, then toned it down — as efficiently as a dimmer switch — as he stepped up to her and Peabody.

"Ladies, I'm sorry, but if you had an appointment with Larinda . . ."

Eve simply took out her badge.

The dimmed smile vanished. Lights out.

"I see. I'll leave you to your business."

"You're part of that business. We have some questions for you."

"I'm afraid I'm very busy."

"Wow, me, too." Eve added a smile of her

own — on the feral side. "We can always coordinate our busy schedules and arrange for you to come down to Central to answer those questions."

"I simply don't see the need —"

"I do, and I've got the badge. We can talk right here about your adulterous, sexual relationship with the deceased, or we could discuss it in your office."

His eyes, a smoky blue-gray, hardened, and the faintest flush — anger or embarrassment — rose to his cheeks. "If you insist."

"It happens I do."

He turned and walked into the office opposite.

Eve supposed he fit the physical mode for screen personalities. He hit about six feet with a trim build that showed off well in the upscale casual look of a dark gray leather jacket over a silky T-shirt a few shades bluer than his eyes.

His hair, a wavy golden mane, flowed around a sharply chiseled face with the added charm of dimples that dipped into his cheeks when he flashed the megawatt smile.

A build that hit in the parameters of the third man leaving the bar, Eve calculated. And a dark watch cap would cover that gilded mane.

He shut the door to his office — though the term didn't really fit, as the room lacked a desk. Instead it held an expansive black leather sofa, a long table in zebra stripes, a massive entertainment screen, a full bar, and an alcove holding rolling racks of clothes and a triple full-length mirror.

"I've just finished shooting bumpers for today's show," he began, "and have to be on set in thirty, so I hope this won't take long. We're all having a difficult day around here, as I'm sure you can imagine."

"I'm sure you are. Larinda Mars had a difficult day yesterday."

He looked away, seeming to study a large framed poster of himself that showcased his chiseled looks and dazzling smile. "I still can't comprehend it, but that's no excuse for my lack of manners. Please, sit. How can I help?"

He arranged himself — really, Eve could think of no other term for the way he sat, crossed one foot over his knee, leaned forward.

"How long had you and Ms. Mars been sexually involved?"

"That sounds so . . . clinical, so careless." His face seemed to open — a little distress, a dash of sorrow, a whole boatload of earnest.

Eve didn't trust any of it.

"Larinda and I have been — were — friends for a long time." He used his hands for emphasis, lifting well-manicured fingers off his thighs, spreading them, palms outstretched. "We had so much in common, enjoyed each other's company. The friendship grew into more, a gradual thing neither of us anticipated. From there, we slipped into a romance."

"Slipped into it? Like on an ice patch?"

The flush returned as he jerked back. "Please, Officer —"

"Lieutenant. Lieutenant Dallas."

"My feelings for Larinda, and hers for me . . ." Now his gaze sharpened on Eve's face. "Dallas? *The Icove Agenda*'s Dallas? Marlo Durn's Dallas?'

"The NYPSD's Dallas."

The smile flashed back, along with the dimples, so his whole face lit with fascinated interest. "I'm campaigning to have you and Marlo on *Second Cup* before the Oscars. I'd love to build an entire hour around the two of you."

Eve simply stared. "Are you serious right now?"

"I'm sure Nadine would join us. It would

be an amazing show."

"Maybe Mars can report on it, on her show, from — you know — beyond the grave."

"I —" He caught himself, bowed his head slightly. "I'm sorry. It's so careless of me, just thoughtless. It's that I live and breathe *Second Cup,* and am always focused on what I can bring my loyal viewers."

"Right. How did your wife feel about you slipping?"

"Sashay and I . . ." He trailed off again, a habit, Eve decided. He sighed, long and heartfelt. "The demands of our individual careers took a toll on the marriage. So often we were dealing with our own pursuits and agendas. It's very difficult when a marriage begins to fail, and I'm afraid we were at odds more than in tune, even as we struggled to make it work. But . . . it became clear what had begun so hopefully couldn't last. I admit I found solace during that difficult time with Larinda. You can say I was weak, and yet —" That sigh again. "I found some happiness."

When someone shoveled bullshit by the ton, Eve thought, it was hard to keep your boots out of the muck. But she had plenty of experience, and just kept her tone conversational.

"You found some happiness banging a coworker while still married to someone else?"

The smile didn't just dim. His whole face went classically prudish. "I don't appreciate the crudeness. There was much more between Larinda and me than the physical."

"How about Monicka Poole? Was there more there than the physical?"

The flush rose, this time with a hint of fear flickering in his eyes. "I'm afraid you have some bad information. Monicka misunderstood my affection and generosity."

He stopped, and when Eve said nothing, letting silence pull him deeper, he cleared his throat and continued, "She's young, you see? Impressionable, even a bit . . . needy," he added. "Her misinterpretation is somewhat understandable, and I take partial responsibility for not seeing how she . . . But when she, I'm sorry to say, threw herself at me, made inappropriate demands and overtures, I had to let her go."

"You're denying a sexual relationship with her?"

"Absolutely." His eyes widened, and Eve decided she'd rarely seen anyone lie so poorly. "Not only does Seventy-Five have very clear rules and guidelines regarding sexual overtures with subordinates, but I have my own ethics. Rumors run rampant in my world, Lieutenant, but I will put my reputation and behavior against rumors always."

He might coat himself in outrage, Eve thought, but it didn't fit him well. "Uh-huh. Where were you yesterday evening — from six to seven o'clock?"

He lifted his head, actually tossed his mane of hair. "You would *dare* to insinuate I killed Larinda?"

No, outrage didn't fit him, but that touch of fear worked. "Peabody, would I dare?"

"Yes, sir, you totally would."

"Even so, I didn't hear any insinuation. I heard a question. Should I repeat it?"

"I believe I'll contact my attorney!"

"You go ahead." Eve rose. "He can meet you at Central. Peabody, see if Interview A's available."

Adding grief to the outrage, Day laid a hand over his heart. "Do you understand I've lost a *friend*?"

"Then cooperate with the investigation looking into who took her life."

"I was at home." He sat back now, crossing his arms defiantly.

"Alone?"

"That's none of your business."

"Jesus. Do you want to go around this

again?" She pulled out her badge, held it six inches from his face. "This *is* my business. Keep dancing, Day, and you're going to end up my prime suspect. You've already lied about Poole, and that could come back to bite you in the ass. Whereabouts, six to seven P.M. yesterday. Bullshit me again, and I'm hauling your ass in for obstruction and all-around dickishness."

"I've never harmed anyone in my life! I was home, from five to eight-thirty. And I was on my way out to meet Larinda. We had a nine o'clock reservation at Divine."

The words tumbled out of him now, and had more of the ring of truth. "The bulletin came across my 'link. I was in utter shock. Utter. My driver will attest to it. I had a complete breakdown, and came here, directly here to the station, hoping against hope it had been some sort of mistake, or a terrible prank."

"That covers you after eight-thirty. I'll ask again, were you home alone between six and seven P.M.?"

"I . . . I was in a meeting."

"With?"

"A potential guest."

"Name?"

"If you won't take my word for —"

"I won't. Answer the question, or you can

contact your lawyer from Central."

Not just a flush this time, but a harsh stain of red on his cheeks. "A fresh young actress I hoped to introduce to more of my viewership, to help advance her career."

"Name."

He spent some time picking invisible lint off his sleeve. "Scarlet Silk."

"Contact information."

"I'd have to look that up."

"Then do that. You were with Ms. Silk," Eve continued as he pulled out his memo book, "from six to seven?"

"Yes." He rattled off the contact information. "Now, I need to prepare for my show. This has been very upsetting. I need to compose myself and prepare."

"All right." Eve rose as he did. "Ms. Mars made her living on secrets, rumors, innuendo. Did she share any concerns with you over anyone who wished her harm?"

"She was fearless." He laid his hand on his heart, made a fist there like a salute.

"Did you share with her any secrets, rumors, or innuendo you learned through your own channels?"

She saw the flicker, the way his eyes cut away. "I host a friendly, comfortable show for my viewership. I maintain a friendly *and* respectful relationship with my guests."

"How about yes or no on the question?"

"Absolutely no."

"All right. Thank you for your time."

Eve stepped out, over to Mars's door, cut the seal. "Peabody, run the fresh young actress with the porn name."

"Already on that."

They stepped in. Like her apartment, Mars kept her work space in complete darkness. Eve called for lights.

Unlike Day's space, it held a desk, fussy, fancy, but a working desk with a slick little data and communication center. Floor-to-ceiling curtains of pale gold covered the windows behind it.

The sitting area, in the fancy/cozy style, used deeper golds and shimmering blues.

Like Day's, hers offered a full bar and a dressing area.

Eve started to speak, then Nadine stepped to the doorway.

"Need something?" Eve asked her.

"This is you doing your job." Nadine leaned on the jamb. "And me doing mine. If you're about to do something the public doesn't have the right to know, I can come in, close the door — and hold whatever needs to be held until. Otherwise, this can go into the pool."

"Christ." Eve chose to ignore her. "Peabody, alert EDD, the electronics will be tagged and waiting for pickup and transport."

"Already did. Scarlet Silk — you nailed it, Dallas. I guess she could be called fresh and young. I guess she could be called an actress. And her name reflects her current videography. Her latest is *Hard, Hot, and Hammered.*"

"Figured. Contact her, verify his alibi."

"Mitch's?"

"You got your one-on-one, Nadine," Eve reminded her, pulling open a drawer in the desk.

Unused memo cubes, a passcoded tablet, a couple of pens, a couple of cubes of sticky notes. Eve held up the notes. "Did she use these?"

Nadine shrugged. "You had your interview, Dallas."

Already fed up by the swamp of bullshit in Day's office, Eve rounded on her. "Don't fuck with me."

"Then don't treat me like somebody who does." Nadine stepped in, shut the door. "Larinda was well-known for slapping stupid stickies on comp screens, doors — even on the foreheads of her staff."

"Where is her staff?"

"Mostly in cubes, in the area to the right.

Neither she nor Mitch wanted their staff on top of them. Mitch, I think, because he likes his quiet time. Larinda because she enjoyed having them run back and forth at her beck. And she used them on a board — like you, sort of."

"What board?"

"This one." Peabody rolled out a white board covered in colored stickies. "I guess we could call it her case board."

Some of the stickies held names, others what Eve thought of as motivations or acts: sex, dollar signs, illegals, abuser, rapist. Some feel-good on there, too: engaged, expecting, honeymoon, charitable interests. Arrows connected some of the notes, and on some she'd tagged initials in the corners.

"Too accessible to be her marks. These would be her, well, marks, but professionally. People she's digging to dish on. Not illegal — it's her job. But let's tally up the names, coordinate them with the suspected dirt or offense. It could be somebody got wind of her scratching around and decided to take her out first."

Eve wandered over to the clothes racks. "These are for on screen?"

"She never wore the same outfit twice on screen," Nadine confirmed. "Wardrobe provides. And she often walked off with what she wore — which isn't part of the deal. You can buy it at a discount or return it to the rack for return to the vendor — who'll sell it at a discount — or the station buys it outright and somebody else uses it."

She collects, Eve thought. Information, secrets, people, money, jewelry, clothes. Hoarder.

She had to have another place to stash her collections.

And her own secrets.

Peabody looked at her signaling 'link. "Scarlet Silk, tagging me back. Ms. Silk," she said, moving away as she spoke.

"Who's the porn star?"

Eve considered, decided she'd get more, potentially, by sharing. "Day's alibi for the time in question."

"Not surprising, really. We keep it in the family, but it's pretty well-known Mitch is a complete dog. A happy, friendly one, but a dog. I assumed Larinda had him on a leash, but I guess he slipped the collar here and there. I'm not sorry to hear he's covered. I couldn't see him killing anybody. It's just not in his makeup."

"You like him? He spent most of the interview lying his ass off or puffing up whatever emotion seemed right at the time."

"Not surprised by that, either. Still, I do

like him. While understanding he's a dog that's going to hump legs, and knows better than to try humping mine."

"He gave Mars information on people. He says otherwise, but he's also a lying dog."

Nadine sighed. "I was afraid of that, and that's over the line. I'm sorry to hear it."

"Silk covers him — ha ha." Peabody stepped back. "She came right out and said he'd contacted her five minutes ago, frantic, asked her not to mention they'd enacted a few of her more memorable scenes, but she doesn't see the problem. In any case, she verifies Day was naked, handcuffed, and covered in passion fruit body gel when Mars was bleeding out."

"I did not need that image in my head," Nadine said. "Really, really didn't."

"And he likes to be spanked."

"Stop it," Nadine begged.

"Arrange for the electronics and the board to be transported," Eve said. "Give the office a good look. I'll start with her staff. I have to get back for the damn media conference, but we're going to squeeze in a talk with Ongar on the way."

She got a lot of tears from Mars's staff. Though clearly Mars had been demanding, often edging close to abusive, she'd gained some loyalty there.

"She was sort of their queen," Peabody said as they left Seventy-Five. "Maybe not always benevolent, but they all looked up to her. She gave them swag — little gifts. Worked them like slaves, but, oh, here's some perfume or this scarf or whatever Mars got in a swag bag at some event and didn't want or like. I don't think any of them were in on her sideline."

"Nope." Eve negotiated traffic. "Mars worked that line alone. She didn't share. Shit she didn't want, sure. Stuff she got tired of, maybe. Rewards to ensure loyalty. But she worked her hobby all by herself."

She brooded a moment. Mitch L. Day clicked some boxes — regardless of his cover of Silk — ha — but she judged him to be a dog, a lying dog. And unfortunately, a lying coward of a dog.

Tough to see him killing in cold blood.

She wanted to do another walk-through of the crime scene, push on Mars's electronics, start digging into her work board. Actual work. But after Ongar — home on a sick day, according to his office — she had to deal with the media.

It felt as if she'd dealt with them all damn day.

She really wanted to hit the lab, bug the shit out of DeWinter for some results.

A new face for Mars. Why?

"Why would you change your face?"

"Me?" Peabody tipped down the vanity mirror, studied herself, smiled at Trina's work. "If I had nothing but money, didn't get the wigs at the idea of it, I'd change some features. Not my whole face. I want to look like me, but better."

"You change your face because you want to be somebody else," Eve insisted. "Or need to be somebody else. Who she was before may play into this." Eve glanced over. "What features?"

"Oh, I'd have them round my jawline, soften it up."

"What's wrong with it?"

"It's really square."

"It's strong. What kind of cop wants a soft jaw?"

"Just a softer line. And I wouldn't mind more defined cheekbones. Maybe slim down the nose some."

"I'm sorry I asked. All of that's just stupid. If you want to look like you, you don't have them change your face."

"Mostly I'd like to be taller." Peabody continued with the dream. "If I could be a couple inches taller, just have them stretch me out, my ass would be smaller."

When Eve rolled her eyes, Peabody

shrugged. "Didn't you ever want to be different?"

"I wanted to be a cop, so the shape of my jaw didn't factor in."

She pulled up, stunned to find a curb spot, in front of a four-unit townhome. Ongar and Case had the east side ground level.

They'd painted their door a glossy blue. Eve rang the buzzer.

"Decent neighborhood," she observed. "Easy walk to the bar."

She rang it a second time. "Home sick?"

"His office said."

No palm plate, she noted, no comm security. Solid locks, a standard cam. She considered buzzing again, but heard the locks *clunk*.

Ongar pulled the door open to the length of the security chain.

"Can I help you?" His eyes, heavy, blurry, focused on her badge. His face was pale as death. "What's the — Cheyenne?"

The door slapped shut, swung open seconds later off the chain. "Cheyenne, is she —"

"She's fine as far as I know. We're not here about your cohab."

He sagged a little. "She just left about . . . God, what time is it? I'm pretty out of it." He scrubbed his hands over his face.

"What's this about?"

"Can we come in?"

"Yeah, after you tell me what this is about."

"It's about an incident at Du Vin last night."

"The bar? We were there. There wasn't any . . . Can I see your badge again? I'm still foggy. I was down for the count."

She offered the badge, let him study it.

"Yours?" he asked Peabody and repeated the process.

"Okay, come on in. Jeez, it's really cold out there. Look, I'm going to just sit down, okay?"

He went into a living area off a short foyer, dropped down onto an oversized couch splashed with sweeping curves of red over cream. "Sorry, sit, okay? What about the bar?"

"I take it you haven't watched any screen, checked for media reports."

"I'm lucky I can see you."

"You look pale, Mr. Ongar," Peabody said.

"You should've seen me about two this morning." His attempt at a smile came off as a grimace. "We tried a new restaurant last night. Do not order the seafood medley at Jamaica Joy. Trust me. Touch of food poisoning, I guess, and a touch is bad enough."

"Can I get you something?" Peabody offered. "Some water?"

"No, that's — Actually, there's some ginger ale back in the kitchen. It's helped. If you don't mind."

"No problem."

Peabody left the room while Eve took stock of Ongar. Pale, heavy-eyed, his hair sticking up everywhere. He still wore what she took as pajamas — cotton pants, a long-sleeved tee, heavy socks. And pulled a red throw over him.

"A woman was killed last evening."

"At the bar?" He started to push himself up, then eased back again. "No sudden moves. It's not the sort of place you expect trouble."

"I'm sure the victim thought the same. You were there with a small party?"

"Yeah, but there wasn't any trouble."

"Who were you with?"

"My fiancée, Cheyenne Case; my best friend, Nick Patelli — we work together — and his date, Sylvie MacGruder."

"Just the four of you?"

"Yeah. Double date. We had drinks at Du Vin, then Sylvie wanted to try this new place. I must make her pay." He smiled wanly when Peabody came back with a glass holding ice and ginger ale. "Thanks, really."

Closing his eyes, he sipped slowly. "Easy, stomach. Everything was fine when we left. I guess it was about six-thirty or six-forty. You don't need reservations for Jamaica Joy. I can currently attest to why."

"Did you notice anyone who left when you did?"

"I wasn't paying attention. I was pushing for Italian, and we were sort of joking around because I pretty much always push for Italian."

"A man, right behind you," Eve prompted.

"Like I said, I wasn't . . . Yeah, yeah, now that you mention it. I guess there was this guy who stepped out when we did, and we were talking. I guess blocking his way. He might've had to wait a minute before we started moving again."

"Any sort of description?"

"I really didn't see him. More sensed him, the way you do, and honestly wouldn't have remembered if you hadn't pushed on it. Maybe I caught a glimpse out of the corner of my eye for a second. Not really his face, just the presence. He killed somebody? In the bar?"

"We're hoping to identify him, speak with him."

"But nothing happened when we were in

there, and he left when we did, so . . ."

"A woman was attacked downstairs minutes before you and your party and this individual left."

"Holy shit. Shit." He bolted straight again, one hand going to his stomach. "Cheyenne and Sylvie were down there like ten or fifteen minutes before we left. God."

"We'll want to speak with them, and with Mr. Patelli."

"Sure. Do you want me to tag them up?"

"We'll contact them. If you speak to them in the meantime, and if you, or they, have anything to add, you can contact me at Central. Peabody, leave a card."

"Mr. Ongar, is there anything more we can do for you?" Peabody set the card on the coffee table.

"No, but thanks. Chey's only going in to work for a couple hours. She'll be back soon. You can let yourselves out, okay, because I'm just going to lie down here for a minute."

"Where's your 'link?" Eve asked him.

"My 'link? I don't honestly know."

"There was one in the kitchen. Good thinking," Peabody said to Eve. "I'll get it."

"If you need medical assistance before your fiancée gets back, call for it," Eve told him.

"Okay, but I'm actually better. Just hollowed out."

Peabody came back with the 'link, set it within easy reach, then pulled the throw more securely over him.

"Thanks, really. If any of us think of anything, we'll contact you. We really like that bar."

Eve stepped out, took a breath. "Well, that was a long shot anyway. You can contact the others while I'm doing this stupid media conference."

Peabody offered a big smile. "At least you'll look really good for it."

"That's, of course, my primary concern. Get in the damn car."

11

Eve hit her office first, frowning at the insulated tote on her desk. Wary, she gave it a poke, then twisted off the top.

The scent hit her first. Meat, a little grease, salt.

Tucked inside on a fancy disposable plate sat a fat burger and a large sleeve of fries. And in Roarke's oddly artistic handwriting around the lip of the plate, looped the one-word order:

Eat

First, she wondered how the hell he'd pulled it off, and second, as she ate a fry, how food of any kind had managed to survive the ravagers in her bullpen.

She supposed the answer was the same for both questions: Roarke was Roarke.

She'd intended to have coffee, but a burger and fries demanded, in her mind, a cold tube of Pepsi. She thought she probably had enough time to scarf it all down, update her board, and think for five damn minutes before dragging her ass to the media center.

Stuffing in another fry, she shrugged out of her coat, turned to the AutoChef.

"Hey, Dallas, I just checked in with . . ." Peabody stopped, sniffed the air like a hound. "I smell — Oh my God, is that a burger? It's a burger. And it's fries."

Saying nothing, accepting her duty — which was not the primal instinct to stuff the entire burger in her own mouth — Eve pulled out the knife in her pocket, flipped open the blade.

Peabody's hopeful eyes watched as Eve cut the burger in half.

"No drooling," Eve ordered and handed Peabody her share.

"Oh, man. Thanks." Peabody bit in, then hummed like a woman being gently stroked like a lover. "It's cow. It's a cowburger. Here is joy and rapture."

After her own bite, Eve just thought: good. And continued to eat one-handed as she updated her board. "Why are you in here eating half my burger instead of contacting the wits?"

Peabody swallowed the tiny bite of burger

— had to make it last. "Got a tag in to all three in Ongar's party. And I had one from McNab, which is why. Can I have a fry, too?"

"Half of them. Not a single fry over half."

"I'm not going to eat half because loose pants, but a quarter. I can eat a quarter." She selected one, bit in, hummed again. "McNab said they're into her home and purse electronics — and the shields were serious. Serious moolah to pay for them," she added after another bite and hum. "Now they're working on the encryption."

Eve glanced back. "She has data encrypted?"

"Not all of it, but considerable. He thinks what he's prioritizing is her list of marks, probably payments and maybe contact info. And Roarke's there now, helping out."

"I figured, since I'm eating half a cow-burger."

"One day I might develop your really casual relationship with food." With a glance at what was left of her half a burger, Peabody sighed. "Except I don't think so, as we have a lifelong love affair."

Eve continued to work on her board. "Let's eliminate the intern, this Monicka Poole. The wits didn't see the suspect's face, but they all lean toward male. But maybe that was deliberate. Poke around there, determine if we should bring her in."

"Will do," Peabody said around a mouthful of fries. "Maybe, as the kill was so quick and clean, somebody hired it out. I can see if she had the finances to pay for a hit."

"Hit's unlikely. A pro's not going to box himself into a public restroom with only one way in and out. But we should tie the possibility off. Work the wits. Take a look at the bar layout again, pull up the receipt list. Follow up on any customers who sat with an eyeline on the suspect's table. We could get lucky."

"On it. Thanks for the burger. Mega time."

Eve only nodded, and as Peabody went out again, sat on the corner of her desk, idly nibbling on fries while she studied her updated board.

Alibis, she mused. Even seemingly solid ones — like Day's — often cracked. But she didn't believe his would. If he'd wanted to cover his ass, he'd have done it with something a lot less humiliating than being oiled up by a porn princess.

Plus, she didn't see him as a killer — not a cold-blooded, stone-spined one. He definitely rated lying dog, but she also saw him as a weak sister.

Fabio Bellami. Lower on her list than Day.

His statement, reaction, demeanor had rung true. Plus, the timing simply didn't work.

Two more known marks — if Trina's information was accurate, and it likely was.

Annie Knight, successful screen personality. Wylee Stamford, superior athlete and baseball star.

What secrets had Mars dug up on them, and hoarded away?

She sat, thinking to start a run on both, to get a sense of them beyond ratings and baseball stats. Then both her desk unit and her 'link signaled.

Kyung, on both, she noted.

Lieutenant, you're needed in the media center. K

"Yeah, yeah, yeah."

But she got up, headed out.

Both Whitney and Kyung waited for her. Kyung gave her a long look, eyebrows arched. And smiled.

"Don't start on me."

"Only to say you look . . . quite prepared, Lieutenant. And to add your one-on-one with Nadine hit the right tone. I've already prepped them, and the commander will give an opening statement. You can go straight to questions. Do you have any of your own?"

"No. Let's just get it done."

She scanned the rows of reporters, the

cameras, while Whitney stepped to the podium to give the official statement.

"The primary investigator, Lieutenant Dallas, will take questions."

He stepped back, she stepped up, and the barrage began.

She ignored the shouts, said nothing at all, wondering why they never learned that she didn't play this game.

When a hand shot up several rows back, she pointed.

"It's been confirmed you were in Du Vin, a bar owned by your husband, when Larinda Mars was killed. Did you speak with her, interact with her?"

"I, along with two doctors on scene, attempted to save her life. Unsuccessfully. You could call that interaction."

"I'm sorry, I meant before she was attacked."

"No."

"But you knew her. Personally."

"I met her briefly three years ago in the course of another investigation." And since they'd ask. "At that time, she asked for and was given an invitation to a party at Roarke's home. Since that time I haven't seen or spoken to her until the events that transpired at Du Vin."

Another hand shot up — maybe they

could learn.

"Isn't the fact you were a witness to this crime a conflict of interest to your function as the primary investigator?"

"I didn't witness the crime, but the result of it." A fine line, Eve thought, but a line. "If I had witnessed the crime, the perpetrator of same would now be in custody. However, the fact I was on scene, thereby able to secure the scene and any witnesses quickly, serves as an investigative advantage. I imagine the individual who killed Ms. Mars would have preferred otherwise."

"Would it be accurate to say, as you were there, you most likely saw her killer?"

She'd asked herself the same damn question. "I can't say, with accuracy. It's a good-sized bar, with a spreading layout, and was, at the time, near full capacity."

The questions went on, a lot of the usual bullshit about leads, motive, details she couldn't and wouldn't answer or answered only in generalities.

When she felt herself running out of patience, she wrapped it up.

"Let me finish up with a statement. Investigative work must remain objective. In the usual course of my job, I stand over the dead, and I do my best by them, as does everyone who works in this department. In this case, I didn't come on scene after a body had been discovered or a crime reported. I watched Larinda Mars die. The two medicals on scene with me watched her die despite their best efforts. The people in that bar, there to have a drink with a friend after their workday, and those serving them, watched her die. I will do my best by her, as will everyone on the investigative team."

She stepped back, ignored the ensuing barrage of questions. She looked at Kyung, got his nod.

And left to do her best.

Hoping EDD had more forward progress, she aimed there first. She skirted the madness, went straight to the geek lab.

Through the glass she saw McNab, skinny butt bopping on his stool, along with Feeney, his hair in an explosive bush, which told her he'd been pulling at it. And Roarke, slick suit coat off, sleeves rolled up, hair tied back.

Not done yet, she concluded, but walked in anyway.

"If we had the Cat's-Paw first layer," Roarke said as he continued to play with a touch screen, "it may be an Armed Defense next."

"Maybe, maybe." Feeney pulled at his hair again. "It's sneaky. I'm already working it."

"Hot shiny shit!" McNab swiveled his narrow shoulders enthusiastically enough to have his long tail of blond hair swaying at his back. "I'm in the bitch now."

"Well done, Ian." Glancing over, Roarke spotted Eve. "Fine timing, Lieutenant. Our boy here just cleared his way into your victim's bedside tablet."

"You'd think she was freaking NSA, the shields and blocks and bullshit she used on her personal e's." McNab grabbed a vending cup, guzzled. "And she encrypted everything — different code patterns on every damn device."

"Can you put what's on that on screen?"

"I can now."

Once he did, Eve looked at a blue screen with a bunch of colorful symbols.

"First layer under the shields," McNab told her. "Standard icons. Hey, she played Killer Bees. Tight game. Anyway, we'll go through all those and check it, but let me just . . ."

He did something to the tablet. Another bunch of symbols scrolled on along with incomprehensible geek code.

"Okay, maybe this."

He did something else. The screen wavered, then actual words came on.

"Okay, just her calendar. Let me —"

"Wait. Hold it." Eve poked his arm to stop him, stepped closer to the screen.

"Travel from last October — eight through twelve. Majestic Resort and Spa, CI."

"Canary Islands," Roarke supplied.

"Okay. See notation on October eight? Durante, with two stars. Person, place, thing? And later in the month, October twenty, she's got Durante again, six P.M., Gino's — bar, restaurant, potentially a person — with three stars. And once more on the twenty-third, five-thirty, DV — that's going to be Du Vin — followed by two dollar signs and one of those stupid smiley faces."

"Person," Feeney said. "A mark."

"Yeah, goes to the resort maybe to loll around and get some tune-ups, and to troll this Durante. People rate with stars, right? Maybe it's a rating system. She ups the rating with a follow-up meeting, then the dollar signs. Durante pays. Move to November, McNab. And yeah. Keep going, month to month."

"You've got Durante, every month — dollar signs." McNab shifted calendar pages. "Other names, too. Durante, third or fourth week of every month, right through January."

She gestured, then fisted her hands on her

hips. "She's got Bellami down for last night, at the bar, the stars — no dollar signs yet, as he hadn't made the first payment. Appointments through the month, Gino's again, DV again. Send this to me, and we'll run the names that repeat."

She nodded. "Nice work, McNab."

"Thanks. Not done yet."

"Keep me posted. I'm in the field."

But she sent Roarke a look before she started out.

He followed her. "Since you look particularly refreshed, I assume you found the burger."

"Yeah, appreciated. Plus, Trina had some juice about Mars. I had to let her snip and buzz and play with my damn face, but it's going to be worth it."

"Your face is always worth it to me."

"Sap time." She poked him. "Anyway, I did something and realized I should've run it by you before I did it, but now it's done. About Peabody and McNab."

"Unless it involves a naked foursome, I'm likely fine with it."

"I hate when you sneak stuff like that into my head. It involves the villa in Mexico and one of your shuttles. She told me he's burnt — and I could see he's looking, well, a little hollow."

Roarke glanced back briefly. "I noticed, yes. A little hollow around the eyes, and not as, well, bouncy as our Ian."

Eve looked through the glass herself, watched McNab's shoulders, hips, feet all jiggle at the same time as he worked.

"Still got plenty of bounce, but . . . Anyway, Peabody was trying to put together a couple of days away once this is wrapped, give him some downtime, and I said she should take like five days, and then I offered the villa before I thought about it."

"You don't have to think about it. It's there, and it would give them a good break from the winter and the work."

"Yeah, but it's —" She caught herself before she said *yours,* as that would just piss him off. "It's probably in the Marriage Rules that you consult."

"Very fine save, Lieutenant." He skimmed his finger down the dent in her chin. "Let's say the consult should be simply to make sure whatever's offered is available during a specific time frame. And this is available, as it's unoccupied at the moment."

"Okay. I've got to get moving." She stepped away, stopped. "Did you know . . ." Checked to make sure no one stood within earshot. "Did you know there's been bullshit in some of the tabloids about you and

Nadine and me and three-way sex?"

"Now look what you've put in my head." He smiled, shrugged. "It's the nature of tabloids, darling, and easily dismissed. If and when they go too far, legal handles it, but if it troubles you, they can take a harder line."

"I don't worry about it. It's just weird what people put out there and other people scoop up like bullshit ice cream."

"Well now, it's hard to see many would enjoy that particular flavor, but you're not wrong about the appetite for salacious gossip."

"Salacious bullshit then. It's only relevant as it's something Mars did — marginally classier than her sideline, but in the same universe. Except she couldn't lie, just fabricate," Eve considered. "She wouldn't have lasted at Seventy-Five if she'd just made things up. And she wouldn't get payoffs unless she hit truths.

"You're not going to hit truth every time," Eve speculated. "Something to think about. I'll see you."

"If you're not coming back, let me know. Otherwise, I'll hitch a ride home with you."

"I'll be back," she called out, striding to the closest glide.

When she walked into Homicide, Peabody, her desk 'link in one hand, signaled with the other. She veered straight into her office, grabbed her coat. As she turned, Santiago stepped to her doorway.

"I need a minute."

"Okay."

"Carmichael's sitting on a woman and her teenage daughter at the hospital. We got the call, DB, male, in a private residence in the East Village. The woman and the kid had both been taken in for medical treatment. Vic's got about a half dozen holes in him from a kitchen knife. Household knife."

"How'd he get the holes?"

"According to the woman — the kid's sedated — she came home early from work to check on the kid, who was home from school on a sick day. That checks out. Found her ex in the kitchen, raping the kid. Rape kit and medical exam also verify, and the kid was beat up pretty good. The mother states she grabbed the knife out of the block, at which time the ex went at her, knocked her down, ripped at her clothes, threatened to kill both of them. She says she managed to get clear, and when he went for the kid again — whom she states was barely conscious on the kitchen floor — she stabbed him. Kept stabbing him until he was down."

"What doesn't check out?"

"The angles, LT, the movements. The kid — she's fifteen — was assaulted, was raped, that's solid. The mother has injuries to her face, to her breasts, and her throat. The DB had a good fifty pounds on her, facial scratches, and on the back of his neck — and both females had skin under their nails — and the stab wounds are all in the back."

She could see it, and could see where her detective was going, but let him lay it all out.

"The angle and placement and depth — we'll get the ME to verify — but, Dallas, it wasn't the mother who stabbed him. She's sticking to it, won't budge an inch. But you can see by the body, the angles, the blood patterns on the mother's clothes, the kid's."

Yeah, she could see it. "The kid stabbed him."

"Had to, boss. He goes after the mother, who tried to drag him off, scratching the back of his neck in the attempt. He gets off the kid, clocks the mom, knocks her down and back, then jumps her. The kid gets up, gets the knife, and makes him stop."

"Did you relate this to the mother?"

"Yeah, we did, but she won't budge, and she's not going to let us talk to the kid until she has time with her. She's not going to let us talk to the kid without her being present."

He took a breath, rubbed his jaw. "I can't blame her for it. Lieutenant, he beat the hell out of that girl, raped her, blackened the mother's eye, choked her. We ran background, and the mother's solid, a publishing exec with eighteen years in, no criminal. Kid's a good student, no trouble. Father — he doesn't live with them — is a lawyer, and you can bet she's tagged him. He's out of Charlotte now, but I'll guarantee he's on his way."

And they'd flank their daughter, their traumatized, likely terrified daughter. Who could blame them?

"The thing is," Santiago continued, "we're going to prove she's lying, and that's just going to make things messier for them. But she won't budge. Carmichael tried the woman-to-woman thing while I stepped out, told her it was clearly self-defense, but she's sticking with her story. Doesn't deviate."

"How about the vic? Any priors?"

"Two, both sexual assaults, both vics recanted. She says they started seeing each other last fall, and she broke it off a couple weeks ago. She didn't know about the priors, but claims he got over possessive, and the daughter told her he'd 'accidentally' touched her breasts or ass too many times. So the mother booted him, and he got bitchy about it, but she figured he'd move on."

"Contact the father — you, not Carmichael," Eve added. "Keep it male, cop to father, looking after the best interests of a child. He's a lawyer. Lay it out for him straight. If and when the ME confirms, if and when — and it sounds like when — you verify all the steps, relay it all to the PA's office, to Reo, because let's stick with a female there. She'll talk lawyer-to-lawyer so they're assured not only will no charges be brought, but it'll be kept out of the media. Nobody talks to the kid without one or both of her parents present."

"The father. Yeah, that could work. I'll push on that."

"And, Santiago? Let them see they matter. Take off the cop face and let them see. If you can't wrap it up, let me know."

"Okay. Thanks." He started out, paused. "He ripped off the kid's sick-day pajamas. They had bunnies on them. Fricking bunnies."

Eve let out a long sigh, let herself close her eyes for one moment. She knew exactly what that girl still had to face. Then she set it aside, put on her coat, and walked out.

"Peabody, with me."

"I talked to all three of Ongar's party. Sylvie MacGruder thinks, and it's a big maybe, the man who came out behind them was about six feet. She bases that on the fact that Patelli is about five-ten, and the man was taller. She thinks. She only has the vaguest impression of him, and thinks Caucasian, and her best guess would be between maybe thirty and sixty, but wouldn't swear to any of it. The others didn't even notice him."

"But she, again, believes male?"

"I asked if she'd noticed an individual walk out behind them. She said there was a guy a couple steps behind them. So she thinks male."

"Well, that gives us next to nothing. Let's see if DeWinter has more. E-geeks are bringing it in," she added, giving Peabody a rundown as they rode down to the garage.

"That'll give McNab some juice. Did you say the Canary Islands?"

"Yeah."

"Durante?" Peabody bundled into the car. "I bet that's Missy Lee Durante. I remember reading she had a fall break in the Canary Islands. She plays Elsie on *City Girl*. Screen series," Peabody explained. "It's really popular. She's the sweet, naive teenager who moved to New York from Iowa when her father got a new job."

"Teenager?"

"Well, she plays one. I think she's about sixteen on the series now, but I'm pretty sure she's more like eighteen or nineteen. Wholesome character, wholesome rep."

"I'm going to guess whatever Mars dug up on her isn't wholesome. Where's she based?"

"Pretty sure in New York, they shoot the series here. I can do my own digging. But no way she'd be mistaken for a six foot male. She's little. More like five-two."

"We'll talk to her. It's unlikely some random person with that name went to the same place at the same time as Mars. She preys on rich and famous."

"And we'll be interviewing the rich and famous: Annie Knight, Wylee Stamford, and Missy Lee Durante. And yeah, she's based in New York," Peabody continued as they crossed the garage. "I'll pin down where she'll be when we want to work her in."

"DeWinter first." Eve settled behind the wheel. "Plot out the best timing for the potential marks, and we'll take all three where they are, or push for a conversation at Central."

Eve backed out of her slot, turned toward the exit. "And make sure the teenage actress is of legal age."

"Hold on. Nineteen." Peabody tightened her safety harness as Eve shot out onto the street. "No need for a child services rep."

Eve maneuvered through traffic while Peabody worked her 'link and PPC to access schedules.

"Stamford's easy," Peabody announced. "He's doing an event at Sports World in Brooklyn, from three to five today. We should be able to catch Knight at her offices-slash-studio up until five-thirty."

"I thought you said she did some late-night thing. That's not late."

"It's recorded from like four to five-thirty, then broadcast later."

"Why?"

"Because . . . I don't know, exactly."

"Never mind."

"I haven't pinned down Durante yet."

"Stamford, Knight, Durante, unless the kid turns out to be sooner and closer."

Once they entered the hive of the lab, Eve aimed straight for the stairs, past workstations, cubes, glass work spaces where techs did their odd and geeky work.

She found DeWinter, dark eyes huge behind microgoggles, holding a skull.

"Is that Mars?"

"It is." DeWinter chose some sort of thin gauge, turned the skull, switched on the narrow beam of light. And said, "Hmm."

"What does that mean?" Eve demanded.

"She had superior work. Whoever operated on her face was — or is — an artist, and one with exceptional skill. I suspect the same on her body work, but I've only taken a cursory study there."

"Are you going to be able to give me a face?"

"We're working on it," DeWinter replied, and angled the gauge toward the jaw. "I've seen this sort of reconstruction on accident victims who'd suffered severe facial damage. In those cases, you can see the damage as well as the repair or alterations, can date both."

"In this case?"

"No indications of previous trauma or damage."

She turned to a screen, ordered magnification. Studied the skull in her hand and on screen. "This complete reconstruction rarely falls under the umbrella of vanity — though some can and do become addicted to cosmetic surgery. However, what I see indicates all of the work was done at the same time. Minor work here and there after, what would be considered tune-ups. But the initial work — jawline, cheekbones, nose, eyes, forehead? All done between twenty to twenty-five years ago. I should be able to narrow that window."

DeWinter turned back, pulled down the goggles. "I've worked on cases where the remains were identified through DNA, and like this, the dead had undergone a facial transformation. Criminals seeking to escape either the law or a rival, for instance. Someone with the connections and the finances — and the need — to completely change identities."

"And her DNA coordinates with Larinda Mars," Eve said.

"Yes."

"Which means either she changed her face but not her name, or she had enough scratch to alter her records of origin. And I'm betting it's the second. You get me a face, and I'll get those records of origin."

"It's going to take time, but we'll get it." DeWinter crooked a finger, starting out with her candy-pink lab coat flapping.

"You remember Elsie."

Eve eyed the woman in the white smock over black pants. "Sure."

"I lost a little weight." Elsie Kendrick grinned, patting what Eve recalled had been a monster baby mound.

"Twins, right?" Peabody asked.

"Right. One of each variety. Amber Grace and Austen Dean."

"Great names," Peabody said before Eve could pull the conversation back to business. "How are you all doing?"

"We're all doing mag. Due to our two-for-one sale, Daddy and I are sharing extended family leave, each working part-time. Plus, we can both do some work at home, so it's pretty smooth. If you don't count sleep deprivation."

She laughed again, gestured to a couple of easels. "And I don't, when I consider my gorgeous babies and fascinating work."

Eve studied the first easel and the sketches of Mars's face. Straight on, right and left profiles, even the back of the head.

The second showed lines, curves, arrows, numbers.

"Working the measurements and angles." Elsie turned to a wall of screens. "The body type, before and after, is going to be quick and easy. Dr. Morris removes the fill from the breasts, for instance, gives me the weight. He measures the uplift, and I can reconstruct the originals. I can do the same with the calves — from the fill. And I can approximate the butt — suck job there and a lift. I go with probabilities, and we have this body shape and type."

The screen came on — arrows and numbers again, but a full-length study of a female form.

"Bottom heavy, right?"

"Ouch," Peabody commented and subtly checked to see if her pants were still loose.

"A little on the hippy side," Elsie agreed, "considering the smaller bust. Thicker through the thighs — also suck and tuck there. Muscle implants — bi's and tri's — so you have less muscle tone here in the before image. Dr. Morris and our flesh-and-muscle tech consulted — that's why we're really just getting started here — and agree the subject was, before various body sculpting treatments, carrying more weight, less muscle, and in consult with Dr. DeWinter, estimate the subject's age to have been between forty and forty-five at time of death."

"Some of her teeth had been pulled and replaced with implants," DeWinter added. "The rest capped. And again, a superior job. Harvo will verify, but it's our opinion, as Morris concluded, she also underwent painful and expensive hair replacement. A kind of permanent color change."

As Harvo was queen of hair and fiber, Eve

expected to know whatever could be known in that area, and soon.

"How long will it take you to do with the face what you've done with the body?"

"Longer. We need to do a lot of precise measurements and testing." DeWinter put her hand on Elsie's shoulder. "But if anyone can do this, it's Elsie."

"It's going to be like a giant jigsaw puzzle. I love puzzles." Hands on hips, Elsie narrowed her eyes at the second easel. "I can tell you I'm close to sure her jaw's going to be rounder, wider, her forehead broader. Same with the nose — most likely. Broader. We determined her eyes were brown before she had them changed, so highest probability brown hair. Harvo may be able to do some magic and tell us more there."

"She won't have been really pretty."

DeWinter raised her eyebrows at Peabody.

"It's just — if she'd been really pretty, it would be harder for her to change everything. She'd have some feature she liked. Her eyes or her mouth, something."

"That's completely unscientific, but it makes sense," DeWinter allowed.

"I don't care if she was kick-in-the-nuts gorgeous or scare-the-kids ugly," Eve said. "I just need a face when you can get it. Appreciate the update," she said to Elsie. "It gives me a sense for now."

As she started out, Peabody said, "Can I see a picture of the babies?"

"Are you kidding?"

At Peabody's first *"Awwwww,"* Eve stepped out.

"She's the best," DeWinter began.

"I remember. She did good, solid work on the unidentified girls at The Sanctuary."

"I could have assigned someone else, and you might have gotten some results quicker that would have been more than good enough. But with Elsie, though it may take a bit longer, you'll have the next thing to a photograph."

"I'll wait for it. How much do you figure Mars paid to have all the work done?"

"I honestly don't know, but certainly hundreds of thousands, just for the face work."

"Not just for vanity," Eve mused. "Nobody's that vain."

"Vanity and ego would be more Dr. Mira's area than mine," DeWinter commented, "but I've certainly worked on bones of subjects who'd paid for a great deal of vanity."

"Not just," Eve said again. "There's a secret in her real face. She had secrets of her own. Peabody, now! Or walk to freaking Brooklyn."

12

Since she moved her ass fast enough and didn't have to walk to Brooklyn, Peabody used the drive time to gather information on Wylee Stamford.

"So, Stamford's a Brooklyn native. His parents — thirty-three years married — live in Brooklyn Heights. The mother, originally from San Juan, came here as an au pair on a work visa, married the father, who was, at that time, employed as a city maintenance worker. The mother now owns and operates Your Kids, a day care and preschool. It gets a Class A rating, so it's a really good one," Peabody put in. "The father owns and operates a home repair and maintenance company. Interestingly, one sister works with the mother, the other with the father in their respective businesses."

Peabody continued to scroll through as Eve crossed the bridge into Brooklyn. "A lot of baseball stats, which you probably already know. Like him being rookie of the year in '55, various MVP deals and Golden Gloves. Blah-blah. But on the personal side, no marriages or cohabs. He's still based in Brooklyn, and lives on the same street as his parents. His best pal since childhood is his personal manager. Four years ago he started the Stamford Family Foundation. The main mission is to expose underprivileged youths to sports — which includes a sports camp, scholarships, donated equipment, mentoring, transportation.

"Aw, he arranges, every year, for groups of kids to not only attend a home game, but to meet the other players. That's nice. He sounds nice."

"People who sound nice and can field like a god can still kill. Solid family ties," Eve continued. "Loyalty — keeps old friends — gives back. But something in there sent up a flag for Mars, and she exploited it."

"There's a lot of information on him, a lot of articles, features, bios. He comes off as a sports phenom from a hardworking middle-class family who values his roots. No scandals, no pissy behavior. Went to NYU on a scholarship, played for the Violets . . . isn't that kind of a sissy name for a ball team?"

"It's team colors."

"Okay." But Peabody mentally rolled her eyes. "Kept up his grades — not dean's list, but a more than respectable three-point-three. Not shabby academically in high school, either," she said, scrolling back. "Kept up that low- to mid-three average all the way . . . Whoops, pretty big dip in — let's see — seventh grade and into eighth. Barely scraped by there. Puberty can be a bitch, I guess."

A flag shot up, high and bright, in Eve's mind. "Check his juvie and medical records for that period."

"Really? He'd've been like twelve."

"If you're Mars looking for dirt and you see that inconsistency, what do you do?"

"I dig deeper."

As Peabody dug, Eve hunted for parking, settled on a lot.

Still digging as they got out, Peabody shook her head. "I'm not finding any juvie tags or . . . Wait, something. Urgent-care visit, records sealed."

"Just one?"

"It's all I can see. I mean he's got other injuries and treatments — clearly sports related — but this one's sealed."

"Look for follow-ups, check the parents' financials for medical bills. Later," Eve said as she studied the block-long spread of

Sports World.

They stepped in through the sliding glass doors.

If you played sports — or pretended to — she thought, you'd find everything you needed here. The retail section, bright and open, was divided into generous sections by sport: football, arena ball, baseball, basketball, soccer, hockey, lacrosse, and more. Screens played games going on somewhere in the world or highlights of games already done.

And all under a big, wide dome, like an arena.

The staff wore warm-up suits and high-top rollers so, when needed, they could flip out wheels and zip over the floor.

Eve snagged one on the zip.

"Where do I find Wylee Stamford?"

"He's on level three south. If you're here for the demonstration, that's at four, and you'll need tickets. They're free, but you have to sign up at the main desk, and they're going fast."

"Right, thanks."

She let him continue to glide, turned away from the main desk, and headed for the wide, open stairs.

The second floor, more retail, held sports clothes — jerseys, sideline jackets, yoga gear, running gear, racks and shelves of shorts and pants, shoes, cleats, skates.

She kept going, up another long flight.

People practiced their putts or swings on an indoor green. Others worked heavy or speed bags in a boxing section. What looked like a friendly pickup game played out on a half court.

Through a glass wall she saw a martial arts class performing a pretty decent kata.

And on the south side, Stamford signed baseball cards, balls, posters, caps, mitts for a throng of fans.

He wore his wildly curling black hair in a high, short tail, had an easy, cheerful smile on his carved-out-of-polished-granite face. His rangy body showed off well in black baggies and a thin, snow-white sweater.

Eve could admit to feeling a little tug — she considered him a true artist on the field and a magician at the plate. But tug or not, he was, at the moment, a suspect.

With a quick, practiced glance around, she picked out security, and headed toward the man with a burly build and suspicious eyes.

She angled herself, palmed her badge, tipped it up. "Lieutenant Dallas, NYPSD. I need to speak with Mr. Stamford."

"What about?"

"We'll speak to him about that."

He frowned, head signaled a woman positioned on the other side of the crowd. She made her way over, and the two security guards had a quick, murmured conversation.

After a hard look at Eve, the woman headed off to yet another man. Not security, Eve thought. Too slight, too well dressed.

She got another look, another frown from him. Then he cleared his face to pleasant, strolled over.

"How can I help you, officers?"

"Lieutenant, Detective," Eve corrected. "We need a conversation with Mr. Stamford."

"I'm Brian O'Keefe." He offered a hand along with the pleasant smile. "Wylee's manager. As you can see he's pretty busy just now."

"We'll wait."

"If you could give me some idea what this is about, I might be able to help. Wylee's schedule's really tight today."

"He can make time to speak to us here, or he can adjust his tight schedule to include a conversation at Cop Central. Maybe you should ask him which he'd prefer."

The smile bobbled, fell away. "If there's some problem —"

"Don't you figure this indicates a problem?" Eve tapped her badge. "Here or Central. Simple or complicated. Choose."

"He's got a ten-minute break coming up shortly."

"Fine."

"Jed, why don't you show these officers back to the locker area. It's closed off for this event," O'Keefe told Eve, "and should be private. If Wylee stays out here, they'll keep coming."

"Sure, Bri." The big man led the way.

"Have you worked for Wylee long?" Eve asked him.

"Awhile." He skirted behind a trio of batting cages, swiped a card on a door. "Don't see why you have to bother him."

"It's my job. What was yours before this? Linebacker?"

His mouth curved, just a little. "Semipro. Bunged up my knee pretty bad, and that was that. Wylee hired me on."

"Same neighborhood, right?"

If you couldn't hear Brooklyn in his voice, you needed to have your ears checked.

"Yeah. Me and Bri and Wylee, we go back. You can wait in here."

He went out, closed the door.

The room held two walls of stainless-steel lockers, a trio of sinks, a couple of toilet stalls, and a pair of low benches.

"See about that medical data," Eve told Peabody, pulling out her own handheld to do a run on Brian O'Keefe.

No marriage, no cohabs, no offspring on record. Studied at Carnegie Mellon, double majors in comp science and accounting.

Nerd, Eve decided.

And the nerd had taken a job in IT right out of college, then ditched it to manage the sports star.

Eve poked around in O'Keefe's life until Peabody swore under her breath.

"I'm not going to be able to pull this out on a handheld, Dallas. The data's too old. I probably couldn't pull it anyway. It's going to take an e-man. I can send it to McNab."

Eve started to tell her to go ahead, remembered McNab was already overworked. "Send it to Roarke."

"Really? That's okay?"

"Nothing he likes better than prying around in somebody's personal business."

Then she looked up, stood up, as Wylee Stamford came in.

He smiled as he did, extended a hand. "Sorry to keep you waiting."

Maybe she felt another tug as she shook the hand that could wing a ball from third to first like the stream of a laser rifle.

"We appreciate your time, Mr. Stamford."

"Wylee, okay? Lieutenant — sorry."

"Dallas, and Detective Peabody."

"Well." He sat on the bench. "How can I help a couple of New York's finest?"

"We need to talk to you about Larinda Mars."

"I . . . Who?"

Eve saw two things simultaneously. He hadn't been prepared to hear that name, and he was going to lie.

"What was your relationship with Larinda Mars?"

"I'm not sure I know who that is," he began, looking relieved when O'Keefe came in.

"Sorry. Got a little hung up." He dropped down on the opposite bench.

Eve considered booting him out, then decided to get the two for one.

"Larinda Mars," Eve repeated. "Gossip reporter, Channel Seventy-Five. She was murdered yesterday. You might have heard about it."

"I did," O'Keefe said before Stamford could answer. "Something about her being attacked in a bar, or a restaurant?"

"That's right. Why don't each of you tell me where you were yesterday between six and seven P.M."

"Excuse me?" O'Keefe said it with a quick laugh. "Are you serious?"

"Murder always strikes me as serious. You first." She turned to Stamford. "Six to seven."

"I'm going to contact Gretchen," O'Keefe interrupted. "Wylee's lawyer."

"Go ahead. We can wait."

"No. Just, no." Wylee waved a hand in the air. "It's simple. I was at my parents' house. Or walking down there around six. I'd've been having a beer with my dad by around ten after. We ate about seven. No, wait — I was late. Mr. Aaron was out walking his dog, and he caught me. He's a talker. I probably didn't get to the house until about twenty after. I'm not sure exactly."

"Mr. Aaron's a neighbor?"

"Yeah, he lives two doors down from my dad."

"All right. We'll verify that. Mr. O'Keefe?"

"I was home at six. I work at home unless we're going to an event or I have an outside meeting. I was home until about seven. I had a date, and I left to meet her about seven."

"Her?"

O'Keefe blew out a breath, shot a glance at Stamford. "Gretchen Johannsen."

"Gretchen? You and Gretch? This is news."

Coloring a little, O'Keefe shrugged at Stamford's grin. "We're just sort of . . . testing the waters."

"You've been swimming in the same pool since you were ten. Gretchen's one of the old neighborhood gang," Stamford continued, then stopped, lost the easy smile. "Sorry. It's not important."

"You never know what is," Eve countered. "When did Ms. Mars first contact you?"

"I really don't know who or what you're talking about."

Eve stared straight into his eyes. "Mr. Stamford — Wylee — I admire the way you field a ball like your glove has radar, and your power — and brains — with a bat. From my perspective you bring integrity to your game, so I'm going to give you just a little room. I'm going to assume you're lying to me for the same reason you let Mars blackmail you."

"You can't —"

"Quiet," she snapped at O'Keefe, "or the room gets a lot smaller. We have her electronics. We have your name among her list of victims. She made you a victim by exploiting something you'd pay to stop her from exposing. Maybe you got tired of paying, maybe she asked for too much, maybe you just snapped. Maybe you decided to kill instead of pay."

"I was at my parents'."

"A lot of people admire you. Some of them might kill for you. Like your old friend here. Or Jed. Maybe Gretchen."

Wylee's eyes turned hard, his face into polished stone. "You don't drag my friends into this."

Loyalty, Eve thought, and continued to use it. "Then stop lying to me or I won't have a choice. I need you to tell me the truth. The faster and more detailed that truth, the less chance there is I'll have to discuss any of this outside this room or bring your friends, your family, into it."

"I don't want my family to know."

"Wylee —"

"No, Bri, enough. It's enough." He braced his elbows on his thighs a moment, scrubbed hard at his face. "I don't want them to know what you found on her lists, in her fucking files."

"Then lay it out for me, and I'll do everything I can to protect your privacy. As long as it's the truth."

"I'm not sorry she's dead. That's the truth." He shoved up, paced the narrow area between benches. "She came up to me a couple years ago, at a sports banquet. She gave me her card, and on the back was a name, and her private number. The name, the number, and an order to contact her."

"What name?"

He shut his eyes. "Big Rod. I had to get up and make a speech. I felt sick, but I had to get up and make a speech. All those kids . . . I was a kid. I was just a kid."

And she knew, by the look in his eyes, the tone of his voice. The child in her knew the child in him.

"Give me his full name."

"Rod C. Keith. My hero." He all but spat the word. "My mentor. Guardian angel of the neighborhood kids — that's what people called him back then. If you needed someone to play catch, shoot hoops, go long, you could count on Big Rod. You could hang out at the youth center for hours. He'd listen to your dreams, push you to get good grades, and sharpen your batting stance."

"How old were you when it started?"

His eyes, haunted now, met hers. "Twelve. Maybe it started before, just subtle things. I trusted him. I loved him. My family trusted him. They loved him."

He paused, breathed in and out, slow.

"Sure you can go watch the game on screen with Big Rod. No problem having some catch with Big Rod. I'd feel special when it was just the two of us in his place."

Wylee closed his eyes. When he opened them again, he stared blindly at the wall of lockers.

"I felt grown-up when he said I could have some of his beer — and we wouldn't tell anybody. He gave me half a beer before the first time. I was dizzy and I didn't understand, and it was Big Rod. He said it was a rite of passage. And after, when I was sick, he said I was his number one. His number one, and if I said anything, I'd be nothing. If I said anything, nobody would believe me. If I said anything, something bad might happen to one of my sisters. And . . ."

He sat again, let his hands dangle between his knees. "I don't want to talk about what he did, and what I let him do for almost a year until he found another number one."

"You didn't tell your parents."

"No. I was ashamed and afraid. I've never told them. I don't want to tell them now." He lifted his head to look at Eve and his hands balled to fists.

"It's over. He's dead. I didn't kill him, but somebody did. They found him beaten to death in an alley a couple blocks from the youth center. He got a hero's funeral, the son of a bitch. I was in therapy by then. I put my family through hell first. Stealing beer, buying street illegals. Sneaking out of the house at night whenever I could, but I couldn't get away from feeling his hands on me, so I broke into Mr. Aaron's house."

When his voice cracked, Eve gave him a moment. "Your neighbor," she prompted.

"Yeah. He had whiskey. I got his whiskey and the pills I bought, and I took them all with all the whiskey I could drink. Just end it, that's what I wanted to do. Just make it stop."

He closed his eyes, breathed out.

"Thirteen years old, and I just wanted to make it all stop. But I wasn't very smart about it, and took too much at once, sicked it all up again."

Pausing, he pressed his fingers to his eyes, dropped them. "My parents heard me, realized what I'd tried to do. They got me to the clinic. I can still see my mother's face, still hear her praying. They made me go to therapy. I didn't want to at first, and I fought it, but they made me."

"They had your back, Wyl," O'Keefe soothed. "They always had your back."

"Yeah, they did, and it pissed me off back then. But . . . Dr. Preston. I guess he saved my life, and making me go to him saved my life. He never told them about Big Rod because when I finally got close to breaking down enough to tell him, I made him promise. He said he couldn't and wouldn't break my confidence."

Wylee cleared his throat. "I started to get better. After I said it all, after Dr. Preston listened, after we talked, week after week, I started to get better.

"I don't know how she — how Mars found out because Dr. Preston wouldn't have told her. I went to him after she hit on me, and he told me to go to the police."

"Good advice," Eve commented.

"Yeah, I knew it, in my head I knew he was right, but I couldn't do it, just couldn't. I don't know how she knew, but she knew enough. She put enough together, even insinuated she could make people think I'd killed Big Rod. End my career, shame my family, destroy the work we're doing with the foundation. Unless I paid her to keep my secret."

"How much?"

"It wasn't consistent, and not that much really. Six or eight thousand a month. Like a business expense. I put it out of my mind."

"In cash."

"Always," he concurred. "She wanted me to deliver it whenever I was in town, but I wouldn't. Take the money, or don't — at least I had the balls for that. I'd have it messengered, or Brian would."

Eve's attention shifted to O'Keefe. "You knew about the arrangement, and the reason for it?"

"Yeah. Wylee told me about Big Rod when we were teenagers. After Big Rod was dead, after Wylee got better. He finally told me."

"He never abused you?"

"I wasn't his type. Not an athletic bone in my body. Skinny, scrawny, brainy. I used to envy all the kids he'd take under his wing. Until I realized I was lucky he barely noticed me. I hated that she used what happened to Wylee for money, but it wasn't worth killing her. Because you're wrong," he said to Wylee. "You've always been wrong — and it's something Dr. Preston couldn't get you to believe. If it had come out then, since, now? Nobody would be ashamed of you. Nobody would blame you. And a lot of people would do what I do."

Emotion shook O'Keefe's voice as he gripped Wylee's shoulder. "They'd spit on that goddamn plaque with his name on it in the youth center. And that bitch would go into a cell where she belongs. Or belonged. I'm not sorry she's dead, either, but I'd rather think of her living in a cage. That's just me."

"You're a good friend," Peabody added.

"I'm going to verify your alibis." Eve rose.

"Do either of you have a vehicle, one you keep here?"

"Yeah, I've got a truck I keep garaged. Brian's got an all-terrain."

"Let's go with the truck. Give Detective Peabody the description — make, color, year. We'll verify the alibis, checking if a vehicle with that general description was involved in an incident in Manhattan during that time frame."

"Thank you. Thank you for that." He gave Peabody the information on the truck, held out his hand to Eve. "I guess I should say I hope you find who killed her, but I don't think I'm going to be sorry if you don't."

"You should listen to your friend. She didn't deserve to die. She deserved to sit in a cell. Humiliated and locked up. You're entitled to your privacy," she told Wylee. "A twelve- and thirteen-year-old's bound to be scared and ashamed and not know what the fuck to do when a trusted adult twists a relationship into the sick and selfish. A grown man who's a goddamn miracle on the ball field, one with a strong family and solid friends behind him, ought to have the sense to know when to go to the cops."

"Yeah. Yeah. I guess there's still some of that kid in there."

"I hear you."

As they walked back to the car, Eve glanced at Peabody. "Your take?"

"I could maybe see him losing his temper and punching Mars in the face. I can't see him plotting, executing, or conspiring to execute cold-blooded murder."

"Agreed. He caved to her, and he'd have kept on caving because there's a part of him that's still ashamed and guilty over what happened to him. So far as we know, at this point, Mars was cagey enough not to demand more than her marks could afford. For Wylee, at least, it was better to pay than risk or fight back."

"Would you? Sorry," Peabody said immediately. "I shouldn't ask, or even bring it up."

Eve waited until they'd reached the car, then stood at the driver's door, looking over the roof at Peabody. "It applies. Not the same situation, but close enough it applies. It took me a long time to remember what happened to me, to be strong enough to get through the protective blocks. And longer to get past the guilt and shame of what happened to me, and what I did to stop it from happening."

She got in the car, settled behind the wheel, considered another moment. "I couldn't, wouldn't have allowed her to victimize me. And whatever Roarke's instincts might have been to protect me, he'd have stood by that. For me. It's the badge that gave me the will to survive — the goal of getting it, the work of upholding it. To survive and to be open enough to let Roarke push his way into my life. Betraying the badge, him, you — everyone I know would stand by me? Betraying myself?"

Not a question, Eve thought. Not an option.

"Couldn't do it. I'd make sure she'd have done her time in a cage even if it was the last thing I could do with that badge."

"Nobody would take your badge for what happened to you, or for what you did to make it stop."

With a shake of her head, Eve began to drive out of the lot. "I killed Richard Troy. Patricide's got an ugly ring."

"Patricide, my ass. An eight-year-old girl defending herself against an incestuous pedophile monster after years of abuse," Peabody corrected, with a bite. "You should get past thinking anybody — *anybody* — would call for your badge over it. You should get past thinking they'd have a right to."

As she waited for the lot scanner to read her tag for billing, Eve flicked a glance at her partner's rigid profile.

"I guess you've got a point. It may take a little more work to get there."

Eve drove out of the lot. "But it applies. Someone killed Wylee Stamford's monster, and maybe whoever did killed his blackmailer. Let's get the case file on Big Rod."

Still simmering, Peabody started to snap something back, then frowned. "Somebody's still protecting him. I didn't think of that."

"That's why my badge says *Lieutenant,* and yours doesn't."

The frown eased into a smile. "For now," she said, getting an easy laugh out of Eve. "How about some coffee for the drive?"

"Yeah." Eve's shoulders relaxed. "How about some coffee? And we're going to look at O'Keefe and his alibi. Loyalty runs deep in both of them. I heard him saying she should squat in a cage, and it rang like truth. But we take a good look. After you program which of Mars's marks we're cornering next."

"On that."

13

City Girl was shooting some exterior scenes in the West Village. Fans, Eve assumed, and those who just liked watching, gathered behind barricades with their cameras. Civilian paparazzi, braving the bitter cold for the prize of a photo or short vid.

Extras plucked from who knew where hustled over the sidewalk as Missy Lee Durante, a pink-and-white polka-dotted backpack over her fashionable purple coat, raced tearfully by on pink airboots.

Her colorful scarf flew out like ribbons; the pom-poms on her hat bounced madly. She fumbled with the latch of a little courtyard gate, burst through it, then ran toward the door of a tidy brick townhouse.

"I bet that jerk Tad dumped her," Peabody muttered.

"What?"

"Just thinking why she's crying. See, Tad's the high school football quarterback she's been crushing on even though he's a shitbag under it. And he's been playing her so she'd do his assignments, but . . ."

Peabody trailed off when Eve simply held her under a cool, cool stare.

"Anyway."

Somebody yelled, *"Cut."* Then swarms of people began moving around. A couple of them dashed to Missy Lee, began fussing with her face, the flowing blond hair under her winter cap, the line of the coat.

NYPSD barricades blocked off the sidewalk for a full block. Eve had to badge her way through. Crew, equipment, security for crew and equipment formed more barricades. While people repaired Missy Lee's makeup so she could cry on cue, Eve flashed her badge again.

"NYPSD. We need to speak to Missy Lee Durante."

"She's a little busy right now." The man in the earflap cap gave Eve a big, toothy smile. "I can see about arranging a quick hello after we get this scene. *City Girl*'s grateful to the NYPSD."

"I'm not after a quick hello. This is official police business."

Now he rolled his eyes. "Yeah, we get that a lot. Look, we're setting up for another take, so I really need you to just step back for a minute until —"

"Would you like to be arrested for obstruction?"

"Hey, trying to be cooperative. Just —"

Now somebody yelled, *"And action!"* Toothy Grin held up a hand, turned his back on Eve. Peabody grabbed Eve's arm, shook her head fiercely.

"It can wait just a minute," she whispered as the same pedestrians began the same hustle.

Missy Lee flew down the sidewalk, tears streaming. Fumbled with the latch, and this time let out a choked sob as she fought it open. Cameras followed her, angled to catch her run, her rush through the gate.

Eve struggled to find patience as people swarmed again, as cameras reangled to record the same scene from the front, the side.

Someone brought the star a cup of something that steamed as she consulted with a plump woman in combat boots.

"Now," Eve told Toothy Grin, "or I'm having the barricades removed."

"You can't do that!"

She shoved the badge in his face. "Can you read that?"

His face reflected a lot more annoyance than fear, and so did the finger he jabbed at her. "You just wait here!"

Eve thought, Bullshit, and followed him as he strode indignantly through the crew and equipment.

"Clarice, there's a cop back there who —"

"I'm right here. Lieutenant Dallas, NYPSD. My partner and I need to speak with Miss Durante. Now."

"Clarice Jenner, director, and we're in the middle of shooting a key and very emotional scene. Miss Durante can't be disturbed."

"It's all right, Clarice. Can I have five?" With tears still drying on her face, Missy Lee smiled, rubbed a hand over Clarice's arm. "Just five."

Clarice shot Eve one hard, angry look. "Clear back. Take five."

Missy Lee kept the smile on her pert, pretty face, sipping from the go-cup until everyone was out of earshot. "I've sort of been expecting you — or somebody with a badge. I can't talk about this here, and I'd really appreciate it if you'd make this look like a fan moment. A lot of people depend on me and this show."

"Then why don't we clear this up?"

"Have you got something to write on?"

At Eve's glance, Peabody pulled out one of her cards. Missy Lee took it and dug a small pen out of her coat pocket. "I'm writing down an address, and a time. I'll meet you there," she continued with her smile still beaming. "I'm going to bring my lawyer. I'm entitled to that."

"You are. I'll give you this, Miss Durante. But if you're not where you say when you say, that'll change. It won't look like a fan moment."

"I'll be there. I want to clear this up. I just want to clear it up quietly." Her eyes, summer blue in winter's bite, met Eve's straight on. "I know who you are, both of you. If the book and vid weren't bullshit, I figure I can trust you. But if I don't get back to work, we're going to run into overtime, and the producers are going to scream."

She held out a hand, shook Eve's, shook Peabody's.

"Ah, it's Tad, right?"

Missy Lee laughed, a quick, infectious gurgle. "Yeah. He dumped me, with mega humiliation."

"He's a prick."

"He really is. I gotta go."

Eve let her walk back to the hair and face fussers, and moved with Peabody through the crew under the twin glares of Clarice and Toothy Grin.

"Check the address on the card," Eve told Peabody. "What it is, where it is, who lives or works there."

They'd reached the end of the barricade when Peabody stopped dead. "It's Tad!" Absolute shock covered her face.

"The fictional prick?"

"It's Tad," Peabody repeated. "Marshall Poster, who plays Tad. It's his place — Upper West."

Eve took the card, stuck it in her pocket. "I'll take that going home. We'll hit Knight next. You can run Tad — crap — Poster in the car."

"Why would she want to meet us at his place? He's a total dick."

"Fictional, Peabody. He may be a dick in reality, which is why you're going to run him."

"She's staying up late doing his assignments while he's laughing behind her back and cruising with that little bitch Jade Potts."

"Peabody." Eve climbed into the car. "You're going to have to get over it."

"I had a crush on a guy like that when I was fifteen." Peabody yanked out her PPC. "You never get over it."

Eve let Peabody stew while she drove to Knight's Midtown studio.

After a small parking nightmare, they joined the hordes crowded into the pedestrian walkway. Tourists bagging souvenirs or taking pictures, hanging over the rail to watch the skaters.

And presenting prime targets for street thieves.

Though she resented the time, Eve tripped one, sent him sprawling seconds after he'd lifted a purse stupidly left hanging from one of those baby-pushers while his partner neatly picked the wallet out of the probable father's rear pocket because he was so busy taking a home vid.

"Hold him," Eve ordered. "Call for a couple of beat droids."

Then, as Peabody quickly put a boot on the fallen thief's back, Eve fast walked after the partner, who strolled along projecting innocence.

Two arm spans away, Eve saw the body language change, go on alert. Communication, she thought, cursed as the thief broke into a sprint.

Fast, she's fast, Eve concluded as the thief poured it on, bowling down pedestrians. Fast, Eve thought again as she leaped over a man who'd gone down flat on his back.

But Eve was faster.

She considered a tackle, opted to snag the thief by the collar of her coat. The thief was nearly quick and agile enough to spin right out of it, but Eve whipped her around, tangling her in her own coat.

The girl — she couldn't have been much more than sixteen — gave Eve one fierce look. Then her eyes filled with tears and fears.

"Help! Help! She's hurting me."

"Hey, lady —" The first Good Samaritan pushed forward.

"NYPSD."

"She's lying! She's trying to kidnap me!"

The Samaritan firmed an iron jaw. "You're going to want to let her go."

And with a crowd moving in, he grabbed Eve's arm.

"Sorry," Eve said, before she kneed him hard in the groin, sending him down. "NYPSD! I'm the police."

"Help! Oh, please, somebody help me!"

"You're good," Eve told her as the young thief screamed and wriggled. "I'm better."

She managed to get out her badge and hold it up. She didn't think it made her any friends while she manhandled a pretty, petite teenager, but most backed off.

Once she muscled the kid to her knees, worked on the restraints, she opened the girl's coat to reveal the loot pockets inside.

And the wrist units and wallets in them.

The Good Samaritan, still wheezing,

stared at one of the wrist units Eve held out as proof.

"I . . . That's mine!" He looked down at his naked wrist, at the one in Eve's hand, at the girl now wearing a defiant smirk.

"You'll need to come down to Cop Central, sir, to make a claim. I'm sorry for the inconvenience. And for the knee."

He just continued to goggle. "She stole my wrist unit."

The girl shrugged. "I gotta eat, don't I?"

He stopped goggling long enough to snarl, "Get a job."

As a couple of beat droids marched up, Eve hauled the girl to her feet, turned her over, gave terse orders. Winding her way back to Peabody, she rubbed her jaw where the girl had rammed her head during the scuffle.

"Remind me to avoid this area in the future," Eve said.

"I didn't spot the girl. Spotted the boy a couple seconds after you, but I didn't make her until you went after her. Which is why your badge says *Lieutenant.* He had ear comms."

"Yeah, her, too. Slick. Just not slick enough."

"Well, that was fun," Peabody said on a quick breath. "I contacted Knight's offices to let them know we're heading in. This time the receptionist said Knight's unavailable, in meetings."

"We'll see about that," Eve said and kept walking.

"Here's the thing, it's the same one I spoke with before, but this time she came off flustered, hedging — like she'd been given orders to push back."

"Interesting. We'll push back harder."

"I guess that'll be fun, too."

They pushed through several levels of building security — and skirted two tours — to reach the lofty level of Knight Productions.

Annie Knight's offices spread over the fifty-first floor in a style that struck Eve as homey efficiency.

Its central lobby ran to soft, soothing colors, deep-cushioned sofas and chairs, and was equipped with refreshment and entertainment programs. A lot of lush greenery and cheery flowers mixed in.

The reception counter formed a gentle curve, manned by people in more soft, soothing colors, and backed by a huge portrait of Annie Knight with a let's-talk-about-it smile.

"Middle one," Peabody said, so Eve aimed for the center receptionist.

She decided to start off discreetly by palming her badge, angling it and her body so those waiting in those cozy sofas and chairs wouldn't see.

"NYPSD. Lieutenant Dallas and Detective Peabody."

The woman flicked a glance at Peabody, flicked that glance away. "Building security informed us you were coming up."

"Uh-huh, and did you inform building security to give us the runaround?"

"No! No, ma'am. I . . . but as I explained before, Ms. Knight's not available. I'd be happy to make an appointment for you for, ah, later in the week."

"How about if I made one for Ms. Knight right about now at Cop Central?"

Pure distress covered her face as she lifted her hands. "She really is in a meeting. And she needs to be on set for bumpers in fifty-three minutes."

"Try this. Inform Ms. Knight we're here, and should be able to complete our business in under that fifty-three minutes if we see her now. Otherwise . . ."

"Listen." The woman leaned toward Eve, lowered her voice. "Her PA already came down on me for giving Detective Peabody the schedule, and I've got direct orders that Annie — Ms. Knight — is not to be disturbed. I'm trying to do my job."

"I'm going to do mine. Let me worry about the PA. Tell Ms. Knight we're here."

"I . . . Listen," she repeated, "just let me contact her PA, explain you're here and you're insisting. He's a little protective of Ms. Knight, and it'll give me some cover. You can take it up with him. Okay?"

"Okay. What's your name?"

"Melissa Forenski."

"Melissa, inform the PA in question that I will speak to Ms. Knight here or at Central, today. Easy or messy, his choice."

"I need a minute." She swiveled around, tapped her earpiece, did a lot of whispering. And when she swiveled back, looked a little sick. "I'll escort you back to Mr. Hyatt's office. Her personal assistant."

"Good enough. You did your job, Melissa, and he'll end up so pissed at me he won't swipe at you for it."

"We can hope."

She led the way through a pair of glass doors down an open area of big, important-looking offices. And around a turn straight into another.

Hyatt wore a navy sweater over dark brown trousers. His hair formed a dark, close-cropped cap over a strong, rawboned face. Though he smiled personably, his eyes remained a cold, hard blue.

"Thank you, Melissa, you can go back to your station."

She left, fast.

"Lieutenant, Detective, what can I do for you?"

He didn't ask them to sit, though the office boasted a long sofa, two high-backed visitor chairs as well as his desk.

"You already know we're here to speak to your boss. You can inform Ms. Knight we're waiting."

"As you were told, repeatedly, I believe, Ms. Knight's in a meeting and then has to prepare for a promotional spot prior to her show. She can't be disturbed, but I'll try to assist you."

Eve kept her gaze, cold and flat, on his face. "Peabody, start generating the paperwork that will require Ms. Knight to report to Central for questioning in a murder investigation."

"Just one moment!"

"Already given you more than that. Time's up."

"I'll contact Ms. Knight's attorneys, and your superior."

"Go ahead. Peabody."

"Yes, sir."

Hyatt strode to his desk, grabbed his 'link.

"Get me Turnbill, immediately, and then contact the mayor."

"Ooh, the mayor." Eve just grinned. "Shudder. Hey, Peabody, maybe Channel Seventy-Five would be interested in reporting Annie Knight's being detained, possibly arrested for obstructing a police investigation."

"If you dare to — Bob? There are two police officers in my office threatening to have Annie detained. Yes, that's what I said."

At the quick rap on the doorjamb, Hyatt's eyes flashed. He broke transmission, but before he could speak, the woman with her hair in a curly topknot, wearing worn skids, skin pants, and a baggy sweater, whirled a finger in the air.

"Sorry to interrupt. I need five when you're free."

"Ms. Knight?" Eve said.

"Yes, sorry." She pushed at her hair. "I had a meeting right after my workout, didn't have a chance to clean up."

"No problem." Eve took out her badge. "Lieutenant Dallas, NYPSD, and Detective Peabody. We need to speak with you."

"I've already spoken to Bob Turnbill," Hyatt began.

"Bill, calm down. What's this about?" Then she lifted a hand, pressed it into a fist over her heart. "Oh. Oh, I see. I see. It's all right, Bill."

"Annie, you need to let me handle this," he insisted.

"I've got it. Why don't we go to my office?"

"Annie, I can have Bob here in twenty minutes. You absolutely don't have to speak to these people."

"I said it's all right, Bill." She turned, started down the corridor. "He's fiercely protective," she said in a voice that trembled a little. "And he'll insist on contacting Bob — one of my attorneys. Sorry," she added, pulling out her pocket 'link.

She listened for a couple seconds. "Bob, it's fine. Bill overreacted. No, it's fine, please don't. I'll let you know."

She replaced the 'link. "My lawyer. I'm afraid Bill gave him the impression I'm about to be hauled off in restraints."

"Were you informed we were coming, Ms. Knight?"

"No." She let out a sigh.

"We contacted your offices," Peabody told her, "in order for you to be prepared for our arrival."

"Fiercely protective," she repeated, and gestured them into the spacious corner office.

A man — mid-sixties, mixed race, wearing a salt-and-pepper beard and a Knicks sweatshirt — sat in a bold red scoop chair drinking what smelled like decent coffee and working on a PPC.

"That was quick," he said, then looked up and saw Eve and Peabody. Smiled with considerable charm. "Hello."

"Bic, this is Lieutenant Dallas and Detective Peabody. My partner, Terrance Bicford."

"Bic to one and all." He rose, stepped over to shake hands. Then he looked at Knight, said, "Well."

"Yeah. Let's sit down." She didn't go behind the impressive black lacquered desk centered in between the wide windows, but took the chair beside Bic's.

"Can I get you ladies some coffee, tea?" Bic offered.

Weighing the different vibe — nerves from Knight, supporting and soothing from Bicford — from the all-out battleground of the PA's office, Eve opted to give them a little time to settle.

"Thanks, coffee, black. My partner goes for coffee regular."

"Annie?"

"I could use some of my go juice. Protein drink," she explained. "I live on them. I'm nervous. I'm going to get that out there. I'm never nervous," she said as Bic walked by her, rubbed a hand on her shoulder before he continued to the refreshment center. "But I am."

"Do you have reason to be?"

Knight leveled direct and dark brown eyes at Eve. "Yes, I do. I'm also going to disclose, right away, I've already consulted with my attorney just in case we ended up here. He can be here by holo in two minutes, or in person within a half hour."

"Do you have reason to need an attorney?"

"I don't know. Bic's also a lawyer."

"Haven't practiced in a few years," he added as he served the drinks.

"But still, I'm comfortable with his presence and his advice."

"Since you have an attorney present, I'm going to record this interview, and read you your rights." Eve recited the Revised Miranda. "Do you understand your rights and obligations, Ms. Knight?"

"Yes. And I'm going to make a statement. As you're here, it's clear you've learned Larinda Mars has been extorting money from me for the past year and a half."

"Twenty-one months," Bic corrected quietly.

"Twenty-one months. I intend to cooperate with you, to some extent against the advice of my attorney. Not Bic." Knight reached out, took his hand. "Bic's with me on this."

"Always."

"I'm going to ask . . . I know your reputation. Not only do I pay attention, but I have excellent researchers. By cooperating, I'm going to give you information that could damage my own reputation. That could, worst case, ruin me."

"Never happen." Bic squeezed her hand.

"Bic has a sunnier view of human nature than I do. I'm going to ask you, on the record, for your word that the information I share will be held in confidence, and if any legal action needs to be taken against me, you'll give me twenty-four hours to prepare."

"Did you kill Larinda Mars or conspire in her murder?"

"No. No, I didn't."

"Have you committed a crime?"

Her lips trembled once, firmed. "You'll decide that, and if you decide I have and that requires my arrest, I need those twenty-four hours. I don't intend to run, Lieutenant. One way or the other, I've been running for a very long time. Will you agree to those terms?"

"I'll give you the twenty-four, on the condition you surrender your passport, agree to having your accounts frozen for that period, and understand that for that period, you'll be under surveillance."

Knight let out a half laugh, looked at Bic. "You called it."

"Relax, baby. It's going to be fine."

"No going back now," Knight said to Eve. "I'm in."

"Let's start with where you were yesterday from six P.M. until seven P.M."

"We finished the show at four-thirty. I did about a half hour of goodwill — posing for photos, signing autographs. Then I changed, and Bic and I went home. We'd have been home by six. We had a drink. I intended to unwind, then work on some ideas for a special we're doing in the spring. We're taking the show to Europe for a week in May. But Bic and I got into a discussion about —" She paused when he let out a sharp, rude snort. "All right, a very *heated* discussion about Larinda."

"It's called a fight, Annie. It's coming — or was coming up on the payment time," he continued. "I felt, strongly, it was time to stop."

"You knew about the blackmail?" Eve

asked Bic.

"Yes, of course. I disagreed with Annie's decision to pay, but . . . I let it go because the idea of exposure upset her so much. But the fact is, it would never stop until Annie stopped it. And would only get worse. We . . . discussed for some time."

"A monumental discussion. My stand has always been the money didn't matter. She wanted more, wanted information about other people, but that was a line I wouldn't cross. And the money didn't matter. I kept repeating that, to myself. Every month. But I knew it wasn't about the money. I knew Bic was right, and that only made me madder."

She sent Bic a look full of regret. "I said terrible things to you. I crossed a line with you. I did," she said as Bic shook his head. "I'm glad I did because when I did, it made me realize what I was doing, what I was allowing to be done to me, what I really felt about the money doesn't matter."

She paused, sipping slowly from her pale gold drink.

"I stopped fighting Bic, stopped fighting myself. I'm not a pushover, Lieutenant, but I'd let myself be pushed. I decided to stop that, too. Instead of the next payment, I'd send her a message. No more. It would give me a week to do what I needed to do. I contacted Bob — my attorney — asked him to come over. I told him everything. He advised we all take a day to absorb everything, and for him to begin some work."

"When Annie and I finally began to wind down, we heard the reports. We heard about the murder."

"Change of plans." Annie lifted a hand. "And here we are."

"When's the last time you had contact with Mars?"

"About a week ago. Two weeks before payment, she would either text or e-mail. Or she'd come in, just waltz into the studios," Knight added, with a flash of anger. "I wouldn't take any 'link tags from her. She'd send me a chatty message, as if we were friends. In it would be a number. Like: 'There had to be eight thousand people at the party,' or 'I feel as if I've walked seven thousand miles in these shoes.' Always between seven and nine thousand. So I could easily justify paying it. This month was to be the full nine."

"How would you get the payment to her?"

"I wouldn't meet with her — which is what she wanted. For us to be seen having drinks together, like friends. No, she wouldn't have that from me. In her message to me she'd routinely suggest meeting at a certain day, time, at a certain location. Du Vin, where she was killed, or Gino's, uptown. Once or twice, the Russian Tea Room. I'd arrange for a bonded messenger to deliver. I used different companies."

"You have records of the deliveries?"

"I have records of everything. Her e-mails and texts, her v-mails on my personal 'link. I've changed 'links three times since this started, but she always dug out the new one."

Knight paused, drank again. "She was good at her job, had a way on screen. She didn't have to do this, it couldn't have been only the money. Do you understand? She *liked* squeezing me."

"Yes, I understand that."

"I have a file, and I'll give you a copy of everything. I always knew I'd be here. Not that she'd be dead, but that I'd be talking to the police about all of it. I knew, no matter how I tried to pretend otherwise, Bic was right all along."

"What did she have on you?"

"Okay." Annie closed her eyes a moment. "Okay. My mother was a prostitute. Not my mother of record, not the woman who'll always be my mother. That's technically my aunt. But I'm going to call her my mother, and call her sister Carly. My mother took me in, made me hers, when I was barely two weeks old and Carly left me with her. She was only twenty-two years old, my mother, had worked her way through college, had just started a job teaching kindergarten in her hometown in Missouri. I found all this out years later, you understand. She'd raised me as her own, given me everything that mattered. To protect me, she'd moved to St. Louis, taken a job there. Moved away from her friends, her family. My grandparents were and are good people. Carly . . . was what she was."

She shifted, took Bic's hand again. "When I was thirteen, Carly showed up. It all came out, and this woman, this junkie, this prostitute, who'd only given birth to me because she'd been too stupid to even realize she was pregnant, and too afraid of terminating the pregnancy once she did. And calculated my grandparents would buy me from her. She was right about that — I learned that, too. They gave her ten thousand dollars when she threatened to take me away again, and just dump me in a ditch.

"I was thirteen, and I learned everything about my life was a lie. I was so angry, so shocked, so *young,* it's all I could see. Instead of embracing my mother, my real mother, not Carly, I rejected her, I attacked her, and while she was trying to explain to me, to reason with me, scrambling to scrape up the money Carly wanted, I locked myself in my room. Later, I snuck out, and I went to the address Carly left with her. A part of the city my mom would never, never have let me go to. She was on the street, soliciting. She wasn't licensed, you understand — this was before licensing — and the clientele she served wasn't interested in licenses anyway. Junkies and whores and dealers, a brew of the worst, and I walked right into it."

Knight shook back the hair that tumbled into her face, a quick, impatient move.

"She was high. I'm not sure I fully understood that, as I'd been so sheltered. I was going to get answers, I was going to get the *truth.* Not from the woman who'd lied to me every day of my life, but from her. God, thirteen."

She paused, drank again, slower now, thoughtfully. "It can be such a pissy, know-it-all age. Both fierce and fragile. She laughed at me, put her arm around me, and said how I had plenty of sass, just like her. This man came up — he was high, too — and he said he'd pay her a hundred for a two-fer. I didn't even know what he meant.

She said, 'Double that, handsome.' I remember those exact words. She kept that arm around me, so tight, and I was still demanding she tell me the truth, too wrapped up in my own world to see the world around me. They pulled me into the alley. I didn't even scream, I didn't know what was happening until he shoved me against the wall, ground against me. I tried to fight, and I can hear her laughing. 'Not so rough now, handsome, let me warm her up. God, let me warm her up.' "

Blindly, she reached out and Bic gripped her hand in both of his.

"It's all right. You're all right."

"He hit her," Knight continued, "backslapped her away. Her nose started bleeding, and she hit him. He had a knife, he waved the knife, and they were cursing at each other. So high, just flying high. Him waving the knife, and it cut my hand a little. I grabbed the knife from him, full of fear and rage and shock, and I stabbed him. In the throat. I know it was in the throat. The blood was gushing, and she was laughing again. I dropped the knife, and when he turned on her, I ran. That part's a blur. Running, getting on a bus again, getting back, running home. I told Mom, told her everything. I'd barely been gone an hour."

Knight breathed deep. “A lifetime can only take an hour. She bagged my clothes. We’d go to the police. She made sure I wasn’t hurt, I wasn’t hurt. Just some scrapes and bruises, that shallow cut on my hand. She held me all night, rocked me like a baby all night. We’d go to the police in the morning, she told me, and not to worry. But in the morning, there was a media report about a man and a woman found dead in an alley. Multiple stab wounds on both. They showed the photos — the ID photos. Carly and the man.”

Now Knight’s eyes swam. “The truth, the absolute truth? I don’t know if I killed him or if she did. I don’t know if he killed her before he bled to death from where I’d stabbed him with her knife. The media said it appeared they’d fought, both of them high on illegals, and they’d succumbed to their injuries. My mother burned the clothes I’d been wearing. She said we’d let the dead bury the dead, and there was no need to put me through what going to the police would put me through. It wouldn’t change anything. She said it wasn’t my fault. She said she loved me from the first instant, but she hadn’t been honest with me, so it was her fault.”

Her eyes, dark and wet, met Eve’s,

pleaded.

"But it wasn't her fault, and I can't blame a scared and angry child. It was Carly's fault. Carly Ellison, and his fault, Wayne Sarvino. We moved back home, and put it behind us. When I was sixteen, Mom married Abe Knight, and we both took his name. She told him everything, all of it. They gave me a good life, they built a good life. I have a brother and a sister. They're good people with good families of their own. So when Larinda threatened to expose all of this, I paid. I kept it from them, as Mom had kept things from me. I was going to go home this weekend and tell them, and talk to the police in St. Louis. I was going to take that weapon out of Larinda's hand."

Eve said nothing, let it all play out until Knight finished. "How did she find out?"

"She never told me, wouldn't. Just said she had lots of clever birds and they loved to chirp. My mother registered my birth — an at-home birth — with her as mother, and father unknown. But if anyone really wanted to dig down, it wouldn't be hard to find our connection to Carly Ellison — my mom changed her last name to her mother's maiden when she moved to St. Louis. But it wouldn't be hard to dig down and find Carly, then how she died, where Mom and

I lived."

"All right." Eve rose.

"Are you going to arrest me?"

"I'm going to talk to St. Louis, I'm going to review the facts, the evidence, and the investigative steps in the two deaths. I want your files, and I want a copy of your home-security feed for the night in question. If after we've studied and evaluated all the above and determine an arrest is in order, you'll have your twenty-four."

"All right."

"Who else knows this story?"

"Nobody. Well, Bob Turnbill now, as of last night. Otherwise, my mom and dad, my grandparents."

"Who else knew about the extortion?"

"No one. I didn't tell my family. Only Bic, and now Bob."

"Your PA?"

"Bill? No. He's loyal and protective — maybe overly — and all-around terrific, but no. This is personal business."

"Okay. We need the file and the feed."

"They're both at home. I have to be on set in — God, twenty minutes."

"I'll go. I'll get them," Bic told her.

"Always got my back." She gripped his hand, pressed her lips to it.

"Always will."

"We'll arrange for a uniformed officer to meet you at your residence and transport. Thank you for your cooperation. Record off."

She stood a moment, then went with her gut. "If you've told me the truth, if you haven't left out salient details or slanted the angles, no one's going to arrest or prosecute you for defending yourself against an assault, or arrest or prosecute the woman who protected her minor child from additional trauma."

As her eyes welled, Knight got shakily to her feet, reached out a hand. "Thank you."

"If you left anything out, now's the time."

"You have it all. If I'd listened to Bic — and I won't hear the end of that anytime soon — I'd have come to you or someone like you twenty-one months ago."

"Next time, listen to Bic," Eve suggested.

14

Because as Peabody had said, it could be fun, Eve decided to make it so and wove back to Hyatt's office.

He shoved up from his desk, outrage in every pore, and flicked at his ear 'link.

"I intend to file a complaint on Ms. Knight's behalf."

"Okay, then you can add one on your own behalf after you give me your whereabouts last evening from six to seven P.M."

He stared down his nose in a way that made her think Summerset did it a lot better. "I'm under no obligation to tell you a thing."

"Maybe you should get that lawyer back on the phone, see what he has to say." Wanting to goad him, Eve took another step toward his desk.

And had the satisfaction of watching him take a step back. "I'm going to have you both escorted from the building."

She bared her teeth. "Try it. Peabody, make a note, Mr. Hyatt is unable to verify his whereabouts during the time in question."

"So noted."

"You can go to hell," he said. "I was here, here in my office until shortly after seven. If you knew how to do the job my tax dollars pay you to do, you could easily determine this by checking the log for these offices and studios. Log in and out is required, by ID swipe. Now get out."

"Do you often stay more than an hour after your boss?"

"I do my job. I do what has to be done. And I don't answer to you."

"You will if you're lying," Eve said easily. As she left, she heard him demand someone contact his lawyer.

It was a little bit of fun.

After they'd wound their way back down, Eve took the long route around the pedestrian area.

"Let's take a closer look at Bill Hyatt. I just don't like him."

"Happy to. I didn't like him, either. I liked her, and Bic."

"People you like can still be murdering bastards."

"But you don't think so, not these two."

"I don't think so," Eve confirmed, "but I'll be checking their stories, right down the line. How much is public about Knight's background?"

"Well, the Missouri girl, raised by her single mother, the teacher. I think I knew about them moving back to the hometown. And if you know anything about her or the show, you get she's tight with family — considers her stepfather her dad. I know she started in broadcasting back in St. Louis, worked her way up. She hit pretty big by the time she was like thirty, got a New York gig as part of a morning talk-show ensemble, and brokered that popularity into her own. She's an icon there. I know she's been with Bic a long time. Easy to find out how long, but long."

"We'll take a look at him, too. He's devoted, that comes across. Devoted enough, you can do something stupid. Doesn't ring for me, but we'll tug that line."

A lot of lines, she thought, and time to tug them.

Back in her office, Eve updated her board, did a full run on Terrance Bicford.

New York native, law degree from Columbia. Hotshot in a hotshot firm all the way up to partner. Estate law, financial law. One marriage and divorce before Knight. One offspring — daughter, also a hotshot lawyer.

Cohabbed with Knight for — huh — nineteen years. He sat on the board of her foundation, and her company — which wasn't peanuts.

A lot of money in the Knight world, Eve noted. But then again, he'd had a very nice pile of his own when they hooked up.

It wasn't about money, she thought. It was about secrets.

She got up to program coffee, sat down, coffee in hand, putting her boots up and letting her mind wander.

At some point, it wasn't the money for Mars, either. It was the having of it, the taking of it, and the mining for more.

It was the knack she'd had — a kind of primal instinct — for finding vulnerabilities, and for exploiting people who could afford to pay.

Who would pay rather than have those secrets and vulnerabilities exposed?

Hit the rich, the rich and the really fucking rich, Eve mused. A few thousand a month meant nothing. Image? Priceless.

She'd miscalculated. Either sucked too hard and long on a mark, hit on someone who'd kill rather than risk exposure. Or somebody who, under the image, couldn't afford the payments.

Protection. A child defending herself, a mother protecting her child, a man covering a shakedown, trying to shield the woman he loved.

Another pattern. Marks not just covering themselves, but those they loved. And those they loved protecting them.

Isn't that what Mars had tried with Roarke? Another miscalculation. Probably she'd made others. And maybe one of those others had flipped her off, as Roarke had. But had also decided to silence her.

Dropping her boots back on the ground, she contacted St. Louis.

It took time, and she had to work her way up to her counterpart in St. Louis Homicide before she got close to anywhere.

"You want us to dig up the file on a john/prossy case from better than forty fricking years ago."

"I understand it's more than forty years, Lieutenant, but dead's still dead. And there may be a connection to an open case here."

Her counterpart gave her a sour look, added a curled lip. "And how's that?"

"I don't know until I see the file. If I could speak to the investigating officers —"

"Forty years," he repeated. "I can't even tell you right off if the investigating officers are still alive, for Christ's sake."

"I would appreciate it very much" — you lazy fuckhead — "if you'd check on that. I'll make myself available at any time." And though she hated pulling the Whitney card, she wasn't in the mood to screw around. "I can have my commander contact yours, Lieutenant, if that would expedite the matter."

"We got open cases here, too. We may not be New York City, but cops do the job here, too."

"And as one cop to another, I need to review that case file and, if possible, speak to one of the investigators. Once again, the DBs were Carly Ellison and Wayne Sarvino."

"I heard you the first time. We'll get to it when we get to it."

"Have you got a problem with me personally or just New York City cops?"

"I got a problem with New York City cops telling me to jump and expecting me to say how high."

"You're going to like me less when I tell you if I don't have that case file within two hours, I'll be contacting not only your commanding officer with a formal complaint, but your IAB."

"Now, you look here —"

"Getting me that file's no skin off your

ass, but I'll damn well take a bite out of said ass if you keep fucking with me. One more thing? This communication has been recorded, as is SOP for my own case file. Dallas out."

She broke communication. "Asshole."

"He seemed remarkably uncooperative."

She spun around in her chair to where Roarke leaned against her doorjamb. "Lazy is what he is. He doesn't want to deal with the paperwork, and doesn't seem to like New York."

"He doesn't like female rank," Roarke corrected.

"Come on."

"My take." Roarke shrugged, stepping in to sit on the corner of her desk. "And young female rank — young, female New York rank — that just ices the cake for that type."

"Just makes him a bigger asshole."

"It does, doesn't it?"

"I don't care how big an asshole he is, as long as I get the case files. Progress in the e-world?"

"Considerable. Feeney's sending you the data and a report. We've got more names, amounts, but she's got books elsewhere. What she kept with her, at home, even at work, is sketchy. More of, in my opinion, a kind of pocket guide."

"So we're back to her having another place somewhere."

"And I haven't found any such place in the names she used for alternate accounts, or variations of them. Yet."

She angled her head. "You're having fun with it."

"Why wouldn't I? It's a fine puzzle, isn't it? And as it appears bodies won't be piling up, the urgency is lessened."

Eve turned back to the board. "You never know about those bodies."

"Do you have any reason to think he'll kill again? For what purpose?"

"No reason, but once you kill, the purpose can get murky. Hey, that went well! And now that I think about it, my landlord, neighbor, brother, ex-wife, really piss me off."

"You're a cynical soul, Lieutenant. Only one of the countless reasons I love you. And now."

He rose, went to the door, shut it. "What is it?"

"What's what?"

"What's troubling you under it all?"

"I've got nearly twenty-four in on a case that happened under my nose. And I'm not feeling the wind at my back."

"Under it all," he repeated, cupping her

chin in his hand. "I can see it."

He always could, she thought and, with a shrug, wandered away to her narrow window. "*Evil*'s one of those words people toss around too much, or other people say people use too easily. But the fact is, there are a lot of degrees of evil. Plain, simple evil. Cops end up seeing pretty much every form of it. You take it down when you can, just like you take down the petty bullshit. Like the pair of street thieves Peabody and I collared today."

"Which explains the bit of bruising on your jaw."

"Head butt." Absently, Eve rubbed at it. "I had to at least half admire her style. Not evil, but the potential's always there, depending on circumstance. You could have turned evil. Me, too. The potential's there," she said as she shifted to look at him again.

"That may be. While I've done my share in cold blood, and more than my share of deeds the cop in you may understand and will never approve of. And still, I've looked at myself before and after you, and come to realize that as lost as I was before you, there were lines I couldn't and wouldn't cross. And you, Lieutenant?"

He studied her as she did him. "You? Your lines are, and have always been, closer and deeper than mine. There's mean in you, just another of the countless reasons I adore you. But your potential for evil — and I agree that's in all of us — is far, far outweighed by your absolute dedication to protecting and serving, not just people, but that amorphous goal of justice."

"I can see myself before and after you, just as clearly. And I can see me doing the job I'm doing now. With this." She gestured to the board. "And not letting myself feel what I'm feeling. Not admitting it to myself, much less anyone else."

There it was, Roarke thought, the under it all. "What are you feeling?"

"Those degrees of evil. Mars? She's on the scale. She doesn't ring the bell, but she's on the scale. She didn't kill or rape or beat small children. She didn't disembowel some stranger for kicks. I've seen worse. We've seen worse."

He had to touch her now, just glide a hand down her back.

"And you've stood for dead higher on that scale than Mars. What troubles you?"

"Her victims, because that's what they are, every one. We say *marks* — it's an easier word, and even puts some of the blame on them. Well, some of it is on them, as they made a choice. But they're still her victims.

Some of them hit close to home, but it's not even that."

"How close?"

She scrubbed her hands over her face. "Annie Knight. You know who she is."

"I do."

"At thirteen she found out the good, loving woman she thought was her mother was her aunt, and her mother was a junkie whore. So the kid did the stupid, ran off to confront the junkie whore, and ended up stabbing a junkie john who tried, with the whore's cooperation, to rape her."

Saying nothing, he crossed the room, took her face in his hands, kissed her gently.

"It's not like me. She gave him a jab and ran. She had a mother — because the aunt *was* her mother — to run to. And unless the case file from the asshole in St. Louis leads me in a different direction, she didn't kill him like she thinks she did. He and the whore ended up putting several holes in each other. But she's carried that around, and that I understand. We've got another mother trying to protect her kid from rape by sick fuck ex, and the kid ends up killing him. Santiago and Carmichael caught that one. We've got people, so far on this one, mostly trying to protect loved ones as much, maybe more, than themselves. That was

Mars's skill."

"She sniffed out people with dark secrets who could pay."

"Had to have some misses, like with you, but I think she, yeah, *sniff*'s a good word. She had a sense, at least about where to start looking. Maybe she had some form of sensitivity, maybe who she was will help us pin that down. She sniffed out, then she preyed. In at least one case, she had somebody drug a potential mark's drink, set him up so she could squeeze him. It likely wasn't the first time she helped her hobby along. Was it business or pleasure, or a mix? I should talk to Mira, get her take."

"Because the more you understand the victim, the more you might the killer."

"Usually." Her computer signaled an incoming. "Feeney's report," she said after a glance. "Excellent."

"I'll leave you to it."

"I have a seven o'clock interview with another mark, close to home — I mean our literal home this time."

"I'll wait and go with you. I'll find a place to work in the meantime."

"Where do you hole up?"

"Here and there." He kissed the top of her head when she sat back down at her desk. "Just tag me when you're ready to go."

"Will — Shit, wait. I'll walk out with you. I want to cut Peabody and McNab loose."

"Now who's being a mother?"

Mildly insulted, she scowled. "I'm being a lieutenant. If my team's burnt, they're useless to me."

She walked out and up to Peabody's desk. "Do you have the run on Hyatt?"

"Just finished. Hey," she said to Roarke. "You guys push through?"

"We did, or near enough."

"Send me the data," Eve said to Peabody, "then go cut McNab loose. I've got the case files from St. Louis coming in shortly." Or there would be hell to pay. "Anything there that needs a closer look, I'll let you know."

"Solid. I went ahead and — Have you got a minute?"

"I'm standing here," Eve pointed out.

"I'll leave you to your cop talk," Roarke said and wandered over to Jenkinson and his eye-burning tie.

"I went ahead and did quick runs on Knight's family. They come off clean and normal. A couple of minor bumps here and there. I could take a closer look at those, but I don't think it'd lead anywhere. And I checked travel, because sometimes you don't think your family knows stuff, but they do. None of them were in New York yesterday, or for months."

"Good thinking. So for now, we cross any of them off. We'll take a look at that angle on the other marks. Somebody protecting somebody who was protecting themselves or others. Copy me the data on Hyatt, and take off."

She turned to go back to her office, saw both Jenkinson, his tie, and Roarke were gone.

Back at her desk, she read Feeney's data. Fifteen more names — a few of which she actually recognized. A couple more sports figures, a defense attorney she'd faced off with a time or two in court, one other who rang a dim bell she thought might be an actor.

She scanned the amounts paid.

"You had more. You've got more on your list," Eve muttered to herself. "A cool mil in your home safe? Plus those buried accounts, the art and jewelry. You've got a longer list somewhere."

As she started runs on the names she had, her 'link signaled. She nearly ignored it, but decided maybe Nadine had something worth the interruption.

"Don't talk to me unless you've got information," Eve said.

"I'm fine, how are you?"

"About to cut you off."

"How about instead you come by my place. I could come to Central, but I just got home and I'd like to stay here. You're still at work."

"Do you have something for me worth the trip?"

"I might."

"Then just spill it."

"Dallas, I want a big glass of wine, and I don't want to do this on the 'link."

"Fine. On the way."

She cut Nadine off, tagged Roarke with a text.

Need to go by Nadine's, so leaving now. Sorry.

Even as she grabbed her coat, he answered.

Meet you in the garage.

She ordered all applicable files and data transferred to her home unit, filled a file bag with more. And, taking one last look at her murder board, started out.

She ran into a grim-faced Trueheart, stopped, as he very rarely managed a grim face.

"Problem, Detective?"

"Asshole killed his own sister over a vid game. Fractured her skull with one of his father's golf clubs because she beat his score and crowed about it. The parents are off on a winter cruise, left him in charge. Seventeen, and he's in charge? For ten days? Now his fifteen-year-old sister's dead over a game of Marauders."

"Is he in the box?"

"With Baxter, an APA, and child services. I needed to step out for a minute."

The hands he'd balled into fists at his sides mirrored the outrage, the disgust in his voice.

"He keeps saying she was being a shithead for dancing around and laughing, that she cheated. So he shut her up."

"The parents?"

"On their way back from some stupid island. Who leaves a couple of teenagers on their own for ten days, LT? What kind of people do that?"

She didn't mention the number of teenagers living with worse, living on the streets. Trueheart had come to her from sidewalk sleeper detail. He already knew. "Which APA?"

"Fruinski."

"He'll push for adult status. He'll probably get it. Walk it off before you go back in. Tie it up, write it up, then go have a beer with Baxter."

"I've got a date."

There were times cops needed cops. "Have a beer with Baxter first."

He sighed, and the grim faded a little. "Yeah, good idea. Thanks, Lieutenant."

She opted for the glide as far as it would take her. He'd walk it off, she mused. He'd shake it off. Baxter would help him talk it out. And tomorrow, he'd be back on the job, dealing with the next.

Trueheart was too good a cop for otherwise.

When forced to, she squeezed on an elevator, rode the rest of the way to her level of the garage.

Roarke already waited, leaning back against her car in the magic coat she'd given him for Christmas — still working on his PPC.

"Got hung up," she said.

"No problem. You drive, as I'm finishing up something here."

She kept her silence as he worked and she maneuvered through traffic. Glanced over when he slipped the handheld back into a pocket.

"Buy something?"

"Sold, actually, for a tidy profit, a property in Nevada I bought just for that purpose."

"Why did you buy something in Nevada to sell it?"

As she appeared to want to make small talk — non-cop talk — he obliged. "Because it was being sold well under market value, had considerable potential if updated and transformed with a bit of imagination and money, particularly considering its location. With that imagination and money, we pocket that tidy profit, and look for another underrated property."

"How do you know about underrated properties in Nevada?"

"The same way I know about them anywhere else." He smiled at her. "We'll say I sniff them out."

"How about if I said why don't you buy some underrated property in — I have to think of somewhere weird. In Nebraska?"

"Why is Nebraska, in particular, weird?"

"Not in particular. It's weird because it's out there." She gestured vaguely to indicate, he knew, not New York.

"Of course. Nebraska it is. Urban or rural?"

"Urban? Are you sure they have cities out there?"

"I'm quite sure of it, yes."

"Actual cities," she specified. "Not just a few buildings huddled together around a couple of streets."

"Actual cities, darling. Even west of the

Mississippi there are actual cities."

She mulled. "Rural. That's got to be harder than urban."

"Rural Nebraska. When I find the property, it goes in your name."

"Wait a minute."

"Your challenge, your name. I may lose you your shirt."

"I've got plenty of shirts," she countered. "You just keep buying them."

She drove into visitor's parking at Nadine's swanky new building. The scanner read her plate, flashed a level and slot.

"Looks like Nadine reserved something."

Once parked, they walked to one of the corner elevators, stepped in.

"Roarke and Dallas for Nadine Furst," Roarke said.

You are cleared directly to Ms. Furst's penthouse. Enjoy your visit.

"Why does it care if we enjoy anything?"

Roarke smiled at her. "It's simply polite."

"Computers don't have to be polite. Efficient. That's all I want out of a machine."

It proved efficient, sending them up, angling them over, and up again with barely a sense of movement.

"Did you buy this building when it was under market?"

He grinned, smugly. "And then some."

"But you didn't sell it."

"Some things you keep." He took her hand as they stepped off into the hushed, wide hallway. "I'm fond of this building, and happy Nadine chose it."

"Suits her down to the ground."

She pressed the buzzer on Nadine's well-secured, tri-level penthouse.

Nadine, dressed in at-home wear of snug black pants and sweater, opened the double doors to the entrance foyer.

"I got two for one." She smiled, moving in to kiss Roarke. "I'm glad I can show off more of what I've done with the apartment."

"The entrance is lovely," Roarke said, studying the colorful bottles in wall niches, the flowering plants, the matching love seats.

"I love living here more every day." Ignoring Eve, Nadine took Roarke's hand, drew him into the living area. "I'm still finding pieces — that's half the fun — but it's already home."

"Eve's right. It suits you."

Bold colors, strong art, a zillion — to Eve's eye — fancy pillows bunched together over sofas in what was probably an artistic way.

"What is that?" Eve pointed.

"It's a table. It's a dragon table. A blue

glass dragon. I don't know why I fell in love with it, but I did."

"It's charming." Roarke crossed to it, admired the sinuous body, the gleaming shades of blue. "Daum?"

"Yes!"

"If you think it's dumb, why did you buy it?"

"Daum," Roarke corrected Eve with a laugh. "Gorgeous craftmanship."

"I'm enjoying finding interesting art and furnishings. I never knew I'd enjoy it as much as I do. And still, it's really all about that."

She gestured to the window of glass, and the city lights glittering behind it.

That, at least, Eve could appreciate. When she had the time.

"I've got a seven o'clock uptown, so give me what you've got."

"Then you've got time for a glass of wine while I do."

"I'm on duty."

"I'm not," Roarke put in, "and I'd love one."

"Have a seat. One minute."

She moved off. Eve remembered the dining room — huge red table. And the kitchen — sleek and loaded.

Roarke sat; Eve paced.

"She'll have a party soon, I imagine," he commented. "Now that I've seen how she's filling out her space, I've an idea where to find her housewarming gift."

The thought of another party, another gift had Eve casting her eyes to the ceiling. It never, just never, ended.

Nadine came back with a tray holding two glasses of wine. Since a big mug of coffee stood with them, Eve couldn't bitch.

Roarke clinked his glass to Nadine's, said something in Irish.

"I take it that's a good thing?"

"Loosely, 'welcome home.' "

"Thanks." Nadine sat, sipped. "My second glass. It was a long one. I had to spend a lot of time in studio and on screen, talking about Larinda, the investigation, you," she added, lifting her glass toward Eve. "And participate in some sorrowful panel discussions about her. But I put my best team on the research, dug into it myself when I could."

"And?"

"Her background, which you've already looked at. How she came to New York as an eager young reporter straight out of college in the Midwest, landed a job as a gofer, an intern at *Behind the Stars,* worked her way up to field assignments, then moved to

Seventy-Five with screen time and eventually her own show."

"It's going to be bogus," Eve said, "at least until the New York section."

"I wouldn't be a bit surprised. The college records all check out. But absolutely no one remembers her. Not one student or teacher or administrator we were able to track down and speak with has any memory. Some of them made things up — vague things, and clearly fabricated to get some screen time of their own. I knew something was tilted there."

Nadine shook her head, sipped more wine. "But she did her job, I did mine. Her data claims she and her parents, who died tragically when she was eighteen, moved around a lot. And still, no one remembers her or them. Not clearly. But mostly, it's all too perfect."

"Exactly," Eve agreed. "Nomadic childhood, death of parents just when she came of age, exceptional student — homeschooled until college. No siblings, no family ties whatsoever. An absolutely perfect and pristine record. No medical issues on record, no criminal or legal issues prior to New York — and she's been sued several times since. No cohabs, no connections. Just a girl, pure and clean, coming to New York from college, where she graduated in the top ten percent of her class."

"That no one remembers."

"Hadn't gotten that far yet," Eve said. "So thanks. It saves me a few hours tonight. But mostly that's not much new."

"Try this." Nadine leaned back, crossed her legs. "I've got you one more of Larinda's marks."

"Name?"

"Phoebe Michaelson."

Not on Feeney's list, Eve thought as she ran through it in her mind. "She's a celebrity?"

"Not hardly. She's an assistant to Larinda's assistant."

"Family money?"

"No."

"Access to information then."

"Bingo. Let me explain. I huddled my team together, told them the work was on the down low, gave them bare bones. One of them came to me privately. She told me she'd seen Phoebe with Larinda a couple of times, at a local bar. Huddled together, Phoebe close to tears. And she walked in the ladies' room once as Larinda streamed out. Phoebe's still inside, crying in a stall. She couldn't get anything out of Phoebe but was smart enough, curious enough to keep her eyes and ears open. Mostly she figured they were having an affair, but it didn't play that way. She'd see Phoebe slipping into Larinda's office after hours. And the kicker is: Phoebe was promoted out of IT. She's an e-geek."

"When you want to dig, an e-shovel's an excellent tool."

"I pulled Phoebe into my office, started asking her a few questions. She broke in two minutes. I'm good," Nadine said, "but not that good. She was ready to break. She's terrified, Dallas, has been terrified."

"What did Mars have on her?"

"You can ask her yourself. She'll be here in about five minutes. I think it's better if you hear the rest from her, and I'm counting on you not pushing for an arrest. She's going to resign from Seventy-Five, or I'll have to tell Bebe and she'll be fired. No way out of that. But she's not a criminal. She's another victim."

Nadine's house computer gave a quiet *ping.*

Your visitor Phoebe Michaelson has arrived in the main lobby.

"Clear her up. She's a little early."

15

Phoebe Michaelson trembled as Nadine led her into the room with an arm around her waist. Her brown eyes, swollen and reddened from weeping, dominated her ghost-pale face.

She looked at Eve as if Eve routinely kicked little puppies off a bridge into a roiling river.

If Eve could have generated the classic picture of a patsy, she would have Phoebe's face.

"Phoebe, this is Lieutenant Dallas and Roarke. You just have to tell them what you told me. You just have to answer their questions, tell the truth."

"I know." Her voice gave a little mouse squeak.

"How about a glass of wine?"

"I . . . I . . . Can I?"

"Sure. I'll just —"

But Phoebe clung to Nadine's hand, as if

being kicked off the bridge into that roiling river along with the puppies, and stared fearfully at Eve.

"Why don't I get that?" Roarke rose. "Nobody's here to hurt you, Phoebe," he said, before leaving the room.

Tears plopped onto Phoebe's cheeks. Nadine steered her toward a sofa, sat with her.

"I'm going to record this," Eve began, "and read you your rights." At Phoebe's broken gasp, Eve let out a breath. "It's procedure, and it's to protect you. Nadine's right about telling the truth. It'll help us, and you. You have the right to remain silent," she began.

She finished as Roarke stepped back in, pressed the glass into both of Phoebe's hands.

"Do you understand your rights and obligations?"

"Yes." Phoebe took a deep gulp of wine. When she spoke again, the mouse squeak was gone. Now there was abject despair. "I don't deserve an attorney."

"It's not about deserve. It's your right."

"I don't want one. I just want to get this over with. I knew it was wrong, I knew, but I didn't know what else to do, so I did it, and I'm sorry. I'm so, so sorry."

"You knew what was wrong?"

"Hacking into people's personal information. Into their correspondence and their private data. Cyberstalking them."

"Why did you?"

"She said I had to. Ms. Mars."

"She forced you?" Eve spoke mildly. "Held a weapon to your throat?"

"Sort of," Phoebe said as Nadine shot Eve a hard look.

"What was the weapon?"

"Okay." Phoebe drank again, took two long breaths. "My father is Larson K. Derick."

Eve drew a blank, but Roarke jumped on it. "Black Hat Derick?"

Phoebe nodded, stared at her wine. One fat tear popped into it.

"Black hat hacker extraordinaire," Roarke explained. "Twenty-five years ago or so, he used his considerable skills to drain financial accounts, briefly turned Wall Street inside out. While he could have bought his own country and retired by the time he was done there, he turned to politics, you could say. I'm sorry," Roarke added to Phoebe, "this is difficult for you."

"It's easier if you tell her."

"All right. He became somewhat of a fanatic."

"He went crazy," Phoebe whispered. "He was a terrorist."

"Yes. He broke into government facilities, exposed or held ransom highly sensitive information. He instigated a fire sale in East Washington — that's e-talk for shutting down the city. The communications, the utilities. He chose to do this in the dead of winter."

"People died," Phoebe continued. "In traffic accidents. Some died of the cold because there was no heat, no way to get heat into buildings. Looting, people panicking and hurting one another."

"I know this," Eve said. "I know something about this."

"He demanded the president, vice president, and their families be executed. He'd come to believe all government was corrupt, and needed to be leveled," Roarke explained. "He believed the people would rise up and create a new society, a pure one. A utopia without leaders or the need for them."

"They caught him, they stopped him, but people died. He was my father."

"And nobody was going to give an e-job to the daughter of a notorious hacker," Eve concluded.

"Any job, probably. I was only two when

they caught him, and my mother had left him right after I was born because he started getting crazy. They put us in lockdown when he broke into the Pentagon and said who he was. They put my mother and me in lockdown, and questioned her for days and days. She told them all she knew, but she hadn't been with him for two years. Still, some of what she told them helped them find him, stop him. They put us in witness protection. New names, new place, new everything. My mom wasn't allowed to do any e-work, but I was only two. Nobody said I couldn't. And I'm good at it. I never did any hacking, I swear."

"Okay. But Larinda found out."

Phoebe knuckled a tear away. "She found out. I didn't lie exactly on my job app. I gave the data we'd been given. But she found out. She called me into her office. I thought she needed help with her comp, but she told me she knew, and she'd ruin me and my mom. When people found out who we really were, they'd turn on us, and how she'd make sure everybody knew. We're just regular people, Lieutenant Dallas, but all my life we've been afraid somebody would find out who we used to be. And she did."

"What did she ask you to do?"

"It was little things at first, like hacking into Valerie Race's communications so Ms. Mars could see who she was talking to and where she planned to be. Her travel. I didn't want to, but she showed me a picture of my mom at work. She works for a landscaper in New Jersey. I got scared, so I did it. I never hacked before in my life, I swear it. But I did it, and I did it again and again when she told me to. I begged her not to make me do it. She promoted me, made me an assistant. And she showed me she'd kept records of everything I'd done, and when she told Ms. Hewitt they'd believe I'd done it on my own, they'd believe it because I was my father's daughter. She —"

Phoebe broke off, drank more wine. "She told me to hack into your systems."

Roarke simply smiled. "Mine?"

"Anything of yours I could get into, she said, but your personal data was key. If I got into that, maybe, just maybe she'd let me off the hook. I couldn't. I mean, I tried. I really tried, but I couldn't get through. When I told her, she got mad, she got crazy mad, and slapped me."

"I'm sorry for that."

"Did anyone else know what you were doing?" Eve asked her.

"No. Well, Ms. Furst figured it out. I'm

glad you did," she said to Nadine. "I'm glad it's out. I know I have to leave Seventy-Five. I really liked working there before Ms. Mars . . . Since then, it's been horrible. If I don't go to prison, I'm going home, I'm going to get a job working with my mom. If I don't go to prison."

"Did you kill her?"

"I — God — oh, no." Her face turned white as bone under the tear streaks. "No, no. I swear."

"Do you know who did?"

"No. I don't know who killed her. But . . . when I heard she was dead, I was glad. That's the truth, too. I was glad, and then I felt sick inside because I was glad."

"Where were you last night between six and seven."

"Um. I had to work till six, maybe a little after. I was getting ready to go home and Dory got a text from her new boyfriend. He broke up with her in a text, and that's just mean. She was upset so I stayed with her awhile. Dory's nice. We went out together. I guess it may have been six-thirty. She just wanted to go home. I got the subway, and I stopped for takeaway from the Chinese place. It's just a couple blocks from where I live. I don't know how to kill anybody."

"Then you won't be going to prison," Eve

said briskly. "Do you have a record of the names of people you hacked?"

"I remember all of them. You don't forget when you do something mean to somebody."

"I'm going to need those names."

After Eve recorded them, Nadine gave Phoebe a pat on the shoulder. "It's over now, and Lieutenant Dallas will take care of it from here. I've got a car waiting downstairs to take you home."

"Oh, Ms. Furst, you don't have to do that. I can take the subway."

"You're taking the car. You go down, give the doorman your name. He'll have it brought around for you. Tomorrow, you give your notice at Seventy-Five, and if you need a reference for a job, you can give my name."

"I'm ashamed of what I did."

"You had a weapon at your throat." Again, Eve spoke briskly. "Next time you do? Call a cop."

"I wish I had. The marshals were good to us, even after what my father did. I should have known to go to the police."

Nadine led her to the door, let out a long sigh when she came back. "I wish I could take her onto my team. I think she's brutally honest and she's a hard worker. But I can't, and she's better off back home planting bushes. I should take on an intern." Nadine picked up her wine, drained it. "Someone young and smart and looking to learn. Someone I can mentor, and someone I can teach."

"Seriously?"

Nadine shrugged at Eve. "Yeah. A protégé. I think I'd like having a protégé."

"You're good at your job."

Nadine lifted her glass. "So are we all."

"I may know somebody. Somebody young and smart. Cocky, but that can be a plus. She'd probably be willing to learn."

"Really? Who?"

"I'll let you know."

"Black Hat Derick," Roarke said as he and Eve rode down to the garage.

"You're not going to tell me you admired him?"

"Well now, there was a time in my youth when he was a hero for certain, scooping up funds like candy drops and bolloxing up the system with keystrokes and vision. No question at all he was bleeding deadly, but he went full mentaller, and that's the tragic."

Eve stood a moment, brows knit. "What? What language is that?"

"Sorry, a mental and linguistic trip to that

youth. I'm saying he was brilliant, but went mad with it. I can admire the brilliance, and feel that what he ended up doing with it and becoming was a tragedy."

"Okay."

"You feel for his daughter, and so do I. Twice victimized, once by her father's deeds, then by a cunning woman."

"Mars had to do some work to find out who she was. I can see her — Mars — homing in on Phoebe as a target. She looks soft, easy to intimidate, and obviously has e-skills. Sniffed her out," Eve said as they crossed the garage.

"Then some background, finds her the only child of a single mother. Pushes a bit on that. Where's the father, who's the father?" This time Roarke took the wheel. "But it would take some skill to lever under the false front and pull out Black Hat Derick."

"Agreed. Missy Lee Durante's next." She gave him the address. "If she managed to very successfully create her own false front, that might have given her some skill, some instincts. She finds a couple dots, starts connecting them, finds more."

"She — Mars again — should have been able to do her own e-shoveling."

"More fun to have someone else under

her thumb. And it gave her a scapegoat. She puts Phoebe on her team, gets information from her. Anything leans south, she tosses Phoebe under the truck."

"Bus," Roarke corrected absently. "And if Phoebe claims Mars blackmailed her, gives out about her father, she's only more fucked. Again, you'd have to say it was bleeding deadly."

"That's Irish for smart?"

"Very. A sad girl with a sad story. You've heard sad stories all day. It's not a wonder you look tired."

"And not one of them goes to the cops, or even to the station head. What are the odds?"

He heard the frustration, sympathized. "I'd say Mars knew her targets well before shooting the first arrow."

"She aimed at you."

"Not really, no. She took the arrow out of the quiver, you could say, but didn't notch it. And was wise enough not to."

"There had to be other times she backed off, or just missed. And there are going to be others she was busy laying the groundwork on."

"Which is one more reason I'm sure she has records kept elsewhere."

Because she agreed, Eve wondered how

hard she could push DeWinter. She needed that face. Mars's true face.

"It's smart to weave some truth through a false ID," she speculated. "Maybe she did go to a college in the Midwest, or move around a lot as a kid." She added, "Her underground accounts used planets, so maybe that's a pattern that carried over. You've got, what, Mercury, Venus, Jupiter."

"Uranus is always popular."

"That's such a lame guy thing."

"Sadly true. Saturn, Neptune," Roarke added, "and Pluto depending on your stand there. Trying to find the name of a female of her age that has a connection to a planet — or perhaps a moon or important star — who attended a Midwest college could take . . . next to forever."

"You're supposed to be bleeding deadly."

Appreciating her, he laughed. "Now you force me to at least play with it, which makes you fecking wily."

"Really smart?"

"Very sly."

"I'll take it," she said as he pulled up at a dignified old building.

Its redbrick rose unmarred, its windows tall and screened. It stood on its corner quietly, its wide glass entrance doors unmanned.

Until they stopped the DLE at the curb.

The doorman wore unembellished black, with a cap over his square, sober face.

As Roarke stepped out of the car, the doorman nodded and said, "Sir. How can I assist you?"

Before Eve could pull out her badge, make any demand, Roarke spoke smoothly. "We're here to see Missy Lee Durante. We're expected."

"Of course."

As he stepped back to open the door, Eve noted the doorman discreetly checking a memo book he eased from his pocket.

The lobby was as dignified and understated as the exterior, with a wide, well-lit expanse of black-grained white marble floor and soft gray walls.

Lobby security also wore unembellished black, sans cap.

"Mr. Roarke and Lieutenant Dallas for three five three."

"Of course." Security left the desk to lead them to a trio of elevators, swiped them on. "Three five three," she said. "Enjoy your visit."

The doors closed silently.

"You didn't mention it's your building."

"I didn't realize it until we pulled up. I don't carry the address of every property in my head."

"It's a lot different than Nadine's."

"Variety is essential to a vibrant city, I think. This is early twentieth century, and though it took some ugly knocks during the Urbans, it survived well intact. A great deal of the interior is original, and what couldn't be saved or preserved was replaced."

"How long have you had it?"

"About six years, I think. Might be seven." He glanced around the car, at the subtle sheen of the walls. "The staff keeps it well maintained."

The car opened to a central area with a long glossy table holding white roses in a clear vase bisecting hallways to the right and left. They went left, to the corner unit, pressed the buzzer.

Eve knew the man who answered could buy a legal brew, as she'd scanned his data when reviewing Missy Lee. But he looked about sixteen with long, shaggy blond hair, a pretty-boy face highlighted by bold green eyes.

"Hey," he said, sticking out a hand. "I'm Marshall, nice to meetcha. Love the vid, gotta read the book. Come on in."

He held the door wide into a living area comprised of a mix-match of furnishings and decors, colors and carelessness. If she subtracted most of the space, the views, and the rest of the apartment, it wasn't much different from her own first apartment in New York.

Missy Lee, in floral skin pants and a long blue sweater, sat on a lumpy sofa beside a suited man with black hair touched with silver wings.

He looked like a lawyer, Eve thought, while the others looked like a couple of attractive teenagers.

"Got brew," Marshall said. "Got wine."

"You can't call that bug juice wine, Marsh."

He just grinned at Missy Lee. "It's not so bad. Anyway, *mi casa* and all that." So saying, he grabbed a coat from the back of a chair that wobbled a little as he brushed against it. He pulled it on, then an earflap cap, wound an enormous scarf around his neck.

"Cha."

"Thanks, Marsh."

"Hey," he said, stepping over to give her a kiss. "Tag me," he added, and strolled out.

"The brew's decent," Missy began. "The wine's foul."

"We're fine," Eve told her.

"It's Marshall's place."

"That's Poster," Eve said. "He plays the

Tad character on your show."

"Yeah. Chief dick, who's actually a complete sweetheart. *City Girl* was his first break, and as you can see . . ." She gestured. "While he talked himself into this place, a good, secure building with some impressive history, he still gets his furniture in flea markets or off the street."

She glanced toward the door. "He agreed to let us have this meeting here and leave, without asking why, because that's the kind of man he is."

She let out a breath. "I live here about half the time, and we're keeping our relationship private. Even the rest of the cast doesn't know yet."

"Did Mars?"

"I can't say, probably not or she'd have brought it up. Could be she was holding that back, but it wouldn't have mattered. It's not going to shake the earth when the fans find out Marsh and I are a thing."

"She didn't know," Eve said. "Breaking it would've given her a spike. She wouldn't have resisted it."

"You know, you're right. I guess keeping tabs on me didn't matter once she got what she wanted. Anyway, I trust Marshall, completely, and maybe one day I'll tell him what I'm going to tell you. But right now, it's personal family business. This is my attorney, Anson Gregory."

Gregory rose, extended a hand to Eve, then to Roarke. "Miss Durante has apprised me of the circumstances. I'm here to protect her interests, of course."

"I'm sorry." Missy Lee rose. "Let me take your coats, and please sit down. There's no coffee because neither of us drinks it, but I could probably scrounge something up."

"We're fine," Eve repeated, and tossed her coat where Marshall's had been. "I'm going to record this, and read you your rights."

Gregory nodded, and both he and Missy Lee sat again.

"Do you understand your rights and obligations?" Eve asked when she finished.

"Yeah, I do. I'm going to say first that if anything I tell you here gets out, goes public, I'm going to sue you and the NYPSD, sue hard. It may not get me anywhere, but I'll make sure it's really unpleasant."

Gregory lifted the briefcase at his feet, set it on his lap, and opened it. "I prepared confidentiality agreements," he began.

Eve simply said, "No. Neither I nor the NYPSD's civilian consultant will sign any such documents. We can, however, compel your client to come into Central for formal questioning. Or we can do this here, with our word that nothing said will be made public until and unless it becomes necessary due to investigative needs or in the event of criminal charges."

"It was worth a try." Missy Lee put a hand on Gregory's arm before he could respond. "I'm prepared to do this, just like I'm prepared to sue their asses off if it becomes necessary. So."

"You can start by telling me where you were last night between six and seven."

"We shot until six, maybe six-fifteen. In studio. Then I ducked out and came here. You can review building security and see when I came in. I'll be wearing a short wig, a black coat. We're keeping our relationship private," she said again. "The doormen know, and the lobby staff, but they also know gossip isn't worth their jobs. Plus, they've been really frosty about it. Marshall got here about fifteen minutes after me. We don't come and go together. He picked up a pizza on the way, we had dinner, ran some lines, and . . . stuff," she said with a quick smile. "I stayed till about ten-thirty. I don't usually stay the night when we're on call. I went home."

"How'd you get here from work?"

"The production gives me a driver. I had

him drop me off at a restaurant a couple blocks from here, told him I was meeting my family for dinner. Then I ducked into a doorway, pulled on the wig, walked the rest of the way."

She stopped, let out that gurgle of a laugh. "And, you know, hearing myself I'm starting to feel really stupid about all the bullshit. I'm going to talk to Marshall about just coming out with it."

"Canary Islands?"

Missy Lee's eyes widened. "And, wow, maybe you're as good as hyped. Yeah, a family vacay. That's where she nailed me. At first, I just thought: Well, crap, the gossip queen's going to hound me when all I want's a little sun and surf. But the smart move is, cooperate a little, give them some feed, and they'll leave you be. Except she wasn't looking for a little of anything."

"What did she have on you?"

"Me personally? Nothing. My family? A whole bunch of too much. Shit, shit, shit. I'm going to have some really awful wine after all. Give me a second."

When Missy Lee left the room, Gregory shifted in his seat. "Missy Lee is a fine young woman, a hardworking actress. If you've researched her background, as I'm sure you have, you know she's never been in trouble, gives back not only to her fans but to her community."

"Did she tell you when Mars approached her?"

He hesitated. "Given the circumstances and Missy Lee's decision here, I feel I can tell you no, she did not. I regret that, as the circumstances would be markedly different if she had."

Missy Lee came back in with a juice glass holding a couple thimblefuls of white wine that read yellow.

"Foul," she said, sitting and taking a wincing sip. "Okay. I've been an actor nearly all my life. First gig, I played the baby of a long-suffering character in a daytime drama. I did modeling, toddler gigs, and so on. My parents both supported it. My dad managed me until we all agreed I needed a professional, and someone not so personally attached. But he's still a big part of my career. My mother isn't. She's peripheral."

Another tiny sip and wince. "My mother has, we'll say, an issue with a certain illegal substance. She has, after the reboot of rehab, gone for long stretches without a stumble. Then she stumbles. Right now, and for about two years now, she's been good. It won't last. I accept that. I accept her. I even love her. She's my mother."

Pausing, she took another sip, grimaced. "Every time she reboots, my father absolutely believes it's the last time, and she'll never stumble again. Maybe she believes it, too. But the point is: He doesn't just love her, he adores her, and blindly. He adores his girls, as he calls us. Whatever it's cost, and it's cost plenty, we've kept her issue private. Not just a financial cost, but in every way."

"Mars found out, threatened to expose that."

"That, yes, and more. It's the more I paid her to lock away because part of me wonders, if my mother's issue came out, it might help end the cycle, one way or the other. I might have paid, for my father's sake, but I'm not sure."

"Whose sake then?"

Missy Lee closed her eyes a moment, then opened them. Clear and direct. "Fourteen years ago, my mother stumbled, badly. Badly enough they separated for several months. I wasn't a big enough name at that time for it to make any real splash in the gossips and tabs. We were living in New L.A. then, and Mom took off with the slug who was supplying her. She was bad enough she cleaned out one of their accounts, and tapped into the one set up for my education, out of my earnings. Later, when she was back, when she was clean and straight again, she told us they'd gone on a South Sea Island binge. Island-hopped, getting high, and living high on her money. Until the money got thinner and she got a little straighter, and he started knocking her around. So she came running home, and Dad took her back."

She shrugged with that, showing Eve she'd grown used to — and cynical about — her parents' pattern.

"A couple weeks later, right after she agreed to another round of rehab, she realized she was pregnant."

"The supplier's baby?" Eve asked when Missy Lee fell silent.

Shrugging, she sipped again. "Maybe, probably likely, but not for certain, as my parents had consummated her return. My father was adamant the baby was his, refused to so much as consider a paternity test. My mother, being my mother, was fine with that. I didn't know any of this at the time, or didn't fully understand, but kids find things out. Kids figure things out."

Missy Lee frowned down at the thimbleful of wine still in her glass, and for a moment or two — just a moment or two — her voice was young and wistful.

"We had a good run after that. She stayed clean during the pregnancy, ate healthy, stayed healthy. We all probably glowed like suns. I was working pretty steady — I always loved the work — my dad was still managing me. My mother did the domestic thing, decorated, gave parties, ran the house. And that held until Jenny was three. Just a little stumble that time, just a quick adjustment. Another stretch, another stumble. Blah-blah."

Any trace of the wistful dried up into the cool and flat.

"She's been clean for almost three years now, so you take the good when you get it. Jenny's the good. The star, the shine, the everything. I love my mother as much as I can. I'd throw her to the wolves without a second thought to spare Jenny a minute's grief or shame. She's my sister, she's my joy. She's the world to me."

"You paid Mars to protect your sister."

"My family. Jenny first — first, last, and always. My father next — but he's a big boy. I'd throw him to the wolves, but I'd have a second or third thought first. Jenny? Whatever it takes to keep her safe and happy. Jenny's a sweet, uncomplicated, loving kid. She's beautiful, in and out. Smart, funny, kind."

A smile flickered on, quick and charming. "When she hit puberty, her head spun around a couple of times, she cried and screamed for about five minutes, then it was finished. I love her more than anything or anyone in the world."

Now she took a shaky breath. "I can be a hard-assed bitch when I need to be, and there are times you need to be. I know how to protect me and mine from the parasites, the hangers-on, and the leeches. I know how to play the game. Killing this leech, and that's what Mars was, just didn't occur to me. I guess my brain doesn't work that way. If it had, I might have tried to figure out how to do it."

"Missy Lee."

Almost indulgently, she patted Gregory's arm. "I'm being honest here, and it feels, well, fucking righteous. I recognize another hard-assed bitch when she's looking at me so I'm talking hard-ass to hard-ass. Got me?"

"I do," Eve said, and felt simple respect.

"I might've tried to figure a way, but I didn't. I paid. It's just money, and I can make more. I've made it all my life, and intend to keep on making it. As long as I paid, she didn't have a reason to go public. I hated her — and *hate*'s a weak word for it

— but I'm pretty smart. Hell."

She gestured with the glass and its little skim of yellow wine. "I'm being honest, so I'll say I'm really pretty damn smart. If my brain had worked around to, hey, rip that damn leech off and stomp her dead, it would've worked around to she's probably more dangerous dead. You're here, and I'm talking about this, because she's dead."

Though Eve didn't respond, she thought: Yeah, you're smart, and you're right.

"Dead," Missy Lee continued, "somebody's going to find her dirty data, and then, well. Boom.

"Jenny's my sister. She's my father's daughter in every way but, possibly, DNA. He loves her, she loves him. It would break her heart to find out she might have come from someone else. Someone like that fucktoid my mother went off with. Paying to make sure she didn't have to face that? It was nothing."

"How did you pay her?"

"Cash. She'd set the amount. Seven, eight, nine thousand, depending, I don't know, on her mood maybe. I'd meet her at a bistro downtown or she'd tell me to just bring it to that night's event if we were both attending one. I've never been in the bar where she was whiffed. Not legal." She lifted her glass, smiled. “Can’t buy a drink yet, and drinking’s bad for the image. Anyway, I’m no wild child. I’m a working actor, and I intend to stay one.”

She set down the glass, looked straight into Eve’s eyes. “Don’t screw with my sister.”

“I don’t intend to. Did your father know you were paying?”

“Are you kidding?” She let out an easy laugh, an indulgent one, like an adult about a child’s antics. “No way. I’m in charge of my own money, and my own life, and my own choices. I love him, okay, but he has weak spots. You can’t deal with someone like Larinda Mars when you have weak spots. He’d tell my mother — he couldn’t stop himself — and she’d use that as an excuse to find a new supplier.”

Missy Lee circled her finger in the air. “And around and around we go.”

“You didn’t tell anyone.”

“I’ve been with Marsh for almost a year now. I know how to keep secrets.”

“Did she ever ask you to meet her anywhere private? Her place, or another?”

“No.” Her lips pursed in thought. “Weird, right? Always a public place. Maybe she got off knowing it was just a little humiliating that way. Or maybe she figured it kept me from punching her. Not just me," Missy Lee said. "I wasn't the only one, was I?"

Eve rose. "I know how to keep secrets, too."

"That's the perfect answer." Missy Lee got to her feet, held out a hand. "I'm trusting you. I'm pretty good at figuring out who I can trust, and haven't been burned yet." Now she held out a hand to Roarke. "I'm trusting you."

"I imagine your sister loves you very much," Roarke said.

"She does. And I'm never going to let her down."

16

On the way down to the lobby, Eve pulled out her PPC.

"You don't suspect her," Roarke said.

"I think the money didn't matter to her — as it's not going to have mattered to most of the marks. The threat, the invasion of privacy would have mattered more as time went by. But as time went by, I think she'd have had a sit-down with her sister. A few years down the line, then she'd have told Mars to stick it."

As she spoke Eve scanned the screen on her handheld. "And I think she was telling us the truth. As she knows it."

"Ah."

"Yeah, so . . ." She let that settle as they stepped out of the elevator, moved outside. Picked it up again as they got into the car. "She believes her parents and her boyfriend don't know anything about it. But her believing it doesn't necessarily make it so."

"Who are you running first?"

"The father. He'd be the most likely. If she gave us a clear picture of him, and it seemed to fit, he's a protect-the-women sort. And he's weak."

"Those factors seem to contradict."

"Only a man would think that straight off. He's weak because he continues to take the wife back knowing she's going to cycle again, put his kids — and it seems clear the younger sister is his kid in everything but, possibly, biology — through upheaval. He wants the wife, and puts that ahead of the welfare of his daughters. That's weak."

"It is, isn't it? Love can make you so."

With a cynicism Missy Lee would have understood, and respected, Eve shook her head. "He loves an illusion, leans on the illusion instead of shoring up the foundation for his children. To preserve the illusion, to convince himself he has to protect his family, he eliminates a threat."

"And the weak kill as often as the strong."

"More. Missy Lee loves him, but doesn't respect him — he forfeited her respect for the illusion. She doesn't think he knows, and she may be right, but she believes that first and foremost because she doesn't respect him. He wouldn't have to scratch too far under the surface to figure out something was up. Scratch a little deeper, find out what it is."

"It makes more sense to you that someone connected to one of the marks did the deed than the mark."

"We don't know all her marks yet, and there are bound to be some where the money did matter, where the risk of exposure was too much to risk. But the pattern so far? Yeah, a connection strikes me as more likely."

"And the mother?"

She glanced up, then over at him. "What do you think?"

"I think the mother has connections to dealers, and for some dealers, murder is simply part of business. But the method isn't business as usual, is it? Setting up a kill in a public place, in a space with only one way in and out isn't professional."

Eve gave it a minute. "You'll be happier if I say you think like a criminal rather than like a cop."

"There is considerable overlap, after all."

"Yeah." She tapped her finger on her knee as he drove through the gates toward home. "And she's an addict, one who slides back into that behavior. Most likely if she'd gotten wind of this, she'd have grabbed for her drug of choice. I'm going to look at her, but the father's more probable. Then there's the boyfriend."

"Seriously?"

"She, by her own statement, lives with him half the time. She works with him. He may know a lot more than she thinks. But."

"But," Roarke agreed as he stopped in front of the house. "The young and in love, or at least in cheerful lust, would most likely want to talk about it. He'd have told her he found out, and if she told us the truth as she knows it, she'd have told us that as well, and wouldn't have asked him to leave."

"That's how I see it." She got out, gathered her file bag. "I'll look at him, too, but he's low on my current list. I've got others ahead of him."

"Let's take a bit of time." He slid an arm around her as they walked to the door. "Have a meal before you dive straight into it. You can tell me about those others."

Summerset and Galahad waited, the long and the bony, the short and the chubby. It struck her that for all the flaws and faults she could pin on Summerset — don't get her started — he and the cat were, and always had been, completely in tune.

"You made it home before the storm."

The words stopped Eve cold. One day left — because today and departure day didn't count — until she had a Summerset-free house for three glorious weeks.

"What storm?"

"The one currently sweeping down from New England." His face cracked into what might have been a smile as Galahad busied himself rubbing his pudgy body against her legs and Roarke's in turn. "Only some sleet expected in the city tonight, along with high winds. Possibly worse on the way in a day or so. A good night to be inside, with a fire."

"A cozy night then." Roarke handed over his coat.

"You might enjoy it with some *cocido.*"

"Sounds just the thing. You'll be glad to get out of the winter for a while."

"I will. A few details to see to tomorrow. I'll speak to you about some of them in the morning."

"Watch your step." Eve tossed her coat over the newel post as Summerset lifted his eyebrows. "No tripping over the cat," she said as she started upstairs.

Roarke gave her a poke in the ribs as he walked up with her.

"Well, it happened," she reminded him. "What the hell is *cocido,* and why would we enjoy it?"

"A hearty Spanish stew, which he likely made himself, and would have taken considerable time and trouble. So it wouldn't hurt you to be nice."

"I didn't insult him, did I? I could've said stuff about just letting those high winds blow him away or how I thought vampires didn't feel the cold anyway. But I didn't."

"Your restraint is heroic."

"See?" She turned toward her office. He steered her toward the bedroom. "What?"

"Cozy night suggests we get out of work clothes."

She was a suspicious woman by both nature and training. "Is that just some sly way of getting me naked?"

"It could be, but I was of the mind to enjoy some wine and that *cocido* in something besides a suit."

"I figured you liked suits, since you own five or six thousand of them."

"Like or not, it'll be pleasant to enjoy wine and stew and a fire on a winter's night with my wife in something less businesslike."

She felt a little tug of guilt. "We don't have to eat in my office."

"We don't, no." As they moved into the bedroom, he unknotted his tie. "But we have a lovely setup there now, don't we? It works quite well all around."

Because he'd pushed for it, she remembered. She tugged off his tie herself, tossed it aside before cupping his face for a kiss.

His lips curved. “And is this your sly way of getting me naked?”

“It could be.” She brushed a hand through his hair before she stepped back. “Let’s consider it a preview.”

“Then I’ll look forward to the feature.”

She chose cotton pants, warm and soft as a hug, a years-old NYPSD sweatshirt, and house skids. Roarke chose black, managing to look both dangerous and elegant despite the casual wear.

“Let’s have that wine and dinner before you update your board.”

She could give him that, she thought as they walked to her office. But . . .

“I just want to check on something. It hit me when we were talking about connections. Question for you: You excel at keeping the private private, but how much could either Caro or Summerset dig out if they wanted?”

“I can’t think of anything, offhand, Summerset would need to dig for. And Caro? While I trust her, and rely on her, she wouldn’t be able to get through anything I didn’t want her to get through.”

“Yeah, but that’s you.”

“It’s me you asked,” he said as he walked over to choose a wine.

"Right. I'm thinking more admins and PAs and like that in general. Summerset would throw himself into any breech before he'd let anyone get through."

"Well now," Roarke replied, "listen to you."

"I know where his loyalties are, and they're unquestionable, unassailable. I'd say the same for Caro. Mira's admin would block God himself from getting through her door if Mira was in a session. It's loyalty, and it's a kind of possessiveness, too. I've never had an admin, thank Christ, but I could say when Peabody was my aide, she'd have put up shields."

"And so?" he prompted as he brought her a glass of wine.

"Annie Knight's personal assistant, admin, whatever the hell he is. I didn't like him. He put up blocks, unnecessary ones. He was aggressively territorial. He was obnoxious about keeping us away from her. Even when we made contact with her, he tried to push in."

"That's rather the job, darling."

"Maybe, and maybe that's a reason I don't like admins in general. Caro being the exception — and I probably wouldn't like her if I were a schmoe trying to get a meet with you. But he got seriously pissed, ordered an underling to lie, then went straight to lawyer. Knight herself was already prepared to talk — but didn't know, as he hadn't told her, we were coming in. He blocked her, too, as much as he could."

Roarke reconsidered. "I rarely meet with schmoes. But an important visitor, an official one? Caro wouldn't block me, or filter it."

"Exactly. And Caro knows who you do meet with, and that's a point. Like Missy Lee, Annie Knight probably believes this asshole didn't know anything about her problem with Mars. But maybe he did. And her partner, who did know, seems like a solid sort, but maybe. I'd lean more to the asshole than the partner."

"You really didn't like him."

"Really didn't, which is why I got back in his face after I'd talked to her. He had that smirky, sneery, superior attitude, had me and Peabody tangled up at every level to get to Knight. What would Caro have done, say, if a couple of cops said they needed to speak to you?"

"She'd have tangled them up until she'd spoken with me, then would have followed my lead."

"Yeah, that's my thought, too. He didn't speak to Knight, tell her we were there. Unless she lied to us, and since she was immediately cooperative, I don't see the lie. And he jumps to lawyer before consulting her. Anyway, I want to check with security, find out if he told me the truth about when he logged out yesterday, and if he had a window to get to Mars."

"To kill her because she was shaking down his boss? That's some serious dislike you have there."

"Maybe. Or maybe he just gave off a vibe. I don't know yet."

"Do you think he's romantically involved, or wishes to be, with Knight?"

She considered it; dismissed it. "No, she and the partner are solid, and the asshole gave off another vibe. The I-like-guys-better vibe, so I don't think he's into that or wants to be with Knight in that way. Anyway, it might take me a few minutes to wind my way through security and get the answer."

"Then I'll see about that stew."

It didn't take as long as she'd calculated. It helped that the man on the desk used to be on the job, and had even worked under Feeney before he'd switched from Homicide to EDD.

When she had what she needed, she sat back, frowned at her board.

"No window?" Roarke asked.

"He logged out at nineteen-six, pretty much when he said. TOD is about thirty minutes earlier, so no. No window. Asshole's clear."

"Come console yourself with *cocido.*"

"It smells pretty good." She walked to the table, studied the stew in thick blue bowls. "Looks like a lot of vegetables in there."

"As there's also a lot of meat, that should balance it for you."

Suspicious, she sat, spooned up a little as Roarke cut pieces from a small round loaf of warm bread. Even as she wondered why they couldn't just have regular stew, she warily tasted.

Flavors exploded in her mouth.

"Okay, it's really good."

Smiling, he handed her a chunk of bread. "Now you can relax and enjoy it."

"Did you ever cook anything? I mean where you put stuff with other stuff and add more stuff?"

"I have actually. When I came to Summerset, he insisted on teaching me — or attempting to — how to prepare a few basic meals. I hated every bleeding moment of it, and surely did my best to turn it all to shite."

He grinned, ate. "Likely I didn't have to try that hard. It's the one area where he gave up on me, to the great relief of both of us. You?"

"One of the state schools I was in had a required course. They called it Life Science, and we had to learn how to cook some basics. I did the fake scrambled eggs. They'd either come out hard and dry or runny and mostly raw. The instructor finally gave me the check mark, I figure out of pity or desperation."

"She and Summerset could have commiserated," Roarke supposed.

Eve shoveled in more. Vegetables didn't taste so healthy when they had a kick and swam around in the really damn good.

"Life Science, my ass," she said between bites. "I was always coming to New York, and you can always get pizza, so cooking was as useless as knowing what year that guy on the elephants crossed the mountains. The strategy, that's useful. But what the fuck does it matter what year it was? That was then, this is now."

Amused, Roarke drank some wine. "Summerset's angle was what if I found myself in some situation where it was cook or starve. And my angle was, I knew how to be hungry, didn't I, and I could always steal food come to that."

"He likes doing it." She dug into the stew

again, though she was pretty sure some of the green stuff was cabbage. "It takes all kinds."

"Even after I was with him weeks, and he saw to it I never went hungry, I stole food. Stashed it away — just in case. After a time, he sat me down, told me I was taking that food out of someone else's mouth, who might go hungry. And I should have a care for those who had less than I."

Eve brushed a hand over the back of his because it touched her. And still, she puzzled over it. "But he didn't have a problem with you stealing otherwise."

"It's a process, isn't it?" With a shrug, Roarke ate. "Over time he pressed that point on me. Have a care for those who have less. In a way you'd find perverse, I became a better thief because I began to take that to heart and aimed higher."

"It *is* perverse," she agreed.

"And yet. It might have been easier to lift the shaky locks on this little flat and pull out the bit of cash the family had stashed in the potato bin, but I'd think: They have less than I, so leave that be. But that fine house there, with all that security to wrangle through? They have a great deal more."

He shrugged again, unrepentant. "He had, for a time, two young mouths to feed and clothe and house and care for. And our world was a hard place."

He smiled over at her. "You were born to be a cop, and I was born to be something else entirely. I'd likely still be that, if only in small ways that entertained me, if not for you. You finished the process, we'll say."

She thought of him, and thought of herself. Sitting there in the big, beautiful house, having a good meal with good wine before she went back to the job.

"I guess you finished me, too."

"And here we are."

"If we ever find ourselves in a situation, I could probably make bad, semi-disgusting fake scrambled eggs."

"I wager I could steal enough to keep our bellies full."

"Then I could arrest us both and we'd get three hots in a cage."

"I do adore you, Eve. Every bit of you."

"Mutual." She nudged her empty bowl aside. "Don't ever tell me what was in that."

"There's a promise. You want to get to your updates."

"Yeah, and the case file the St. Louis asshole finally sent."

"What can I do for my cop?"

"If your own decks are clear, there's that angle about Mars going for pattern under another name. Maybe using another name to buy or rent another place. It's all speculation, but it's a good angle."

"I can play with that. Once I get that set up, it's going to run primarily on auto. I can clear what's left on my decks while it does. I'll start that in my office."

Following their tacit agreement, since he'd put the meal on, she cleared it off before updating her board and book.

She let the updates simmer while she read the St. Louis file.

Not really sloppy work, she thought, not altogether careless work, but borderline on both. One witness had mentioned a teenage girl running out of the alley, but the investigating officers didn't follow up or through on it. And obviously didn't put much faith in the statement of another junkie whore.

Partially the times, she thought, partially the area. And far too much who-gives-a-shit because the dead were the dregs.

A cop had to give that shit, no matter the dregs, or didn't deserve the badge.

In any case, the ME had done his job, she decided. The throat wound on the male vic had been severe, as had two chest wounds and a gash on the arm — but the gut wound had been determined as COD. A few defensive wounds as well — both vics. Female vic, two facial gashes, three chest wounds. Including the heart stab (a lucky shot, in Eve's opinion) that had killed her. The vics' TODs were within two minutes of each other, with the male bleeding out last as he attempted to crawl out of the alley.

Eve read it all a second time, considered, then engaged her 'link.

A woman with a pleasant face, a pleasant voice answered. "Good evening, Knight residence."

"Lieutenant Dallas to speak with Ms. Knight."

"I'm sorry, Ms. Knight has retired for the evening and asked not to be disturbed."

"Disturb her with my name, see what she says."

"One moment, please."

It took barely more than that for Knight to come on — making Eve think of the personal assistant again.

"Lieutenant."

"I thought you'd want to know, I received and reviewed the case files from St. Louis."

"Oh. I see."

"You didn't kill anyone."

"I — what?" Knight lifted a hand and pressed it to her mouth. "I'm sorry?"

"Sarvino might have died from the throat wound you inflicted if he hadn't sought medical assistance. But, in point of fact, that didn't cause his death. They killed each other, sloppily and stupidly, because, in my opinion, they were high and pissed off. Carly Ellison died because she dragged a thirteen-year-old girl into an alley so she could make some money by allowing a junkie to rape her. You didn't kill anyone, so put it away. Tell your mother to put it away."

"I . . ."

"This is what I do for a living, Ms. Knight. I'm telling you, you weren't responsible for what happened in that alley. I'm telling you that as an investigator. Mars had to know you weren't responsible. If she dug deep enough, she knew, but she exploited you anyway."

Tears glittered in Knight's eyes. "We didn't go to the police."

"I'm the police," Eve said. "Better late than never."

"I don't know how to thank you."

"I'm doing my job. Put it away."

"I think I can at least start to. I think I finally can. Thank you. Good night, Lieutenant."

Eve clicked off, began her deeper runs on connecting names she felt were low probability. Get them out of the way, she thought.

From there, she moved on to what she thought of as the next tier. Unlikely, but more possible.

She programmed coffee, gathered data, added notes to her murder book.

Then she went back to Guy and Iris Durante. Missy Lee's parents — father leading — were most probable of her current crop to her mind. But she'd added Wylee Stamford's sports agent and his two other friends from back in his old neighborhood who fit the pattern of victims of the abuser.

If Stamford's story had come out, theirs might, too.

When Roarke came in, she noted his warning look when she reached for more coffee. Instantly annoyed, she started to snap something, then noted the time.

Okay, he had a point.

"It'll continue to run on auto," he told her. "Nothing substantial as yet. I did find a Starr — that's two *r*'s — Venus with a flat downtown, but she's actually an over-the-'link psychic, born Karen Leibowitz. Did some time under that name for fraud. And how about you?"

"I've moved the bulk of connections to the bottom of the list. No one there has a probability over ten percent. I've got a couple who hit low twenties. Guy Durante's at sixty-five and change with current data, so he bears more study. And I've got a couple of possibles connected to Wylee Stamford. Very likely victims of the same fucking pedophile. If I keep on them, I'm going to find who killed the fucking pedophile. I lean toward the father of one of them."

He read the conflict on her face. "Will you push on that?"

She stood, paced. "Rock, hard place. It's my job. But I can tell myself it's not my case. I can take the straight-arrow line and start peeling things back. And the man I'd peel things back on has two more kids, has worked at the same company for thirty years, volunteers at a youth crisis center — he started there six months after the fuck's death. He also coaches a Little League team."

"He, if you're right, would have been protecting his son."

"He should have gone to the cops."

"Who knows how the boy would have reacted? Who knows if he'd have been believed? What would it serve, after all these years? We both know what it is to be abused as a child. For me, it was neglect or beatings, but you and that boy have more in common. Summerset saved me," Roarke continued, more passionately than he'd intended. "And someone did me the favor of putting a knife in Patrick Roarke, as he'd have found me and likely done for me sooner or later."

Eve slid her hands into her pockets, looked away, walked to the window to look out.

She didn't respond, just stared out the window.

"You saved yourself," Roarke continued. "We don't know what it is to have a child, but we know what it is to be one. What wouldn't we do, either of us, to protect what we loved and cherished?"

"I need to look — for my own case, not for someone else's. If it turns out either the father or the son learned what Mars was doing to Stamford and took action to stop her, it all comes out. If not . . . I don't know. I need to let it settle."

"Fair enough." He walked to her, took her hand. "Let it all settle for the night."

She'd disappointed him, she could see it. And still felt herself torn. She had a duty, and yet . . .

She believed she knew who'd killed a man — or a monster disguised as a man. Just as she knew who'd killed Patrick Roarke.

So she knew just how far a man might go

to protect — or avenge — his son. Or the boy he'd made his son.

17

Even tucked in, Roarke's arm around her, the cat curled at the small of her back, dreams slipping through. Alleyways, crumbling projects marred and scarred with graffiti, the stench of garbage gone ripe with the undertone of brew-fueled piss.

Deep shadows and muddy pools of light from failing security lamps smeared the stained ground.

She knew it to be that urban, hopeless anywhere.

She'd hidden in one like it as a broken child. Though the bloody body of the man who'd broken her lay at her feet, she knew it wasn't the alley in Dallas.

It was anywhere. It was nowhere. It was everywhere.

Another body lay to the right, a knife protruding from its throat. Dazzling blue eyes, Patrick Roarke's eyes, stared up at her.

To the left, another. A big man, beaten

ruthlessly into shattered bones and torn flesh. She imagined his face haunted Wylee Stamford's dreams.

Three monsters disguised as men. Three secrets of violence and pain and terror.

She knew the secrets. How they'd died, why they'd died, and who had ended them.

Her badge weighed heavy.

"What about me?"

Larinda Mars strolled into the alley on the high, thin heels of her green boots, her pink skin suit highlighting every curve, her golden hair sweeping around her expertly crafted face.

"What are you doing about me?"

"My job," Eve said, and got a dismissive *pftt* in return.

"Your *job*? Dreaming about three men long dead while I'm still fresh in a drawer at the fucking morgue is your *job*?"

"Maybe. What was yours?"

As Mars stood hipshot, she waved a hand in the air. "To get the dish, to dig it out, cook it up, and serve it to millions on a silver platter. Nobody did it better."

Even in death, even in dreams, Mars projected sheer, unapologetic arrogance.

"That might be because others in your line of work don't stoop to blackmail and extortion."

Larinda threw back her head and laughed — a good, hearty one that echoed down the fetid alley. "Oh, don't be naive. Besides, if someone chooses to pay or barter to keep a secret buried, it's their choice, isn't it? They should've gone to the police," she added in a sneering mimic of Eve's words. "But they didn't. That's not on me."

"It's all on you."

"So I deserved to die?"

"No. That's on your killer."

Hands on hips now, Mars gave an exaggerated look around the alley. "Well, my killer's not here, is he? So why are you?"

Eve studied the bodies. "Sometimes old business crawls up over the new."

"What bullshit!" Anger now, the fierce lash of it skinned with disgust. "You're wallowing. You'd kill him again, wouldn't you? Stick that knife in him a thousand times again to save yourself. Go to the police, my ass. You made your choice."

"He was raping me."

"Oh, boo hoo! And that dead Irish bastard? You wouldn't have minded a shot at him. You didn't get one, but you're protecting the man who got one, and took it. That's personal, sister. Murder's murder, but you let it ride. And that last one, the little boy diddler? Same goes. You feel for the man who bashed his head in, broke his bones. Go to the cops?"

She snarled it as blood began to run down her arm.

"You were there, right there, and you let me die. What good are you?"

Truth, Eve thought, enough truth mixed in with the accusations and dismissals, she wouldn't deny it.

But she could answer it with truth.

"Good enough to look at you," she said, "to know you were a stone bitch and still work my ass off to find who killed you, to gather the evidence to put them away for it. Just the way I'd have put you away for screwing with people's lives."

"You're not so pure, *Lieutenant.* Three dead men at your feet, and two of them are yours. I kept secrets — for a price, but I kept them. Not everybody can, not everybody will. Think about that. Secrets have a way of crawling their way out no matter how deep you bury them.

"I'm not going to die in this stinking alley even in your stupid dream. The dead don't always rest," Larinda said as she walked back into the shadows. "I can promise you that."

As she spoke Patrick Roarke's eyes blinked, fixed on Eve's. Richard Troy turned his head, grinned at her. Big Rod's fingers crawled over the littered ground toward her ankle.

Dread crawled into her heart.

"Call a cop," Eve said coolly, drawing her weapon.

"That's enough now," Roarke murmured as he held her close and the cat bumped his head between her shoulder blades. "Enough."

"I'm all right." She pressed her face into Roarke's shoulder as the dream broke. "I'm okay."

At the sound of her voice, Galahad climbed onto her hip, stared at her until she stroked a hand over him. "I'm okay," she repeated. "It wasn't a nightmare. Just . . . a lot of weird."

Roarke tipped her face up toward his, studied her as the cat had done. "Tell me."

Couldn't, she thought. Just couldn't. So she hedged instead. "A conversation with Larinda Mars. She's a little pissed off at me." On a sigh, Eve closed her eyes. "I can live with that. Arguing with a dead woman's annoying and useless. Sorry it woke you up."

Not a lie, Eve decided as Roarke rubbed her back and the cat settled down again. Just not a full disclosure.

She shoved it away, willfully shoved it all

away, and concentrated on Roarke's scent, Galahad's breathing, the simmer of the bedroom fire.

And, willfully, pushed herself into dreamless sleep.

Roarke lay awake even after he felt her slip off. Lay with his arm around her and his thoughts circling.

Not a lie, he thought in nearly a mirror of her own. But not altogether the truth.

And why was that?

Considering the whys, he backtracked over the evening as he would over a negotiation before its next round. Picking at details, tones, body language.

As possibilities came and went, he slept little. And rose early, as always.

He showered and dressed, handled a 'link conference, a holo meeting before dawn. His work energized him as much as sleep, as did his need to involve himself in the details, small and large, of all the arms of all the reaches of what he'd built.

Through wile and guile, through brains and sweat. Through a fierce and focused determination since childhood.

Once money had mattered utmost, because money equaled survival. Then power had joined that ambition, because power brought respect. And with both, a man could adjust his life as he pleased, toss off — at least in appearances — the ragged and violent beginnings.

Then came the building, and the wonder of it, the all but shocking realization that he could truly create. With that, the revelation of simple satisfaction.

Buy, sell, build, own, innovate, expand. Risk and reward. Take what was neglected, make it shine again. Create where a vacuum had once existed. Risk and reward — and yes, even when survival had been assured, some of that risk had involved snaking over and under and across the line of the law.

Habits, particularly enjoyable ones, are hard to break, after all.

But then Eve. Just Eve. Only Eve. Difficult, cynical, troubled, and fascinating Eve had changed him, saved him, completed him. And habits had been as easily broken as a dry twig under a boot.

Even then he'd never seen himself as now. As a man who could and would shuffle his own work, check on hers, contribute to hers. Never imagined that satisfaction.

He read through the results of the auto-search he'd run for her — his cop — considered those results from both sides of the line he straddled now.

The criminal past, the Eve present.

As dawn approached, he continued his habit — checked on her through house security, saw she slept yet, and the cat felt confident enough in her comfort to have left her.

He rose and, diverging from habit, went downstairs.

As he approached the kitchen, he heard Summerset's voice, the murmur of some early media show under it.

Talking to the cat, Roarke realized. The conversational tone amused him — as he often found himself doing the same, as if expecting the cat to talk back.

"I expect you'll behave while I'm gone, and keep an eye on the children."

Roarke paused to take in the scene. Summerset, a baker's apron over shirtsleeves, was kneading dough while Galahad sat on a counter stool and watched, apparently listening as well.

"I'm leaving it to you," Summerset continued, his long, thin hands working methodically and with what looked like an easy enjoyment. "You'll have to see they get a decent meal in them."

"He's generally more worried about his own meals."

Summerset glanced over, eyebrows lifting. "He'll keep his clever eyes on you nonetheless. Is all well?"

Roarke made a sound of affirmation, wandered in. He rarely came to the kitchen. It, like the rooms beyond, were Summerset's domain — an arrangement that suited them both.

"You're about ready to be off, I'd think."

Summerset continued to knead. "Early tomorrow. I'm entertaining myself by baking and cooking. You and the lieutenant won't starve while I'm gone. Do you want coffee?"

Shaking his head, Roarke continued to wander, restless. "You and I, we've evaded with each other now and again over the years. That's natural enough, isn't it?"

Summerset turned the dough into a bowl, covered it with a cloth before walking to the sink to wash his hands. "What's on your mind, boy?"

"I don't recall either of us lying outright to the other. Well, not since my beginnings with you when lying was my default. And you saw through that, more than I thought then. Though I may have slipped a few by you."

"I doubt it."

Roarke smiled, leaning on the counter as Summerset dried his hands. "Those were the days. And still, after those raw beginnings, after trust and respect and affection, I don't see either of us lying to the other if a question was asked straight and direct."

"What's your question?"

"Did you kill Patrick Roarke?"

Summerset laid the dish towel aside, and simply said, "Yes."

"Ah, well." On a nod, Roarke kept his eyes on Summerset. "All this time, you never said a word."

"For what purpose?"

"You couldn't think I would have cared? That I would have turned even an inch away from you for it."

"No, not that." Summerset walked over to the breakfast area, sat, waiting for Roarke to join him. "You were just a boy, beaten down and barely beginning to believe you could have a life without the fist. Why burden you? As time passed, again, what purpose would there have been to tell you? I wondered when she would. The lieutenant's scale weighs different than mine. No less right or wrong, just different measures."

"She didn't tell me. Why did you tell her? And when?"

Obviously surprised, Summerset sat back. "I may never get a true handle on your wife, boy. Not one that holds firm. I didn't tell her, not in so many words. She has a way of finding out, of . . . interpreting and intuiting. I didn't confirm or deny, but she knew. It was when I fell down the stairs, when I was healing from breaking my own careless leg. I suppose I was a bit less guarded."

Roarke looked back to the accident, the aftermath, and wondered how he hadn't seen. "A considerable time for her as well, to keep that secret from me."

Summerset's narrow shoulders stiffened. "You won't blame her for that or you'll disappoint me."

How they protect each other, Roarke thought, though both would be appalled to have it pointed out.

"I won't blame her for that, no, nor you. But neither of you needed to carry this for my sake. Will you tell me why you decided to end him?"

Summerset sighed. "I want coffee."

"I'll get it."

"Sit. I know my way around here better than you, more's the pity."

Rising, Summerset walked to one of the three AutoChefs, programmed coffee for both of them. "He had contacts, as you know, and some of them had badges. I won't call them cops as I did then. I've come to understand and admire the difference between having a badge and honoring it."

He brought the coffee back — a dollop of cream in his own — and sat again. "He knew where you were, bided his time it seems. If you'd died after that last beating, he'd have been fine with that, but you hadn't. So he wanted his property back, as he put it. He had uses for you. He knew talent when he saw it, I can give him that. You were, even then, skilled and clever."

Summerset sipped his coffee, looked back. "We had a decent place."

"It seemed a palace to me," Roarke replied.

"His view wasn't palace, but he assumed there'd be money, so he was agreeable to a deal. I could buy you."

Unsurprised, unmoved, Roarke nodded. "How much was I worth?"

"To me? A great deal more than the price he set. It wouldn't have ended there, and we both knew that. He'd come for more."

"A leech," Roarke said, thinking of Missy Lee's word for Mars, "never tires of sucking blood."

"So paying wouldn't have solved the matter. I thought about taking you and Marlena and leaving. Though Patrick Roarke had those contacts beyond Dublin, so did

I. And better ones, so I considered that."

Summerset paused, sipping at his coffee. "So did he. He had those badges, and he'd use them, he told me. They'd come knocking before I could pack the first bag, and I'd be charged with abusing you, and my girl. Sexually."

"Christ Jesus." Surprised now, sickened now, Roarke shoved his coffee aside.

His voice calm, matter-of-fact, Summerset continued on, "And of selling you to others for that purpose. There'd be proof of it, he guaranteed me, and I believed him. I had not a doubt he'd have seen both of you raped and beaten and traumatized. The money might have put that off for a time, and maybe I could have gotten you safe. But I chose to end it before it could begin. I wouldn't risk either of you."

The man who sat across from him had had a life before he'd brought a beaten street rat into it. He'd had a child of his own.

"You could've given me back to him, left with Marlena. He'd have had nothing."

"He'd have had you," Summerset said simply. "That was never an option. Never. I put the knife in him without a moment's regret. He never saw it coming, with all his contacts and blustering. He saw me as a weak man he could bully and frighten."

"You've never been weak."

"His mistake."

Roarke sat a moment in silence, absorbing it all. "I went back to the alley where they'd found him, and I wished it had been me that had done him." He looked up again, met Summerset's eyes. "Next best thing."

"I took no pleasure in it."

"No. I would have — then." Roarke laid his hand over Summerset's, left it there for a quiet moment. "I'm not what I was."

"You were never what he wanted you to be. And more than even I hoped. In weak moments, I might credit the lieutenant for some of that."

Roarke smiled again. "In her weak moments, she might credit you. It's a sum of work, isn't it?"

"You'll tell her all this?"

"Her scale's different than ours, and it's weighing on her. I'll tell her, yes, and it'll lighten." Roarke rose. "I'll see you before you go."

"Of course."

"You were right not to tell me before. I would have celebrated it, even a handful of years ago."

"And now?"

"Now, I can be grateful for the man you

were and are. That's more than enough."

As Roarke started out, the cat leaped down and trotted behind him.

"He's been fed," Summerset called out.

"It rarely makes a bit of difference to him."

Eve woke, frowned at the sofa where she'd expected to see Roarke drinking coffee, watching the stocks, maybe working on his PPC or a tablet.

World-domination meeting ran over, she decided, pushing herself out of bed. She hit coffee first, let it fire up her brain.

She needed to check the search results, nag DeWinter, push through more interviews, she thought as she headed for the shower.

The search results might give her a new path to pursue, and nagging DeWinter in person could prove more productive than a text. Then there was Guy Durante — some possibilities there. Time to press.

She stepped out of the shower, into the drying tube, let the warm air swirl.

It occurred to her she could beat Roarke to breakfast. There could be anything but oatmeal.

She jumped out, grabbed a soft white robe, and was shoving her arms into it as she stepped out.

And thought, Damn it, when she saw

Roarke already at the Auto-Chef.

"Did buying Uruguay run over?"

"Uruguay?"

"It sounds buyable." She shrugged, resigned herself to oatmeal. "Where is Uruguay?"

"South and, though I have a few interests there, I haven't considered buying it outright. I've got this, and since you're up and about, why don't you get us a pot of coffee?"

He carried the tray to the sitting area; she got the coffee.

"If not Uruguay, what?"

"This and that."

He lifted the warming domes. Oatmeal — oh well. Berries, brown sugar, bacon. It could be worse.

"Summerset's making bread."

She said, "Huh?"

"He was kneading dough when I went down to see him, so I assume it's bread." He poured coffee for both of them. "Do you want to know why he killed Patrick Roarke?"

Her hand froze before it reached the cup. "What?"

"I should have seen it before," he said easily now. "In him, in you. As a boy there was only relief, and I never thought of Summerset. He knew violence, and certainly had used violence during the wars, but he heals. His instincts are to heal, so I never thought of him for it. And, in truth, I thought of it all very rarely. You should eat."

She only shook her head, so he covered both plates again.

"It's secrets, isn't it, and it dovetails with your case. Maybe that's why it opened for me now. After your dream you say wasn't a nightmare, though I suspect it came close, you wouldn't tell me. You brushed it off. Evaded, and looking back, I realized you'd done the same earlier in your office when we talked of Mars, of her murder possibly being done to protect a child or another. Then of Patrick Roarke. You turned away, but I'd seen it, just something on your face for an instant. It didn't strike home until I thought back, and I began to see. So I asked him, and he told me. He assumed you'd told me."

"I —" She started to get up, but Roarke simply took her hand, held her in place. "I didn't *know.* I suspected. I didn't push on it. It wasn't like I pushed him to . . ."

"Confess?"

Everything inside her went tight and cold. "I wasn't after a confession."

"Eve." His voice quiet, Roarke gripped

her hand tighter. "I know that. Just as I know it was hard for you to know that a crime had been committed, that murder had been done, and do and say nothing."

"I didn't have evidence. I don't have proof."

"Stop it." He brought her hand to his lips, kissed it. "Stop now."

"I should've told you, but —"

"No. You did exactly the right thing."

"How? How is it the right thing? You have to be able to trust me. The Marriage Rules —"

A half laugh escaped him. "Oh, bugger the Marriage Rules over this."

"If you bugger them over one thing, you start buggering them over the next."

Because he understood her genuine distress, he pushed away all amusement, shook his head. "The world's not so black-and-white, as both of us know well. We've lived in the gray. You didn't tell me even though it would've unburdened you because it would be a betrayal, and because it may have burdened me. So I'm telling you it doesn't. And it wouldn't even if I didn't know the whole of it now. I'd like to tell you why."

"I know why. It doesn't take a cop to understand he was protecting you and his daughter. It's clear. I want to say he should have gone to the police, but they were corrupt, careless, cruel."

"And a lot of them were in Patrick Roarke's pocket. And still, for you, one who stands for the dead, whoever they were, it's very hard. I hope to make it a little easier. He'd found me," Roarke began.

He told her all, letting her go when she pushed up to pace.

"Would the cops have been complicit in this?" she demanded. "Would they have looked away while two children were sexually and physically abused?"

"There may have been some good or at least decent cops in that area back then, but the ones he had, the ones he knew? Not just looked away, Eve. They'd have participated."

"In the brutalization of children."

"Homeland looked away when a child was being brutalized by her father because it didn't fit their agenda," Roarke reminded her. "In my world then, the garda lined their pockets and did dark deeds more often than not."

It sickened, and somehow steadied. "If what I did was self-defense, what he did was in defense of the defenseless."

"And can you let it go? I don't mean legally. I mean inside you. Can you breathe out what you've surely been holding in since you came to know?"

"Patrick Roarke killed your mother because she was inconvenient. He nearly beat you to death. He threatened you and an innocent girl. I can't say what Summerset did was right. But I can believe it was just."

She walked back, sat. "I saw him in my dream, dead on the ground of an alley. With Richard Troy and Big Rod Keith."

So now she told him all.

"I believe I know who killed Keith."

More weight she carried, Roarke thought. "What will you do?"

"It's not for me to judge, to decide. I believe I know who, I believe I know why. It's possible I could prove it. But it isn't my investigation, and unless it crosses clearly into mine, I'm not going to pursue it. That's the gray, and I'm not altogether comfortable there, but I can live with it. I'm not sure I could live with destroying the lives of good people to walk the straight line."

She picked up her coffee, stared into it. "If it does cross clearly, if that changes, I will pursue, and I will prove it. I can't do otherwise. Mars is my dead, and has to get my best. Or I don't deserve the badge."

"You're right, all the way down the line. Black or white or gray, you're right." Gently, he stroked a hand over her hair. "And I'm with you."

As she had in the night, she shifted, pressed her face to his shoulder. He wrapped his arms around her.

"There now, we're fine, aren't we?"

She held on, then realized she'd done just what he'd asked. She'd breathed it out. "We're okay."

She lifted her face, met his lips with hers, lingered there.

When she eased back, he started to run a hand down her hair again, then his eyes narrowed.

"Oh, that's well beyond the pale."

At the snap in his voice she jerked a little, glanced back in time to see Galahad leap off the table, bound over to the bed, leap up, and sprawl out as though exhausted.

"What?"

"Well, he was trying to get under the warming domes, wasn't he? Sneaking his paw under the edge."

"For oatmeal? Seriously?"

Galahad merely rolled over, giving them his back. Switching his tail.

"There's bacon as well." Roarke lifted off the domes again. "So have at it."

She thought it too bad the cat hadn't been quicker, but doctored her oatmeal up enough that she could claim it wasn't all that bad.

Plus, bacon.

"I'm heading out a little early," Eve began. "I want to go by the lab, give DeWinter and team another push. I want that face. Who she was is going to be important. I need to do a quick check on your search, on the names and locations, see if we hit anything that rings."

"We hit a few that might."

"What? You already looked?"

"Well, since I didn't buy Uruguay, I had a moment or two to spare."

"Have you got a list? I need to run them. I need to —"

"Only three that hit the mark, and I transferred the results. You can look at them on screen here."

"Why didn't you say so before?"

"I had other things to say."

She hissed out a breath, had to gnaw over his response. Was forced to see his point. "So we're all fine and good, right? Let's see what you got."

"I'll do just that. Eat your oatmeal."

Eve rolled her eyes, but shoveled in more.

18

Roarke brought a half dozen names and ID shots on screen. Eve dismissed two instinctively.

"Take off the top left, bottom right."

"Why?"

"She was vain, pretty seriously vain. I don't see her using an ID that hits significantly older than she was. Both of those are."

Though he wasn't sure he agreed — clever concealment trumped vanity to his mind — he pulled the two off screen, enlarged the others.

Studying the four remaining, Eve ate her oatmeal without thinking about it. "Ditch top right."

"Because?"

"Average looks."

"That's certainly scientific," he said, but complied.

"That one, bottom right. Angela Terra.

Terra's not a planet, is it?"

"Earth."

"A fancy name for Earth? Interesting." She switched to bacon. "And possible. What about Juno? Carly Mae Juno."

"Juno's an asteroid between Mars and Jupiter."

"Hmm. Connected to Mars, so you'd think maybe. But it's not big enough. Important enough."

"You could take another angle. She's the wife of Zeus. A goddess."

"Goddess ranks high on the scale." Not bad, Eve thought, then reading the data, waved the bacon at the screen. "An assistant manager of a twenty-four/seven? No way Mars would settle. And that one, Brite Luna — seriously? — the proprietor of Moonstruck Life Embracing Therapy? It's just embarrassing."

"Which leaves you with Angela Terra. I'm not a cop," Roarke began. "But I have some experience with alternate identification."

"Really?" Eve's voice was desert dry as she picked up her coffee.

"In some cases, it's strategic to create something close to reality, and in others it's advantageous to go in the other direction, particularly if that direction is average, quiet, something that goes unnoticed. A low-level job, an unremarkable face."

She wondered how many he'd used — how many times he'd become someone else to slip through the fingers of authority, to outwit a competitor or enemy.

"Maybe, but I don't figure she's using this ID for anything but establishing another residence, maybe some financials. It's not for traveling, for daily use," Eve pointed out. "See there, Terra's the president and CEO of Terra Consultants. Top dog, that's the style. Age thirty-six, put on a red wig and fiddle with some facial enhancements, Mars could pull off that face if she had to use the ID. Height and weight are in line. And check the address? It's just a couple blocks from Du Vin, a location she used routinely."

"You make some points."

"We'll check all of them. It's easy enough. We do runs, we knock on doors. But I start with Angela Terra."

Eve rose, walked to her closet while Roarke brought the six images back to study them.

"Who'd be second on your list?"

"The goddess," she called out. "Because she might have gone for, what's it? Irony. Maybe she amused herself with the twenty-four/seven clerk. I'll start the runs in the car on the way, have Peabody meet me at the first address."

"You could simply contact each of these by 'link."

"Face-to-face is better. If there's a face to — ha — face. If we hit, one of those faces is in the morgue and unavailable for interview. Why are there so many clothes in here? It makes me clothes-blind."

He got up, walked to where she stood in a pair of slate-gray trousers and a support tank and a look of baffled frustration. Tapping a drawer on one of the built-ins, he glanced at the contents, pulled out a sweater with a modest V-neck.

"Try this."

She stared suspiciously. "I was working toward black."

He tossed the aubergine cashmere to her. "Shock the world and go for a bit of color."

"You should talk."

"I might be wearing red boxers as we speak."

"Yeah?" She dragged the sweater on. "Let's see."

Smiling, eyebrows arched, he reached for his belt buckle. "Well now, there's plenty of room in here, isn't there?"

"Never mind." She stared at the line of jackets in the gray section, decided to just save time. Waved her hand at them.

Roarke stepped over, plucked one out that had thin cuffs of leather that matched the sweater. She might have bitched, but she had that weakness for leather, and he knew it.

He strolled to the boots, lifted a pair the precise color of the sweater. Then laughed at her horrified expression.

"It was worth it. If you never wear them, it was worth having them made just for the look on your face."

"They're purple."

"Aubergine," he corrected.

"Auber my ass, those are fricking purple boots."

"And would look very well on you, but . . ." He exchanged them for a pair in more acceptable murder-cop gray.

She snatched them, carried them and the jacket out to strap on her weapon harness, to fill pockets with her daily paraphernalia.

It wasn't until she sat to pull on the boots that it struck her. " 'Made'? Made for me? You have the boots made?"

"Someone has to."

"I mean, specifically?"

"Why wouldn't I? My cop walks miles on any given day, and often runs after bad guys. As we already discussed, her feet are rather precious to me."

"Precious feet," she grumbled. "You're a madman." Standing, she rolled from heel to toe and back again. "I gotta go." On impulse, she linked her arms around his neck, finished it off with a long, deep kiss. "Catch you later."

He held her in place a moment. "Take care of my cop."

"I've got the boots for it."

She jogged downstairs, grabbed her outdoor gear, and stepped out into the sharp jaws of February.

They really needed to work on eliminating February from the calendar, she thought as she bulleted to her car — heater already running. There had to be a way; they must have the technology.

As she drove, she tagged Peabody, relayed the address. If they struck out there, they'd move to the next. It was a good angle to pursue. And she followed it up by starting a run on Angela Terra on the in-dash.

"Clean as a whistle," she mused. "A clean, shiny whistle. Why are whistles so clean? What does that even mean?"

She didn't realize she'd spoken out loud until the in-dash comp answered.

The phrase suggests the clean, pure sound a whistle makes. It indicates that to emit this clear sound, the tube must be

clean and dry.

"Huh." Eve pursed her lips, whistled. Let it go.

The clean-as-a-whistle Angela Terra had lived at the downtown address for seven years. The data stated she'd been born in Canton, Ohio, parents deceased, no siblings. No marriages or cohabs.

No connections, Eve thought, following the scent.

Graduated from an online university — interesting. Started the consulting business twelve years prior — with no other employment listed. Also interesting.

She pushed on to the consulting business, found absolutely zero. No data, no web page, no client list, no referrals. That wasn't just interesting, she thought.

That was telling.

Angela Terra was bogus. The odds she wasn't an alias for Larinda Mars were very, very slim.

"Sometimes you get lucky," Eve noted aloud as she fought her way downtown.

She found the address — a quiet, dignified duplex. Since the residents of the neighborhood hogged all the curbside parking, she double-parked, ignoring the outraged horns. Flipping up her On Duty light, she stepped onto the sidewalk.

Sedate, she decided. The kind of sedate that took money to claim. The sort of neighborhood that ran to dog walkers and nannies, where the residents walked to their favorite restaurants and shops.

She approached the left-side entrance, walked up the short stairs to the door. Narrowed her eyes at it. Designed to look like old, rich wood, but a quick tap of the knuckles told her it was steel. A quick glance showed her high-level security. The cam, the palm plate, the double swipe, the trio of sturdy police locks.

No buzzer or bell, she noted, so knocked loud and long.

And received the expected response. None.

She walked down, and crossed to the neighboring door.

Standard door, she thought, good but standard security. And a buzzer.

She pressed it.

"Bonjour! Comment vous appelez-vous, s'il vous plaît?"

"Say what?" Eve buzzed again, holding her badge up to the scanner. "NYPSD."

"Un moment, s'il vous plaît."

"For Christ's sake." Eve leaned on the buzzer.

Finally she heard the locks *thump.* The

door opened a couple inches with a woman in a red robe, her hair scooped up in a disordered chestnut mass on her head, peeking through the crack.

"Yes?"

Eve held her badge up again.

"Yes, the police. Is there some wrong? Some*thing* wrong?" she corrected.

English, Eve thought, heavily accented, but English.

"I have some questions about your neighbor, about Angela Terra."

"I'm sorry. We don't know the neighbors."

"Could I have your name?" Eve glanced back as Peabody mounted the steps, her cheeks pink with cold. "My partner. Peabody show the woman your badge."

"Sure. Morning," Peabody said as she pulled out her badge.

Somewhere behind the woman a young male voice shouted out, *"Maman, dépêche-toi!'*

"Elles sont les officiers de police!"

That caused some rapid-fire responses Eve couldn't interpret. "Ma'am, if we could come in for a minute. We have some questions about the individual who lives next door."

"Yes, come in. It's cold. We don't know the next-door person."

She let them in a narrow foyer where a coatrack with cubbies held various and colorful outdoor gear. The young male voice belonged to a gangly teenager with dark, fascinated eyes.

"You are police? Someone has been murdered!"

He said it with a kind of relish that had his mother — Eve assumed — giving him a look that translated in every language.

Shut up.

A girl a few years younger than the boy with flyaway blond hair and feet in pink bunny slippers ran in, with a man — a less gangly, taller version of the boy — following. Since he wore pajama pants, like the boy, and a New York City sweatshirt, Eve concluded the family hadn't gotten a full start on their day.

"Is there a problem?" he asked in perfect English, with the charm of the accent.

"Lieutenant Dallas, Detective Peabody, NYPSD. We're looking for information on the individual who lives next door. Angela Terra."

"I'm sorry. We arrived only last week."

"I like your coats very much," the girl piped in. "I would like the long like you, but in the pink like you."

The mother stepped back, stroked a hand

over the girl's head, and whispered something that had the kid shrugging.

"I don't know how we can help," the man said.

"Could we have your names?"

"Of course, excuse me. I'm Jean-Paul Laroche. My wife, Marie-Clare, our son, Julian, and our daughter, Claudette."

"Would you like to sit?" Marie-Clare asked.

"If we could, for a minute."

They trooped, the entire group, into a living area with colorful disorder — a couple of stuffed animals, a tossed sweater, some striped house skids — over what struck as bland furnishings.

They'd brightened them a bit with bowls and vases of flowers and some framed photos.

"We haven't settled in." Marie-Clare gestured to chairs. "May I offer you the coffee?"

"No, thanks. We won't take much of your time."

The entire family sat on the couch, looked expectantly at Eve.

"You're moving to New York?"

"For three months," Jean-Paul said. "I have business, and Marie-Clare has family."

"My aunt and my cousins. It's an opportunity to experience. The children will start school here on Monday."

That got an eye roll from the boy, a wide grin from the girl.

"We have taken the house for the three months," Jean-Paul continued. "And are having a short holiday before work and school begin."

"Have you seen anyone next door since you arrived?"

"No." He glanced at his family, got head shakes.

"It's always dark," Claudette added, "the windows."

"Okay." Dead end here, Eve thought. "So you found the property through your work?"

"I work for Travel Home. We are a global agency listing homes and flats for travelers who prefer this rather than a hotel, you see?"

"My cousin lives only one block," Marie-Clare told Eve. "We can walk to see each other, and she has children close to the ages of ours. I worked with my husband's assistant to find this house, this neighborhood. Through my husband's business people can travel and stay in homes, a night, a year."

"Handy," Eve said, getting a polite, if puzzled, smile in return.

Wouldn't it be really handy? she thought.

"The properties you — and clients — can

rent belong to this Travel Home?"

"Listed with," Jean-Paul corrected. "We take applications, you see, and screen the owners and the properties, visit them to be certain they are as they claim to be."

"Got it. You'd probably know who owns this house."

"I could not tell you from the top of my head, but it would be easy to find out."

"I'd appreciate that."

He rose. "Excuse me one moment."

"Maybe somebody's dead in the next door," the boy said when his father walked out.

"I doubt it," Eve said.

"Maybe."

His mother sighed and patted his knee.

"I like also your boots very much," Claudette told Peabody.

"Thanks."

"Yours are very nice," she added for Eve.

"They do the job."

Jean-Paul came back in with a PPC. "The owner is Terra Consultants, and the address for the owner is next door. The property has our highest rating or I would not have brought my family into it. Is there a worry here?"

"No. No worry. We appreciate your time

and your help. Enjoy your time in New York."

Outside, Eve started toward the houses on the other side. "Get us a search warrant, Peabody. The ID for Angela Terra and her company is very shaky, and we believe this is an alias and front for Larinda Mars. Go ahead and move my vehicle before we start an insurrection — bring my field kit back with you. I'll knock on some doors."

"Buy the whole duplex, rent out the connecting half to people who come and go — and don't look to make pals. Smart."

"Yeah, she had brains."

Eve had knocked on four doors by the time Peabody got back, and they hit two more together — with the same negative results — by the time the warrant came through.

Eve used her master, got through one lock, then one more. But the third held firm.

"She put in a cop-proof lock here. Bad girl." Puffing out a breath, Eve dug in her kit. "Let's see how much I've learned."

Peabody frowned as Eve took out a set of lock picks. "We could call for EDD, or a battering ram."

"I can do this."

Eventually, Eve thought. Probably.

Ten minutes later, with Peabody shivering

and stomping her feet in the biting wind, Eve felt something give.

"Nearly got it."

"Sing hallelujah."

When the last tooth snicked, Eve did an internal happy dance. Peabody did an actual one right on the stoop.

"Let there be heat."

"Record on." Eve drew her weapon, waited for Peabody to do the same. "Dallas, Lieutenant Eve, and Peabody, Detective Delia, entering residence under the name of Terra, Angela. We are duly authorized."

She booted the door open, went in smooth, fast, and low.

A dim light eased on at the movement, showing a narrow foyer crammed with furniture. Eve gestured Peabody to the right.

"Let's clear it. This is the police," Eve called out. "We have entered the premises. We are armed," she continued as she swept and moved forward.

Things, she thought, lots of things. Tables, lamps, vases, paintings. But no sign of life.

She worked her way back to the kitchen and found the dust of disuse. She called out, "Clear!" as Peabody did the same.

They backtracked, started up the stairs.

"Nobody lives here," Peabody said. "There isn't room with all the stuff."

"It's her warehouse."

They cleared two bedrooms — jammed, a closet loaded with furs, some with the tags still attached. A room loaded with shoes, boots, handbags.

Then the master.

"Here's where she worked."

Satisfied, Eve holstered her weapon. "A lot of fussy stuff, but actually arranged, the sofa — pillows and one of those throw things — the desk, the d and c.

"Adjoining bath's got fresh towels — fresh-ish," Peabody said. "And soaps and bath oils, lotions. Enough of them for a department store, but she used at least some of them."

Eve didn't care about the lotions and oils. She went straight to the desk. She sat, tried to engage the computer.

Passcode required.

"Yeah, figured. Pull in EDD, and see who we have in the bullpen who isn't on something hot. Add a couple of uniforms. It's going to be a bitch to search and inventory."

"You want sweepers?"

"Let's see what we find first."

With a nod, Peabody opened the double closet doors. "Holy shit. Look at this, Dallas." Peabody stepped back. "It's a freaking vault."

Rising, Eve walked over to study the sheer steel. She pulled out her 'link. When Roarke came on, she said, "Want a challenge?" and angled the 'link to show him the vault.

"Well now, that's a Podark, and a fine, big girl she is, as well. Would you be in the Terra residence?"

"Terra's bogus, but yeah."

"I believe I'd enjoy a challenge. Let me clear a thing or two up. I should be there in thirty minutes. Forty at the outside."

"Works for me."

"A Podark," he said, with what Eve could only think of as a happy sigh. "It's been some time."

Eve went back to the desk. "Start checking drawers," she told Peabody, opening one in the desk.

She pulled out a thick leather binder, opened it. "Well, you just don't expect to hit pay dirt. That's another one: Why does dirt pay? But you don't expect it right off the jump."

"Whatcha got?"

"A research file, I'd say. There are several in here. Marks, potential marks, maybe. Clippings. She printed stuff out, made her little scrapbooks. Photos, too. And some of them she must've taken herself, maybe using a long-range lens. Portable this way. She could pull one out, lounge on the sofa, hit the AC. I bet it's fully stocked. Weave her webs. The suspect list is going to . . ."

Peabody glanced back, then turned completely when she saw the fury lighting Eve's eyes.

"What?"

"She has Mavis in here." Eve flipped a page. "Mavis, Leonardo, the baby. Goddamn it. Some data, just basic shit. Some question marks, Roman numerals, but just your basic shit from a standard run or from interviews, articles."

She slapped at the computer as she rose. She wanted in. If there was anything more, it would be in the comp.

She pulled out her 'link.

Mavis, sleepy eyes, tousled Caribbean-blue hair, smiled. "Hey."

"Where are you?"

"Huh? Oh, Aruba, remember? We buzzed down for a couple weeks. I've got a gig, and it's maxi-mag-lush down here. You should completely come. We could —"

"Mavis, did Larinda Mars ever put the arm on you, or Leonardo?"

"Larinda?" Mavis yawned and stretched. "Sure. Interviews, photos, exclusives, the dish. It's part of the life. Why?"

"She's dead, and she has a file on you."

"Dead? Like *dead*? How? When?"

"A couple days ago. The kind of dead that has me looking for who made her that way. She has a file on you, Mavis."

"Well, I guess she would. I mean, I guess people in her business would. Holy crapola, Dallas. I mean she was kind of a bitch, but —"

Somewhere in the background Bella laughed and said, very clearly, "Bitch!"

"Damn it," Mavis muttered. "I forgot. Mama said 'fish,' Bellamina. We're going to go see fish later."

"What kind of bitch?"

"Fish," Mavis insisted. "She was a pushy fish. Like — barracuda! That's a fish. She had that kind of smile — you know, shiny and sharp — if you didn't give her what she was after. But we got along okay, no probs. I didn't bump into her all that often anyway."

"She was a blackmailing fish."

"Oh." Mavis strung the word out into multiple syllables. "She never tried to work me. She got pushy, like I said, and pushed about you more than once. I shut that down. I know how. I mean when you've worked the . . . g-r-i-f-t like me, you know how to slip and slide."

"Ask Leonardo. Ask if she tried to work him."

"He'd have told me."

"Ask him. No bullshit. Straight ask, straight answer."

"Okay, okay. Let me . . . Talk to Bella. Bellisimo, it's Dallas."

"Das!"

The screen filled with Bella's pretty, happy face and her crown of blond curls. She jabbered for a full minute without pause, then laughed like a mental patient.

"I bet," Eve said, without a single clue.

"Oook, oook, oook!" The screen jiggled and zipped and rocked, then showed an expanse of golden sand, blue seas, and waving green palms. "Mama say mago-oso."

Despite everything, Eve laughed. "Yeah, she would."

"Ove Das, Das come. Mago-oso."

"Maybe sometime."

"Hey, my Bella, say bye to Dallas. Daddy's got your berries."

"Mmm. Bye, Das, bye! Slooch!"

Bella pressed her lips to the screen, smearing it with toddler spit.

"Yeah, slooch."

Mavis swiped the screen with something, gave Eve a look. "Straight no. She pushed some, about me, about you and Roarke, but my honey bear knows how to hold the line. He said he let her think he wasn't too bright, or clued in, and she backed off."

"Which makes him both bright and clued in."

"That's my moonpie. Should I be worried?"

"I don't think so, and if I'm wrong and there's anything, I'll take care of it."

"I know you will. We're back in the Apple in about four days, I think. Tag me back either way when you know what you know."

"I will. Have fun in the mago-oso."

Mavis laughed. "She'll get those *l*'s in one of these days. Cha, Das."

Satisfied, even if the anger still simmered, Eve sat again. "Take another of these books, Peabody. The way I see this one, it's recording stars and their connections. She's likely got one of vid stars, etc., maybe one on politicians, your basic wealthy types, and like that."

Peabody took two, settled on the couch. "One's vid stars — seems exclusive to that." She flipped open the other. "She's got directors, producers, the industry types in this one. Question marks, exclamations, underlines, those Roman numerals. Those might be how close she thought she was to cashing in. You know, one for first stage, and like that?"

"Yeah, that could work." Eve had already concluded the same. "She had Leonardo at a one, Mavis hit a two. I've got a couple in here with fives, and she writes them in bold red."

Eve set the book aside, pulled out another. And opened the first page to find her own face. "She's got me. I rate a one. A lot of pages on me," she continued as Peabody shoved up, coming over to see for herself. "A lot of question marks. Oh, look, I rated some commentary: *Bullshit, bitch.* Hey, *slut*? Where does she come off calling me a slut? Anyway, lots of articles, some photos. She caught a couple of Summerset. Looks like he was shopping. A few of you and me on the job. And all that fancy shit for the premiere of the vid."

She flipped through, stopped. "And here's Roarke. Lots and lots of Roarke."

Checking, she nodded. "We rate our own book."

"And he ranks a one, just like you."

Peabody flipped back, curious. Then tried to flip a page over quickly to cover. Eve slapped her hand down.

Mars had devoted an entire page to a blown-up still of Roarke and the woman who'd been in his life long before Eve. The woman who'd come back into his life — their lives — briefly to try to destroy their marriage.

"Magdelana," Eve murmured. "The picture she set up."

Her arms around Roarke, their bodies close, and her face turned — cheating out, Mavis had called it — so the camera could capture her full beauty.

She had notes there — Magdelana's name, her ex-husbands, some of her data — most of it probably as bogus as Larinda's had been.

Does one operator recognize another? Eve wondered.

Eve turned the page, found more notes on the next page.

Where the hell did she go? Did Roarke sleep with her?

Weak spot? Possible seduction route? How much does she know? Have on him? On Dallas?

"That's the door." Peabody cleared her throat. "Probably McNab."

"Mmm-hmm."

"Don't take in that bitch's bullshit, Dallas."

"Huh? No." Eve looked up. "I'm not." To prove it, she closed the book, pulled out another.

But when Peabody left to let in EDD, Eve sat a moment, looking back, seeing the stunning blond in the red dress.

19

When McNab bounced up the stairs, Eve turned the comp over to him. She carted a couple more books over to the sofa, opened a fresh one.

"Broadcasting marks and potentials. Roman numeral fives, her high score, hits a few here. The assistant she screwed with, Phoebe Michaelson, earned one with a star instead of a dollar sign. And I've got some guy with three stars she connects to Bellami — to using sex drugs, having access to questionable sex workers."

"That'll be who doctored Bellami's drink for the setup."

"Yeah." Eve nodded absently at Peabody. "We'll be paying him a visit before we're done. Some more names here, some from Channel Seventy-Five," she continued as she turned pages. "Here's Annie Knight — she earns four full pages. Hits the five with dollar signs. Ah, and she had one of Knight's team on the hook. Ilene Riff, in wardrobe, two stars for information."

"What did she have on her?" Peabody asked.

"Daughter's an addict with emotional issues. Eating disorder, a cutter with a taste for punch. Bumps for solicitation without a license, petty theft, assault. Two rounds of rehab, two short stints in a cage. Currently in a halfway house and clean according to the copy of the report Mars got her hands on. Looks like Riff's working nights waiting tables to pay off the second round of rehab.

"We'll talk to her," Eve said as she turned another page. "And here's Nadine."

Peabody puffed out a breath. "I guess that's expected."

"Low score and, knowing Nadine, she's going to be pretty pleased with just how much Mars disliked her."

"I'm in," McNab announced. "Want me to start pulling things out?"

"I'll start that." Eve noticed his gaze shift and lock on the vault. Wistfully. "Have you ever cracked a Podark?"

"No, but I'd sure like to play."

"Roarke's on the way."

Now came a sigh. Wistful. "Better idea."

"How about checking security, seeing if you can find the last time Mars came in and out? And there's a domestic droid in the kitchen, disengaged. Mars must have used it for basic cleaning. Whatever you can get."

"Can do." He rose. "Hey, Dallas, thanks for Mexico. All of it. Serious gratitude."

"Let's close this case so you can get gone."

"I'm all about it."

"Peabody, go ahead and give him a hand." Eve rose to walk back to the desk. As they bounced and clomped away, she opened the comp to a general search.

It didn't surprise her to find files that mirrored the theme of the books. Screen, Music, Business, Politics, and so on. She'd go through them for comparisons, but first she wanted to study the marks, priority on males.

She'd save the financial files for later.

Helpfully, Mars had her marks listed in alpha order. Eve started on the *A*'s. She'd barely moved into the *B*'s when Roarke came in.

"I didn't hear you knock."

"I didn't." Like McNab's, his gaze shifted and locked on the vault. Eve could only interpret his expression as a look of love.

"Ah, there she is." He crossed to it, skimmed his fingers lightly over the polished surface. "Quite the beauty."

"Should I leave the two of you alone?"

He tossed Eve a grin and set down what looked like a high-class field kit. "I owe you a solid for this, as you'd say," he told her as he took off his coat. "So I won't say too much about all the signs you left that you'd picked the lock on the main door."

"I had a warrant. I wasn't worried about leaving signs."

He all but tsked at her as he took off his suit jacket. "Have some pride in your work, darling."

"I'm in, aren't I? I could've used a battering ram."

He only smiled, removed his tie, rolled up his sleeves. "It's an excellent lock, with illegal master blocks. How long did it take you to lift it?"

When she shrugged, he took a leather strip out of his pocket, tied back his hair. "That long then? We'll get more practice in."

"If you owe me a solid, why are you pissing me off?"

He walked back to her, bent down to kiss the top of her head. "Then I'll tell you: An amateur or third-rate thief would have needed a drill or that battering ram."

She nearly got to mollified, then pulled back, eyes narrowed. "Does that make me second-rate?"

"It makes you an excellent student with

considerable, innate skill."

He picked up his kit, walked back to the vault. "Now, let's have a good look at you, my lovely."

So saying, he sat on the floor, began to take various tools — many she didn't recognize — from the kit.

"What is all that?"

He turned, glanced meaningfully at her recorder.

She put it on pause.

"Mementos, you could say, from a past life," he said, getting down to it again. "I cracked my first Podark in a lovely and graceful Tuscan villa. And a lovely night it was — I can still smell the lemon blossoms. I believe I was about twenty. I had my last . . ." He glanced back. "Before I had you."

"How long before?"

"Long enough."

"Hmm. Resume record."

He chose a device about as long and wide as his hand, attached it to the sheer front of the vault. He played his fingers over it, hummed in his throat.

She watched him work for a few minutes as, apparently satisfied with whatever the first device told him, he attached a smaller one to it, slipped a comm unit over his ear.

She spotted a flash of codes, as incomprehensible to her as his morning stock reports, then left him to it to go back to her own work.

He muttered to himself now and then, sometimes in Irish, as she worked through the *B*'s and into the *C*'s. She heard McNab bounce back in, then stop.

She looked up to see his attention riveted on Roarke.

McNab whispered, "Search team's here. She-Body's getting them started. How long's he been at it?"

"I don't know. Fifteen, twenty minutes."

"Is it okay if I watch until . . . No way!" McNab exclaimed, and bounced forward. "No way you can open a Podark — that's a TXR-2000. I looked it up. No way you can open it in twenty freaking minutes!"

"Eighteen and thirty-two seconds." Roarke slid off his earpiece. "She's a shy one."

"It has twenty-eight locking bolts, up to six passcodes and two fail-safes. Kick my ass and call me Sally, you've *gotta* show me how you did that. It would've taken freaking hours to drill through."

"Drilling wouldn't do it," Roarke said. "She's built to snap drill bits like dry twigs under a bootheel. If you're crude enough to try explosives, she'll laugh at you. You don't force or bully a lady like this." He trailed his fingers over the surface again. "You . . . convince her."

"Do the three of you need a moment?" Eve asked. "Or can we open the damn door on that thing, and see what's in it?"

"She's all yours, Lieutenant." Roarke gathered up his tools.

Pushing away from the desk, Eve walked over. She gripped the ship-wheel handle, pulled. Put her back into it, braced her feet, and pulled again.

"Hot, juicy wow!"

She couldn't argue with McNab's assessment. The vault wasn't full — obviously Mars had planned for more — but there was plenty of wow.

Two shelves of neatly banded bills, rows of jewelry laid out on black velvet nestled in thin drawers. The glitter of gold and silver, the gleam of bronze, the shine of porcelain in objets d'art.

Eve scanned over it all, focused on the back shelf. "Her own ID kit."

"You would latch onto that and overlook these rather exquisite emeralds."

She saw the damn emeralds, and the other glitters, and stuck her hands on her hips. "We're going to need an armored to transport all this. Which detectives are on the search team?"

McNab, eyes a bit glazed, blinked. "Ah, Jenkinson and Reineke."

"Good. They can log it all." She moved into the vault, poked into a box. "Full of bugs — the e-sort. That's one way to get personal information. The list of people with motive is going to be ridiculous. Box of discs. At least they're labeled. Names, dates. Likely copies of whatever the listening devices picked up. So."

She set her hands on her hips again, turned around. "Give me an estimate."

Roarke shook his head. "That's a hard one."

"Try anyway."

"Well now, you've got different denominations in the paper money, and some of it's foreign currency. I'd start at about sixty million."

"Some start," McNab noted.

"For the baubles, that's even more plucking out of the air, but from the look of things, about triple that. And the rest . . . a hundred, a hundred and twenty."

"Million again."

"Of course."

"Round it up," she said, circling a finger.

"All in all, you've somewhere in the vicinity of three hundred and sixty. You might hit four hundred."

As McNab would say, Eve thought, some vicinity.

"How about the building? All of it, both units."

At this Roarke looked a little pained. "Well, I haven't seen the second unit at all, have I? And haven't done more than walk straight up here in this one."

"Just basically."

"The location, the space, not factoring how well or how poorly maintained, what might be needed to put it on the market? A very rough fifty, and it could be as much as twice that. And don't be asking me about the contents, as I couldn't begin."

Close enough, she thought. Plenty close enough.

"What I'm seeing with what's here, what was at her apartment, what's in her accounts? She hit the billion mark. But instead of buying herself a damn country and spending her days sipping mai tais, she kept working, kept blackmailing, and kept hoarding. That tells me she couldn't stop. It would never have been enough. It might be her killer figured out the same."

She stepped out as Peabody came in. "Get Jenkinson and Reineke up here."

"Okay, but . . ." Peabody looked in the

vault. Her jaw dropped; her eyes went wide and dazed. She said, "Ooooh, shiny."

"Never mind." Eve pushed by to get her detectives herself. As she strode out, she heard McNab.

"He opened it in like eighteen minutes."

She just shook her head and kept going.

Roarke wandered down with his coat and kit while she called in for additions to the search team, an armored vehicle, guards.

"The commander's taking over the transfer details, thank God," she told Roarke. "Thanks for the assist."

"My very genuine pleasure." He smiled at the steady look she aimed at him. "Should I turn out my pockets?"

"You're too good to get caught that easy." She shoved a hand through her hair as she looked around the cluttered foyer. "Plus, you stopped. Could stop. She couldn't. Not the digging, the knowing, the taking, the using, and the acquiring. Not evil, but sick. Seriously sick. And still . . ."

"You're pissed," he said, shrugging into his coat.

"Yeah. She has books up there. Record books of marks and potentials. You and I are in there. I need to talk to you about that, but not here. Mavis and Leonardo and the baby, them, too."

"You're right to be pissed. They're family."

She nodded. "And Nadine. I talked to Mavis, just to check if she'd gotten pushed any."

"She'd have told you if she had."

"Yeah. Yeah. I'm circling. I'm pissed and I'm circling. And some stupid part of me feels sorry for Mars because it's like she had a disease."

"It's not stupid."

"It's useless. The same as being pissed is useless. The useful is to stand for her, do the job."

"You are."

Since there was no one to see, she didn't resist when he pressed his lips to her forehead.

"To keep doing it I need to get to DeWinter, see if there's any progress on that facial reconstruction. Finding out who she was before she was Larinda Mars may help."

"Good luck with it. I'll see you at home. Unless you find another vault for me."

She went back upstairs where her detectives photographed and recorded every item in the vault. She heard the commentary.

"Jesus, look at the size of this rock."

"Is something this fugly actually worth money?"

She turned to where McNab loaded up the electronics. She started to ask about Peabody, then heard her partner's voice. From inside the vault.

"Oh! A tiara!"

"You put that thing on your head," Eve called out, "I'll bury you with it. Today."

"Might be worth it! Just kidding!"

Grinning, McNab finished loading up. "I sent copies of all content to your office and home comps, LT. I'll get started on the data after I get back, log it all in."

"Start at the end of alpha order, work up halfway. Feeney's standing by to work with you." She'd tagged him to make sure of it. "You know the parameters. Get me the list of most likely first."

"Can and will. I've got the listening devices. I've got the discs here. Want me to take them in?"

"I'll take those."

He patted the evidence bag, sealed and marked, on the desk. "All yours. Hey, She-Body, I'm rolling."

She poked her head out. Eve didn't see anything glittering on her but her eyes. "See you later. This is fun!"

He grinned, hefted his evidence box. "Cha, all. Eighteen minutes," he repeated as he pranced out. "It's freaking magic."

"Peabody, with me."

"Aw." But she came out, grabbed her coat. "I can't get over it. She had her own jewelry store, and she kept it all locked up."

"Because having was the thing." She took the evidence bag; the boxes of books would go straight to Central. "We're swinging by to see if DeWinter has any answers."

"Maybe she grew up in poverty," Peabody speculated as they walked down and out. "On the streets, maybe. You know how sidewalk sleepers can hoard things. It's a kind of survival, and security. It could've grown out of that."

"Maybe. Where's my vehicle?"

"Oh. Two blocks down, around the corner."

That being the case, Eve pulled her snowflake hat out of her pocket, dragged it on.

"You know," Peabody said conversationally, "it's a real advantage that Roarke designs and manufactures security devices, safes, vaults, like that. The guys and I were saying how otherwise we'd have had to call in a specialist, and probably still be waiting. But we already had one."

Eve flicked a glance at Peabody's innocent smile. "You and the guys decided that?"

"Yeah. All of us agreed. A real advantage for the department, and how it fits with our squad slogan, how we protect and serve no matter, blah-blah — even our expert consultant, civilian — even when the one who got dead was an asshole. And she pretty much was."

"Yeah, that works all around." Touched, as she'd intended to write it up exactly that way — minus the slogan and the asshole — Eve kept walking.

In the lab, she headed straight up to DeWinter's domain, prepared to execute a good, hard push if necessary. In fact, she looked forward to the execution.

But the only one in DeWinter's domain was Mars — or her remains. Eve noted someone — likely DeWinter — had marked areas of the skull. The skull and the markings, along with numerous equations, covered the wall screen.

Eve turned on her heel, walked to the next area.

DeWinter, a bold blue lab coat over a bold green dress, worked off a tablet while the artist, snug black pants, her braid falling down the back of a hip-skimming white tunic, keyed data into her own tablet.

"I need the face," Eve said, and had both women turning.

"We're working on it. It requires considerable measuring, calculations."

"We're making progress," Elsie told her.

"Show me."

DeWinter looked annoyed. Elsie simply looked mildly distressed. "I could use a few more hours before —"

"Just let me see what you've got."

At DeWinter's nod, Elsie used the tablet to bring up a screen image.

"Wider face," Eve noted. "Nose, too. Higher forehead, right? The eyes look rounder, the mouth thinner."

"Using Dr. Morris's measurements — that's flesh and muscle — and Dr. DeWinter's on bone, we've been able to estimate at — I'm confident — a ninety-five percent probability on this structure.

"Projecting . . ." And she did just that, bringing up a three-sixty holo. "Using the DNA results, and Harvo's findings, I'm reasonably confident of this skin tone and coloring. I've gone the hair medium length just for the visual, as there's no way to know."

"How about sketches? Do you have any?"

"Those, right now? Guesswork. Not supposed to say guess," Elsie added, with a quick grin at DeWinter. "Speculations based more on estimates, projections, and personal sensibilities than scientific fact."

"Screw science and let's see the sketches."

"We live and die by science here," DeWinter reminded her.

"Science got you this." Eve gestured to the screen. "And it's a good start, but it's not enough to use for face recognition. So we guess and see what we have."

"Go ahead." DeWinter waved a hand. "It wouldn't hold up under analysis, and certainly couldn't be used in court."

"We're not in court."

Eve studied the offered sketch pad. The face took on more life. In the sketch the hair formed curls, the eyebrows ran thick and nearly straight over the eyes. The jaw, more square than rounded, suited the wider face.

"This we could run, but . . . Can you do another, cut some years off? What would she look like at ten or twelve? She covered her tracks, but why would she delete or alter her ID from that far back?"

"Give me a second. If I program this sketch in, the computer will give us an image projection of that age range."

"If you'd give us another day —" DeWinter began as Elsie went to work.

"We try this. If it doesn't work, you take another day. I've got a list of her marks, and we've got another of people she was working to victimize. I'd like to know who she was."

"If the sketch is anywhere close," Elsie said, "she would have looked like this at the age of ten."

A rounder face — that was youth. Softer, and more innocent.

"Calculate the date, and run it."

"Then hydrate," DeWinter ordered.

"Happy to. I could use a hit. Anybody else?"

"I could. How's the coffee in Vending here?" Peabody asked.

"Bilge," DeWinter said.

"Tube of Pepsi?"

Eve nodded, watching images flash by on screen.

"We're working as diligently as you," DeWinter began when the others left for Vending.

"Never thought or said otherwise. We just work differently."

"I don't gamble, but if I did, I'd say the odds of getting a hit on what we have now are a few hundred thousand to one."

Eve smiled as the screen signaled, and the ID shot shared the screen with the sketch. "Pay up."

"You can't be sure that's —"

"Lari Jane Mercury — Larinda Mars. She

has a thing for planets. Lawrence, Kansas — that's the Midwest and slides right in, too. Got her parents and a female sibling."

"It's still speculation."

Eve pulled out her PPC, did a run on the name. "Nothing. Doesn't exist as of now." She took it back ten years. "Nothing ten years back. Let's plug in age ten and take it forward. There she is again. Every other year for ID shots until the age of eighteen is standard, but . . . Got one at twelve. And . . . that's it. Poof."

DeWinter's eyebrows beetled. "The child might have died."

"Jesus, you're stubborn, and that's supposed to be my job. She had it erased, back to age twelve. It costs to have ID scrubbed," Eve pointed out. "Twelve should have done it, would have done it. Who's going to go back, especially after she changes her looks that dramatically, changes her background? Who'd know to look," she added, "and for what reason?"

"I'll point out we are."

"We are because she's dead, and even then no investigator would have looked except Morris knew she'd changed her face, her body, and that's a flag.

"Larinda Mars was born Lari Jane Mercury." Eve gestured at the screen. "You were wrong. You ought to admit when you're wrong."

"I hate to be wrong. And I wasn't. You were just, in this case, more right."

Eve let out a laugh. "That actually works."

Peabody and Elsie came back with tubes of juice and soft drinks. Elsie gaped, then did a quick dance. "You hit."

"You hit," Eve corrected. "I'm impressed with your personal sensibilities."

"Regardless of this result, we'll continue the facial analysis and restructuring," De-Winter insisted.

"Knock yourself out." Eve shrugged.

"The investigation — and the family — deserve thoroughness and accuracy."

This time Eve nodded. "Now you're more right than wrong. I'll update when you're finished and satisfied. Smart work," Eve commended, studying the images. "Slick, smart work."

"Science," DeWinter corrected, but smiled with it. "Slick, smart science." Then surprised Eve by grinning at Elsie. "And superb sensibilities."

"Sold. Can you get me a couple of hard copies and a disc copy?"

Elsie all but rubbed her hands together. "You bet."

Eve cracked the tube, studied the face of

the child. "Okay, Lari Jane, let's find out what the fuck, and see if it helps tell us who killed Larinda. Thanks." She took the hard copies and the disc. "Let's go, Peabody. We have a really strange notification to deal with."

She moved fast, down the steps, through the labyrinth of the lab. "Quick run on the parents' current status."

"Working it. It pretty much slaps down any theory about poverty or street time. James Mercury," Peabody read off her PPC as they worked their way out. "Dr. Mercury — private practice pediatrician, still practicing after more than fifty years. Marilee Mercury, coowner of Kansas Gardens, a nursery and landscaping company — owns it with her sister, and has for thirty-seven years."

When she settled in the car, Peabody took a large gulp from her cherry fizzy — diet — then continued, "They own their own home — outright now — and have lived in it for about forty-five years. The other daughter, Clara, age thirty-nine, owns a twenty-two-acre farm with her husband of eleven years. Two children, one of each kind. The family comes off solid upper middle class, financially solvent, community active, and rooted."

"Look for smears. Idyllic often has a dark underbelly."

"Poking there, but I'm not getting one. Both parents have received kudos and awards in their respective professions. Both volunteer time and services for a local kids' camp."

"Death notice or missing persons on Lari Jane Mercury."

Eve pulled into Central's garage.

"Did that. Zip."

"Okay. I'll talk to the parents. See if you can hook me up with Mira for a quick consult." Eve sat a moment in her parking slot. "We know who and what she was when she died. We'll fill in who she was before. Maybe the combo helps us work through what's going to be a bitch of a suspect list."

20

After considerable time spent on a 'link conference with the next of kin, Eve worked to organize her thoughts on the way to Mira.

At least Mira's dragon of an admin gestured her straight in.

Mira sat at her desk, likely writing up some report, and held up a finger to signal she needed another moment.

She wore her rich brown hair soft around her pretty face. A suit with small gold buttons marching to the throat showed off her trim build while the strong blue brought out the softer blue of her eyes. High thin heels, watercolor swirls of blues, showed off excellent legs.

She looked female and as fashionable as any of the ladies who lunched in the most trendy bistros of Manhattan. And had the sharpest mind and steeliest spine of anyone Eve knew.

"Sorry." Mira swiveled in her chair to face

Eve. "Busy day."

"I appreciate you fitting me in."

"Never a problem. Tea?" she offered as she rose.

"No, really, I just had a hit. I won't keep you long."

Mira rose, moved to one of her two blue scoop chairs. "Larinda Mars," she said as she sat and gestured for Eve to join her.

"Or Lari Jane Mercury. We've ID'd her birth name, her family, gotten background."

"That should be helpful."

"I think." Eve sat. "DeWinter and her team were able to put together a sketch, and we hit on facial recognition. She'd scrubbed the ID back to the age of twelve. It's a costly process, and I imagine she figured she'd spent enough. And with Roarke's help we were able to locate a building she owned under the name Angela Terra."

"Sticking to planetary names."

"Yeah. Duplex, upscale neighborhood. She owns the whole building and rents the one side out through an agency that caters to short-term tenants. One night to one year. Vacationers, business travelers, like that. Her side? Loaded with things. Furniture, dust catchers, unpacked boxes of more things. It's going to take weeks to catalog.

In her office we found a series of books she'd put together, photos and data — with some personal notes — on people she considered possible marks or who became marks. While I'd say the things in her place were stuffed in there without much thought, the data — in the books and on her comp — that's meticulously organized."

"Her work as opposed to her possessions."

"Yeah. I'm thinking her work was mostly her life, plus the work was how she accumulated the possessions. Once she had them, they're just stuff. Mavis and Leonardo were in her books. Nadine. Roarke and me."

Nodding, Mira crossed her legs. "I'd have been surprised otherwise. You're all successful and/or prominent. And Nadine? Though they worked in different areas of the same business, she would be seen as a rival. Add Nadine's access to you and Roarke, to Mavis and Leonardo as well? An envied rival."

"She had a ranking system. We all ranked low, but some of the data was current, so she wasn't giving up."

"Was there anything in her background you discovered that correlated to her pathology?"

"I spoke with both her parents and her

younger sister. Upper middle-class background. Father's a private practice kid doctor, mother owns and operates a successful business, as does the sister. What I found, and my take from the interviews, says grounded, well-off financially, good, stable home."

Because she got twitchy sitting, Eve rose, moved around the room.

"What also came out? The maternal grandmother favored Lari. First grandchild, and they'd named the baby for her — more or less. Her name was Larinda. She was well-off — widowed, a kind of socialite, and she'd feed Lari all the gossip."

Mira made an agreeable sound, continued to listen.

"She kept books — along the same lines as we found. Photos, clippings, her own notes and observations. She often took Lari along to parties and events."

"And so Mars developed the enjoyment of finer things, society of a certain level, and gossip. Certainly not unusual hobbies and habits."

"Yeah. The upshot is the parents figured it was an indulgence, and the kid kept her grades up, got to experience some things. She and her sister butted heads some, but the younger one wasn't interested in the parties and glamour end. She liked athletics, and was into the whole gardening/nature thing like their mother."

"And the change, the defining moment?"

"Lari's nineteen when the grandmother drowns in her own backyard pool. No evidence of foul play. She had a habit of swimming in the middle of the night, often after she'd had a few. She'd had a few.

"Grandmother leaves the whole ball to Lari."

"Only Lari?" Mira asked.

"She tossed some small bequests to her daughter, her other granddaughter, but the big bulk, all to Lari Jane. The house, the things, the jewelry — she collected it like gumdrops — the money. About five million, and triple that with the sale of the house and the stuff."

"Young," Mira commented. "Nineteen is very young to come into that large an inheritance, with no guidance or backstops."

"She sold the house, had some of the stuff sold, some shipped off, though the family didn't know the details of that."

"She'd already shut them out of her life."

"Sounds like it. It also sounds like — to me — she already had another place, a place she sent the larger items she wanted to keep. Once the estate settled, she took off. No good-bye, no see you around, no forwarding address. Just packed up what she decided she wanted, took the money, and left. They never heard from her again."

"And there's no evidence of abuse at home?"

"Zero. The sister told me Lari played a role. That's how she put it. She played the role in school — kept her grades decent, but had no interest in anyone or anything that didn't directly benefit her. Same at home. Mostly stayed out of trouble, did what was expected — no more. And played it up with the grandmother. Where the money and influence were."

"No emotion, no familial feelings or ties," Mira commented. "Some sociopathic tendencies, certainly. To cut herself off from her entire family, without cause or explanation."

"By that time she was twenty-one," Eve continued, "and there was nothing they could do. It shows it stunned them, cut pretty deep, but that was that. She'd cancelled all her communications — 'link account, e-mail, v-mail — giving them no way to reach her."

"She had the capacity to sever all ties with her family, her roots, her friends, and her social circle. The inheritance gave her the means to do so."

"She'd been seeing someone the family thought she was fairly serious about. They liked him, thought he was a steady influence on her, as they saw she'd become — me, I think it was more started to show — the shallow, the selfish, the calculating. She didn't even bother to dump him before she left. They'd just spent the weekend together, her and the guy, at his parents' house on the river. Big weekend bash. He wakes up Sunday morning, she's gone. She went down early, told one of the servants to bring her car around, and load her weekender into it. The servant — they got a cop connection to look into it — stated she'd had more luggage in the trunk. Two others saw her get into her car and drive away. The guy, his family, the other guests, the house staff, all stated she'd appeared to be very happy, sociable, had discussed upcoming parties and events some of them planned to attend. Then she rolls out of bed, gets dressed, drives away."

Mira sat a moment, absorbing. "She may have felt something for the grandmother who indulged her, but even that would have been surface. She simply wasn't capable of forming a true connection emotionally. Without the grandmother to lavish her with things and opportunities, she had no reason to remain. Still, she was smart enough, calculating enough, to stay until she had all she wanted, to maintain a kind of illusion."

"I figure she used that couple of years to decide on who she'd become, and how. The face and body she wanted to inhabit," Eve explained. "I could probably track her from Kansas to the sort of high-end, specialist doctors who did her work, but it's not going to apply to the now."

"I could certainly help with that, but I agree. The doctor or doctors who transformed her physically were only a step along the way. The name she chose, a nod to her past, was a kind of private joke. The woman she became symbolically eliminated her sister altogether in her bio, and made herself an orphan. Indeed they meant nothing to her. She felt no bond. Her emotions, her loyalties are all self-directed. A narcissist's narcissist with the sociopath's lack of feeling. Yet in her own way, she was devoted to her work. Dedicated."

"It was her window into the blackmail."

"Yes, but she was no less devoted or dedicated," Mira insisted. "Or ambitious. The work fed her. The secrets discovered — those she revealed publicly to her audience, those she held close for profit."

"She was hitting close to a billion in personal wealth, but she didn't stop. Couldn't. Okay," Eve allowed, "devoted. Dedicated."

"And addicted," Mira added. "Not only to what she did, but to the rewards."

Eve sat back down. "The more I look at this, the more I add information, get a fuller picture of her and her . . . process, the more it's leading me away from her marks. She chose carefully. She calculated, and was damn good at it. Yeah, she had data on Roarke, for instance, and that's a rich mine. But she only gave him a single nudge — which he shut down in his Roarke way."

Mira's lips curved, her soft blue eyes danced. "I'm sure he did."

"She kept collecting data there, but it doesn't amount to anything that he doesn't want anybody to know. She couldn't dig down. So he gets the low rank. And it's my take she collected the data more for her public work than her private. When I look at the ones she exploited — though we've got a lot more to talk to now — they follow a pattern."

Mira nodded. "A secret that usually embarrasses another, and the financial power to pay easily."

"Yeah, it's a fertile field. Or the ones she

hit for favors instead of cash? Easily intimidated, those afraid to do otherwise. Not the sort who'd kill. Everybody's capable under the right circumstances, but she picked types who'd cave and cooperate. She read people and well."

"She might have had a touch of the sensitive."

As she'd thought the same, Eve gave a shrug of agreement. "So where did she make the mistake in her read? Who did she pick who could and would kill? Or is it not a mark? Someone connected to one somehow. Someone who made it his business to eliminate her."

She pushed up again, restless. "Not one of them goes to the cops. Not *one.* Even Roarke. He didn't tell me she'd tried to put the arm on him."

"Do you tell him every time a suspect threatens you?"

Hissing out a breath, Eve jammed her hands in her pockets. "I say that's different because it is. And I'm saying if somebody she successfully put the arm on had gone to the authorities, she'd be alive. Probably, hopefully, doing some time, but alive."

She paced the confines of Mira's office. "It's none of the marks I've talked to. Somebody connected maybe. I've got dozens more to look at now, but if the pattern holds . . ."

She turned back to Mira. "Looking at the pattern, what's your take?"

"Anyone under pressure may snap. Someone being victimized can strike back, end the victimization."

"When you snap, you punch somebody in the face." Frustrated, Eve jabbed the air. "Throw them out a window. Grab a heavy object and whale away. This was planned out, and carefully. But I get it. You can snap, then start planning. He had to stalk her, at least enough to get her routine. Any of the marks she shook down at that bar would know she used it, know how the place is set up. But they wouldn't know she'd be there at that particular time unless he'd clocked her habits and routines."

So Eve circled back.

"He'd been in the bar enough to have cased it, scoped out the security. What if she hadn't gone down to the restroom? Could have taken her outside," Eve continued, talking as much to herself as Mira now. "Maybe that was the preferred plan. Take her right on the street. Just a quick swipe, and keep walking."

Once again, she sat. "The bathroom was of the moment. That makes more sense. She goes down, he thinks: I can do it now. He's been sitting there, sitting there, it's building up — or maybe it's ebbing. He's starting to lose his nerve. Then she goes downstairs, and he straps on his balls and goes after her."

"The killer had the control to plan. It wasn't impulse," Mira said. "While it's certainly possible the killer and his victim just happened to be in the same place at the same time, he had a weapon. Morris's opinion is scalpel. While a medical might have a scalpel in a medical bag or kit, your witnesses never mention one. And the security feed doesn't show the person you've identified with one. So he armed himself for this purpose.

"I'd say he has medical knowledge, as the strike was accurate, and lethal. However," Mira qualified, "it takes only a little research to learn about this kind of injury, and a bit of practice to successfully inflict that injury. If he didn't have previous medical knowledge or training, he also has the intellect and control to research and practice."

"She wasn't afraid of him. He walked into a private area, one where a man isn't supposed to walk. But she wasn't afraid. She doesn't try to get her defenses out of her bag — right there where she'd been primping. She knew him, which leans back toward a mark or a connection she knew. She had an ex-lover, but he just doesn't ring. I should take a closer look there anyway, another look."

"She was confident," Mira put in. "Used to having the upper hand. She needed to have it. When she came up against someone like Roarke, or you, Nadine, she backed off. She couldn't gain the upper hand so she retreated. It's likely she believed she had that upper hand with her killer."

"Agreed. So maybe he's in her books, or it's someone at Seventy-Five, or in the business. Another lover maybe, or someone she kept on the back burner. She made a mistake with him, underestimated him. Not the snap. I can't buy the snap and blow."

"Let's use your back burner then. A slow simmer can hit boil."

"That's a cooking thing, but I get it." And, as she liked it, Eve nodded. "You think you've got it on just enough heat, right, but maybe it gets turned up while you're not paying attention. The planning time, the research, the practicing. That adds more heat. He walks in. She thinks: I've got this. Maybe she tosses out an insult or a come-on, depending where he fits. And that's the snap, the blow, the boil. But he's still smart enough to walk right out, to walk right the hell past me and out the damn door."

"I wondered how much that troubled you."

"Pisses me off." Eve expected it always would. "I don't see him. I can describe at least a dozen people in that bar from before it happened, and every single one of them left in there once I secured the scene. But I don't see him."

"You will. Despite the lack of respect you feel, justifiably, for the victim, you'll look until you see him. If he blended in the bar —"

"See, that's it." Eve pointed a finger. "He did blend. Stood out just enough because he kept the outdoor gear on, but the servers just didn't really *look* at him. He was not important. Not a celebrity."

She circled the office again as that planted in her mind. "A well-known figure doesn't risk that kind of public display. Sitting there like that in a bar where somebody might look, might see. Just like the wits he merged with when they left. One of them looked enough to see a little, but didn't get a buzz. Not a famous face. I'm bumping the famous faces down," she decided on the spot. "Connected to, possible. One of the ones, the unimportant types, she intimidated. That's possible. A bad read on her part, but possible. You can't hit every time, right? Somebody connected to, or a wrong read that simmered and boiled. Snap. That's the direction."

She focused on Mira again. "Sorry. I said I wouldn't keep you long, and I've gone overtime. I'm just thinking out loud now."

"The process is very interesting. I'm finding myself seeing exactly what you're thinking and why. Just as I find myself agreeing with that direction. We may both be wrong, but it fits. He's old enough to control impulse, educated enough to have that medical knowledge or to have the skills and intelligence to gain it. Patient enough to learn her routine. And yes, very likely, able to easily blend into a crowd at an upscale, trendy bar. I'll add, as he had or acquired this medical knowledge, he could have acquired the same to have killed her more quickly."

"She bled to death. She bled people. I'd say he appreciated the symbolism."

"I absolutely agree. That wasn't random. Nothing here was random."

"No. I've got to get on this. I appreciate the time."

"If you find more, send it to me. I'll try to add some meat to the profile."

"I will. Thanks." She started for the door, stopped. "You and Mr. Mira weren't in her books."

"Why would we be?"

"Besides being connected to me, Nadine, Mavis, you're at the top of your profession — a kind of celebrity — you're socially active and well connected, financially solid."

"I doubt my profession held much interest for her."

"I disagree, majorly, there. You know secrets, and she was dedicated and devoted to uncovering secrets. You know a lot of mine."

"Eve. I'd never betray your confidence."

"I know that. I never doubt that. She didn't know that, but you weren't in her books. Here's why. She looked at you, and at Mr. Mira, and she saw the unassailable. You weren't worth the time or trouble. That's not just why you're at the top of your profession. It's why you, both of you, are who and what you are."

Touched, deeply, Mira rose. "I want you to know, if she had — as you put it — tried to put the arm on me or Dennis, we would have come to you. Without hesitation."

"I know that, too. So, good. Thanks again."

When Eve left, Mira sat back down, smiled to herself. Trust built slowly for some, but once constructed, became strong as steel.

Eve went straight back to Homicide, turned to her office in time to see Santiago stroll out of it.

"What were you doing in there?"

He stopped short at her tone. "Ah, giving Peabody a hand. Evidence boxes. On your desk."

Her eyes stayed narrowed. "Yeah?"

"Well, yeah. A couple of them, and they had some weight."

"You've got nothing else to do?"

"We just closed one. Carmichael's writing it up."

Since they stood there, and she continued to give him the hard eye, Santiago ran it down.

"Guy breaks into a loft in SoHo. Female occupant is home sick instead of at work as she normally would've been at that time of day. She wakes up while the thief's banging around unhooking electronics, comes out of the bedroom upstairs thinking it's her co-hab. She's half naked, just wearing this big T-shirt. Thief's coming up, goes for her, knocks her around a little, as she's medicated. But she bounces back and beats the crap out of him."

A hint of admiration glinted in his eyes.

"Turns out she's a boxer — competitor and an instructor at a local gym. She gives him a solid roundhouse, and he takes a header down the stairs, breaks his neck. She calls it in."

"How fast?" Eve asked, mostly for form.

"Nine-one-one came in under two minutes after TOD. Uniforms respond, secure the scene. Her statement holds up, boss, and it reads self-defense. The DB has a sheet a mile wide. B and E — he goes for female households — assaults, again he goes for women. The locks and security were compromised, he'd piled up all the easily portable electronics and valuables on the first floor. Had an empty sack with him going up, and dropped it when he charged her. Looks like he tripped over it when she fought back.

"She took some solid hits in the first round," he added, with that admiration glinting again, "but she came back at him. She says he turned to run away, got his feet tangled in the sack, and took the dive down. That's how it reads."

Eve folded her arms. "KO'd the DB."

"You got it."

"Okay. What about the kid? The rape and stabbing."

"You had the right angle, boss. I was able

to talk straight to the dad, and when we brought Reo in, between her and Carmichael — and the dad again — we got the mother to tell the truth. Reo had to practically sign off in blood for the mom, but we got it worked out, we closed it."

"How's the kid?"

"Medicals say she'll be fine. Rape counselor's working with her and the mom. She's got good parents. She'll get through."

"Okay. Beat it."

She turned into her office, studied the boxes on her desk. Confirming Santiago's statement, but still.

She closed and locked her door. She walked to the AutoChef, rolled her shoulders, lifted it high enough to see the bottom, where she'd used black tape to affix her secret candy bar. She'd tried hiding it *in* the AC, programming it as something healthy and unappealing. That hadn't fooled the infamous Candy Thief.

But so far, her secret stash remained. Satisfied, she set the machine down again, and rolled her shoulders one more time. The ancient AC weighed a freaking ton.

Which might be why the Candy Thief had yet to find her newest hiding place.

Score one for Dallas, she thought, and programmed coffee.

She took the mug to the door, unlocked it before anyone noticed.

Sitting, she considered the books. The slow simmer — if that theory held — would have started there, but likely graduated to the top rating and the comp ledger.

Unless the killer was never a target, but someone connected to one. She stacked the books on the floor, broke the seal on the top one, brought the ledger up on her comp.

And heard the brisk *click* of heels coming toward her office.

Nadine walked in.

"What did you bribe the bullpen with?"

"I went for the classic."

"What kind of donuts?"

"Variety."

When Eve simply sat, head angled, Nadine reached into her enormous purse, pulled out a small take-out bag. "Separated yours."

"Smart." Eve looked in, sniffed. The scent of yeast and sugar stirred the appetite she'd forgotten through the day. She took the fat, golden pastry out, bit in. Found cream.

Bonus.

"You earned a seat."

Nadine glanced dubiously at the visitor's chair. "I earned better than that."

With a shrug, Eve rose, gave Nadine her desk chair.

"I'll go first," Nadine said. "There's a lot more underlying animosity mixed with trepidation about Mars than I knew. Most just kept their heads down with her. I may not be a cop, but I report on them. I'm going to say I didn't brush up against anyone who appears to have had enough animosity or trepidation to kill her."

"People have a tendency to be careful how they appear to cops and those who report on them."

"True, but good cops, and good reporters, can see through that. I know a lot of these people personally, and I'm torn about this, but I'm going to give you a couple more names of people I think she might have been blackmailing."

"Okay."

"In addition to that, I have a source at Seventy-Five who's romantically involved with someone at *Knight at Night.* Mars made herself at home over there, according to my source, more than anyone could figure. She'd breeze in and out, and often timed it when Annie had interviews or meetings with A-list celebs. She'd end up with her own little snippets and scoops that way. I know Annie, and like her. I especially like Bic, her partner. It's hard to see Annie giving someone like Mars that kind of access unless she was being pressured."

"Okay," Eve said again.

Nadine's gaze sharpened, catlike. "And you already knew that, or some of it. It's common knowledge in our world that Mars was screwing around with Mitch L. Day, and you already know Day's wife gave him the boot, and Mars dumped him — just as you've likely concluded by now Mitch couldn't plan a two-car parade much less a murder. So, let's try the research portion."

Nadine pointed toward the AutoChef. Eve shrugged.

"My team's been going at this hard, and I picked up the shovel myself. Dig down and Mars's data doesn't hold. The background, lineage, education, it all starts to shake and slide if you get far enough below the surface. I've got some more work to do, but I'm going to have to break that story within a day or two, before someone beats me to it."

Nadine came back with her coffee, sat down. "I'm not too worried, as there's not much reason for another reporter to dig down too deep, but a good one could smell something and keep going. If Mars is going to be exposed, Channel Seventy-Five needs to do it, or we look like fools."

Logical, Eve thought. Hard to argue with logic — and what Nadine and her team were finding on their own. "You've talked to the big guns about it?"

"Had to. I can't hold something like this. The woman we're now officially mourning, one who had a prime spot on our network, was a fraud. Worse. The worse will start tumbling, too. I need you to give me the go."

"Can't do it. Yet," Eve added before Nadine exploded. "Think of it this way: When I can give you the go, you'll be able to break bigger. We'll have arrested or at least detained a suspect in Mars's murder, and part of what led the investigation to that suspect is you and your team's independent investigation."

Nadine narrowed her eyes again. "Would that be accurate?"

"It's not inaccurate. You're here corroborating information and data that my investigation has found, and is pursuing. And when I can, I'll give you details on how our investigation, with the skills and dedication of various arms of the NYPSD, uncovered the truth about the victim and identified her killer."

Nadine held up a finger. "A one-on-one, and a full-spot interview on *Now.*"

"Agreed." With DeWinter, Eve thought, or Elsie Kendrick. But she wouldn't add that just yet.

"That was too easy."

"Maybe it's the donut. Or maybe it's because this one's different. Off the record, Nadine."

Nadine knocked her fists against her temples in frustration. "You ought to be bringing me donuts. Off the damn record."

"She had another place, and in her other place she had records and lists and books. Of her marks, of the transactions. Her data on them, the meets. And in the books were pages dedicated to individual potential marks. Photos — some of which appear to have been taken without the person's knowledge — articles, interviews, connections to other people. They're ranked low to high — for potential. You're in there."

"What?" Nadine came straight out of the chair. *"What?"*

"She looked into you, fairly hard, and she's thorough. She lists your favorite shops, restaurants, where you work out, where you buy cop-bribing donuts. And she has a list of people in those places she's either talked to about you, or hopes to find something on so they'll dish it out on you."

"That goes too far. That fucking bitch."

"You're mine."

"What?" Nadine stopped pacing.

"According to Mars you're Dallas's bitch. And I don't think she was talking sexy three-way on that."

Nadine kicked at the visitor's chair with a foot clad in a skyscraper red heel. "I wish she was still alive so I could slap her stupid."

"You make a lousy bitch then. A good, solid bitch punches. Slaps are for little girls."

"Slaps are humiliating for the slapee — and don't bruise the slapper's knuckles." Stunned and angry enough to forget about the ass-biting properties of the visitor's chair, Nadine dropped down into it. "She never approached me other than what I told you before. I swear. I'd have told you. I told her to go to hell, basically, had that recording to back it up. Thought that was that."

"I got that. I'd have gotten that even if she didn't have the ranking system, and you never rated above a one. But she tried, even after you metaphorically slapped her. She talked to some guy you dated in college. Scotty. How could you have dated some dude who called himself Scotty and sells used sporting equipment in a mall in Poughkeepsie?"

"Because he was gorgeous, and I only dated him for . . ." Nadine bapped her fists against her temples again. "Are you kidding me?"

"He said you were a bitch, too. Ambitious and nosy."

"He would," Nadine shot back.

"She got a few people you've pushed, cornered, harangued by doing your job to say some uncomplimentary things along the way."

That earned no more than a satisfied smirk. "That means I *did* my job."

"But she couldn't get any solid dirt. She threw out a wide net, and she got lucky with plenty."

"How many books like that?"

Eve pointed to the boxes on the floor by her desk, and Nadine leaped up.

"You have to let me see them."

"No."

"Damn it. At least let me see what she gathered on me."

"I can't, and you know I can't. What I'm telling you here is between friends. Mavis is in there, and Leonardo. She even has data on Bella — where she plays, where she takes her baby classes."

At her sides, Nadine's hands balled into fists. "Maybe I would have bruised my knuckles on her bitch face. For that, maybe I would have."

"And maybe I feel the same, but somewhere in here, in the other records of her targets, her marks, those connected to them, is her killer. It's my job to find him, to stand for her and bring her killer to justice. She deserved a few punches in the face, and some years in a cage. She didn't deserve to bleed out on the floor of a bar."

To calm herself, Nadine took two long breaths. "You're in there, too, aren't you?"

"Yeah."

"And Roarke. Of course Roarke." Taking another breath, Nadine unclenched her fists. "If you have another avenue you want me to explore, I'll go there. Anything I can do, or have my team do. Not only for the story, and not for her. You have to stand for her. I don't. But I'll sure as hell stand with you and whoever else is in those books."

And that, Eve thought, was a primary reason they were friends.

"Nudge your source at Seventy-Five. It could be interesting to get a different perspective on Knight Productions. I'll be going through the data we collected, and may find others she targeted there. And at Seventy-Five. And see what you can find about Missy Lee Durante."

"The actress?"

"She's clear, but she has a lot of people surrounding her. Family, managers, hangers-on. A lot of people connected to her show and her career who might have been targets, or objected to her being targeted."

"We'll get right on it."

"You heading down to the garage?"

"Looks like."

"Good." Eve swung on her coat, grabbed a file bag, hefted one of the boxes. "I'm going to work at home, in the quiet. Grab the other box."

Nadine bent down, lifted it two inches. "It's heavy!"

"Put your back into it, bitch."

Nadine hauled it up, teetered a little. "Let me show you how this is done."

Struggling some, she walked out with Eve, then angled toward Baxter's desk. She didn't flutter her lashes, Eve noted, but it was implied.

Baxter swiveled away from his work, rose. "Hey, let me get that for you."

"Thanks. I was going to help Dallas take all this down to her car."

"Too heavy for you."

Eve didn't roll her eyes, but it was implied. "Hold on a minute." She carted her box, which was apparently not too heavy for her, to Peabody's desk. "Taking these home to work. Keep on the comp data, and keep a running loop on it to me. Clock out at end of shift."

"I don't think I'll make a serious dent by then."

"Clock out. You can work at home on some of it." She shifted the weight of the box. The damn thing *was* heavy. "Let's go."

21

Against the snapping cold, Eve carried the first box into the house. She had a Summerset snark set and felt annoyance when she found the foyer empty, and her snark at the ready.

Still, without him there, she didn't feel honor bound to cart the damn box up the stairs, and walked back to the elevator, used the box to hold the door open until she went back for the second.

Then, shoving them both in, stepped in and ordered her office. She decided Summerset would likely be dealing with packing. He'd need at least a dozen black suits, right? He probably sat on the beach wearing one, with a carefully knotted tie.

At least, she didn't want to imagine him wearing anything else. Or less.

The idea made her shudder.

When the elevator opened, she shoved the boxes out. She bent to lift one, heard

Roarke's voice from his adjoining office.

Leaving the boxes where they were, she crossed over.

"I'm looking at it now, yes," he said into the 'link as he studied some sort of schematic on screen. "Hold a moment." He put the 'link on pause. "You're earlier than I expected."

"You, too."

"I only got here shortly ago."

Long enough, she thought, to have taken off his jacket and tie, rolled up his sleeves, and tied back his hair.

The cat stretched across his command center, yawned.

"Just a bit of work I wanted to handle in the quiet."

"Same here."

"I should be wrapped up with this in about twenty minutes."

"Okay." She started to step back. "Summerset packing?"

"Unpacking by now, I'd hope. We have weather coming in late tonight into the morning. I nudged him along."

She stopped stepping back. " 'Along' as in out? Out of the house?"

"I didn't like the idea of him flying out in bad weather, so persuaded him to leave today."

Eve held up a hand like a stop sign. "You're saying — let's be absolutely clear — this house is Summerset-free?"

"I expect he and Ivanna are enjoying blue skies and balmy breezes, so yes."

"Okay. Okay," she repeated. "Don't let me interrupt."

She moved just out of his eyeline, heard him go back to the 'link. And boogied her way back to the elevator with the cat trotting behind her. She started to pick up a box, straightened again.

And decided to go with impulse.

Roarke finished the meeting. It ran a bit longer than he'd estimated, but the small changes he and the engineer made would, he was sure, be worth the time and trouble.

Plus, though he had a few things that could keep him busy, this cleared his slate enough he could see what his wife was up to.

He walked in, glanced at her board, noted some updates, then looked toward her command center.

She sat, in nothing but a couple of tiny swaths of lace, purple boots propped on the desk. When his gaze traveled up, up those long, bare legs, over the lean torso, those firm, lace-frothed breasts, to meet hers, she smiled.

"I figured since I've got the boots anyway, they ought to get some wear."

His wife, Roarke thought, his cop, so often a creature of habit and straight lines, could and did pull out the most fascinating curves.

"They look . . . perfect."

She jiggled one. "Comfortable, too. You all done?"

"Oh, I believe I'm just about to start."

He crossed over, trailed a finger up her leg. "How about you?"

"I've got work that's going to keep me chained here for hours. No reason I can't take a little personal time first."

"Good, as I believe this is going to be very personal."

She smiled again. "Want to sit on my lap?"

He laughed and simply plucked her out of the chair and off her feet. In response, she hooked her legs around his waist.

"I had a donut," she warned, "and came home to a Summerset-free zone. I'm riding a high."

"Let's see if we can keep you there."

He took her mouth, ferociously. With her legs clamped tight, she dragged at the leather strip so she could fill her hands with his hair. Then she levered her hands between them to fight with buttons until she got to skin.

She could luxuriate there, mouth feeding on mouth, skin pressed hot to skin, and his fingers, long and strong, sliding over and under lace.

The big house empty around them, and all the world locked outside.

When he set her on the command center, she kept her legs hooked to bring him close. Reaching up, she tugged his shirt away before she nipped her teeth at his throat.

"Better than a donut," she murmured.

His hands played over her, curves and angles, tough and smooth. He took her lips again, more tenderly now, and let the taste of her fill him, fill him even as it stirred deeper cravings.

He'd planned to set up a romantic meal before she got home — candles and wine, music playing low, and a fire simmering. A dance with her, a seduction, a long, slow build to passion.

A quiet intimacy before death and duty pulled them both back in.

Instead she'd seduced him, in a finger snap, with humor and sex — so intimately theirs.

A part of him wished he could hold on, just endlessly hold on to this moment. But he contented himself, was more than content, to know there would be others, scores of other moments.

Intimately theirs.

He trailed his fingers over the lace, over those firm breasts, teasing them both, then flicked open the tiny front hook to free her to his hands.

And when her heartbeat quickened, to his mouth.

Her breath caught. It always did. That rush, that *punch* of feelings, the impossible knots of them tangled in that mad swirl of sensation as he took her over as no one else ever had, ever could.

Just him, only him, the one who knew her, knew her mind, her body, her often shaky soul. And loved her, simply loved her.

That, just that? The miracle in her life.

She let him take, surrendered herself to his needs and to her own, as here, always here, they became one and the same. Let herself tremble and ache as those hands, that mouth, possessed.

Then as they roamed over her body, roamed down.

His thumbs gliding along those sensitive lines where the white lace rode high, his tongue sliding under where it lay over her center turned the trembles into shudders. And shudders to writhing as he slowly, so slowly, eased the lace lower.

The pleasure all but drowned her, and still he took her down, further down, into the thick and the hot and the glorious. Soft, slow, dreamy touches that left her utterly helpless.

Blissfully so.

He loved the sound she made, between a moan and a purr, when she was steeped in what he gave her, when she yielded to herself. Then the explosion of her, the break and shock when, with fingers or tongue or both, he slid into the hot and wet.

Her body arched, it quaked as she rode that wild burst of release. Her hands flailed, then gripped the edges of the counter as he pushed her higher, gave her more until she cried out once, twice.

Her world reeled and spun, and there was nothing in it but him. She arched up, wrapped around him, her breath ragged, her skin slick. Clinging there, she gathered herself while his lips pressed to her throat.

Then her hands grappled with his belt, tugged. "I want." She tossed her head back, met those wild blue eyes. "I want."

He kissed her, and the ferocity was back. "I want."

One and the same.

She dragged at his zipper, desperate now, greedy now. Her hands raced over his chest, his back, his hips, as he stripped.

As desperate, as greedy as she, he pushed her back, drove into her. Thrusting hard, deep, over and over, with her long legs hooked around him like chains so he was steeped, he was lost. With his blood racing under his skin, her hands clutched in his hair, her eyes fixed on his, he let himself go into the madness.

Then through it, with her, into the bliss.

When her body went lax, he simply had no choice but to drop his weight on her. He wasn't sure he had a muscle or bone left in him.

Her voice, when she spoke, came both husky and smug.

"Command center sex. I've been saving it up."

"Saving it up?" He wondered if his brains had been scrambled.

"Until the first Summerset-free night. It was worth it."

He managed a laugh. "I'm in no position to argue."

"Maybe we could just slide to the floor, then try to get up again in two or three days." She locked her arms around him a moment in a tight hug. "Except."

"Except." He eased up enough to look down at her. "You know, now every time

Summerset goes on holiday, I'll be expecting command center sex."

"I figure we mix it up, that way you'll never know." After a long sigh, she poked a finger into his chest. "I've got to get dressed. I've got that work."

He reached over, picked up a discarded scrap of lace, offered it.

"Get real, pal. I can't work in that. Or these purple boots."

"I have a new and extreme fondness for those boots. What do you say we shower, get into comfortable clothes. We can have a meal while you catch me up on the investigation."

"I want spaghetti, and big, fat meatballs."

"I could use the same."

He made her laugh by plucking her up again, tossing her over his shoulder before he started out of the room.

"Now you're looking for shower sex."

"And I know just where to find it."

Over the meal, and a little wine, she filled him in and explained how she intended to approach the data.

"I need to pull out any five ratings from the books, cross-check them with the financial ledger. Some of them might not have made the initial payment, and they all have to be checked. Not all of them are from New York, or New Jersey, or within an easy distance. She hit some, I've already seen, from other areas, even out of the country. I need to separate those out, check travel."

They cleared the table together. "I can help with that."

"I was hoping you would. It's going to be a long slog. I want to look for anybody we might be able to connect with Lari Jane Mercury. It's a long shot she dipped into that pool, but I'm betting she started this business of hers a long time back. Why else change her face? She was of age, nobody could have forced her back to Kansas."

"It's just as likely, for someone like her, the appeal of remaking herself, sloughing off all the old — and improving on her looks was enough."

"She looked okay before, but yeah. Yeah, vanity. She died a knockout. Still, it's a thread to tug."

With the dishes in the machine, she walked back into the office where the cat lay in front of the fire, his back to the room.

"I'm pretty good at reading Galahad's body language. He's a little pissed off at us."

Roarke gave the cat a thoughtful study. "Well, we did pay more attention to each other than we did to him."

"He was working with you when I got here."

"He was, wasn't he? And how did we thank him? We had command center and shower sex, pasta and meatballs, and he got low-cal kibble."

Put that way, it sounded just wrong.

"Maybe a little tuna wouldn't hurt. It makes us patsies," Eve admitted, "but . . ."

"We are his patsies, aren't we? I'll get it," Roarke told her. "You can start setting us up, and I expect we'll need a pot of coffee."

"Got it covered." She walked over to the cat, stared down at him as he studiously ignored her. "Do you want tuna or not, fat boy?"

He rolled over, eyed her, eyed Roarke. Then followed Roarke into the kitchen as if doing them a favor.

"Patsies," Eve grumbled, walking over to program the coffee and set up.

They fell into the rhythm of the work. It could still surprise her how easily he adapted to the elemental tedium of cop drudgery. The reading, analyzing, checking, rechecking, all that comprised so much of the job.

He worked on her auxiliary while the tuna-content cat dozed on her sleep chair.

For nearly an hour they worked in silence, each studying and assessing the names, the lives, of those Mars had targeted.

"I'm sending you two batches," Roarke told her. "Those I find more than an hour's commute outside the city, and a second, smaller group who ranked a five and aren't on her financial ledger."

She leaned back, poured more coffee for both of them. "I'll fold it into what I have. Business-brain question."

"I happen to have one of those."

"What I'm seeing here when you go through her payment schedules are some she started collecting from four or five years ago. A scattering of six years ago. And there are some names that drop off. A check shows me two of them are deceased, but the others aren't. She marks the last payment shown with a red check mark. When I add them up, the cumulative amounts vary, just as the monthly payments varied, so that eliminates a final amount she might have designated."

"But it wouldn't." He picked up the coffee. "Not if it was a final amount she designated per individual, calculating just how much they might pay before balking or becoming angry or despairing enough to do as you wish they had at the start. Go to the authorities."

"Okay, I was playing with that. She looked at the individual, calculated how much she could suck out of them, and/or how long she could so suck, before they started to waver. And/or again, she cut them loose when she sensed she was reaching that threshold."

"Either/or," he agreed. "It makes good business sense. Know when to settle and move on. From what I'm seeing, she had a head for it. Determine how much a target would pay per month, how long they would pay, and if and when they would reach their limit."

"Maybe she miscalculated with one, and he hit his limit."

"Which, logically, eliminates those with a red check mark from your suspect list."

"Unless." Calculating, she drank coffee. "One who she cut loose when he hit that threshold, or was, in her estimation, approaching it, is connected in some way to another target. Target A is now off the hook — but you'd simmer awhile, right? You've shelled out in the neighborhood of a half million or more to this conniving bitch. It's a pisser. Then you find out Target B — maybe a friend, an associate, a relative — is being skinned, and the simmer goes to boil.

It's never going to stop, you think, never going to stop until *she*'s stopped."

"Interesting, and logical." He leaned toward her, tapped the side of her head. "Cop brain."

"Yeah, and the cop brain says even the dead ones can't be eliminated because someone connected to one of them might have found out, sought revenge. She knew the killer, I'm sure of that, but she knew a lot of people.

"I need a minute."

She rose, paced, circled her board. Roarke took the minute with her, drank his coffee.

"It's not going to be the data," she decided. "It's not going to be someone she used for information."

"Why not?"

"When you reach the threshold there, you're more likely to pack it in. Get yourself fired or transferred, find a way to be of less use to her. Not impossible you decide to kill her to end it, but she went for lower-level there, the easily intimidated, the rank and file most don't notice. And I'm betting some of those she used enjoyed it. Like playing spy — and what's the big deal? Wouldn't surprise me to find out she fed the source now and then, too. Slip them a little cash, keep them going."

She circled again. "She did that now and then — has it deducted as an expense. Like she deducted the expense of the two street LCs she paid to have sex with Bellami. Likely they knew he was drugged. Maybe they didn't care, or maybe they thought that's how he wanted it."

"You'll interview them."

"Yeah, since she has their names listed. And the guy she blackmailed into dosing Bellami's drink, I'll do more than interview him."

"Good news, blackmail days are over," Roarke said, "bad news, you're under arrest."

"I'll look forward to that." Hands on her hips, she stared at her board, the faces. Shook her head. "Miscalculation on Mars's part, maybe. Maybe, but she had a knack, like you said. She was damn good at this. The people she was bleeding? It's upsetting, sure, it's a pisser, yeah, but roughly eight thousand a month, a half million over a period of years? It's no big. It doesn't change their standard of living."

"It's insulting."

"If it's so insulting, you stop or you never start. She gave you a little nudge, and you slapped her back — and she stepped off. Because she read you right. If it's so insulting, you tell her go ahead, try it. She'd have hit that a time or two and done just what she did with you. She stepped off."

Eve walked back, dropped into her chair, blew out a breath. "Damn it."

"You're saying you don't think her killer's in this mass of books and ledgers."

"Somewhere," she muttered. "Somewhere. I just — It's not clicking. Why kill her? Missy Lee had that right. You'd know the cops would come into it. You don't know she's got a secret place under another name. You'd have to figure the cops would find what we found, some sort of record, and we'd uncover your secret anyway. Killing her risks exposure, too."

"Fight-or-flight's not logical but instinctive. He snaps."

"But he didn't," she insisted. "I went around this with Mira when she used that same term. He planned, he calculated, he timed, he prepared. This wasn't a crime of passion, but of cold calculation. He's not going to have been a target. I just don't see it. But he'll be connected to one. He'll care about one. And he has to be close enough to know the target's being exploited. A spouse, a relative, a friend, a trusted coworker. One who decided the target could weather the exposure of the secret if it came out, but shouldn't bear the stress, the insult. He decided for them."

Eve tapped a finger on one of the open books. "He'd handle it, take care of it, he'd clear it up."

"Because that's what he does?" Roarke prompted. "Handles things for this person? Takes care of this person?"

"Does or wants to. Killer's male — determined. Target's most likely female, or possibly a male perceived by the killer as vulnerable, too weak to take care of himself. I'm leaning female, and the killer's the shiny knight."

"That's white knight, in shining armor."

"If the knight's wearing the armor, he's shiny. If he's not, he's probably got a spear in his guts anyway."

Roarke hesitated only a moment, then decided, "Inarguable."

"Let's try this. We'll separate the female targets, then look for connected males. Spouses, fathers, brothers, partners, handlers. Like Missy Lee: her father — though he comes off a weak sister to me — her business manager, her agent. I'm leaning away from her only because she comes off as someone who knows how to keep a secret — you tell no one."

"All right. Hold on." His fingers raced

over his keyboard. "Done," he told her. "Both machines."

"I could've done my own."

"Now you don't have to."

She scowled over it for a moment, then turned to do the work.

"Connections," she said again. "There are scores of them in the books — celebrities with their entourages, high-end execs with their staffs. You and me rate our own book, and plenty of connections. Nadine, Mavis, Summerset, Whitney, Caro. Even the red dress earned a few pages."

Barely listening, he glanced up. "Red dress?"

"I . . . Just thinking out loud."

He read it on her face. "Magdelana?"

"It's not important. I didn't mean to bring it up."

He reached over, laid a hand on hers. "I'm sorry." Always would be.

"It's not important. Really, just thinking out loud." But he, deliberately, turned her hand over, intertwined their fingers in a firm grip.

"Okay." Better to get it out, she decided, as those blue eyes held hers just as his hand held hers. She didn't think it would fester, but . . . "Mars did some research on her, speculated about the two of you. It looks like she considered taking a pass or two in that direction to see what she could stir up, but then Magdelana left town, and that's that.

"That's that," Eve repeated.

"We're both fully aware Magdelana would have enjoyed using Mars, as Mars used her, to stir things up. I regret even the possibility of that."

"It didn't happen. Mars didn't make her move there soon enough, and Magdelana's gone."

"She is, and will stay gone." When he hesitated, just a fraction of a second, Eve's hand stiffened in his.

"You've got something you're not telling me."

"I detest bringing her into our lives even for an instant, but you should know. She arrived in Port-au-Prince a few days ago."

"You're keeping tabs on her?" Eve said carefully.

"I'm not, no. I don't give a bleeding, buggering fuck where she is or what she's up to." Temper, brutally cold, edged his voice. "But I do keep track of my holdings, and if my directives are met. Perhaps testing the waters, or my reach, she attempted to stay in my hotel there in the company of another guest. As per my orders, she was turned out and away."

He let out a breath. "I hope you can take at least some satisfaction from knowing security very firmly showed her the door."

"More than some. Is there feed? Might be fun to watch."

He smiled, but it didn't reach those marvelous eyes. "I promise you, she won't touch you or anything of ours again."

"It doesn't matter. She doesn't matter." In saying it, Eve realized she meant it. "Seeing her in the book gave me a bad half minute. Maybe a minute and a half," she corrected as he simply looked at her. "We're good."

"She doesn't matter," Roarke echoed. "All that does matter to me is right here."

Maybe it hurt him more, she thought, that faint shadow Magdelana cast. So she shrugged. "I gotta figure that's true the way you stock my closet with boots."

He murmured to her in Irish as he kissed the hand he held. She'd heard him tell her he loved her in his heart's tongue often enough to recognize the words.

The way he said it, the way he looked at her when he did, made her throat ache. She leaned over, kissed him, then pulled back before she got sloppy.

"Okay, that's enough sap. We're working

here. Connections," she repeated.

The comm she'd brought in with her signaled.

"Crap. Crap." She snatched it up, frowned. "Baxter," she said, and responded. "Dallas."

"Boss, we caught one. I think it links to yours."

"Who's the vic?"

"Female vic ID'd as Kellie Lowry, she's employed by Knight Productions. We're outside 30 Rock now, and the scene's secure."

"I'm — we're," she corrected when Roarke raised his eyebrows, "on our way. Do you have an on-scene determination on COD?"

"Yeah. It probably has to do with the gash in her right thigh. She bled out. Coincidence? I don't think so."

"Hold the line," Eve told him, and ended the communication.

"She's not on the list," Roarke told Eve before she could do a search of her own. "We could go through the books, but I assume you want to get there quickly."

"Let's move."

She retrieved her badge, her weapon, changed skids for boots before rushing down to where Roarke already had her vehicle waiting. "You can drive," she said. "I want more info on the vic."

She pulled out her PPC as he drove, keyed in the data she had. "Lowry, Kellie, age twenty-four, unmarried, no offspring. Employed by Knight Productions for two and a half years. Assistant to an assistant producer. Residence in the West Nineties, born in Queens, studied broadcasting at NYU. No criminal."

She lowered the handheld. "Why does he kill her? Was she a source, an accomplice who had to be cut off? Did she see or hear something? Knight was a target, Mars — according to Nadine's source — breezed in and out of the studio at will, and often when someone screen and gossip worthy was there. Somebody fed her that info. Might have been Knight herself, but she never mentioned that and she told me things a lot more damaging. Maybe Mars had something on Lowry. The killer, protecting Knight, kills them both."

"Knight's longtime partner?"

"He's protective, devoted. He loves her. But . . . he respects her. At least that was my sense. Does the shiny knight respect the — what's it? Maiden?"

"Love and devotion do not preclude respect."

"No, but a couple of murders do, at least

in my book."

Roarke pulled up to the police barricades blocking off Rockefeller Center at Forty-ninth.

People massed. Plenty of tourists, she thought as she badged them through and worked her way to the crime scene tape, the shields erected. Tourists who'd come out on a cold night to watch the skaters, eat hot pretzels from a cart, throng along the gardens, the shops.

And now got the bonus of a murder to tell their friends back home about.

She ducked under the tape, pushed through the shield.

Lowry's long, wavy black hair spread like wings over the sidewalk. She lay faceup, brown eyes staring out of a pretty face gone slack with death. It bore a raw, bruising scrape on the right side of the forehead, another on the right cheek. Blood soaked her cheerfully flowered pants. The trail of blood, much of it smeared by foot traffic, ran east.

"TOD's nineteen-eighteen, LT," Baxter told her. "We've got a couple wits inside the lobby who saw her go down, tried to help her. They turned her over."

"Yeah, I see where she hit the pavement." She crouched down, sealed her hands, then carefully spread the slice in the bloody pants to examine the wound. "It looks pretty deep. He wasn't taking chances."

Looking up, she studied the blood trail. "How far did she get?"

"Sir, the blood trail starts fifteen feet, seven inches from the main doors." Trueheart gestured back. "Security has her logging out of Knight Productions at nineteen-oh-eight."

"Alone?"

"The guard's still at the desk inside. He doesn't have anyone logging out with her. I went up to Knight Productions, inquired. She left alone according to the swipe log up there. And I brought down a coworker — a friend, Lieutenant. One of the vic's roommates. I've got her with a uniform. She spoke with the victim before she left. She's pretty broken up."

"Any shot on security feed?"

"In the lobby — we've got that, and she walked out alone," Baxter told her. "Out here — nada. She was about a couple feet out of range of the door cams."

"He'd have known." Looking up, Eve visualized it. "Had to know when she was coming out, that she — at least usually — came out alone. Walking toward her, that's how it looks, weapon down at his side. Does he bump into her? Does he just give her the slash? Either way, he can just keep walking.

"Your wits give you anything?"

"A couple of guys here from Boston. A pal's getting married. They noticed her staggering, thought she'd had one too many. She bumped into some people, kept staggering, then went down. When she hit, they were right behind her. Still thought she was drunk, until they tried to help, turned her over. Saw the blood, called for a cop, a medic. She was gone before either got here."

Slick, fast, done, Eve thought.

"Did you check the purse, that bag?"

"Gym bag — yoga-type clothes, confirmed by office pal. She had a seven-thirty yoga class. A couple blocks away," Trueheart added. "She's got her wallet, her 'link, a mini tablet, her swipe ID for work, and what we assume are her apartment keys. The friend can confirm that. Other personal items, you know, the makeup and hair stuff."

Nodding, Eve checked her wrist unit. She'd hoped Peabody would arrive before she took the roommate.

"You're right." Eve pushed to her feet. "This connects to mine, no way around it. I'm going to step on your toes, Baxter."

He lifted his shoulders, dropped them. "Figured. You want the assist?"

"I do. Peabody's on the way. Trueheart, since the roommate's already talked to you, we'll take her together. You can call it, Baxter. Bagged and tagged, and the sweepers are going to want to do what they do."

"I'll take care of it."

She glanced around, surprised not to find Roarke behind her.

"Whenever Roarke gets back from wherever, tell him —"

She broke off as he stepped inside the shield with a take-out tray of coffee. "It's a cold night," he said.

"You are the man." Baxter helped himself.

"You can be the man with Baxter," she told Roarke. "I have statements to take inside. With me, Trueheart."

They'd blocked off the front lobby area, detouring anyone leaving or coming in for business to alternates.

Eve saw the two male witnesses sitting together with a uniform, and the female, weeping silently, several feet away with another.

"What's her name?"

"Terren Alta."

Eve walked to her. "Miss Alta, I'm Lieutenant Dallas. I'm sorry for your loss."

"Okay." The tears spilled and flowed. "They said I can't tag her mom. Her mom's really nice. We go over and have dinner sometimes."

Trueheart signaled for the uniform to leave, moved in. "Don't worry, Terren. We'll talk to her mom."

"Kellie's just . . . I don't feel like it's real, but I can't stop crying."

"You talked to her before she left tonight." Eve sat.

"Yeah. She said she was heading to yoga, and I said, see you at home. I'm working on *The Glory Hour.* We come into work and leave together otherwise, but I got assigned to *The Glory Hour.* It's new this winter, so I don't come in until later, and don't leave until nine-thirty. Sometimes ten.

"She's my roommate. When Kendra moved out and in with her boyfriend, Haley and I needed another roommate. Kellie and I got to be friends at work, and she was commuting from her mom's in Queens because she couldn't afford a place on her own, so I said how about sharing the apartment with me and Haley, and . . . It doesn't matter, does it?"

"You were friends, and this is hard. Did she have a boyfriend?"

"Nobody special. She dates sometimes, but mostly the work keeps you going, and none of us are much interested in anything serious. Haley had a girlfriend for a few months, but it didn't work out. And that doesn't matter, either. I'm sorry."

"It's okay. Did she date anybody from work, or hang out with anyone in particular?"

"It's not smart to date out of the work pool, and she's smart. It gets sticky. She had friends, sure, but since she moved in — like, six months ago — we've been hanging more. The three of us."

"Was this her usual time to leave?"

"It depends on the work, but yoga nights she'd take off about seven. She'd stay later than usual because the gym's close by. Otherwise, she'd be out by five-thirty or six. Maybe six-thirty like."

"But on Thursday nights, about seven."

"Tuesdays and Thursdays. She really loves yoga. I went with her a few times before I started with *The Glory Hour.*"

"Tuesday." The night Mars was killed. "Did she leave at seven this past Tuesday?"

"Ah." Terren closed her eyes, sighed. "I remember. Yeah, sure, just after seven. I remember because I had a seven-thirty meeting and I checked the time when she came over to say she'd see me at Rush. It's a club, we were going out after I got off work, after her class. Haley was meeting us.

We had a lot of fun."

"Just after seven," Eve said thoughtfully. "Just a second." She rose, moved to Trueheart. "Check the vic's log-out time — I want exact — on Tuesday night."

Eve saw Peabody come in, signaled her to wait. "The swipe cards — the studio security has you log in and log out."

"Yeah," Terren brushed at tears, sniffed. "There was some trouble a few years ago, with some fans getting in. You have to get cleared from the lobby now, or do the swipe."

"Where did she keep hers?"

"Ah, in her purse."

"Always?"

"Well, everybody sort of leaves them on their desk if they have one, or sticks them in their pocket. Or a purse."

"Did she leave hers on her desk?"

"I guess, yeah."

"They all look the same. How do you know whose is whose?"

"You can write your name on them, or initials. Some people draw something. I've got a dragonfly I drew on mine."

"I bet you don't really look when you just grab it up to go."

Terren shrugged. "It's right on the desk, or in my pocket."

"Right. It's got your data inside, programmed in."

"Sure. Your name, your area, your ID number."

"Do you ever grab someone else's by mistake?"

"I haven't, but Wally and Misha got theirs mixed once. I remember because it was just a couple weeks ago."

Trueheart came back, whispered in Eve's ear.

She just nodded.

"Terren, would you like us to contact Haley, make sure she's home, or comes home? We're going to arrange for you to be taken home."

Fresh tears spurted. "I want Haley."

"Detective Trueheart's going to take care of all that."

"Her mom?"

"We'll go see her mom. Thanks for your help. And I am sorry for your loss."

Eve crossed quickly to Peabody. "Take statements from the two male wits, and make it fast. We've got him."

"Who? How?"

"That fucker Hyatt — Knight's admin. I'll fill you in when you're done. Get full statements, but don't screw around."

She went out, took a deep breath of cold

air. She'd get justice for Larinda Mars. That was duty.

But she'd damn sure get it for Kellie Lowry.

22

Eve moved to Baxter.

"Trueheart's arranging the female wit's transpo, making sure her other roommate's home. When he's done, and you're done here, I need you to make the notification."

Though he nodded, Baxter pointed at her. "You hit."

"Apologies for putting you on notification, but we need to move on this."

"Throw me a bone."

"Knight's admin, Bill Hyatt. I knew I didn't like that rat bastard, but he had an alibi — his log-in had him in the building here when Mars was attacked. Except it wasn't his swipe. He switched on Kellie Lowry. She's the one who was in the building until nineteen-six. And he's the one who left — logging her out — at seventeen-fifteen. Plenty of time for him to get downtown when we can place him entering Du Vin."

"He killed that girl, had her bleed out on the sidewalk, for her log-in?"

"He did."

"Get the rat bastard, boss."

"Count on it."

She turned to Roarke, who offered her a go-cup of coffee. "Thanks."

"The knight protecting Knight. Strangely poetic."

"I couldn't connect him to Mars — he's not in her books, on her list, and I looked. Then today, I find out Mars made herself at home up there. He'd have had some dealings with her. He figured out what was going on, didn't like it. It wouldn't surprise me if he confronted her at some point, warned her off, got in her face some like he did with me. And it wouldn't surprise me if she laughed in his face. He's just an assistant, right? A lackey. He didn't worry her."

"Murder's somewhat over and above for an employee," Roarke commented.

"Some people take their job way too serious. You can head out, go on home. I'm going to bag this."

"Mars, whatever she was, bled out on my floor," Roarke reminded her. "I'll see it through."

"Fine. Baxter, you and Trueheart need to

go up to the studio, get more statements. I'll get you a warrant for Hyatt's office and his electronics."

"We know the drill, Dallas. We've got this covered."

Sure of it, she pulled out her PPC, pulled up Hyatt's info. "Handy, he lives about five blocks away."

Pleased, she tagged Reo. "I need some warrants."

By the time Peabody came out, the warrants were in the works.

"Somebody tell me something," Peabody demanded.

"Talk and walk."

In long strides, Eve headed to the car, giving Peabody the details on the way.

"For her log-out," Peabody said as she settled into the backseat. "He killed someone for their log-out. But . . . why? He used it, switched it back obviously. Nobody knew."

It gnawed in Eve's craw. "I pushed him on his alibi, and made sure I pissed him off. And I pushed on it again with security. Nadine worked on a source inside Knight's studio. I'd say he got wind of the second push, he got worried."

Son of a bitch, Eve thought. Son of a bitching bastard.

Blood-soaked flowered pants, black wings of hair spread on the sidewalk. A girl from Queens with a nice mom.

"He killed Lowry," she continued, "to cover his ass, but just like killing Mars exposed Knight's secrets, what he did by taking Lowry's life? He exposed himself and his cowardly white dick of an ass."

" 'Dick of an ass'?" Roarke repeated.

"I'm pissed. I need to get through being pissed. Mars didn't have any problem exploiting lives for profit. She made a goddamn science out of it. But she didn't kill people. He did Mars, more than likely, because he has some pathological obsession with protecting Annie Knight — and you can bet your non-dick of an Irish ass he harbors a strong loathing for Bicford, because Bicford has access to Knight he doesn't, has a relationship he doesn't.

"Lowry he killed because maybe, just maybe, we'd have looked more closely at the log-outs."

"You didn't like him right off," Peabody acknowledged.

"No, I didn't like him. But I don't like a lot of people who don't decide they can kill people. Who don't decide to slice someone's artery so they can bleed out on the floor or on the street. And you know what?"

God, she was pissed!

"Sooner or later, there would've been somebody else. Somebody he deemed didn't treat Knight the way she should be treated, somebody who he judged stood in his way for something. He'd have done it again, because now it's his solution."

Roarke opted for a lot rather than the second-level street spot available. The walk would give his wife, his thoroughly pissed cop, a little more time to cool off.

"It wasn't done for gain, for love, for hate, not because he's just batshit crazy. Not in hot blood, but cold. It was just done."

She took out her 'link when it signaled. "Okay, Reo came through. Both search warrant and arrest warrant. Get us a little backup, Peabody," she added as she got out of the car. "We're going to have him taken in while we go through his place. I'm betting he didn't ditch the weapon, and I know damn well we're going to find some data on his electronics on his killing method, on both vics."

"I can tag McNab for that."

"We've got our e-geek right here. Tag McNab and tell him to pack, you're leaving tonight."

"I — What?" Peabody nearly bobbled her 'link. "Tonight? Now tonight? But —"

"He's a coward, he's an amateur, he's an asshole." Eve ground the words out. "Do you think I can't handle him in the box?"

"Yes, I mean, no. But —"

"Tell McNab to clear it with Feeney. You can have a shuttle for them tonight?" she asked Roarke.

"Anytime."

As Peabody's eyes welled up, Eve jabbed a finger at her. "Don't piss me off a-fucking-gain. I'm just getting through it."

"Okay, but I just have to . . ." She shook her fists in the air, bopped her hips, did a quick dance. Then threw her arms around Roarke. "She'll hurt me if I hug her, too. So this is a double. Thank you, so much."

"I'll take the double." And kissed the top of her head for good measure. "You're more than welcome."

"If you're done now," Eve said coolly, "maybe you could see about that backup. You know, just so we can have this murdering dick-ass taken in."

"I'm going to get the best backup in the history of backups."

She proceeded to do so while Eve studied Hyatt's building. More than decent, she decided, a faux brownstone of twelve stories. One built to look old, with more than decent security.

She mastered through it.

The lobby stood empty and quiet with secondary security requiring guests to register and residents to use swipes for the elevators or the stairwell.

Fucking swipes, she thought.

"Bypass that, will you?" She gestured Roarke toward the security station while Peabody tagged McNab.

"We're wrapping it. Yeah. I'll tell you later. Tag Feeney, okay? Dallas says we can go tonight. Yeah, tonight. Woo! I know, I know."

Eve rolled her eyes at the un-coplike giggle, but she smiled, just a little.

"No, no, stop talking, start packing. Totally, totally. Mag!" Peabody ended with a long, loud kissing sound.

"Sorry," she said to Eve.

"We will never speak of it."

With Roarke grinning, Eve swiped her master to call the elevator. "Eighth floor," she ordered. "Engage recorders. He's not going to want to open the door when he sees me. If he refuses, you can take care of that," she said to Roarke.

"Happy to assist."

"He's eight-eleven." The elevator opened and, as they stepped out, she saw a woman, mid-thirties, bold red coat, a tumble of blond hair, step out of eight-oh-six.

"Excuse me." Eve held up her badge.

"Oh!" The woman's attractive face displayed the typical unease when faced unexpectedly with the police.

"Do you know Bill Hyatt — eight-eleven?"

"I . . . yes. A little. Not really *know,* but —"

"Do me a favor? Just ring his bell."

"Um . . . all right."

"Spoilsport," Roarke commented as they moved down the hall.

The blonde rang the bell.

"Just stand there and smile a minute. Thanks."

So the blonde worked up a slightly nervous smile.

The door opened. Hyatt, obviously fresh out of the shower with his hair still a little damp, the scent of manly pine wafting, beamed. "Hey, Cynthia. What can I —"

"Thanks," Eve said, nudged the blonde aside, put a shoulder against the open door. "William Hyatt, we are duly authorized and warranted to enter and search these premises." She showed the badge she still held. "Remember me? Dallas, Lieutenant Eve. NYPSD."

Though he tried to shove the door closed as she spoke, she muscled her way in, along with Roarke and Peabody.

"This is outrageous!"

"Yeah, it is, and it gets better. William Hyatt, you're under arrest on suspicion of murder — that's first degree, two counts. You weren't going to get away with Mars, Bill, but you had a better shot before you killed Kellie Lowry."

The blonde in the hall gave a little squeak of shock before Peabody closed the door.

Maybe Eve took her time rather than moving straight in to restrain him. And was rewarded when he turned, ran.

"Really?" She let out a little (somewhat pleased) sigh as a door slammed. "I've got this."

"Let her have the moment." Roarke patted Peabody's arm. "She's still working through being pissed."

Eve walked back to the door, angled her head. Interior door, she thought. Not much of a challenge.

And kicked it in.

Across the bedroom, Hyatt struggled to open a window.

"Stop where you are." She said it mildly as she strolled across the room. "I repeat, you're under arrest."

He spun around, took a sloppy swing at her. It gave her time, the sloppiness of it, to decide whether to take the shot or evade it.

She decided she just couldn't let some dick-ass land a weak punch. The record would show the swing.

All she had to do was lean left. His own momentum carried him around. And since Nadine's thoughts on bruised knuckles rang true under the circumstances, Eve just kicked him in the ass and sent him sprawling.

"Okay, we add attempting to flee and resisting, attempting to assault a police officer."

She dragged his hands behind his back as he tried to kick her, tried to inchworm away.

"Lawyer, lawyer!"

"Okay, Bill, you'll have that right along with others. Here they are."

She recited the Revised Miranda. "Do you understand your rights and obligations?"

"Lawyer, lawyer, you bitch. You cunt."

"I take that as a yes."

She hauled him up, pushed him into a chair in the scrupulously clean, absolutely tidy, and obsessively trendy room. "Sit!" She snapped. "If you try to get up, attempt to assault me or flee again, I'll be forced to take measures you won't like. You know, Bill, we've got you locked. More, we'll double the lock once we go through your place because I'm just betting you've got the murder weapon stashed in here."

His eyes flicked to a low, three-drawer bureau — glossy black with silver trim and knobs.

"Seriously? You're making it too easy. Peabody, we need to seal up. We need a field kit."

Roarke took a mini can out of his pocket. "From the center compartment of your vehicle."

"You are handy."

"I'll get the kit. More steps, more calories burned," Peabody said before Roarke could object. "I've got this little bikini."

She dashed out before Eve could snarl at her. Instead, while Roarke leaned on the doorjamb, Eve sealed her hands.

"Now let me guess." She watched Hyatt's stony face as she walked to the bureau. "This one?" She circled a finger in front of the middle drawer as he fought to keep his gaze level.

"Or is it . . ."

His eyes flicked down.

"Made you look." She pulled open the bottom drawer. "I see you work out, and wouldn't be surprised if it's the same gym Kellie Lowry used. Coordinating outfits, very stylish," she added as she pushed through them.

"Get your filthy hands off my things."

"Hey, they're clean enough, and hello, warrant. Why, just look here under this neatly folded stack of gym socks, and in its plastic sheath."

She held up a scalpel. "All clean — or I bet you think so. You think you washed all the blood away. It's really hard to do that. And even if you managed it, the question will be just what is the lapboy of some mediocre talk-show host doing with a medical scalpel under his gym socks?"

"Mediocre! Annie Knight is an *icon*! You aren't fit to speak her name."

Since his reaction gave her just what she'd wanted, she just smiled again. "Aw, are you in love?" She drew out the word, mockingly.

As he started to lunge up, Roarke moved fast as a snake. He only put a hand on Hyatt's shoulder, shoved him back down again. "You'll want to sit where the lieutenant put you."

At the buzzer, Eve said, "That should be the uniforms. Would you mind?"

"Not at all. Just where she put you," Roarke said to Hyatt, and left to let in the uniforms.

"You're cooked, Bill." Eve studied the scalpel.

"That proves nothing."

"Oh, it's going to have weight. Then there's the swipe cards, the log-ins. There's going to be the lineup with the wits you walked out of Du Vin with. And better? What we find on your comp. Because someone like you? An organizer, a planner, somebody who handles details, schedules? You wrote it all out. You researched how to kill them, how long it would take. You timed it and wrote it all out."

"You can't break into my electronics."

"My warrant and badge says different. Officers." She nodded to the two uniforms. "Take this dick-ass to Central. He's invoked his right to counsel, so let him contact a lawyer, then put him in Holding. Roarke, you're on e-duty. Make me proud."

"It's what I live for."

"You're going to arrest me? *Me?* Do you know what she was? What she did? Why didn't you arrest *her*?"

Stir him up, Eve thought. Just keep him stirred up. "Bill, you've invoked your right to counsel, but you keep talking. You really ought to shut the hell up."

"Don't you tell me to shut up! I'll have my say."

With the hand at her side, Eve signaled the uniforms back. "Are you waiving your right to counsel at this time? You want a lawyer, or not? Make up your freaking mind, Bill."

"I'll get a lawyer when I'm ready to get a lawyer. You're going to listen to me."

"Are you waiving your right to counsel at this time?" Eve repeated.

"Yes. And you're going to listen!"

Eve walked over, sat on the side of the bed. "Happy to, I get paid either way. We're on the record here, Bill."

"She was a spider, a leech."

"Who?"

"You know damn well. Larinda Mars. She was blackmailing Annie, threatening to break a story about how Annie defended herself against a *rapist* when she was just a teenager. She bled her month after month. Mars, she held that over Annie's head, said she'd spin the story so it came off Annie was whoring, like her bio mother, and was a junkie, like her bio mother. Annie would lock herself in her office and cry her *heart* out. And what did Bic do about it? *Nothing!* He did nothing to ease her pain, to protect her."

"So you did."

"You're damn right."

"Did she tell you all this? Annie? Did she come to you for help?"

His chin jutted up. "She'd never unburden

herself that way, never let herself lean or ask for help. But I could see, months ago I could see how upset she was. She lost weight, wasn't sleeping. She and Bic would close themselves in her office to talk about it."

"Her private office?" Eve asked. "You listened to conversations they had in her private office? Oh, Bill, did you bug her office?"

His jaw tightened. "I'm Annie's personal assistant, and I need to know what she needs, often before she does. I have to know her moods, her difficulties. I did what had to be done to protect her. I'm the one who looked after Annie, not Bic. I'm the one who confronted that bitch, not Bic."

"When did you confront Mars?"

"Months ago. The way she'd just stroll in whenever she liked, bag little pieces, even in-depth interviews with people Annie had worked, honestly, forthrightly, to get on the show. You can thank Ilene Riff for that. She's the one who fed that bitch names and times. Arrest *her*."

As his venom spewed, Eve thought Riff could consider herself lucky. Hyatt would have killed her eventually.

But she simply said, "So noted. You confronted Mars."

"You're damn right I did. I told her straight out she had to stop tormenting Annie, that I wouldn't tolerate it. And she laughed at me, she insulted me. She dared me to go to the police, and said if I did, Annie would be ruined, and I'd be to blame."

"You realized words wouldn't be enough to stop her."

Lost in his own version of heroism, Hyatt leaned forward.

"Do you understand she wouldn't, couldn't be reasoned with? She was bleeding Annie. It wasn't the money, it was the stress, the constant reminder of something horrible that happened when she was so young, so defenseless."

"You decided to bleed Mars. Literally."

"It was justice. You're supposed to stand for justice, but you didn't stand for Annie, did you? I exterminated a spider. I did what had to be done."

Eve made a noncommittal sound. "It took planning, I'll give you that. Planning and precision — and, you could say, some poetry. You spent the months since she laughed at you planning it out, following her routine."

"She wasn't the only one who could dig up dirt, dig up secrets. I found out she was doing the same thing to a lot of other people. Making them pay so she wouldn't expose them. No doubt some of them deserved it," he said dismissively, "but she was despicable."

"Back to the poetry of it all. How did you come up with the method?"

"I wanted her to bleed — that's the justice. I found out how to make her bleed."

"Smart. And you knew her pickup locations, the routines of them."

"She liked having her victims have to sit there, pay for her drinks. I could see how she liked it."

"How'd you decide on switching swipe cards with Kellie Lowry?"

"She had her routine, too. Twice a week she stayed until between seven and seven-fifteen. Clockwork. Mars met the people she was bleeding at Du Vin on Tuesdays, and she'd finish up with them by about seven, no later than seven-thirty. Logging out with Kellie's card gave me the alibi I needed if anybody asked. Mars usually hit the restroom before she left. Primped herself up for wherever she was going next. I just had to wait."

"You followed her down," Eve prompted.

"Gave her a minute, went down. It had to be fast. I'd timed it out. I could block the door for a minute if I had to, but it had to be in and out and gone, even though it would take her up to four or five minutes to bleed out."

He stopped to take a breath, and looked, for a moment, pensive. "It had to be done," he concluded. "She had to be stopped."

"You walked into the women's restroom."

"She smirked at me when I went in. Smirked, and made some insulting comment about knowing I didn't have a dick so I needed the women's room. I walked right up to her — my ears were buzzing, buzzing, but I walked right up to her. I sliced her arm just where I'd practiced. She didn't smirk then."

Tears gathered in his eyes. " 'That's for Annie,' I said when she grabbed her arm and stumbled back. For Annie. And even though I wanted to keep slicing her, I just walked out. I held the door for ten seconds, just in case. My legs shook a little, and I needed to catch my breath. Then I went up the stairs, walked out right behind a group of people. And it was done. Annie was free."

"Yeah. Smooth."

She'd seen Peabody come back, field kit in hand, seen her partner ease out again. But kept her focus on Hyatt.

"It wasn't smooth to try to block me and my partner from speaking to Annie the next day, contacting the lawyer, pushing back so hard."

His eyes cleared, and a touch of insult crossed his face. "It threw me off a minute. I didn't expect the cops to figure out what Mars was doing so fast. If you could figure it out so fast, why didn't you stop her before?"

"Why didn't you call her bluff and go to the police when you found out what she was doing?"

"And betray Annie?" He looked sincerely shocked. "I'd never betray her. I'd never risk her welfare."

"Right. You killed for her instead."

"I ended the torment. I killed to defend someone. It's not a crime, it's heroism!"

"Okay, you could look at it that way." If you're a dick-ass, she thought. "But then there's Kellie. She didn't do anything. She wasn't a threat to Annie."

"I'm sorry about Kellie. Collateral damage. It happens," he said with a shrug that had Eve's pissed-off level threatening to rise again. "And it's your fault. Not mine, yours."

"It's my fault?"

"Looking at me the way you did. Talking to me the way you did. Pushing, sneering. Do you think I don't know you asked questions about when I left that night, even after I *told* you? Asked questions about me, and when I logged out on Tuesday. And I know damn well Junie was talking to one of Nadine Furst's people about Mars, and that would lead to Annie, and that could lead to me if you started asking if anybody saw me leave. If you started poking around. I did what I had to do to protect myself."

"You waited for Kellie to come out of 30 Rock."

"She was running a little behind, didn't even see me until I bumped into her."

"You went for her leg instead of her arm."

"She had a jacket on, plus the thigh would bleed out faster. I didn't want her to suffer. I'm not cruel."

"You killed Mars to protect Annie. You killed Kellie to protect yourself."

"It protected Annie, too — protecting myself protected Annie. It should have ended it. You shouldn't be here."

"I am here, Bill. I'm here after standing over a young woman who did you no harm. Who, from what I know at this point, harmed no one. I stood over her lifeless body where she collapsed and bled to death on the sidewalk, on a bitter winter night. Because you decided to use her as cover for the murder of another woman. Because you decided to end her life rather than risk exposure. You're exposed anyway, and Kellie Lowry is still dead by your hand."

"What about Annie? What about what she suffered? You heartless bitch! What about Annie?"

"Do you think she'll thank you for this? I've had exactly two conversations with her, and I know — I *know* — it's not thanks you'll get from her. It's disgust, and it's grief, and she'll suffer more now because you used her as an excuse to kill."

"You don't know her. You don't understand her. I protected her!"

"You're pathetic." Eve rose. "William Hyatt, you've confessed, on the record, to the premeditated murders of Larinda Mars and Kellie Lowry. You're under arrest for two counts of first degree murder, and the lesser charges already on record. Other charges may be added. Take him in, out of my sight. Book the son of a bitch."

"I defended Annie!" He struggled when the uniforms flanked him, hauled him out of the chair. "I defended her. I'm a hero! I want a lawyer."

"Yeah, yeah. Let him get his lawyer. Let's see how his lawyer can spin what he's just blathered onto the record. Get him the hell out."

She stood a moment, blocking out his shouts as the uniforms dragged him away. And studied the scalpel. Such a small thing, she thought. Created to save lives. Some would always twist the good into the ugly.

She walked out, saw Peabody conducting the search of the living area.

"I didn't want to interrupt," Peabody said. "I could hear. I knew you had him."

"Yeah. He'll be the PA's problem now. Maybe Mira's." Eve took an evidence bag out of the field kit for the murder weapon. "Roarke?"

"Small second bedroom converted to a home office. He's in there — which is also a little shrine to Annie Knight, with photos of her, posters, photos of the two of them. It looks normal until you know. And when you know, it's a little sick. Anyway, Roarke's got it all."

"Figured he would. Go home, Peabody. Go to Mexico."

"McNab texted he packed for me, which is a little scary, but what the hell. He's going to meet me at the transport when I text him back. I'm stupid with grateful, Dallas. He really needs this break."

"Then go give it to him."

"So going." She grabbed her coat, hat, scarf. Then, moving fast, rushed Eve, hugged hard, then rushed out. *"Adios, amiga!"*

"Yeah, yeah. *Hasta la* whatever the hell."

She walked to the office, where Roarke sat at an orderly desk contentedly working on Hyatt's d and c. "Put it away," Roarke said.

"What away?"

"The idea that if you'd gotten to him sooner, or hadn't pushed at him in a certain way, Kellie Lowry would be alive. It's as much a fallacy — and as egotistic, really — as blaming yourself Mars died while you were having a drink with a colleague."

"I'm working on it because I know better. And I don't like the ego crack."

"Truth is often harsh. It's all here," he continued. "His searches for the method, how long, on average, a human being will bleed to death, how the body shuts down and so on, from those specific wounds. He ordered the scalpel online from a medical supply house about two months ago."

"Planning and practice time." She came around to read the screen over his shoulder.

"Yes. He's meticulously — he had meticulous in common with Mars — detailed Mars's movements, her haunts, and he's listed some of her marks he identified when he shadowed her. He practiced on a droid. In the closet there."

Eve walked over, opened the closet, studied the economy droid with numerous gashes on the arms, on the thighs.

"He has Kellie Lowry in here as well. You were quite right about them using the same gym. He even took a few yoga classes with her. He also has several files dedicated to Annie Knight."

"I'd have been surprised if he didn't have files on her."

"His devotion there is extreme," Roarke said. "She is perfection to him, and he did indeed see himself as — as you put it — her shiny knight. His respect for Bic has been disintegrating over the last months. It's now down to disgust. I believe it may have gone further in time."

Those wild blue eyes flicked up to Eve's. "That's Mira's territory, but if he did kill again, he would have felt justified in eliminating the man he believed allowed his goddess to be tormented."

Roarke reached for Eve's hand. "So consider you very likely saved a life. And this sort of obsession can grow and turn — as you know. He may have devolved until he killed Annie, then himself."

"Mira territory, but yeah, I can see it." Had already gone there in her head. "I'm going to have Baxter and Trueheart finish this up. Finalize the search, take in the electronics. They should have a part in it. I need to write it up. At home." She gave his hand a squeeze. "Let's go home."

"Let's go home," he agreed.

She set the sealed weapon on the desk for Baxter and Trueheart, went back to the living area, got her field kit. "I need to tag DeWinter — I said I would. And Nadine. Nadine'll take longer."

"From home."

"Yeah, from home." She stepped out, sealed the door, took out her 'link to tag Baxter as they walked to the elevator.

Before they reached the car, the snow had started, thin, swirling flakes against the black sky, the brilliant lights of the city.

Home, she thought, where the shadows could be banished. Where all that mattered was right there.

"After I make the tags and write this up, let's crack a bottle of wine and watch a vid. Something funny. Like stupid funny. Something ridiculous."

"I can come up with one of those."

"You never let me down." She stowed the field kit, turned to him.

And, at least for the moment, she put it aside. For the moment she leaned into him, wrapped around him, and kissed him while the snow swirled white against the bitter.

ABOUT THE AUTHOR

J.D. Robb is the pseudonym for #1 *New York Times* bestselling author Nora Roberts. She is the author of over 200 novels, including the futuristic suspense In Death series. There are more than five hundred million copies of her books in print.

The employees of Thorndike Press hope you have enjoyed this Large Print book. All our Thorndike, Wheeler, and Kennebec Large Print titles are designed for easy reading, and all our books are made to last. Other Thorndike Press Large Print books are available at your library, through selected bookstores, or directly from us.

For information about titles, please call:
(800) 223-1244

or visit our website at:
gale.com/thorndike

To share your comments, please write:
Publisher
Thorndike Press
10 Water St., Suite 310
Waterville, ME 04901